HIRED LOVER

We fell to the bed together.

"This is still wrong," she said, "but it's the way I want it."

I wanted to tease her.

Her mouth was wide open for me.

"I'm sure."

"Prove it to me."

She did.

Not once.

Not twice.

Several times.

That night I didn't do any drinking or running around. After supper I went to my cheap room and got into bed.

My only regret was that I was alone.

That girl had it.

She sure did.

And as soon as I got the chance I was going back for more.

A long lost Orrie Hitt novel originally published as by Fred Martin. "The incredible story of a man and woman who loved like animals—and were destroyed the same way!"

HIRED LOVER

·

SUMMER HOTEL

TWO NOVELS BY
Orrie Hitt

Introduction by Jeff Vorzimmer

Stark House Press · Eureka California

HIRED LOVER / SUMMER HOTEL

Published by Stark House Press
1315 H Street
Eureka, CA 95501, USA
griffinskye3@sbcglobal.net
www.starkhousepress.com

HIRED LOVER
Originally published by Midwood Books as by "Fred Martin" and copyright ©
1959 by Tower Publications, New York.

SUMMER HOTEL
Originally published by Beacon Books and copyright © 1958 by Universal
Publishing and Distributing Corporation, New York.

"Hired Man—Hired Lover—Hired Killer" copyright © 2024 by Jeff Vorzimmer

Copyright © 2024 Stark House Press. All rights reserved under International
and Pan-American Copyright Conventions.

ISBN: 979-8-88601-114-2

Book design by ¡caliente!design, Austin, Texas
Cover art by Ernest Chiriacka

PUBLISHER'S NOTE
This is a work of fiction. Names, characters, places and incidents are either the
products of the author's imagination or used fictionally, and any resemblance to
actual persons, living or dead, events or locales, is entirely coincidental.

Without limiting the rights under copyright reserved above, no part of this
publication may be reproduced, stored, or introduced into a retrieval system or
transmitted in any form or by any means (electronic, mechanical, photocopying,
recording or otherwise) without the prior written permission of both the
copyright owner and the above publisher of the book.

First Stark House Press Edition: December 2024

Contents

7

Hired Man—Hired Lover—Hired Killer
by Jeff Vorzimmer

13

Hired Lover
by Orrie Hitt
writing as Fred Martin

141

Summer Hotel
By Orrie Hitt

264

Orrie Hitt
Bibliography

Hired Man–Hired Lover–Hired Killer

by Jeff Vorzimmer

In October of 2009 I read a blog post by my friend and fellow Texan James Reasoner in which he reviewed a book entitled *Hired Lover*, written by Fred Martin and published by Harry Shorten's Midwood Books in 1959. In the opening paragraph he referenced a blog review, 45 days earlier, by Michael Hemmingson, who speculated that the book was actually written by Orrie Hitt. I clicked through the link he provided to Hemmingson's blog to see what he based his theory on.

Hemmingson claimed that the book was easily identifiable as Orrie Hitt's style, though it wasn't exactly clear why the publisher would use a pseudonym for that one book when all previous and subsequent books by Hitt for Midwood appeared under his real name.

Hired Lover was an early offering by Midwood, it was catalog number 13, and interestingly enough, numbers 10, 12 and 16 were Orrie Hitt titles under his own name. This fact gives credence to Hemmingson's theory that the publisher did not want to saturate the market with too many books by a single author as a way of explaining the use of the pseudonym.

As for more external evidence of Hitt as author, Hemmingson sites bookseller and paperback historian Lynn Munroe as claiming in one of his blog posts that most of the first forty Midwood books were written by just five authors: Donald Westlake, Lawrence Block, Robert Silverberg, Hal Dresner, who each had there own pseudonyms, and Orrie Hitt.

What struck me about Munroe's claim was that it setup an ideal situation for running author attribution software, since the control group of texts to run against *Hired Lover* could be limited to samples from just five authors.

I had used author attribution software quite successfully in the past to identify stories in *Manhunt* magazine written under the house pseudonym Roy Carroll. The house pseudonym was used for one of the stories of an author who had contributed more than one to an issue, so that his name wouldn't appear multiple times. The sample data could then be limited to the authors appearing in that particular issue. In the case of *Manhunt*, usually seven or eight authors, an ideally small and finite control group for author attribution software.

To get the most accurate results from author attribution software it's best to get samples of the authors' works as close to the publication date of the unknown work, in this case *Hired Lover*, and as many from the same publisher, or similar publishers, as possible.

The sample data I collected by the five authors to run against *Hired Lover* (Midwood 13) by Fred Martin were:

> *Campus Doll* (Monarch 189) by Donald Westlake, writing as Edwin West
>
> *Man Hungry* (Midwood 147) by Donald Westlake, writing as Alan Marshall
>
> *Passion School* (Nightstand 1515) by Hal Dresner, writing as Don Holliday
>
> *Stud* (Nightstand 1532) by Hal Dresner, writing as Don Holliday
>
> *Born to Be Bad* (Midwood 14) by Lawrence Block, writing as Sheldon Lord
>
> *Carla* (Midwood 8) by Lawrence Block, writing as Sheldon Lord
>
> *As Bad as They Come* (Midwood 23) by Orrie Hitt
>
> *The Cheaters* (Midwood 34) by Orrie Hitt
>
> Connie (Midwood 18) by Robert Silverberg, writing as Loren Beauchamp
>
> *Meg* (Midwood 30) by Robert Silverberg, writing as Loren Beauchamp

When I ran the author attribution software on *Hired Lover* against the above samples, the results were as definitive as I'd ever seen. With a 97% probability, we're talking evidence that would likely hold up in a court of law that *Hired Lover* was written by Orrie Hitt.

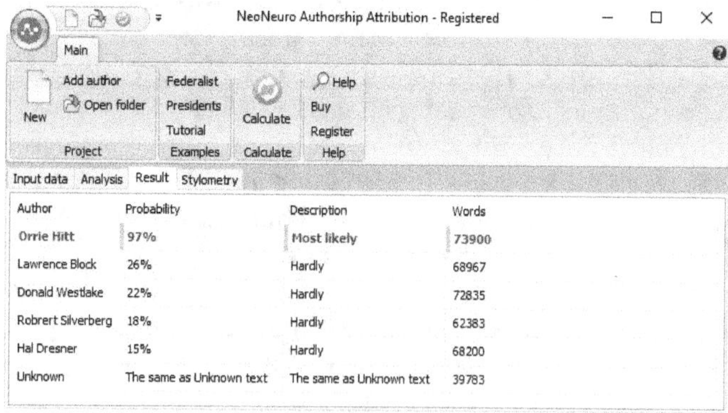

Author	Probability	Description	Words
Orrie Hitt	97%	Most likely	73900
Lawrence Block	26%	Hardly	68967
Donald Westlake	22%	Hardly	72835
Robrert Silverberg	18%	Hardly	62383
Hal Dresner	15%	Hardly	68200
Unknown	The same as Unknown text	The same as Unknown text	39783

The NeoNeuro Authorship Attribution results of Hired Lover.

What gets really interesting, though, is when you look at the text strings that the software used to make that determination. There were 8- 9- and 13-word text strings that matched the Orrie Hitt samples.

For example, the longest string, 13 words, was the following as it appeared in two books:

"She reminded me of a girl I had once seen in a carnival girlie show."

—*Hired Lover* by Fred Martin

"She reminded me of a girl I had once seen in a carnival, big and lush . . ."

—*As Bad as They Come* by Orrie Hitt

The lines in *Hired Lover* that would really have gotten the attention of a reader well-versed in the idiosyncratic phrasing of Orrie Hitt, however, are: "She was quite young, not much over eighteen, and she dripped sex like a leaky faucet." and the line, "She walked over to the light switch and the movements of her body dripped sex."

Variations on phrases that revolve around "dripped sex" can be found throughout Hitt's novels. It's his catchphrase as evidenced by the examples below:

"This girl dripped sex all over the place, like a leaky faucet."

—*Add Flesh to the Fire*

"She dripped sex the way a leaky faucet drips water."

—*As Bad as they Come*

"She drips sex like a leaky roof."

—*Burlesque Girl*

"She dripped sex like a leaky faucet."

—*The Cheaters*

". . . a wet smile that dripped sex."

—*Ex-Virgin*

". . . that shape of hers dripping sex appeal like a leaky faucet drips water."

—*Inflamed Dames*

"Nothing, except that you drip sex like a punctured can of water."

—The Lady Is a Lush

"She didn't drip sex . . . but a girl didn't have to be all sex to be a girl."

—Sexurbia County

". . . walking along, you just dripped sex."

—Sheba

"The redhead had talent and she dripped sex with every movement"

—Unfaithful Wives

Notice that, in addition to the two lines in *Hired Lover*, two more of these lines come from books in our test samples: *As Bad As They Come* and *The Cheaters*. That's the kind of similar phrasing that scores high in author attribution software. For those readers interested in the Regular Expression search string I used to unearth the above examples from Hitt's novels, it is:

```
(drip.{0,4} sex)\W+(?:\w+(?![.!?] )\W+){1,5}?(leaky faucet)?
```

Other characteristics of Hitt's writing that can be found in *Hired Lover.* One is his use of the word *jerk* and variations on the word as a noun, adjective and adverb. The word appears 19 times in *Hired Lover*.

Two other interesting characteristics of Hitt's writing that appear in *Hired Lover* are his dramatic effect of ending chapters in one-sentence paragraphs that compel the reader to turn the page to the next chapter.

The other is his use of a character repeating what another has just said to him or her, but with a twist. He has the other character repeating the line spoken to him, but turning the statement into a question or vice versa or by repeating the words and elaborating on them.

Here are some examples from *Hired Lover*:

How many girls have you had up to this room while you've been waiting for me?"

"You're the first."
"Honest?"
"Honest."

"Do you still love me," she asked.
"Sure."
"Sure, but what?" she asked.

Here are some examples from *The Cheaters*, one of the sample texts used:

"The hell with him."
"The hell with him is right."

You want something else," he said.
"Such as?"
"Such as what's upstairs. You went up there with her last night and you'd like to be with her again, wouldn't you?"

Although other authors employ these techniques, they don't do it quite as often as Orrie Hitt. He has, in fact, written whole novels with every chapter ending in dramatic one-sentence paragraphs. In his novel *The Widow*, Hitt employs the technique of repeating lines ten times.

The result is that *Hired Lover* scores higher than anything Hitt ever wrote under his own name as far as the markers that identify the characteristics of his writing.

Going from a micro view of the text to the macro view of structure, there are similarities in the plots of *Hired Lover* and *Summer Hotel*, a novel Hitt wrote under his own name for Beacon Books in 1958. The two books are both of what has become known as the James M. Cain variety, a femme fatale who entices her lover into killing her husband.

But even though many authors, including Hitt himself, had been down this road before, you don't anticipate the twist in the plots coming in either of these novels. What's unique and specific about Orrie Hitt's version of this love triangle is not that the wife is beautiful and much younger—she is—and the husband is older and sickly—he is—but that the husbands in both these novels are diabetics. It's around this fact that the plots to kill the husband revolve.

Orrie Hitt would use this plot device again in *The Cheaters* in 1960, with an older husband and a young, beautiful wife. In that book Hitt's diabetic older husband uses the more vernacular term *sugar* or *"the sugars,"* which was how diabetes was often referred to in the 1950s and early 60s along with the more common, *"sugar* diabetes."

Another variation of Hitt's on the Cain-style love triangle is that the main character—the husband's employee turned wife's lover—has a somewhat shady past and larcenous heart. In both novels *Hired Lover* and *Summer Hotel*, the back story of the main character shows a man just one step ahead of the law.

In the case of *Hired Lover*, the character of Mike Callahan has been reduced to taking a job as driving instructor after a dust-up with the Mob while running cars to Mexico. *Summer Hotel* opens with bartender Mac Osmund being fired for having a till that was $5 short. Bartending was a job he took after losing his position as a manager of a resort hotel in the Catskills that was busted for doubling as a brothel.

Unlike similar novels by, not only Cain, but Gil Brewer and Charles Williams, where an everyman, honest and hard-working, is seduced by a femme fatale into committing a criminal act, Hitt's characters are not above doing anything for a fast buck or lusting after what belongs to another man.

Nor are they loyal to any one woman. Both the characters of Mike Callahan and Max Osmund have multiple love interests, one of which, in both cases, is interested in traditional family values and marriage. This too is a recurring theme in Hitt's novels—a male character torn between a woman who wants to settle down into a normal home life and the femme fatale who is sexually insatiable, drinks too much but is never boring or predictable.

This, of course is the appeal of an Orrie Hitt novel and why, since his death, he has acquired the kind of cult following he never had in life.

HIRED LOVER

by Orrie Hitt

writing as

Fred Martin

Chapter 1

When I saw her come out of the building and head for my car, I thought she was just another dizzy blonde, but I changed my mind when she got in with me. She wasn't just another blonde. There was something mean about her and she was beautiful. I could tell she had a lot of fire in the furnace when she looked at me and smiled. It was one of those sarcastic smiles that made you want to slap her hard.

But you wanted to kiss her, too. You wanted to kiss those big soft lips of hers and then slap her down and kiss her again.

I wished they hadn't assigned this one to me because she was the kind of girl I could make a fool of myself over and I didn't want to be a fool again. I was trying to come clean and stay away from dames for a while, but I didn't tell her to get out. My resistance wasn't that strong. I knew trouble was coming my way, but it would be nice trouble and even if it was a lot of trouble I knew it would be worth it if she was thrown in with the bargain.

"Mike's the name, Mike Callahan."

When I spoke she looked me up and down like she was guessing my weight.

"I'm Kitty," she said, and I wanted to make a joke right then, but I figured I'd have to know her for half an hour before I could make jokes like that around her.

"You don't look like the kind of girl who'd be taking driving lessons."

"I use to drive, but I had a bad wreck about five years ago and quit. Now I've decided to try it again."

I explained the double controls to her. There was a steering wheel, an accelerator and everything on her side of the car and there was another set on my side so I could take over if anything went wrong while the student was driving. Chicago's not the easiest place to learn how to drive.

After we got going she took over and seemed to be pretty much at home behind the controls. She relaxed a little and glanced over at me again.

"Come to think of it you don't look like the kind of man who would be teaching driving lessons."

"I'm not the type, but I just got in from L. A. last week and this was the first job I could find. I don't plan to stay in this car jockey business forever if that's what you mean."

I guess she was looking at my heavy build and deep sun tan when she said I didn't look the type. She was right. I wasn't the type, but unfortunately I developed a bad habit in my childhood. I got in the habit of eating and this job was strictly from hunger. A year ago I went to L. A. for a big deal with an army buddy of mine. We were going to run used cars down to Mexico and sell them for a small fortune, but like everything else I had ever tried it didn't work out. We got the deal moving all right, but then some big time crooks got wind of it and moved in. Hal joined up with them, but I pulled out. I never could stand working for a big shot. That's one of the reasons I took this lousy job. I don't have to see much of the boss.

But it was a strictly from hunger job. I took it so I could get the lay of the land in Chicago and move into something big later on.

Kitty was doing fine at the wheel. We went down Montrose to the Outer Drive and then turned north. She stepped down on the accelerator and the Ford we were driving shot ahead like a scared rabbit.

"I've got the hang of it now."

"I hope to God you have," I said and watched the road ahead so I could take over if anything went wrong. When we reached the Foster Avenue cut-off she didn't let up one bit and I thought we'd turn over as the tires screeched around the long curve in the drive.

"My nerves aren't built for this kind of thing."

"You don't look like the nervous type to me."

"Maybe not, but I like to live."

"For what?"

"You got me there, sister, but if you don't mind too much will you slow down a little? There's a stop light ahead."

She stopped the car like she started it, with a suddenness that shook your teeth and then she looked over at me and gave one of her contemptuous smiles that made me want to hit her again.

She drove like a lady as we turned up Sheridan Road.

"Do I pass the test?"

"Either you pass or get another teacher."

"Then I pass."

When we got to the Edgewater Beach Hotel she asked me if I'd like a drink and I said yes before I before I remembered I only had five bucks to last me the rest of the week. Instead of pulling up in front of the hotel she drove on up the road a couple of blocks and turned into the drive of one of those pre-Roosevelt mansions that lined the Gold Coast.

"You work here?"

"I live here. Good enough for you?"

"If the whiskey's anything like the house it suits me."

She jumped out of the car and ran up the front steps before I could open the door. Sure she was a crazy kid. I figured she was just another one of those spoiled rich bitches who was born with a silver highball glass in her hand, but later I found that I missed my guess. She wasn't born that way. She just got that way and she did it the hard way.

The front door was open when I got there and I wandered in expecting a butler to throw me out at any minute. I stood there holding my hat looking as awkward as I felt. The house was like those you see in the movies, an English castle with a front hall as big as the Palmer House lobby complete with suit of armor standing at attention. I thought all those places had been sold at auction and turned into apartment houses, but there it was for me to touch if I didn't believe my eyes. I started looking at the heavy paintings on the living room wall to have something to do and I was trying to decide why anybody wanted to buy a picture of a table loaded with fruit when she came running down the stairs.

"Like it?"

"It's O.K., but I don't believe my eyes. I thought all these places went on the block during the depression."

"My husband was very lucky."

"Your husband!"

"That's right."

And then for the first time I looked at her finger and saw the wedding band and the engagement ring with a rock as big as Gibraltar. I usually look at the fourth finger left hand on a dame right off, but this girl was so young and so full of hell that I didn't even think of her as a Mrs.

After she told me she was married to the house she walked up close to me and looked up at me with those bright blue eyes of hers. You can look but you can't touch she was saying. Don't get too close or you'll fund out, I was thinking.

As she was mixing the drinks she told me about her and David. He was over fifty when he married her and all the family had objected because they wanted him to be faithful to the memory of his aristocratic family background. Then too, he had diabetes and they had always planned for him to die without a wife to inherit his money. He was the quiet sort who spent all his time mulling over the business details of his chain of hotels.

"In fact that's about all he does do anymore."

"With you around the house I don't see how he keeps his mind on business."

"Remember he's nearly sixty."

"If I was sixty I'd still figure out something."

"I'll bet you would."

We touched glasses and I took a sip and watched her drain the whole glass without taking a breath. The whiskey was so damned expensive that it didn't even taste like whiskey to me. I like for it to burn a little as it goes down, but this whiskey was too cultured for anything like that. I finished mine and asked her to leave the water out of the next one.

"And how did you meet this David?"

"I was a student nurse. One day he went into a diabetic coma and when he woke up the next morning he found me at his bedside taking his pulse. We got to be good friends while he was in the hospital. I was the first person who understood him. He had always been sensitive about his diabetes and because I was a nurse he could talk about it with me. Later he asked me out to his house for a swim and when he saw me in a bathing suit there was no longer any doubt in his mind. He needed a wife and he needed me because I understood him."

"For a million dollars I'll bet I could understand him."

"For a million dollars I'll bet you'd do more than understand him."

"Cut the cracks."

We sat down to work on the third drink. Maybe that whiskey had culture and didn't taste like much, but it sure had an Indian kick, the kind that sneaks up on you.

I knew it was getting late and that I ought to be headed back to the office, but the whiskey was free and I didn't want to leave before I got the lay of the land. I began to make conversation with the hope that it would lead up to some kind of invitation. It did because when I asked her what she did all the time she told me that she led a very dull life. David was jealous of her and thought that the best way to keep her safe was to give her only five dollars a week allowance.

"So I spend most of my time painting figurines."

"Figurines?"

"Sure you know, china dolls."

"This I got to see to believe."

"Don't I look the type?"

She batted her lashes at me again.

"Somehow I can't picture it."

"Then I'll prove it to you."

She took my hand and led me back out into the hall and up the winding staircase to the second floor. She had one of these things I guess you would call a studio. Anyway it was a room cluttered up with a lot of china dolls sitting on a work bench. There was an easel in the room and some half-finished clay statues and out of the corner of my eyes I saw a comfortable day bed over by the window.

She held one of the white clay figurines up for me to see.

"I buy them at the dime store. You see a girl can't do much on five dollars a week."

I didn't give a damn about those china dolls, but I pretended to be interested as hell in them. I could feel something stirring up in me and my hand trembled a little as I held the doll. It was the same forbidden feeling I had when I was debating whether or not to kiss my first girl.

"You like them?"

She was standing close and she knew she was making it tough for me. I wondered what she felt. What would happen at the Lake Shore Driving School if they got a complaint about me? I didn't much care, except for the fact that I only had five bucks in my pocket. There were other jobs and a guy didn't run into a girl like this one every day.

"They're okay," I said.

"Is that all you can say?"

"They're great."

I was looking at her and thinking things that I shouldn't be thinking. But I couldn't help myself. The booze was in my blood, boiling over, and she was all woman, every inch of her raw woman. She could have been dressed in a burlap bag and she would still have been beautiful. It was just one of those things that hits you, sudden and furious. A wrong move can cost you your job or bring the cops and you don't care.

"Please," she said when I reached for her.

I hesitated but she didn't move. She just stood there, looking up into my face, an amused smile tugging at her full red lips.

"You brought me up here," I said.

"To show you what I do."

"Okay."

"It's one way of passing time."

I looked at the bed and I had an idea how she would be if I could get her over there.

"There are other ways," I said.

"Apparently you think so."

"What man doesn't?"

"There are other things in life."

"Name me one."

She laughed and I knew the laugh didn't tell me yes and it didn't tell me no.

"I'm afraid I can't," she admitted.

This time when I reached for her I didn't stop. My hands found her shoulders, then crept around to the back, pulling her in close.

"Let's not kid each other," I said. "We aren't kids hiding out under a porch. We both know what this is."

I tried to kiss her and she fooled me. She turned her head away and I had to use most of the strength in my right hand to bring it back around so that my mouth could come close to her lips.

"Don't," she murmured.

"Give me one reason."

"It isn't right."

"Because you're married to some guy who's sliding around with one foot in the grave?"

"That isn't a nice thing to say."

"I could tell you something better."

"What?"

"You're lovely."

Her eyes searched my face.

"You aren't so bad yourself."

This time I had no trouble kissing her and I found out why she had been protecting her lips. At first she was passive, almost resisting me, and then, suddenly, she was all fire and flame. It was like the Grand Coolie Dam opening up.

"We shouldn't," she said once.

But she didn't stop kissing me. Her lips were there, hot and willing, and I could feel her hands up there in my hair, straining. She moaned and rocked her head from side to side, her mouth a thing of desire.

"But we are," I managed to say.

"It doesn't make it right."

"What is right?"

Her lips moved against my mouth.

"Perhaps this is," she murmured.

I picked her up and carried her to the bed. She was wild in my arms, an animal of the jungle, and I had all I could do to hold her.

"Lock the door," she said.

"For what?"

"Because."

I left her on the bed and walked over to the door, flipping the lock into place. By the time I turned around she was already out of her dress.

"Who said you weren't anxious?" I asked her.

"You didn't hear me say it."

I helped her with the rest of her things, my hands shaking as I did so. Her flesh was soft, smooth as a piece of velvet, and I ran my hands over her.

"O-o-oh!" she said as she came into my arms.

Her own hands were experienced, filled with need.

"Baby," I breathed.

We fell to the bed together.

"This is still wrong," she said, "but it's the way I want it."

I wanted to tease her.

Her mouth was wide open for me.

"I'm sure."

"Prove it to me."

She did.

Not once.

Not twice.

Several times.

Later, as she dressed, she seemed to be gay and happy.

"I'll see you in class tomorrow, teacher?"

Her bra was tight, filled out, and I wondered how she could get into it.

"For lesson number two," I said.

She laughed and flung her head like a prize mare.

"Am I a good pupil?"

"In more ways than one."

When I left the house, following another drink downstairs, I felt as though I had spent the afternoon in a turkish bath—the kind of a turkish bath you hardly ever find any more.

That night I didn't do any drinking or running around. After supper I went to my cheap room on Kenmore and got into bed. My only regret was that I was alone.

That girl had it.

She sure did.

And as soon as I got the chance I was going back for more.

Chapter 2

Maybe she felt guilty or something, I don't know what it was, but she didn't show up for a driving lesson the next day. In place of her I had a nervous old maid school teacher. She spent the afternoon trying to kill us both in the car and all the time I was watching the traffic I was thinking about Kitty.

Things like Kitty just don't happen to a guy every ten years but by the time the week passed I had put her back in the part of my brain I reserve for happy memories.

Then big as life she showed up again. After waiting a few days maybe women get a head full of memories just like men.

"I thought you'd given up driving."

"It was dangerous."

"But now you think the danger's worth it?"

"You're worth a lot."

She squeezed my hand and looked at me with those big blue eyes. She had been remembering too.

Instead of tearing up the Outer Drive like she did before she drove on down Montrose to the beach.

For a while we just sat there watching the people go by with arms full of blankets and supper baskets as they headed down to the beach. It was the last of May and we were having the first hot weather of the year. Lake Michigan looked cool and green and I felt like we were a couple of kids playing hookey from school to go fishing.

We got out of the car and walked down to the edge of the water. She looked at me again and took my hand as we went on down past the crowd to the point of sand that jutted out into the water. It felt good being close to her again. There was something right about us. We were both young and full of life and we belonged together like that, walking along the beach on a hot May afternoon. When I thought about her being cooped up all the time with that sick old husband of hers it nearly made me sick.

And it was the same way with me. I was young too and full of life and it wasn't right that I should be at loose ends and not have a woman of my own. If you didn't have a woman when you're young when in Hell was the time to have one? And it was the same way about money. Sometimes I watched the rich old dames with the chauffeurs driving them around downtown and thought to myself that it wasn't right. What could dried up old gals like those care for money? Money was made for young people who still knew how to enjoy it.

Hell, the old people had everything and we who were young had nothing. That is we had nothing but sex and before Kitty and I met we didn't even have that, at least not regularly.

We walked on back to the shore and lay down on the grass near a tree.

"Are you happy?" I asked.

She lay on her back and looked up at the white clouds passing over the deep blue sky. It was like she didn't recognize the word.

"You made me happy. I wasn't happy till I met you. I was cooped up in a prison and I could feel everything inside me drying up."

"But you've got lots of money."

"Five dollars a week."

"But look at the place you live, servants, good food, class."

"They don't mean anything."

"Then why did you marry him?"

"I thought they meant something. I thought living in a house like that was all any girl could ever want. And I felt sorry for David."

Suddenly I felt sorry for Kitty. She had everything and she had nothing. She wasn't mean like I had thought at first. She was just a lost kid.

I felt even more sorry for her that afternoon when I took her home.

Her husband was pudgy and bald headed and limped around the living room like a dog sick with the mange. I mean you wanted to shoot him to get him out of his misery. You could tell by his face that he wasn't any happier than Kitty and me. He kept mumbling about his sore foot and then he called in the butler and dressed him down because the chauffeur had quit.

"I don't know when people will learn that they have to work for a living," he was saying to the butler when we went in. "I gave Frank a good room and a good salary and now he leaves without giving any notice."

"That's the way those chauffeurs are," Karl was saying.

"David, this is Mr. Callahan. He's giving me driving lessons."

I shook his fat soft hand.

He kissed Kitty on the cheek and I winced to see his fat red lips that close to her. My mind made pictures of the fat man with his beautiful young wife and I knew I had to get away from there.

Yes, I felt sorry for Kitty all right.

We all sat down and Karl served the before-dinner martinis.

"Mr. Callahan is a wonderful driver. Maybe you could talk him into being our chauffeur. He could go on giving me lessons."

When she said that I could almost see the smile she had inside her.

"Would you consider the job, Mr. Callahan?"

"I don't like my present job."

"I'd see to it that you were well paid and there's a very comfortable room over the garage that goes with the job. You could take your meals here in the house. Uniforms would be furnished and every cent you made would be pure profit."

"It sounds good."

I didn't like the idea of dressing up in a monkey suit, but then I would be near Kitty and then too I thought, he would have a Caddy and a Caddy is the only thing in my book that can come near a beautiful woman.

"What kind of car do you have?"

"Most of your work will be driving the Cadillac. Of course we have a station wagon and another light car, but you won't have much to do with them." He paused a minute like he was trying to think of all my duties. "We have a yacht too. Sometimes you'll be needed to help out there. You aren't afraid of water?"

"No, sir," I said. I hated to say sir to him in front of Kitty, but then you sort of automatically say sir to a man who has three cars and a yacht.

"You look like a good man. I'd like to see you take the job."

I thanked him and told him I would let him know in a few days.

Kitty walked to the front door with me.

"Please take it for my sake, Mike."

"You mean that?"

"Of course I mean it. We can be together every day."

She took my hand in hers and squeezed it and I suddenly felt sorry for her again. Then she stood on her toes and gave my cheek a quick kiss.

"Please."

"It will be dangerous as hell."

"But wonderful."

"God knows how it'll end."

"I love you."

"How can you know?"

"I can feel it down here."

Instead of touching her heart she touched her stomach, but then maybe that's the kind of love we had for each other and maybe that's the only kind of love that's really love.

"I'll give you a ring tomorrow."

"And remember that I love you and that I want to be near you always."

"How can I forget?"

I kissed her and ran down the steps two at a time and got in the car and shot it out into the traffic on Sheridan Road.

That night as I ate my usual fifty-five cent supper at the Marquis Lunchroom on Lawrence Avenue she was still with me begging me to take the job so I could be with her.

But the thing inside me that told me it was dangerous as hell was still with me and it turned my stomach into a leather bag and it made me a little dizzy just to think of the two of us spending the afternoon together in my clean room over the garage. We had tasted love together, but it was only a quick taste. We still had the world of love ahead to explore together with our strong legs locked together.

And the thought of love with her was all the better because it had the sweetness of the forbidden fruit and forbidden fruit is always the sweetest. It was like being a kid again. Was there ever anything more exciting than forbidden moments? And if you took the excitement away from life what did you have left?

I couldn't finish the food.

I didn't want to think about Kitty that night. I wanted to get slightly drunk.

It was just another ironical trick of life that I drove around in a car all day and then had to take an El when I wanted to go someplace at night.

I went to Danny's joint on North Clark Street. He's another one of my buddies I met while I was making the Sahara Desert safe for democracy. Only he was smart when he came home. He got one of these G. I. Business loans and opened a crummy little bar on Clark Street. He made money selling rot gut to bums at twenty cents a throw, and when he had half as much capital saved as any sensible business man would need, he opened a strip joint next door.

It seems like the guys like Danny that don't have any sense are the ones who make all the dough in this country. He's like these Texas millionaires you're always reading about. They get a third-hand set of drilling tools and go out to some God-forsaken desert and start drilling holes in the ground like a gopher that's gone crazy. They get one little well and then they start drilling more holes and the first thing you know these dumb jerks that never had anything in their lives are riding around in Caddies filled with champagne and Texas broads.

Well, that's the kind of guy Danny is. He's got so little sense that he don't know you can't open up a new business on a shoe string.

I pushed open the door at his place and walked in big as day and took a seat at the horseshoe shaped bar that was crowded with conventioneers and just plain everyday degenerates.

"Take it off, take it off," they were calling to the little blonde who was dancing not two feet from their noses. They were beating on the bar with their beer bottles and acting like they don't know she's going to peel. When I didn't get excited and beat on the bar with my bottle, the little queer sitting next to me started giving me the eye so I beat on the bar like all the rest of the degenerates. Who said it was a free country?

By the time the little girl had herself loose for some exercise I saw Danny come out of the back room. He walked past me and I stopped him.

"How's the harem manager?"

"I'm eating and that's more than I can say for some suckers."

"But I don't all the time have to worry about catching something."

We were good friends, but I hadn't seen him since coming back from L. A. He asked me to come in the office for a drink.

You should have seen his office. It was so ritzy that the president of the Bank of America would feel like a country hick there.

"Danny, you've got quite a front here."

"That's how you make the money me boy."

"You talk like that's all there is in the world."

"That ain't all but that's the second most important thing."

He leaned back in the chair to give his beer pot a rest and lighted the stinking Havana cigar he was smoking.

"How come you ain't still in L. A.?"

"That damned house of queers!"

"I heard you liked the coast."

"I did but Hal and I got flim-flammed by some New York sharpies. They found out we had a good racket running cars into Tia Juana and those boys don't let any good rackets stay in private hands. We turned them down at first, but their strong arm boys made it clear as water that we'd get snubbed out if we didn't play ball. Hal joined up with them but I got out. I don't want any trouble like that. A little private racket's one thing, but playing with the big boys is something else again. If you get tired playing in their big league they won't let you quit. I don't want any job I can't quit."

"What you doing here?"

"I'm teaching dames how to drive at the Lake Shore Driving School."

He didn't say it but I could tell from the look in his eyes that he was thinking I was just another guy that would never amount to anything and maybe he was right.

"I might work you into something down here."

"Legitimate work?"

"Almost."

"I'm going straight. I've seen too many of my buddies start out with shady deals and end up in the big house."

"And I've seen too many suckers like you end up in the poor house."

"At least they got dames there."

"Yeah, they got dames but not the kind I got."

While we were talking the door opened and in walked one of his blonde strippers. Her face was still young and pretty and there weren't any marks on it yet from the kind of life she led. Funny how it takes them a year or two before you can see it in their faces. This girl wasn't more than seventeen and I'd guess she was straight in off of some Iowa farm. When young girls like that start going to Hell, they go in a big way. And Danny was just the man to help them.

"We going out to eat?" she asked.

Her voice was still soft.

"Meet Mike Calahan. Mike, this is Bee."

"Glad to know you."

"We going out to eat like you said?"

"Sure thing, baby. Where do you want to eat tonight?"

"Cugat's playing at the Marine Room."

I finished the drink and asked him if he would give me a lift as far as the Edgewater Beach Hotel where they were going for dinner.

You should have seen the car Danny had waiting out front for him. It was one of these cream-colored Caddies with a convertible top. Jeez, when she pulled away from the curb you felt like you were riding on a cloud.

They let me out at the corner. I think Bee had asked him to when she whispered something in his ear as we were leaving. She didn't want the doorman to see her ride up with me in the car.

I stood there on the curb and watched Danny pull away in his Caddy with the little blonde's arm around his neck and it got me way down deep. I didn't envy Danny, (that's a lie, of course I did) but at least what I got I got without putting those little country girls up on the block for a bunch of degenerates to leer at. But, Christ, I didn't have anything. Not a damn thing.

Maybe I did have one thing. Maybe I had Kitty. She was so beautiful and young and clean that she was like something in a dream. She was so much better than me and the kind of people I knew. She was like a drink of clear spring water after months of drinking muddy water purified with G. I. chlorine tablets. Kitty was the real thing and I was lucky to find someone like her. At first I had thought she was mean. But I was wrong. She was too young to be mean.

When I walked up the four flights of steps to my bare room I opened my trunk and took out a fifth I kept stashed away there where the landlady couldn't find it. I sat down on my thin mattressed bed and unscrewed the top of the liquor bottle. Out of habit I wiped the top off with the palm of my hand and then turned the bottle up and gurgled down about five good shots. Then I put the bottle down on the floor beside me and lay down on my squeaky bed to think. I couldn't think. All I could do was see pretty pictures of Kitty floating past me. She was so pure and healthy and right. I'd cut off my right arm up to here for her. As the man said I'd have slaved for her all day just to smell her perfume.

I tried to talk myself out of taking that job as a chauffeur because I was afraid it would mean trouble, but I didn't have a very strong argument with myself. The pretty pictures of Kitty kept interfering with my arguments. Like I said before I never did get along working for big shots, but I couldn't let that stand between Kitty and me.

But if I had been smart I would have dropped the whole thing like a chunk of brimstone.

Chapter 3

"This place gives me the creeps," Kitty said.

We were in my room over the garage.

"It isn't so bad," I said. "The bed springs don't squeak and there's a rug on the floor. It's a lot better than the dump I had on Kenmore."

"But it's too close to everything."

Kitty was sitting on my bed and I was in the chair by the window. She reached over to the night table and pulled out a cigarette.

"We can't have everything."

"Can't we?"

"What do you mean?"

"Nothing. I was just thinking."

"Nobody ever has everything. We got the most important thing. We're together."

"We can never be together as long as David is alive."

I knew what she meant. His picture kept coming up in my dreams. He was always walking up the steps to my room over the garage, opening the door and finding Kitty and me in bed together with our bodies clinched. But I didn't like the way she used the word "alive". There's some things you think about but don't ever say out loud.

She was studying the ceiling above the bed but I could tell from the way she was wiggling her foot that she had something else on her mind. After a while she turned her head and looked at me.

"Mike, we've got to stop."

"What do you mean?"

"We can't go on seeing each other like this."

"Don't start getting soft on me."

The afternoon sun spilled in through the windows, crawled across the room and found our naked bodies lying close together on the bed. I wasn't looking at her but I knew she was there, her needs now satisfied. We had been together since shortly after lunch and the hours had been filled with fury and passion.

She was on the outside and she got up, hunting for her clothes. I watched her, watched the sweeping lines of her body, the high, proud tilt of her breasts.

"It was your idea," I reminded her. "If it hadn't been for you I'd still be pushing cars for that driving school."

She leaned forward and then straightened as she hooked her bra.

"Guilty," she said.

I rolled over and sat up on the edge of the bed.

She struggled into the dress and pulled up the zipper on the side.

"We've been doing all right."

"All right? You call sneaking up here in the afternoon all right?"

I shrugged and got to my feet. I guess I should have been slightly embarrassed that I wasn't wearing anything but I wasn't. She had seen me this way before and she would see me this way again.

"You take what you can get," I told her. "What is it they say? A half a loaf is better than none?"

"Maybe it depends on which half you get."

"Well, I've got the best half."

"With David alive there is no best half."

I closed my eyes for a second and tried to forget about him. In my dreams he was always walking up the steps to my room over the garage, opening the door—there wasn't any lock on it— and finding Kitty and me in bed together. Sometimes the dream woke me up and then I couldn't get back to sleep again. I'd lay there sweating, my guts on fire. What would he do if he ever found us? I didn't know. And what would we do? He didn't give her much, that was true, but what I could give her would be even less.

"Forget about him," I said roughly. "When we're up here together he's out of our world."

She shook her head. "He's never out of our world, Mike. As long as he lives he's a big part of it."

My clothes were on the other side of the room but I never got to them, not then. I grabbed for her, catching her, and she came into my arms, all soft and warm and alive.

"I love you," I said.

"Mike—"

"Get that through your head, baby. I wouldn't have come out here to work if it hadn't been the real thing."

"Let me go, Mike."

"Why?"

"You know why." She strained against me. "You only have to touch me and I go a little crazy wanting you. I've been here for a long time now and what if somebody has been looking for me?"

She was right. We had to be careful. I released her and walked over to where I had thrown my clothes. Or had she thrown them? We had been pretty savage that afternoon and we hadn't cared what we did.

"Tell them you went for a walk," I said.

"It isn't that simple."

"It is if you don't complicate it with a lot of fears."

"I *am* afraid," she said, throwing back her head and taking a deep breath. "I'm scared to death."

"Of what?"

"Supposing I should become—"

"You won't."

"He would know it wasn't his and then where would I be? I'd be done, that's what I would be. Done."

It took me a few seconds to get into my clothes.

"You're making a mountain out of a sand pile."

"No, I'm not."

"Yes, you are. How many other people do you think do these things? Lots of them. They just don't get caught, that's all. And we won't get caught. We play it smart and no one will ever know."

"Only us."

"Well, naturally."

"Isn't that enough?"

I was annoyed with her.

"Say, what are you driving at?" I demanded.

She lowered her head and her eyes returned to my face. She gave it to me straight, without any frills.

"Mike, we've got to stop."

"Come again."

"I said we've got to stop."

"I don't get you."

"We can't go on seeing each other like this."

She had belonged to me, all of her, and I didn't want to let her go. There had been other girls in the past, several of them, but none had had what Kitty had. Kitty was a man's woman, a woman to be loved, a woman who could please a man in a dozen different ways.

"Don't start getting soft on me," I said.

"I can't help it. I can't spend my days here with you and then go to him at night and have him put his fat arms around me."

She was hitting below the belt when she painted that picture for me. I had almost thought of them together like that too, but every time my mind came close to thinking about it, I shifted over to something else. It made my stomach rumble to hear her talk about it.

"And you want to break it off between us just like that?"

"I don't want to. I love you, Mike, and I don't want to ever break it off with you, but not many women can love two men and keep clean."

"You told me you didn't love him."

"I don't, but you know how it is. After all I am married to him."

When she said that I was suddenly as hot as a T model Ford climbing Pike's Peak.

"What do you mean?"

"Mike, you aren't a child."

"Then let's leave. Get your things together and we'll pull out. I can get a job in L.A."

"What if it would wear out?"

"I don't get you."

"What if we don't really love each other? Maybe it's just an infatuation with us and if it were to cool off you'd leave me and then where would I be?"

"I love you."

She didn't say any more. She just took long drags on her cigarette and looked far away into space.

When it was four o'clock and time for me to go downtown and pick up David we got ready to go. She kissed me and opened the door.

"This is the last time, Mike. I love you but I can't go on like this."

"Wait a minute. Let's talk this over a little more before you say that."

But she ran down the steps and out around the edge of the garage without looking back at me.

This was not going to be an easy one to charge off the books. Some girls you could have for a night or a year and just wipe them off your mind like wiping chalk off a blackboard, but Kitty wasn't that kind of a girl. Looking back on it now after all these months it's hard for me to say what she had that was different from other girls. I guess maybe it was her spirit that made her different, that and the way she would look at me—like I was the only real man in the whole world. Yeah, Kitty was differ ent from other girls and it wouldn't be easy to charge her off the books.

I drove the Cadillac down to the Palmolive Building on Michigan Avenue to pick up David. (I had talked about him to Kitty so many times that even now I think of him as David instead of Mr. Grey.) When I saw him come limping out of the building I jumped out and held the door open for him.

"Mike, I want you to take me by the doctor's office before we go home."

"Yes, sir. I hope you aren't feeling worse today."

He must have felt worse because he began talking about his ailments and it was the first time he had ever mentioned them to me.

"I'm afraid I don't feel very well."

He paused for a minute and then went on.

"From your place you must look upon me as a very lucky man, but believe you me we all have our problems. I'm very rich and I live in a beautiful house and I have a very charming wife, but I have diabetes."

"I'm sorry to hear that, sir."

"Yes, I have my troubles too. I have an ulcer on my right leg. That's what makes me limp. Diabetics have a tendency to ulcers on the extremities, and when they come it's next to impossible to cure them. They might have to amputate my leg."

"I'm sorry, sir. I hope the doctor will have good news for you today."

"Thank you, Mike."

As I drove on through the five o'clock traffic on the Outer Drive, I was thinking about this poor bastard in the back seat. I couldn't help but wonder how long he would live and I remembered what I had thought when I first saw him. He was a poor miserable man and like a mangy dog, he would be better off dead. Then I thought about the stinking ulcer on his leg and I thought about him making Kitty sleep in the same bed with him in spite of his rotten leg, but you can't think thoughts like that and stay sane so I put it out of my mind.

After he came out of the doctor's office he seemed to be in better spirits.

"The doctor wants me to take a trip."

"That sounds good, sir."

"It's just the thing for me. I need to get away from it all for a few weeks."

"Where are we going, sir?"

"Hot Springs. He thinks the change would be good for my leg and you know he might be absolutely right."

"I'd like to get away for a while myself."

"That's good because I'll want you to drive me down."

I could see pictures of Kitty and me together again. Down there I would have a regular room in the hotel and she wouldn't worry so much about being caught. He would be taking the baths and stuff and it would give both of us a lot of free time. I thought that I could get Kitty to depend on my loving so much that she couldn't do without it if I just had her with me for a few more weeks. We could run away together, just drop off the face of the earth and it would be wonderful. Dames are all the time hesitating about running away or sleeping with a man or doing anything like that but if you work on them long enough most of them will come around to your way of thinking.

When Karl rang my room that night about nine o'clock and told me that Mr. Grey wanted to talk with me, I thought he was going to tell me all about his plans for the trip.

He was seated in the overstuffed chair by the fireplace reading *The Wall Street Journal* when I came in. Kitty was on the sofa with her legs drawn up under her, reading a magazine. She didn't look up at me. It was like she was afraid to look me straight in the eye. For a crazy moment I was afraid she had told David about our affair. Kitty was a flighty sort of girl, the kind you couldn't always depend on and that's just the type who would run home and tell daddy about the nasty old man.

"We've decided to leave tomorrow for Hot Springs."

"That's fine, sir."

"But Mrs. Grey has talked me out of driving down. She thinks it would be better for me to fly. I telephoned my doctor and he agreed with her, so we won't need you for the trip. I'll rent a car down there if I want to go out anyplace."

It seemed funny that he should explain to me why he didn't want me to drive him. I guess it was because one chauffeur had quit on him and he didn't want to take any chances on losing me.

"You can stay around the house and take it easy until we come back in about two weeks."

"Thank you, sir. Will that be all?"

"That's all, Mike. I might add that I've been very pleased with your services and that it's not because of you that I'm flying down."

Yes, it is, but you just don't know it, I thought.

I tried to catch Kitty's eye before I left the room, but she didn't look up from the magazine in her lap.

It looked like our affair was really ended. Maybe she was one girl who meant it when she said no, but if she was it would be the first girl I'd met who was that way.

Anyway, her going away did something to me. It was like I had owned the whole world for a month and then suddenly had it jerked away from me and given to somebody else. I don't know why I was fool enough to let it hurt me so much. I was thirty years old at the time and I had knocked about the world a good deal. I had known women by the hand full and I tried to make myself believe that Kitty was just another skirt in my life.

But like I said before she did something to me that no other woman ever did. Kitty was so clean and above me that having her made me feel like I really had something for the first time in my life. I was lonesome as hell after she left.

And then something else happened to make things worse. That bastard of a valet named Karl started riding my butt and after a few days I knew why the other chauffeur had quit.

Karl was the butler and the valet and was the one who really ran the house. He was a tall man with a dark soul. There were deep circles under his eyes and you could never guess what he was thinking. His hair was cropped short and he still had a trace of his German accent.

Karl took over after David and Kitty left. The next morning when he called me and asked me to come to the house for a talk you would have thought it was his house. He was sitting in the boss' chair by the fireplace smoking a cigar. I thought he had called me in so he could send me to the store to pick up something for lunch, but he had something else in mind.

"I saw Mrs. Grey coming down from your room the other day."

"Maybe she was looking for me."

"I saw you come down a few minutes later."

"And what does that prove?"

"Mr. Grey is a very jealous man."

"I don't blame him."

"Let's not beat around the bush."

"All right, what are you getting at?"

"If you want to keep your job I'd suggest you leave Mrs. Grey alone."

"I don't know what you're talking about."

"I hope not."

You could tell he didn't believe me. But I was pretty sure he didn't have anything definite on us or he would have gone to Mr. Grey. That was the last thing I wanted him to do. After all, I was sure David would fire me if he had even the least suspicion and I wanted to keep the job, because it meant I could see Kitty. If I had a few more weeks with her I was certain I could talk her into running away with me. If it hadn't been for her I would have told him to take the job and do you-know-what with it.

No, he wasn't sure about anything, but he was sure enough to make life hell for me and know that I wouldn't go to David and complain about it. I guess all of us have a sadistic streak and if we got the chance we'd probably all enjoy giving some poor guy hell. Well, Karl had me and he knew it. He made my life hell. First he told me that there was some heavy work to do in the house and had me down on my knees waxing and polishing the hall steps by hand. I took my time about it, but I didn't complain any. I thought it was just a trick to show me who was boss. When I finished that I went up to my room for a nap and the first thing I knew he was on the phone telling me that there was more work to be done.

"You think this is going to be a vacation just because the boss's gone on a trip?"

"He told me about my duties when I came to work for him and he didn't say anything about polishing the hall stairs."

"But he told you that I run this house?"

"No."

"Then I'm telling you now. I want you to wash the basement windows and then scrub the floors."

The basement was about as big as the Chicago Stadium and it was plenty dirty, but I went to work on it. It was June then and the basement had a musty odor about it that almost smothered me. I was sure I'd catch something down there, but nothing happened. All week I kept at it till I could feel the dirt in my lungs. By the time Saturday night came around I was mad and tired and when I get mad it makes me want a woman. I just couldn't stand waiting till Kitty came home. Maybe I could have waited if I had been sure she was coming back to me. It was either go out on the town or blow my top and take a punch at Karl.

I decided to go to town.

Chapter 4

I'm like other humans, but in a way I'm different, in an important way. When the rest of humanity dreams about doing things and thinks about these things that's the end of it. They don't actually ever do those somethings because something inside them holds them in place. That something is missing in me. I dream about making love to a girl and I think about it till it gets so strong that it's just like reality and then nothing holds me back and I do it.

It had been that way with me all week. Karl had almost worked me to death and Kitty had left me. I was mad and as the week went past the hate grew inside me like a black flower that opens up in the night. And the more hate I felt the worse I had to get drunk and have a woman. It was the only thing I knew that would make me feel clean again. Some people can get clean by praying or confessing or knocking a golf ball, but I'm not that way. Maybe I could have gotten clean that way too if I had learned it from the start, but I never learned how to confess or play golf and I get rid of my bad feeling the best way I can.

Maybe I picked it up from my mother. She ran a gin mill over on the west side, and my first memories go back to her tavern and all the people sitting at the bar on Saturday night and laughing and playing the juke box. And when the laughs were all out they'd start playing with me; They'd start off by giving me beer and then they'd damn near rupture themselves laughing when I'd get enough beer in me to stagger around the room. That's how I got this burn on my left shoulder. One night they got me dizzy and I staggered into the wood stove that heated the joint. But maybe that was funny too, I don't remember.

I did a stretch for six months back in 1940 before I went in the army. It was one of these fancy jails in California where they have baseball teams and all that kind of stuff. This jail was so fancy they even had a psychiatrist to talk to all the prisoners once a month.

After I'd been in this jail about a week they took me up to his office and told me to sit down and wait for the doctor. I was surprised when he treated me like a human and it seemed like he was sort of a queer or something because he just sat there and talked to me. He asked me all kinds of silly questions like where I came from and how far I went in school.

"I don't know who my old man was," I said and I thought he'd kick me out then, but he didn't do a thing but just sit there and wait for me to go on talking. Anyways, this grey-haired doctor and I got to be pretty good friends before my stretch was over and on the day before I left he called me up to his office to tell me goodbye. I asked him why he was interested in me and he said I was an interesting case.

"What do you mean case?" I asked him.

"You are a person who hasn't really grown up."

"I don't get you, doc."

"You see when we are growing up our ego develops so that we are able to distinguish between fact and fiction. We learn to control the primitive part of our personality and not act out on our phantasies. You are what we call a psychopath."

Now I'm sure that psychiatrist knew a lot about me. I couldn't figure out all he said and I don't guess there are many people who could, but I'm sure it was important.

When Saturday came I called Danny and asked him to fix me up with a date. You might not think Danny and I were good friends but we were in a special way. He somehow represented all that was bad in me and when I was in a bad mood like I was that day he was a very good friend of mine. Later when I would get it all out of my system I wouldn't like him at all, but then I knew that the whole cycle would repeat and I would want him as a good friend again. The difference between Danny and me was that Danny was all bad. He made a profession of his badness and mine was just a hobby.

"You want something extra nice?" he asked me.

"I could do it justice tonight."

"I got a new girl down here who's got a sister. How would you like that?"

"It suits my mood right down the line."

"I'll give them a ring. You meet me here at the strip joint about nine."

Karl paid me that afternoon and I went down to the Loop and bought a grey summer suit that had real class. After supper I went to one of these double features at the Roosevelt where everybody gets shot up and where the good guys win over the bad guys at the end.

When I got to Danny's joint the place was just opening up. A flat chested girl who was the M.C. was standing up there on the stage making cracks about her flat chest and stuffing a handkerchief down in the top of her dress and strutting around like she suddenly had something in her dress.

Danny was in a good mood and got up from his desk to slap me on the back when I came in. It always made him happy to find someone who felt the same way he did about the girls. Maybe it made his conscience lighter and made him feel like a better man when he found somebody else who's as low as he is.

"Fran's on next. We'll go out front and watch her do her stuff."

"Is Fran the girl you were talking about?"

"That's the baby. She started working here last Tuesday. Best girl I've had here this year."

We went out front by the bar where Danny ordered a drink for both of us and insisted that I join him in the doubtful pleasure of smoking a stogie.

"That M.C.'s a slut if I ever saw one."

"She's queer as a Chinaman eating spaghetti, but she keeps the customers entertained."

After about five minutes the M.C. ran out of jokes about her flat chest and motioned for the boys in the band to announce the next number.

"I'm sure you boys heard about Fran Sims," the M.C. said in her harsh voice. "If you think I got it wait till you see her."

The music blared again and Fran walked out on the stage. She wasn't as young as some of the others, you could tell she was the kind of girl who would hold up under it. She had long legs like in the Petty drawings and they were the hard legs of a dancer. You could see the long muscles stand out as she walked around in her high heel shoes. And she walked with a cocky air like a marionette pulled in quick movements by a string up above. At first she just walked around the edge of the stage that projected out into the room. She looked down at the faces below her like she hated them all and was going to torture each one individually. She was going to undress the most seductive way she knew how and she was going to dance around out there for the boys, and then she was going to quietly walk to the edge of the stage and leave them with nothing but a cottony taste in their mouths. That was her revenge on mankind.

Fran did a whirling dance as the orchestra played the slow music and then casually she began taking off her gloves and it was funny seeing what that could do to an audience. I guess it was the first thing that started the old chain reaction going and that's why it got them when she casually peeled off her gloves, danced to the back of the stage and gave them to a girl waiting there for them.

The music picked up its tempo and she danced faster. The damned degenerates sitting around the bar started calling out "Take it off, take it off," and beating on the bar with their beer bottles. Now she smiled a little, a mean smile that said "Now you guys have started to suffer. I'm going to put you through hell and then leave you to go back to your empty rooms where you won't be able to sleep from thinking about me. I'll make you suffer the lonely hell that scum deserves."

But as they watched her take off her evening dress and then turn away from them and take off her bra and then turn back to them with her breasts swinging in cadence with the fast music, as they watched her bare from the waist up dancing before them, they did not suffer. They grinned up at her and thought, "Now you cheap little bitch, take it off up there and throw it around in front of us and show the whole world that you're nothing but a bitch."

And that was the way the woman made the men suffer and that was how the men made the woman suffer and neither one was really suffering. The woman and the men were both doing it to get rid of that same feeling that I had. Some take it out in exercise and some take it out in drinking and some take it out in watching.

Now the music was hard and the deep-throated drum beat out a rhythm that was discovered in the jungles a million years ago and Fran danced faster. The tempo of the drums increased and the whole room shook from the sex and the drums and the hips and then the naked girl fell down on the floor in a convulsion as the drums reached their climax and a trumpet blared out from nowhere and all the lights went off so that the girl and the men were alone with their thoughts of full hips and hot naked flesh and jungles a million years old and drums that beat in your stomach.

I took a deep breath like I hadn't been able to breathe for a long time. When the lights came on the girl had disappeared and there was silence among the men for a minute like the silence that comes at eleven o'clock on November the eleventh. Then there was talking again and the bartenders were throwing ice cubes in glasses and the room was back to the Chicago of 1959.

"How did you like her?" Danny asked me.

"Is her sister like that?"

"I don't know. Never met her."

Danny relighted his cigar and I ground mine out on the floor.

"Come on back to my office and we'll meet her sister."

As we picked our way through the crowd to the back room Danny told the M.C. to send Fran and her sister to the office.

Fran had on her green evening dress again and it seemed strange to see her dressed because she looked about like any other show girl with her clothes on, only her face was still a little flushed and her eyes were puffy like she had been making love.

"This is Mike. Remember I was telling you he'd take Ruth out? Mike meet Fran."

"I liked your show."

"Then you're O.K. with me." She shook hands with me.

"Where's your sister?" Danny asked.

"She was lying down. I'll go back and see if she's finished putting on her face."

"Not bad," Danny said when she had gone.

"A lot of woman."

I soon found out that her sister was quite different. She was quite young, not much over eighteen, and she dripped sex like a leaky faucet. Her breasts were bigger than those of her sister and her hips had the roundness of youth. It was her first trip away from home and she looked like a scared kid who was getting into something that she didn't understand. I grinned as we were introduced. If she didn't know what it was all about I would be more than pleased to teach her.

Danny whispered something to Fran and the girl laughed.

"Of course not," she said and put her arm around her sister.

As we left the strip joint Danny looked at my date as though he wished he were walking in my shoes.

Chapter 5

We wrapped the town up fine that night. I really felt like somebody driving up to the door with Danny and the girls in that cream-colored Caddy and having door men all but bow as they helped us out.

First we went down to the loop and caught an ice show at the Boulevard Room and then we went to Barney's for a steak. After that Danny said he wanted to show us how the other half lived and took us to the Buttery at the Ambassador West.

Sitting there watching the college kids drink I got to thinking about Kitty. She was like those college kids, clean and well groomed. It was funny to see how different they were from our dates. They could be wearing the same clothes and eating the same food, but there was a difference that you could always spot. I was sure those college kids raised their bits of hell and that one or two of the girls had probably had as much experience as Fran, but there was a difference and it made me feel big as hell to know Kitty and I wished she'd hurry back.

While I was sitting there drinking I got to thinking about her husband with the stinking ulcer on his leg. I got mad just sitting there thinking about her being married to him.

We were all drinking heavy except Ruth. She just sat there and tried to take it all in without staring. When she took a sip of her drink I could tell she wasn't used to drinking and that she didn't like it. Studying her helped me to get my mind off Kitty and I began to wonder why she came to Chicago to live with a sister like Fran. Somehow you'd picture Ruth going to a country schoolhouse some place and then marrying the farmer's son and having a dozen kids and growing old without ever going to a strip joint in Chicago. Later I learned that she hadn't wanted to come to Chicago at all. She had lived with her father in down-state Illinois and three months before she came to Chicago her father had had a stroke. She took care of him there at home until the doctor told him he would never be able to farm again. He sold the place and went to live with his brother in Davenport. There wasn't room for Ruth too, so it was decided that she should come to Chicago and stay with her older sister. I guess the others in the family thought Fran was acting in plays when she told them she was on the stage.

"Did you see your sister's act tonight?" I asked Ruth when the others got up to dance.

"No."

She looked down at her glass and I could tell she was embarrassed.

"She's quite a girl."

"I didn't know she worked in a place like that."

"Would you have come to live with her if you had known?"

"I guess so. I didn't have much choice," she said, and then told me about her father's sickness.

"You going to work there too?"

"Fran said I'd have to. I don't know how to do office work or anything like that."

"Can you dance?"

"No, but Fran said she'd teach me."

"I'll bet she'll teach you lots of things."

"I'm pretty green about everything, but Fran told me what to do. I'll get along."

"You'd better be careful or your sister'll get you in trouble."

As I was saying this I wondered why I should be warning her. After all she was my date and I had every intention of getting her in as much trouble as possible before the night was over. The kind of get-togethers Danny gave weren't exactly tea parties. Danny liked to start off by hitting the town and drinking enough to mellow up. Then he liked to take everybody to his place and drown himself in booze.

Danny came back to the table puffing and laughing. He sat down without holding the chair for Fran.

"Why don't you two give it a fling?" he wanted to know.

"Would you like to dance?" I asked Ruth.

"I'm afraid I'm not very good."

"I'm not the world's champion either."

"Go on, give it a try," Fran said. "Let him lead and you follow."

Ruth stood up as though she had made up her mind to do everything that her sister told her to do.

Ruth was right. She wasn't a good dancer. She followed me all right, but she was stiff and frightened.

"Relax," I told her.

"I'm trying."

"That doesn't mean that you have to be a foot away from me."

She hesitated a moment and then came in closer. It was good to hold her, to have her body next to mine. Once, when a couple banged into us, she hit me hard and I could feel her breasts down there, round and shoving out. My hand at her back was over her bra strap; it was narrow and taut and I wondered how big she was.

"You'll like Chicago," I said.

"I hope so."

The music ended and we drifted toward our table.

"You'd feel better if you got a few drinks into you," I said.

"Do you think so?"

"A couple of belts will take away the nervous edge."

When we sat down again I ordered a double whiskey for Ruth. She looked at me, smiling faintly, and then drank it all down without taking a breath.

"Look at that girl go. You're getting the spirit now," Danny said and laughed as he told the waiter to give us all another double.

By the time we were at Danny's apartment Ruth was so wobbly I had to help her out of the car.

"Now we'll have a real party," Danny said when we got inside his three-hundred-a-month apartment that overlooked the lake. "You girls can take off your things while I get the whiskey."

I looked around the living room at the fancy modernistic furniture. When he came back with a couple of bottles I was standing in front of the picture window that looked out over the lake twenty stories below.

"That dame of yours is gonna be all right," he said and slapped me on the back.

"She's too young for this kind of party."

"Aw, come off it, Mike, I thought you wanted to have a real party. We'll get the girls a little more liquored up and then let Fran give her sister a lesson in stripping."

Danny was right, I had set my heart on a real party that night, but now that I had been around Ruth for a few hours I had almost changed my mind. She was just a sweet corn-fed girl from Iowa and I didn't want to be the one to introduce her to a big city like Danny knew. Well, I might not be able to talk

Danny out of a big party, but I would certainly keep him away from Ruth even if I ended up slugging it out with him.

"Let's have a couple of shots while the girls are straightening up," I said to Danny. If I could get him drunk enough my job would be a good deal easier. Then I remembered Danny kept some knock-out drops around the apartment someplace to use on girls if they really wanted to hold out on him. I decided to look for the medicine and try to slip some in Danny's drink. Would he ever hate me in the morning if he ever found out what I did to him!

"What else do you have around as a mix?" I asked.

"About everything you ever heard of, ole pal. You name it and Danny has it."

"I'd like to have some cream to make a King Alphonso."

"A what?" he said like I had told him I wanted the S. S. Queen Mary to float in my bathtub.

"I want a King Alphonso. Didn't you ever hear of that?"

"Sure, but I never heard of anybody drinking it on a party."

"Then you've heard of something new tonight," I said. "O. K. if I *go* back in the kitchen for some cream?"

"I'll get it for you. Nothing's too good tonight for my friend Mike Callahan."

After Danny left the room I quickly searched the liquor cabinet for the chloral drops. I couldn't find any there or in the dining room cupboard. Danny came back just as I seated myself in the living room again.

"Here's a King Alphonso for my good friend Mike Callahan."

"Thanks, Danny," I said and took a sip of the sweet drink. He was right, it was a mighty poor drink to have on a party and my stomach objected to mixing it with the bourbon highballs that had gone before, but I had asked for it and now I had to drink it. The girls came back in the room as we sat there nursing our drinks. Fran went over to sit on Danny's knee and Ruth sat down on the sofa beside me.

"Do you feel better now?" I asked her. She nodded her head and looked up at me with her big brown cow eyes. No, I wasn't going to let anything happen to her. I felt very tender towards her and I was sorry that she had come to Chicago to get mixed up in this kind of life. It was times like that that I wished I knew something about life, why the whole world was so screwed up, why you felt good one minute and bad the next, and what was right and what was wrong. I wished I was one of those smart college guys that knew all about everything, and for a minute I even thought about going to night school so I could get all the answers like that college guy I had known in the army. But then I wondered if those college guys knew it all. This college guy I had known in the army had ended up by putting a Ml rifle in his mouth and blowing the top of his head off. But maybe that was because he was so smart. Maybe that was the real answer.

When I finished my drink I told Danny that I was going in the kitchen to get my own cream this time. He was busy turning off the lights and didn't say "no." I looked through the refrigerator and kitchen cabinets for the chloral, but I wasn't able to find any. While I was mixing my drink there in the kitchen I heard a muffled scream from the living room. I put the pony glass down on the sink and ran back towards the living room.

"Don't be such a prig," Danny was saying. The light coming in from the picture windows showed me Danny's beer potted body leaning over Ruth trying to push her down on the couch and kiss her.

That was when I hit him. For a minute his eyes went open wide like he didn't believe it, and then he charged into me and started throwing wild punches at my face, but they weren't all wild because one of them knocked me down and in a second he was on top of me. We went rolling over and over and then he jumped up and the next thing I knew a metal ash tray glanced off my head and struck the floor by my right ear. I rolled over and was able to get my arms around his legs and pull him down on the floor beside me. I crawled on top and smashed him in the jaw with my fist. I could feel his jaw turn to mush under the blow and I knew the fight was over. He just groaned and held both hands against his jaw like it would come off if he let go.

"Let's get out of here," I said to Ruth.

She looked down at Danny lying on the floor.

"I don't know what got into him," she said. "I just don't."

I knew what had gotten into him. He had seen her and he had wanted her. Not that I blamed him so much. She was as ripe as a berry on a vine and somebody was going to enjoy the fruit.

"Let's get out of here," I said again.

Fran was putting cold towels on Danny's face when we left.

She didn't even look at us.

Chapter 6

When Ruth and I reached the street below there was a soft warm early morning breeze coming in from the lake and you could tell from the pearl grey color of the sky over the lake that it was nearly morning.

I didn't know what to do with Ruth. Now that I had taken her away from her sister it was up to me to take care of her.

I reached down and took her hand in mine and without speaking we walked to the underpass at Michigan and Oak and went down the steps and through the dark tunnel over to the beach. We walked on up the beach a little way and sat down to rest. I put my arm around her shoulders and she let her head relax on my arm like she was trusting me to help her.

We sat there for a long time without talking, looking out over the water that was still and grey, letting the warm breeze rumple our hair.

After awhile I began talking softly.

"Ruth, you got yourself in a mess by coming to Chicago."

I waited for her to agree with me, but she didn't say anything. I looked down at her face to see if she was asleep, but she wasn't. I guess she was just too done-in by everything to talk about it.

"I don't care how tough things are with you, you can't go back with your sister. She's bad all the way through. Maybe it's not all her fault but she's not much better than a prostitute and if you stay around her you'll get the same way."

I stopped for a minute trying to think of what to say next, but I wasn't much good at preaching.

"I've knocked around the world a lot and I know some things you couldn't possibly know. I know how girls like your sister end up. Life's a lot of hell raising fun for her now, but in five more years her body will be too old for a stripper and Danny or somebody like him will fire her and then she'll start hustling for sure, and she won't be a first class one either. There'll be lines on her face and dark circles under her eyes from the kind of life she's led and she won't be able to even get a good price for selling herself and she'll drink more and pretty soon any drunk will be able to have her for only a couple of shots of bar whiskey. Then she'll drink more and more to kill all the hate in her that she'll feel and then she'll have a bad liver or she'll go on dope or she'll get pneumonia some cold night lying in a dark alley where some guy will leave her after knocking her in the head, and they'll take her to County Hospital where she'll die and be buried in an unmarked grave.

"And if you start now, something will be killed inside you and you'll go the same way. Do you know that?"

"Yes. I'm afraid. I don't know anybody in Chicago and I don't know how to get a job or a place to live or anything. And I can't go back home. I don't have any home."

It seemed screwy that a girl should feel so lost in a place like Chicago and then I tried to think back to when I was seventeen. I remembered that the world seemed very complicated and strange to me then. If I had come to Chicago from a farm where I had lived a quiet life with my family, I guess Chicago would have seemed even larger. When I pictured myself seventeen again I could understand Ruth better. She didn't know about things like Traveler's Aid or the Y.W.C.A. or night school or employment agencies. They were all things of the city that she had never even heard of. She knew as little about them as I knew of the 4H clubs.

Talking with Ruth and sitting there with my arm around her made me feel like a better man. Here was someone who trusted me enough to leave her own sister and go out into the city with me alone.

I wasn't in love with her or anything but I felt very tender. It must be the same feeling a mother has when she puts her arm around her small child that is so defenseless and that trusts her for food and protection.

I squeezed her shoulder with my hand and I wanted to say foolish things that I had never said before. I wanted to say, "There, there, I'll take care of you. Everything will be all right."

For the first time in my life I wasn't just out to get all I could from the world. It was a good feeling and I wished it would last, but I was sure it would go away when it got light and I would be the same as always. You don't turn soft that easy.

We sat there a long time with her head on my shoulder and my arm around her. When we got up to leave the sun was coming up out of the lake and the cars were beginning to swish past on the Outer Drive behind us.

"I think the Y.W.C.A. would be the best place for you to stay."

"Can I go back to our hotel for my things?"

"Do you have a key to the room?"

"No."

"Then let's skip it."

"But I've got to have some clothes to wear."

"You aren't just trying to find an excuse to go back with your sister?"

I had seen lots of girls who would really like to be strippers. For all I knew that was what Ruth really wanted. She had never said much about really wanting to leave her sister.

"No, it's not that. I've just got to have some clothes to wear."

"You're sure you want to leave your sister for good?"

"Yes."

"Then I'll go to the hotel with you and see that there's no trouble."

As we walked back through the underpass I thought about the crazy deal I had worked myself into. A rough guy like me talking a girl out of staying with her sister didn't make much sense. If she wanted to be a stripper and hit the bottom of the barrel, what business was it of mine? She was old enough to take care of herself. My guess was that she wasn't as innocent as she acted. A girl didn't grow up like she had grown up and not know what life was all about.

We stopped at an all night coffee shop in the Near North Side for breakfast. While we were eating I studied her. She had the build for a chorus girl or a stripper. And a build for something else. I finished my coffee and pushed the cup aside. What was I kidding myself for? She had a hotel room and I was going there for just one reason. I missed Kitty and what she had given me. I had come to town looking for what a man usually looks for and this Ruth was no better than any other girl.

Later we walked over to Fran's hotel on Delaware Street. The old guy on the desk looked us over pretty good and said he wouldn't give us the key.

"For five," I suggested, reaching into my pocket.

The five changed his mind and he came up with the key.

"It happens all the time," he said.

We walked to the elevator and Ruth said she couldn't understand the old man's attitude.

"He's got his mind in the gutter," I explained.

The room was on the fourth floor and it was just a room. There was a bed, two windows, a couple of chairs and a carpet on the floor that had a big burn in it.

"I haven't got much," she said.

I sat down on the bed.

"Take your time."

She moved around the room, getting dresses from the closet and picking up things from one of the dresser drawers. All of this went into a cheap suitcase with a broken strap.

"You've been nice to me," she said.

"You're a nice girl."

The dress hugged her body and when she bent over the suitcase I thought she was going to spill outside of it. She was rich there and if she wasn't thirty-eight she wasn't an inch. She had some trouble with the catch on the suitcase and as I continued to stare at her my head began to pound. We were alone in the room, just the two of us, and what I wanted to do was for two people to do alone.

"I'll help you," I said and got up from the bed.

"It's just an old thing."

"Well, it's better than nothing."

She had part of a garter belt caught in one corner and that was the trouble. I opened the suitcase, pushed the garter belt inside and closed the suitcase without difficulty.

"I wish I had a drink," I said.

"I don't. I still feel them. I never did drink much. My father didn't believe in it and the boys I knew couldn't afford to."

I was near to her, smelling her perfume and the woman smell of her. The pound in my head raced to the back of my neck and my feet were numb.

"She won't be back right away," I said.

"Meaning my sister?"

"She'll stay with Danny. They'll make a night and a day of it. When he goes on a tear it's one for the book."

"How can she stand him?"

"He's her bread and butter."

"Even so."

"If you took a job with him he'd expect the same thing from you."

She made a face.

"The pig," she said. "He reminds me of one of the hogs back on the farm."

I didn't know what I was going to remind her of but I was going to find out. She had what I wanted, enough for any man, and if she got out of the room without giving it to me she would have to fight her way clear.

"I think I like you," I said.

Maybe it was true and maybe it wasn't but what do you tell a girl when you're after her?

"And I like you. You're kind."

"I'm still human."

"Aren't we all?"

I didn't ask her if she was willing or if she would fight me or anything. I just took her in my arms and my mouth went down there to her lips. I kissed her, burning the kiss in, fighting her stiffness and restraint.

"No," she whispered.

"You wanted me to come up here, didn't you?"

She turned her head away.

"I don't—know."

"Don't you trust me?"

"I know what you think I am."

"No, you don't. I think you're a sweet girl. I think there's something here that we shouldn't miss. And you need somebody. You need somebody bad."

This time when I kissed her I knew I had her. Her lips moved, opening up, and her tongue was there to greet me.

"I said this would never happen," she panted.

I didn't know what she meant and I didn't care. I had her over to the bed, pushing her down, everything that she might have said or done clouded by the passion that swelled within me.

"Don't hurt me," she begged.

But I did hurt her.

I couldn't help it.

I was the first.

Later, as we left the building, I told the night man not to say anything about our visit.

"I'd get fired if I did," he said and settled back to sleep in one of the overstuffed chairs in the lobby.

On the way to the McCormick Y.W.CA. on Dearborn Street I told Ruth there were agencies in the city to take care of girls like her.

"You mean, if I get in trouble?"

"No, not that." I started to sweat. "Don't worry about it. Lightning doesn't always strike."

"It would be just my luck."

We walked a short distance in silence.

"Are you mad at me?" I wanted to know.

"No, I'm not mad. It wasn't your fault. We shouldn't have gone up to the room together but after we did there wasn't anything that could stop it." She took my arm, squeezing it. "I'm not sorry, Mike. I'm glad—in a way. Sooner or later there had to be a man and I'm happy that man was you."

"Thanks."

"It's awful nice of you to help me like this."

"Here," I said, reaching into my pocket and getting out two twenty dollar bills. "You'll need something for your first week's rent and use the rest of the money to buy some clothes with. Tomorrow morning find out who's in charge of this place and ask her what kind of clothes to buy and where you can buy them the cheapest."

"I've got enough clothes to last awhile."

"Those clothes you have are O.K. for high school kids, but as of today you're a career girl and they won't do for that."

"I'll pay you back sometime."

"Forget it."

As we stood on the steps of the "Y" I told her to be sure that she got in touch with the woman in charge and did like she said. I gave her the pressed-paper suitcase and watched as she went up the steps and through the front door.

I didn't feel like going to bed, so I took a street car down to the loop and wandered around for awhile trying to find something to do to pass the time. The bars were still closed and the streets were empty except for a few policemen and delivery trucks. A couple of times I passed groups of people in evening clothes going home from some all-night party. At last I settled for a movie.

By the time the movie was over I was sleepy. I walked out of the theatre into the hot air that was already taking the city over for the day. It wouldn't be much of an afternoon to catch up on sleep, even in my room near the lake.

I got off the Sheridan Avenue bus in front of the house and noticed two men in a black Ford parked across the street. At the time I didn't think anything of it and walked on down the drive carrying my coat over my shoulder. I went up the outside stairs to my room over the garage and threw open the windows to let in some air. As I was taking off my shirt I turned around and saw two big bruisers standing in the door. They looked like something that had escaped from the Museum of Natural History.

"You Mike Callahan?" the one in front asked.

"That's right."

"Danny wants to know where you took Fran's sister."

"Tell him to look her up in the phone directory."

"Smart guy."

"I almost finished high school."

"Come on, Little Willie," he said to the man behind him and they came in the room.

I looked around for something to bash their brains out with and came up with a metal lamp that stood on the table by the bed. Maybe they would give me a beating, but they wouldn't come out of it without a few scratches.

"What's holding you?" I stood holding the lamp, waiting for them to get tough.

They knew I wasn't any push over like the little guys they were used to beating up for half a "C" note.

"Come on you bull-necked bastards." I might just as well have some fun. Either way I was going to get a beating.

When I said that, Little Willie started to charge me, but the other guy held him back.

"We got to get the info first," he said.

"I'm gonna kill him."

"Come on tell us what you did with the girl. You just as well tell us now, because you know you'll tell us before we're through with you."

"I got her chained under my bed."

Little Willie was ready to look under the bed when the other guy stopped him. The smart one must have taken a correspondence course at Leavenworth.

"This is the last time I'm gonna ask you."

"Ask me what?"

"It's the last time I'm gonna ask you what you did with the girl."

"What do you mean?"

"You know what I mean. Where did you leave her?"

"On the steps."

"What steps?"

"I forgot."

They started on in the room, Little Willie going to the right and the other big guy coming in on the left. I held the lamp tight in my hand and moved back a little towards the wall so they couldn't get behind me. Little Willie was the first to come in close. He kept edging towards me and then all of a sudden he rushed me. I hit him square on the side of the head with the brass lamp and he went down. Before I could get my balance again the other guy was all over me and the lamp wasn't much good. He tried to get a hammer-lock on my head, but I slipped out of his arm and ran over to the other side of the room. Little Willie was still sitting on the floor feeling his head and wearing a silly look on his ape face.

"Come on over and I'll give it to you," I said. I'm one hell of a big man myself, and there aren't many who'll rush me one at a time, but this one was so dumb he charged right in again. I hit him on the head and the lamp glanced off like it had struck a rock. His fist hit me in the chest and I was thrown back against the wall and then he was mugging me again, I got a good right on his chin as he was trying to get a grip on my head again, and then I felt something around my legs and knew Little Willie was back in circulation. I kicked him in the face and cracked my heel across the back of his hand. It didn't knock him cold, and nothing short of that would stop him. He got both arms around my legs and I went down on the floor. But I was the only one there. The other two guys got up quick and began kicking me. I guess that was their special method because they were good and thorough about it. When I lunged for one of their feet the other one would kick me in the chest so I would pull my arm back in and try to protect myself. After that went on a couple of seconds I got frightened and bloody, and there's nothing stronger than a man who's mad and tasting blood. I lunged up at Little Willie and somehow got him down on the floor with me. I could feel the other guy kicking me but I didn't give a damn. I was going to get one of them. I caught Little Willie's arm and turned him over on his face. When I forced his arm up behind his back I wasn't gentle about it. I didn't do it by degrees and ask him if he had had enough. I just forced his arm up till it got hard to push and then I have a big heave and felt the arm go limp as the bone cracked. He screamed bloody murder and the kicks kept raining down on me from above. A shoe hit me in the temple and for a second I didn't know where I was. After that there wasn't much fight left in me. The last thing I remember was a kick in the groin with a size fourteen shoe while I was trying to cover my face. That kick did it. The whole sky looked like the Milky Way and there were about six too many moons in the room. I turned over, retched on the floor and passed the hell out.

Chapter 7

Pretty soon I opened my eyes enough to see the room spinning around me and feel the pulsating ache where I had been kicked. When I tried to move the pain went down my legs like electric shocks and I threw up again. I must have passed out because the next thing I knew the early afternoon sun was shining down on my face from the west side window. This time I was able to pull myself to the bed and telephone for somebody in the house to come out and help me. I told them to send anybody except Karl, but Karl was the one who came.

"First you make love to Mrs. Grey and now you get mixed up with a bunch of thugs," he said, looking down at me where I lay stretched out on top of the bed.

It hurt too much to move and he had to cut my clothes off. When I was finally undressed I looked down to see what they had done to me. There was not a two-inch spot on my body that had missed being kicked black.

"We'll have to take you to a hospital," Karl said.

I'm sure he hated to lose such a good source of labor, but there wasn't much else he could do about it. He called an ambulance and they took me to Memorial Hospital. The next twenty-four hours weren't so bad because they kept me so doped up with hypos that I didn't even know who I was. Every few hours I would look up to see a pretty nurse sticking a needle in my arm, or an intern starting another bottle of fluid in my vein.

I remember the police asking me what happened. I told them two thugs tried to make me give them information about the location of the family silver. I don't know how I managed to stick to my story with all the dope they gave me, but I did. There wasn't much use in telling them about Danny and Ruth. Fellows like that always have a cop or two they're paying off for protection, and he could buy a hundred men that would swear they had been playing poker with him all night.

But Karl didn't believe my story. You'll have to give him credit for being the smartest one around. Of course the whole thing was fishy. Who ever heard of a couple of robbers operating that way? If I'd been in my right mind I could have made up a lot better tale.

But I decided on a story and stuck to it without any variations and the rest of them believed me before it was all over.

I didn't know I was any kind of hero until the supervisor of nurses told me one day. Miss Watson was a woman about fifty years old with grey hair and a large bosom. Every day she would go around to see the seriously ill patients, and I had come to enjoy my talks with her. She was a little on the holy side and was always preaching to me.

"Mr. Grey is arranging to give you a reward," she told me after settling herself in a chair by the window one morning. Then she went on telling me about how long she had known David Grey and what a fine man he was. After recovering from the coma he had donated a few grand to the hospital for a new laundry machine and in her eyes that made him a fine man.

"I understand Mrs. Grey (meaning Kitty) was a student nurse here when they were married."

"She was a student here when she met him, but she had stopped her training before they were married."

"What made her give up nursing?"

"I would rather not talk about that if you don't mind, Mr. Callahan," she said and then she left the room before I had time to question her any more about the reason for Kitty leaving. I wondered why she avoided the question. After she left the room I tried to think of reasons why student nurses would stop their training program. Maybe some of them found it dull or too hard or too bloody. But none of these reasons would fit Kitty. She was certainly not the type to be frightened by the sight of a little blood. Maybe she was sure she could marry David and didn't see much point in staying on the bedpan detail any longer.

I forgot about the whole thing and went to sleep.

The next morning the old hunchbacked male nurse named Glen was giving me my bath when I got to wondering about Kitty again.

"Glen, did you ever know Kitty Phillips when she was a student nurse here?"

"You mean Mrs. Grey?"

"That's right."

"Sure I remember her. You don't forget a face like hers."

"How long did she stop her job here before she married Mr. Grey?"

"Oh, I'd say she quit here about six months before she was married."

I turned over for him to wash my back and he went on.

"You can't exactly say she quit."

"What do you mean?"

"This is just between you and me."

"Sure thing."

"She was asked to quit."

"What did she do?"

"Nothing was ever proved. It was all hushed up and I don't know exactly why she had to leave. There were lots of tales going around. Some say she stayed out too late one night, and others say she shot off her mouth to Miss Watson. I don't rightly know just what did happen."

I asked him some more questions about it, but he didn't know any more. I made up my mind to ask Kitty the next time I saw her. I was sure there was something funny about it because Mrs. Watson never did come back for any of her friendly chats after that. She would just stick her head in the door long enough to say hello and leave before I had time to ask her any questions.

The x-ray showed that I didn't have anything broken except three ribs. After about a week my left side went down to its usual size and I got out of bed. I was still sore all right, but it wasn't the same kind of sharp pain that I had had at first. Now I just felt like a man about ninety years old.

I was tired as hell after sitting up for twenty minutes. When I climbed back in bed and lay still waiting for supper I got to thinking about my future. I did that every now and then and it always made me get the blues. I knew I didn't have any future. I would always be just a plain jerk who did stinking little things like chauffeuring for a living. I wouldn't ever save any lives or climb any mountains or make any inventions.

But still I got to thinking every now and then. There was something in me somewhere that still had crazy dreams. That something in me wouldn't believe me when I told it that I would always be a tramp and that afternoon something in me that would not be discouraged by the truth got to bothering me.

I thought about the big deal I had lined up on the coast just to see it fall flat. Then I remembered how I had felt when I got when I got back to Chicago. I was going to give driving lessons for a few weeks while I lined up another good deal, but instead I took a job chauffeuring to be around a skirt that had run out on me after a month. I could have worked out something with that bum Danny but now he'd have every sharpie in the city down on me. Anyway, I wanted to go legitimate this time.

I just lay there between the smooth white sheets waiting for supper trying to think of some way I could make a decent living, and all of a sudden it came to me. I would open a hash house somewhere. My old lady had run a combination tavern-restaurant (those are mighty kind words for the dump she ran over on West Madison Street) and I had learned something about the business when I was a kid. It was the only legitimate business besides soldiering that I knew a damn thing about.

Suddenly I could see it all there in front of me. I could see a little hash house somewhere on the North side that would start out as a two-by-four room with burgers and beer, and I could see it grow into a respectable place like Isbell's where you could buy quail and roast venison. I could save enough out of my pay to get started and then I could nurse it along and see that it grew into something I wanted.

When I got through the dream I told myself that it was all just a lot of hot air and that I'd always be a jerk, but that little bastard inside of me didn't believe what I told it. It said "Go on and think about it. What you got to lose except your reputation as a jerk?"

I was lying there on the bed with my eyes closed thinking about the restaurant deal when I heard someone walk up to the bed. I thought it was one of the nurses coming to take my afternoon temperature. I rolled over and saw Kitty.

She was standing there alone by my bed smiling down at me. You never saw anybody look so pretty. She had a new sun tan and her hair had been bleached even blonder by the sun. She was wearing a freshly-starched blue linen dress and she had that smooth, well-groomed look about her that only rich people ever have. Christ, how could I ever fool myself into thinking a gal like that could care about a jerk like me?

"I have a reward for you," she said smiling down at me.

"What for?"

"For saving the house."

"Forget it."

"No, I'm serious. David wants you to have a reward." She opened her purse and handed me a check for a thousand dollars. My hash house looked pretty real right then.

"And I have my own personal reward."

She went to the door and gently closed it. She came back and smiled down at me before bending over and planting a big red kiss on my forehead.

"You can do better than that."

"Is this better?"

She kissed me on the lips this time. My arms went around her and pulled her against me so I could feel her hard breasts against my chest.

"That's better."

"It's good to see you again, Mike."

She rested her head against my shoulder while my hand made circling movements over her.

"Did you miss me?"

"More than I like to admit."

"Are we going to have some more fun when I get out of this rat trap?"

"Sure. I've got it all planned out."

"Let's hear it."

"When you get out of the hospital I'll have them take you to our summer place on Lake Geneva."

"David wouldn't do that."

"Certainly he would. You're a hero. You were almost killed protecting his property. There's nothing too good for you."

"And what if I do get farmed out up there?"

"I'll spend the summer with you."

"Just you?"

"Oh, we'll have a cook and a maid come along."

"What about David?"

"He doesn't like it up there. Believe me we'll have a beautiful summer."

"I believe you."

"You'd better wipe off the lipstick. Here, I'll do it for you."

"Where's your ring?" I asked when I saw she was not wearing it.

"Left it home when I went to Hot Springs."

Then she told me all about her trip, about the plane trip and the hot baths they gave at the resort and how all the dowdy old people sat around on the hotel porch talking about the things they used to do. She said that she had missed me more than she liked to admit.

"But the tennis instructor wasn't old."

"Did you improve your game?"

"Certainly."

She laughed because she could see I was jealous.

"And you stuck to tennis all the time?"

"Nothing but tennis. Would you have minded if I hadn't?"

"You know damned well I would have."

"How much?" she teased.

"Enough to spank you good and hard."

At first, I hadn't been pleased with the fact that I had a private room but now it suited me fine. It was good to have her there with me, the door closed, just the two of us alone. During some of my moments I had thought of Ruth, remembering that night with her, wishing that I could be with her again. But now that Kitty had returned Ruth seemed far away and unreal. Ruth had simply been part of trying to forget and now there was no longer any reason to forget. She had returned and things would be the same for us again.

"If I have a baby," she said, "it'll be yours."

My guts were empty and frozen.

"You're not serious," I said.

"But I am serious. There hasn't been anybody but you, Mike. Not anybody at all."

"You could lock the door and prove it to me."

"What if the nurse comes along?"

"So she doesn't get in. I've got a right to some privacy."

She didn't hesitate, not the way I thought she might. She smiled down at me and then turned and walked to the door. The sound of the key turning in the lock made a loud noise in the room.

"I thought you were sick, Mike."

"Not that sick."

"They told me at the desk you had been kicked and bruised and that it might be several days before you could get around."

"Try me and find out."

I moved on the bed, sitting up, and there was still a lot of pain in my back and right side. If it had been Ruth or any other woman I would simply have laid there and thought about what I wanted to do. I had done that with one of the nurses, the one who always wore her uniform low in front and who liked to lean over my bed, taking my temperature or fussing with the sheets. But this with Kitty was different. This was a forest fire that burned through me, something that I couldn't control.

She sat down beside me on the bed and I put my arm around her, my hand searching for what it wanted to touch and finding her loveliness. She sighed and came close to me, turning her head so that I could kiss her on the mouth. Her mouth was wet, moving, and for a second she closed her eyes.

"I'm jealous of you," she said.

"Why?"

"What have you been doing while I've been gone?"

"Nothing much."

"I'll bet you haven't."

"Well, I haven't. That crazy man out at the house kept me so busy I didn't have time to think."

"Even about me?"

She was in my arms, all of her, and my left hand was where it had to be.

"I thought about you all the time."

"Hating my husband?"

"A little. I kept thinking of that sore on his leg and of you being in bed with him. How can you do that?"

"It's a wife's duty. You put one of these rings on your finger and everything that comes along, good or bad, goes with it."

"I don't know what you've had that's good."

"This is good, Mike."

She knew how to kiss, all wild and hot, and I didn't mind the pain in my back any more. She was as starved as I was, maybe more, and she moaned as we went down on the bed together.

"God, you've been in my dreams," I said huskily.

Our bodies were close, wanting to find each other.

"And you've been in mine, Mike. At night, in the darkness, when he was beside me I tried to think of him as being you. You don't know how I needed you then. You can't understand and you never will."

Our lips were filled with fury as we kissed and kissed. I wanted to undress her, to strip her naked, but she wouldn't let me.

"Somebody will be coming," she said.

"I suppose you're right."

"When you get out of here we'll have fun, loads of fun. There won't be a day that I don't belong to you, a night that I'm not yours. And if anything should happen I don't care. Do you know that? I don't care."

"That trip did change you."

I was over her, looking down, and my mouth was greedy for the nectar of her lips. I had her almost open up at the top and I kissed her there, saying crazy things as I did so.

"I want your baby, Mike."

"It might be a freak."

"No, it wouldn't. It would be beautiful."

I shook my head.

"I don't want you getting that way. I couldn't stand that. I wouldn't want to see you getting big and fat and ugly."

"A pregnant woman is the most beautiful thing in the world. She can be as homely as they come but when she gets pregnant her whole life takes on a new meaning."

"Let's not press our luck."

Her hands were on either side of my face, lifting my head. There was a trace of tears in her eyes but there was a yearning there, too, a yearning that cried out for complete satisfaction.

"Please," she whispered, pulling my mouth down to her lips, "Oh, please, Mike!"

It was too much to refuse.

I tried to give her her wish. Somebody knocked on the door but I didn't pay any attention to that. She gave herself to me, more than once, and more than once I belonged to her. In those moments she was my world, my entire world, and it was a good world, filled with desire and satisfaction, a world in which only the two of us lived.

I didn't eat that night.

I wasn't hungry for food.

She had given me all that I needed.

Chapter 8

I felt bad about taking the reward money, but I couldn't change my story, and after all I had saved somebody in a way. I had saved Ruth from Danny.

Before I left the hospital for Lake Geneva I decided to give some of the money to Ruth so she would have a better chance to get started on the right track. I telephoned the McCormick Y.W.C.A., but they didn't have anybody by that name registered there. I asked them if she had been there and moved, but they just played dumb and said they had no record at all of a Ruth Sims.

That was a hell of a note, I thought, getting beat up like that for a girl you were going to save and then finding out that she didn't stay saved for even one day. That was a woman for you. A man my age should have had more sense about women, but some men never learn.

By the time I left the hospital to go to Lake Geneva I had forgotten all about Ruth. She was just another dame I had met in the night and known well for a few hours and left forever when the sun came up. Ruth wasn't like Kitty. You could forget the run-of-the-mill kind like Ruth.

Chicago was hot as a Bagdad laundry the day Kitty and I left for the lake. You could feel the heat coming down from the sky and you could feel it coming up from the pavement and coming at you from all sides as it was reflected off the buildings.

I mopped my face with a handkerchief as I went down the hospital steps with Kitty.

"And now it's your turn to be the chauffeur," I joked when I saw she had come for me in the station wagon.

"And you're the honored guest."

"And so forth."

"Check, and so forth."

"You're sure David's not going to be there?"

"He's afraid to get that far away from a doctor."

"Won't he be slightly suspicious when he thinks about us being up there all alone?"

"He heard you were seriously injured. Maybe he thinks you'll be incapacitated for a while."

"Maybe I will."

"I'm a good nurse."

"Meaning you'll cure me?"

"That's right."

"You'll probably kill me but I can't think of a nicer way to die."

As she drove out Foster Avenue I leaned back and rolled down the window in the back seat.

"It's too hot to do anything today."

"Wait till we get to the lake."

"Is the cottage in a quiet place?"

"Nothing but trees and our own private beach."

"Who takes care of the place?"

"We have an old man and his wife. They have a separate cottage about a quarter of a mile away."

"Then we'll have the house to ourselves at night?"

"That's right."

"Oh, brother, now I know why I didn't die."

As we left the crowded city and sped over the flat open highway it grew cooler.

After we were out of town ten or fifteen miles we stopped at a drive-in for an ice cold bottle of beer. We just sat there in the car sipping the cold beer and smiling at each other. It was like we were two kids running away together to discover for the first time what love was like. I knew it was wrong for me to be going off like that with another man's wife, but then there was something right about it too. We were both young and we had had such a big yen for each other and it was like owning each other was the only thing we had in the world, and everyone was due to have at least one thing in the world. David had his money and his position. He had a fine mansion on Sheridan Road and a limousine to drive around in, but we had love and right then I felt like the richest guy in the world. I was glad she had missed me while out of town.

We drank another bottle of beer and then Kitty started the car again. I liked the way she drove. It was like everything else she did—full of Kitty. She put the gear in first and started off so fast that the tires screamed and then she threw it into second and held it there till we were hitting about fifty. She was some woman. I'd known my share but I'd never known one with a spirit like hers, as wild and clean and unconquered as a summer storm.

We drove on north over the Illinois state line and into Wisconsin where the countryside looked like real country with rolling hills and creeks and cows and mail boxes beside the road.

As we got near Lake Geneva we kept passing cars filled with people going up for a weekend of rest from the heat of Chicago. The people were laughing and driving crazy and sometimes you could see a bottle passing back and forth. It was the first vacation I'd ever had, but I was getting the spirit of things already.

The "cottage" turned out to be a ten-room house with a big rustic living room made up like a hunting lodge with mounted animals on one wall. Out front there was a wide porch, and past that was a well-kept lawn that ran down to the private beach and landing pier.

Mrs. Hobson, the caretaker's wife, was a buxom old lady who almost bowed when she spoke to you. After Kitty introduced me she told her that she could have the rest of the day off.

I knew why.

I put my suitcase down in the living room and followed Kitty into the bedroom.

"It's been a long time," I said and stood there running my fingers through her fine blonde hair, wanting to make it all last a long time because it was all so good, like a kid with a sucker that only licks now and then so it'll last all day.

"Mike, I'm going to ask something big of you."

Women and their ideas, I thought. Why didn't God make them without tongues and brains?

"All right."

"Mike, you know I'm very fond of you."

"I had an idea."

"Then you'll know how it hurts me to say this."

"Let's have it."

Why did they always want a man to grovel in the dirt at their feet and beg them?

"Mike, I want you to promise me you won't try anything."

"Don't you want me?"

"Of course I want you. All the time we were gone I kept thinking about you and wanting you and remembering the times we had been together. Sure I want you."

"Here I am."

"I can't have you."

"Yes, you can."

"Something inside me keeps me away now. It won't let me have you like I want you."

"Then let's get drunk and put that something to sleep."

"But later it'll wake up and then I'll remember and everything will be all mixed up and I'll hate myself."

"Every person's got a right to love."

"But not me."

"Why?"

"You know why."

"David?"

"Yes."

"Then leave him. Divorce him and marry me."

"He'd never give me a divorce."

"Then leave him. We'll go away someplace together. I'll use the money to open up a hash house and we'll nurse it along till it turns into something big and then everything'll work out all right for both of us. You just need to get away from him."

We were sitting on the bed. I pushed her down very gently and kissed her wide lips and put my arm around her to pull her against me.

"Let's run away together."

"I want to," she said, and I started kissing her again.

"Mike, it's not right."

She leaped up from the bed and ran into the bathroom and locked the door. I could hear the water running and every now and then I could hear her crying.

She wanted to make love as bad as I did. The poor kid was all mixed up inside. It's hell to be thirty but it's even more hell to be twenty-two and not know what the world's about. And any way you look at it, it's more hell to be a woman. They get the short end of every deal in the world.

Pretty soon she came out. She didn't look fresh and well-groomed and rich and happy any longer. She looked all wilted up inside. Her eyes were red from crying, and her dress was all wrinkled and her long blonde hair needed brushing a thousand times.

"I'm sorry, kid."

She came over to where I sat on the bed and kneeled down beside me and looked up at me like a little puppy dog.

"I'm sorry, kid."

I sat there for a long time running my hand through her hair and thinking about what a stinking world it was. You never got what you really wanted. But then you never stopped trying because when you stopped trying you were dead.

"You really love me, don't you, kid?"

"Yes, Mike. I never knew what it was till I met you. That first day when I let you make love to me I'm sure you thought I was just a rich tramp, but I wasn't. I was all dead inside and tied in knots and I had to have you to untie the knots and make everything right again."

"And now everything's all tied in knots again?"

"Yes, everything's all tied in knots again."

"Let's run away together."

"We've got to do something."

"Then you'll leave with me?"

"I guess that's the best thing, Mike. Nothing we can do would be right, but if we ran away together at least it would be better because then I would only have one man."

"We can tell everybody that you're my wife."

"That would help."

"And I'd even buy you a wedding band."

"A plain gold one?"

"That's right, a plain gold one and I'd have our names put inside."

"And the date."

"The date we first met."

"It was wonderful."

"Yes."

"And soon we'll have each other like that all the time."

"That's what I want, Mike."

Then I took her arms and pulled her up on the bed with me. I didn't try again. I just put her head over on the pillow by mine where I could look in her eyes and touch my lips against hers. We didn't really kiss. We just made it so our lips touched and were wet together and we stayed there and talked with our lips touching all the time, and we just lay there and looked at each other.

We went to sleep that way. Suddenly I was in a great black valley with great black clouds overhead. I was running like the wind and I went through a dark tunnel and when I came out on the other side I was a kid back in my mother's run-down tavern on West Madison Street. But mother wasn't old like I remembered her. She was like the picture she had that was taken when she was in high school. Her hair was long and light and hung down to her shoulders, and her body was trim and young and her eyes were still full of dancing lights.

The music from the juke box was blaring and I stood in front of the box watching all the colored lights turning on and off. It was Saturday night and behind me the tavern was full of laughing people who were sitting at the bar drinking.

Suddenly everything was quiet.

An old man was standing in the center of the floor and my mother was walking towards him with her head bowed. When she came up to him he struck her in the face and then I was filled with sickness because the man and my mother were struggling on the floor and I was sure he was going to kill her.

I ran towards them to save my mother and suddenly as I ran there was a knife in my hand and I plunged the knife into the man's back and he rolled over to grab me and I cut his throat and the blood ran out of his neck on to the floor and he lay limp and I just stood there plunging the knife in him even though he was dead.

And then suddenly I was no longer a child. I was a powerful young man and I put my arm around my mother's waist and we walked out of the door together into the dark.

Then I was awake and lying there in the bed with Kitty and for a second it seemed that she was the other woman.

"What's the matter?" she asked.

"I had a dream."

"About me?"

"No, something else. Something a long time ago."

She stirred beside me.

"I had a dream, too. About you. About us."

"And?"

"You think I'm playing hard to get?"

"Maybe."

"I was a little insane there in the hospital. I couldn't help myself. But after I left you I felt cheap."

"Love isn't cheap."

"You can make it that way. You can twist it the way you twist a wire and then it's all out of shape."

I knew how she must feel. She was married to one man and she had come to me, seeking the love that she could not get from him. It was sneaking around corners, cheating in the dark. Maybe she was right. Maybe these things bothered people, destroyed love. But I didn't think so. She was a girl and I was a man and we had a right to take what belonged to us.

"Don't ever leave me, Kitty," I said.

"I won't. Never."

"We'll work something out. I don't want to live without you."

"But this stay up here has to be honest, Mike."

"How honest?"

"You know."

I knew. We would play it straight down the middle and when we returned to the city there would be no guilt, no regrets. She could look her husband in the face and challenge him to prove that anything had been wrong.

"The hell with it," I said, turning to her.

She was dressed, fully dressed, and the buttons ran from the top of her dress all the way down to the bottom. She started to cry when I began undoing the buttons and she rocked her head back and forth.

"Don't make me, Mike," she pleaded.

"I'll make you."

"No."

"I won't bother you for the rest of the week."

"Please, Mike."

I fumbled with the buttons, cursing at them, and sweat dripped from my forehead. A big drop of sweat hit her skin and flattened out. She put her hand up there and nibbed it away.

"I would have bet on it," I said as I pulled her dress open.

She didn't have a thing on underneath.

"Mike!"

I was breathing hard, unfastening the buttons. She had a glorious body and I wanted her to be mine, all mine.

"I don't get it," I told her. "The other day you wanted this—and more. Now you're too good for me."

Hurt crept into her eyes.

"It isn't that, Mike. I told you."

"I know what you said."

"This is the only clean thing that ever happened to me and I don't want to dirty it."

"I suppose going away together won't dirty it?"

"Somehow that's different. That's where I end it with him, where we start a new life. It isn't the same as this."

I didn't follow her reasoning exactly but I didn't argue with her about it. I just got the dress off of her and threw it on the floor.

"You want to as badly as I do," I said. "And you know it."

She looked up at me and smiled.

"Will you keep your promise about the rest of the week?"

"Sure."

She seemed to relax on the bed.

"Then I'm yours," she said. "Take me."

I took her.

Chapter 9

We had a week together up at the lake. We didn't make serious love. It was more like we were sweethearts romping around in the sun. In the mornings we'd go swimming and then fish for awhile or sail the sloop down to the village where we'd go shopping for groceries. One night we sailed over and went to the dance that was given so the bachelor boys and girls could meet each other.

All the laughing and playing together seemed to draw us even closer together. We began having our own jokes about people and soon we got to know each other well enough to say the intimate words that married people say to each other in fun.

Little things like that are what make two people married. They get to know all about each other and there's not a wall between them any more.

By the end of the week we had our escape plans all laid out. I was to cash the check and we would use it to buy a hash house someplace. She had a little money of her own in the bank and she would lend me that if we needed any more. She would write a note to David and we would just leave together without even saying anything about a divorce.

But we weren't going to leave Chicago. Chicago is such a big city that we could be lost from the rest of the world right there. No use going to Omaha or Salt Lake City.

On Saturday night our plans were suddenly changed. While we were eating supper and talking about the dance we were going to, a car drove up and parked outside the dining room window.

Karl was driving and David was sitting in the back seat.

"Here's the end of our picnic," I said.

I could see the disappointment come over her face.

"Damn him, I didn't think he'd ever come up here."

"Maybe he's suspicious. Karl saw you come down from my room one time when we were in town. Maybe he told David about it."

"You should have let me know."

"What good would it have done?"

"I don't know."

We got up and went to the front door to meet them. David put his arm around her and kissed her lips.

"You look much better," he said, turning to me.

"Thanks, everything's healing."

I stood there and watched him as he kissed Kitty again. I hated that fat old man with the bald head. He limped on into the living room and lowered himself into a chair. Kitty got a stool and put it in front of the chair so he could use it to support his leg.

"How's your leg?" I asked.

"Much better. I think the trip did it good."

After we all had a drink he turned to me again.

"Would you like a job as my body guard?" he asked.

"That would be something new."

"You've been very good so far about protecting my property. My lawyer advised me to get a body guard and I thought of you right away. You're large enough to make any criminal think twice."

"Criminal?"

"That's right. I've had a bit of trouble."

"What kind?"

"I found some of the boys were using the third floor of one of my hotels for book making and I put them out. The other day I received a threatening note."

"I'd like a month off before starting."

"That could be arranged. I'll hire a private detective in the meantime."

We didn't go to the dance that night. Instead we played Canasta until I damn near had a hemorrhage from boredom.

That night I lay in my bed listening to David and Kitty going to bed. I knew there wouldn't be many more nights for me to suffer like this. I tossed on the bed and pulled the sheet this way and that until the bed looked like a tornado had slept there. I tried counting sheep and when that didn't work I went over the plans Kitty and I had talked about. It had all seemed very real when we were talking about it, but now that David was back I wondered if they would be just a bunch of dreams cooked up by a couple of moon-struck kids. At last I got up and sat in the chair by the window and smoked a cigarette. I wouldn't be able to take this every night. If David stayed I'd have to leave tomorrow. I wanted to go in the next room and smash his head in and take his wife away from him. No man can stand living thoughts like that all the time.

After I finished smoking the fag I got a drink of water and went back to bed. It was the same story all over again. I tried counting the sheep and then I made up a little game of going back and re-laying all the girls I'd layed. I got lost somewhere around number eighteen and gave that up.

There weren't but two things that could have put me to sleep that night, a woman or a drink. I went out to the kitchen to get a bottle and then decided it would be cooler out on the front porch.

As soon as I stepped out of the door I knew there was somebody else there. I thought about David's threatening letter and gripped the neck of the bottle to use it for a black jack.

"Is that you, Mike?"

"Kitty?"

"Yes."

I went down to the end of the porch where she sat.

"What are you doing out here?" I whispered.

"I couldn't stand him any longer."

I reached down to touch her. My hand felt her cheek and it was wet.

For the first time I felt real murder in my blood.

"What did he do?"

I had my arm around her and I could feel her shiver.

She buried her face against my shoulder and cried like a hurt kid. I stroked her hair and let her cry but I wasn't thinking nice thoughts. I was figuring out ways I could kill David and get away with it. I could kill him and then take his body out in the woods someplace and bury him and if I buried him deep and did a good job of it they would never find the body and the police could not scream murder if they didn't have a body on their hands.

Then I thought about Karl. I'd have to kill him too. Well, that could be done.

Then I thought of the caretakers and then I knew I was thinking in crazy circles. I couldn't kill them all and expect to get away with it. A good murderer should pick his time and place.

The crying let up a little.

"What did the bastard do?"

"I'll be all right."

"I know you will because you're going to leave this place with me right now, tonight."

"Mike, you do love me?"

"I love you so much I'd cut my heart out for you."

"It's nice to have someone love you like that."

"Kitty, we've got to get away from this place."

"I know. I can't stand it any longer."

"Go put on your clothes and I'll meet you here in five minutes."

"We can't do it that way."

"Why not? You said yourself that you couldn't stand it any longer."

"If he knew I left with you he'd hunt you down and kill you. That wouldn't help us."

"Only maybe he would be the one to get killed."

"No, he wouldn't. He'd hire somebody to do it. He wouldn't take any chances. He'd hire gunmen and they'd shoot you down some dark night and nobody would ever know who did it."

"But we've got to get away."

"Why don't you leave tomorrow? David said he'd give you another month's vacation before starting as his body guard."

"What about you?"

"I could meet you some place."

"And you won't back down on me?"

"Of course not."

She looked up at me like she wanted a kiss. I held her face in my hands and kissed her, but it wasn't much of a kiss. We were so worked up that our mouths were dry.

"Where can we meet?"

"Field's would be a good place," she said.

"O. K. Meet me just inside the Randolph Street entrance at nine-thirty Monday morning."

"I'll be there."

"I'm counting on it, honey."

"Kiss me again before we go inside."

Our lips were still dry, but she knew I loved her anyway. We got up to go back inside and I thought about lying awake in my bed the rest of the night knowing that Kitty was in the next room with him. I couldn't do it.

"Kitty, I'm leaving tonight."

"Wouldn't it be better if you waited until morning?"

"I can't stand it any longer."

"I know how you must feel," she said and put her hand on my arm.

"I'll leave a note saying I decided to take the month's vacation he promised."

"I'll miss you, darling."

"Same here but it won't be for long. It's nearly morning now. We'll only be apart today and tonight and then nothing will ever separate us again."

"That's the way I want it."

I kissed her again and then went in my room to pack my clothes and write a note to David.

When I sneaked out of the house it was still dark, but you could tell from the chirping of the birds and the soft wind that it would soon be light.

As I walked down the drive to the dirt road to the highway, I knew that I was still weak from my stay in the hospital. The suitcase got heavier every minute. Before I reached town I opened the bag and took out my toilet articles and a T shirt and dumped the rest by the side of the road.

When the walking was easier I felt more like thinking about Kitty and me. It was like a load had been lifted off of my shoulders to know that we were going to leave David for good and make some kind of life for ourselves. It might not be the best as far as money went, but it would be a good life as long as we had each other. I'd take Kitty and let the money go. A good woman was more than most men ever had.

Maybe some people would think I was a bastard for running off like that with another man's wife, but I didn't look at it that way. He should never have married her in the first place and it wasn't like they were real husband and wife. Nobody could blame a young girl like Kitty for wanting more out of life. She and I were young and full of fire and we just had to have each other.

When I finally got to the town of Lake Geneva I stopped at the station and had a cup of coffee and a sweet roll while I was waiting for the next bus for Chicago.

Because it was Sunday morning the traffic was all coming to Lake Geneva instead of leaving it, so the bus back to Chicago was nearly empty. I got a chance to catch up on some of the sleep I'd missed.

Chapter 10

I got off the bus at the State Street depot about ten o'clock Sunday morning.

I had another lonesome Sunday on my hands. There's no place in the world any deader than Chicago on a Sunday morning in the middle of the summer. And for me it was even deader than it was for the other people because I didn't know anybody in Chicago. Isn't that funny? Here I was born and brought up in the burg and I didn't know anybody. But you know how it is. The old crowd that you went to school with got all broke up during the war and somehow you just never run into them again in a city like Chicago. Maybe it's the same way in small towns too, I don't know.

Of course I did know Danny but I didn't feel quite up to seeing him. You'd think I would have been mad at him but I wasn't. I guess he gave me what I had coming. I did run off with one of his girls.

As I walked down to Grant Park to wait for the bars to open at noon, I got to thinking about Ruth and wondering what had happened to her. I guessed she had gone back with her sister and was learning the trade. Danny was probably making love to her regularly unless he was already tired of her.

I bought some popcorn to feed the pigeons, took off my coat and sat down on a bench to watch the little bastards shimmy up to me for a free handout. I sat there looking at them wondering how they kept their feet warm in cold weather and finally got tired of the whole thing and dumped all the popcorn on the ground and let them fight over it.

I lay down on the bench and closed my eyes and I hadn't been there more than five minutes before some big flatfooted cop comes over and taps the sole of my shoe with his night stick.

"Sleeping's not allowed here," he said like he owned the town.

"Did you hear me snoring?"

"No."

"Then I wasn't asleep. I always snore when I sleep."

He pulled a pad out of his pocket.

"Bud, you wanta get run in on a vagrancy charge?"

I sat up. There wasn't any sense in getting locked up all week-end and missing Kitty on Monday.

"You'd better move on."

"I'm not sleeping. I'm just sitting here."

"Wise guy."

"Thank you. My mother always thought I was pretty smart."

"That does it. Come on."

"I was just leaving."

I hoisted my coat and walked away. I couldn't get in a fight with the bastard and take a chance on getting put in the cooler. After I had walked almost to the street I turned around and saw him watching me. I doubled up my fist and put out one finger. He got the idea and started blowing his damn whistle. I took off across the street and then ran up Van Buren to the alley and cut back. What a hell of a town it is when they won't even let you sit still on a park bench.

But I knew I had asked for it. I had to find something to do or I would get myself in trouble before Monday morning. As I was walking along Wabash I got to thinking about Ruth again and decided to go by the "Y" and see if I could find out anything about her.

At the "Y" I asked to see the woman in charge and the desk girl took me around back to meet a fat middle-aged woman dressed in black.

"I'm looking for Miss Ruth Sims. I sent her over here about two weeks ago and now nobody knows anything about her."

"Won't you have a seat Mr. . . ."

"Callahan's the name."

"Won't you have a seat Mr. Callahan?"

She sat down behind a desk and pulled her skirt down like she was afraid of men.

"We've been very crowded lately. Maybe I sent her someplace else. What did you say the young lady's name was?"

"Sims. Ruth Sims."

"Well, let me just have a look here."

She took some papers out of a folder on her desk and looked through them.

"You say her name was Ruth Sims?"

Christ, I'd already told her a hundred times.

"That's the name."

"She was sent to a girls' club on the south side. I have a follow-up note that says she was given a room there."

I got the telephone number and left.

Ruth had just got in from church when I called. She asked me to come out to see her.

You never saw anybody change so much in a couple of weeks. The girls there at the club ran what they called a beauty clinic and all the new members were given the once-over. Ruth's long stringy hair had been cut short and it was all fluffy with little brown curls. She had touched up her eye lashes with some stuff to make her eyes look larger, and the girls had made her buy a red dress with a lot of flowers on it. The way she walked and everything was changed so she looked more like a career girl who'd been around instead of a scared little mop from down on the farm.

"You like it?" she asked.

She stood in front of me and whirled around so I could get a good look at all the changes.

"It's swell. What happened?"

"The other girls gave me some advice."

"Did they advise you about men too?"

"Yes."

"What?"

"They said a girl was smart to hold out for a ring first, but of course that was off the record."

"But it was good advice."

"You approve!"

As we left the club and walked over the soft green grass covering the center of the Midway I felt very pleased with myself because I had done one thing in my life that was unselfish and right. After all, if it hadn't been for me she would be at Danny's place taking off her clothes in front of a crowd of half-drunk degenerates. I could see the change that had come over Ruth, and now I was sure that she would never go back to her sister.

As we walked on over to 63rd Street to a movie she told me about the job they had helped her find at Field's.

"Of course it's not much, but I'm lucky to have it. I sell kitchen ware in the basement."

"How did they happen to give you that job?"

"I told them I was from downstate Illinois and they asked me what I knew the most about. I laughed and said cooking and milking, so they put me with the kitchen ware."

"Sounds like a good idea."

"All but the money. I'd make more if I were selling women's clothes."

"One step at a time."

"That's right," she said, looking up at me and smiling. For a second I thought she pressed my hand, but I guess she didn't. That part didn't come until much later.

We saw a shoot-em-up movie and when we were outside again I said, "It sure was a shoot-em-up movie."

"It certainly was," she said and I thought about the crack Kitty had made about the movie we had seen at Lake Geneva. Kitty's remark made me feel very near to her and that she belonged to me, but Ruth's remark made me respect her a lot more. I wished to God I was more like Ruth and less like Kitty, but we are what we are and I still don't know how we can do too much about it.

We stopped in one of the joints on Sixty-third Street. Ruth ordered a coke and I got a short beer. While we sat there drinking she got to talking about the things she wanted. She told me how she wanted a house and a bunch of kids someday.

"You look like you're on the way to being a career girl," I said.

"Maybe it looks that way, but you can't believe everything you see. This is just a game I'm playing till the real thing comes along."

"I hope you find the right guy."

She didn't say anything when I made that crack, but she turned her big eyes up from the table and looked at me for a long time, long enough for me to feel sort of funny inside. But, Christ, she wasn't my kind of dame. It was crazy to let a good kid like Ruth make me feel funny. I'm bad medicine.

"And what do you want?"

"I want a million bucks and a blonde to spend it on." That shut her up for awhile. I ordered another beer.

"But why do you want a million dollars?"

"I just said that because it was the first thing that came to me. I don't know what in hell I want. All I know is that life's damn unsatisfactory for me like it is and a million bucks would change it. Maybe I'd be happy with a million bucks and maybe I'd be just the same."

"Do you have a girl?"

"Yeah, I got a girl."

"Tell me about her."

"She's blonde and she's beautiful and she's married to the wrong guy."

"I'm sorry for you, Mike."

"Don't waste your time, kid. I can take care of myself."

"I hope so."

"Drink up and let's go."

I don't know why it was, but suddenly she made me nervous. She was the real thing and I was such a phoney.

I held her hand and we walked down the street without taking any more. She looked in the shop windows and I just sort of followed along. After awhile we cut back to the Midway and walked some more, but we didn't talk again. Talking made me think and I didn't want to think any more right then. Kitty was going to meet me the next morning and we were going to live together forever and run a restaurant. I had the world by the tail on a downhill pull. But at the moment, walking along with Ruth beside me, it wasn't quite enough. There had to be something more.

We stopped in front of a cheap hotel, one of those places that has a small lobby and a thirty dollar a week clerk, and I could tell from the expression in her eyes that she knew what I was going to ask her.

"We can't go to the club where you live," I said. "They wouldn't let me past the front door."

"Hardly."

"And I know what's on your mind."

"I doubt if you do but I know what's on yours."

A man came along, walking a dog, and I watched the man and the dog move off down the street.

"You're a beautiful girl," I said. "You can't blame me if I think what I'm thinking."

"But you've already got a girl."

"Does it matter?"

She didn't say anything. She took a deep breath, filling out that red dress in two of its most prominent spots, and looked down at her shoes.

"Does it matter, Ruth?"

"It should."

"But it doesn't?"

Her voice was far away. "No. No, it doesn't matter. When I'm with you nothing seems to matter."

We entered the hotel and I noticed that she turned the ring around on her finger, concealing the red stone, so that it looked like a wedding band. I wondered, vaguely, who had told her about doing that and I guessed that some of the girls at the club had.

The room was five dollars, in advance, and I paid the clerk behind the desk. Ruth stood off to one side, sort of scared, and I found the situation somewhat amusing. She wanted to go up to the room as badly as I did but she was ashamed about how she felt.

There wasn't any elevator and we walked up to the second floor. She held my arm, clinging to me on the way.

"I shouldn't be doing this," she said.

"Give me one reason why not."

"Because it isn't real with you and it's real with me. As far as you're concerned I'm just another girl, Mike."

I stopped and stared at her.

"We don't have to go on," I said.

She tugged at my arm.

"I want to go on. The time to have changed my mind was on the street, not now. We'd look foolish walking out so soon." She hesitated. "Besides, I'm not afraid. I trust you."

She leaned against me and we continued on up the stairs. She was trusting the wrong guy but maybe she didn't know it.

"Just don't give me a baby," she said as I unlocked the door.

"No."

"There's a girl at the club and she's going to have a baby. The man who is the father is married and he can't do anything for her. She cries all the time."

The room was like any room you get for five bucks, a bed and not much else. But we didn't need anything else. It was hot in there and the first thing I did was to open the window. The room faced the front and the smell of burned gasoline followed the heat up from the pavement. I took off my shirt and threw it on the one chair the management had been kind enough to leave in the room. She stood there in the middle of the room, still nervous, not knowing quite what to do. I didn't blame her. She was a nice kid, strange in the city, and she was caught in something that was almost too big for her.

"So you sell pots and pans," I said.

"Yes, but they don't pay very much."

"None of those jobs do."

"Probably I'll get used to it. People have to be sold and I'm a little backward about that yet."

"You'll get the hang."

"It's better than stripping."

I lit a cigarette and blew the smoke toward the ceiling. "Anything would be better than that."

"I don't know how my sister does it. If you think something of a man you don't mind him seeing you but if you don't know the men there can't be anything clean in it."

"Hardly."

"With you, for instance, I know you're going to see me undressed. I know what you're going to do. But I don't mind. I like to see you, too."

"Do you?"

"I never saw a man before. The girls in school had pictures but I didn't look at them. Some of the pictures were with women."

"They would be. There's nothing attractive about a man's body."

She shook her head and fluffed out her hair.

"Oh, I don't know, Mike. There is about you. You're big and strong and—well, I think you know what I mean. Looking at you isn't like looking at a picture. There seems to be something right about it."

No matter how I tried I couldn't figure her. She was a sweet kid, unspoiled, yet there was a boldness about her, too, a boldness that I didn't understand. Maybe she was that way because I had been her first man.

"You're too good to touch," I said, meaning it.

It was plenty hot in the room but that wasn't the only reason I was sweating. I'd had no business bringing her up to this room, of deciding to take from her what I wanted to take. She deserved something better than a love affair that could only like for a few minutes. She was the kind of a girl a guy married and settled down with to raise kids. And I wasn't that guy. I was in love with Kitty and if I had to have somebody this way I should pick up a chippie off the street. There were plenty of that kind in Chicago, just as there are plenty in every city. They do it for money or for the hell of it and they don't care. You can't hurt them because they are beyond hurting. Not so of a girl of Ruth's type. Ruth played the game not for the sport but for keeps.

"Let's get out of here," I said, reaching for my shirt.

"Don't you—want me?"

"It isn't that. It's something else. The first time wasn't right and this won't be right either."

"I like you, Mike." Her tone was soft. "I'm willing to take what I can get."

I stood there with the shirt in my hand, holding it. There was something else that I had missed about her—she was honest.

"Hell," I said.

"You're nice, Mike."

"Not very."

"But you are. You steered me right and I appreciate that. If it hadn't been for you I'd be a stripper and I'd be ashamed every minute that I worked." She reached for the zipper on her dress. "Before I came to Chicago I read about strippers and I used to practice in front of a minor I had in my room. I didn't know what I was supposed to do but I practiced anyway. Like this."

I started to tell her to stop, to cut it out, but I didn't. She was quick, for one thing, and for another I guess I wanted to see what she was going to do.

"Watch," she said.

She moved around the room, pulling the dress up over her head slowly. I saw her legs to a point above her knees, to where the slip began, and then the dress crept higher. The slip was a half slip and it ended at her middle, just below her tiny little stomach that was now moving in and out as she breathed.

"They don't do it this way," she said. "They have things that come off easier."

My tongue was thick, my mouth dry and I couldn't say a word.

"After the dress I began to get the idea."

The dress came free and she dropped it onto the floor. All she had up above was a black bra that was so thin I could almost see through it.

"You take it slow and easy," she said.

She moved back and forth across the room, her body alive and all woman, and when she was out of the slip I sucked in my breath. There was nothing professional about her movements, just sex, raw sex. It was the kind of sex that blazed down inside of you, a roaring fire that just kept growing and growing until it became an inferno.

"You like?"

She was there before me in just her bra and panties. She didn't wear a garter belt or stockings. I meant to ask her why she had gone to church without wearing stockings but I didn't. Just then it didn't seem important.

I threw the shirt onto the chair.

"I'd be crazy if I didn't." I said.

She was smiling and her head was held up high and proud.

"There's more to it than that," she told me, reaching behind her. "This comes off, too."

"Not always."

"In most of the clubs it does. It's what the men come to see and you have to give them what they pay for."

I wasn't paying anything but she gave it to me anyway. The bra joined the rest of her clothes on the floor and she was bigger than I had remembered. They were saucy, far apart and big, and I knew she was excited because of the way they were lifting and falling.

"You do the rest," she said.

She didn't have to ask me twice. She didn't even have to ask me once. I was already after her, wanting her, needing her, everything else forgotten.

"Love me," she begged. "Just give me a chance with you."

The bed was hard but I didn't mind that. I kissed her and buried her head in the pillow.

"You'd make a good stripper," I said.

"Would I?"

"You've got what it takes."

"And for you? Do I have that, too?"

I didn't lie to her. I didn't have to. She knew how things were with me and she was taking her chances. Inside I felt a pang of doubt but it quickly slipped away. She knew the truth and she was doing this because she wanted to do it. What more could I ask?

"You live for today," I replied.

"Does everybody?"

"Almost. One minute you're alive and the next minute you're dead. You get only what you take."

"Or receive?"

"If you're a woman that fits."

She began to tremble.

"Don't make me that way, Mike."

"What way?"

"I told you about the girl at the club. I couldn't stand that."

"Don't worry."

"But I do worry."

My hands were all over her, all over, and she lifted to me.

"Maybe we shouldn't," I said, knowing that she was burning up, certain that she wouldn't stop.

"Don't torture me, Mike."

"All right."

"And don't hurt me."

I don't think I hurt her. It was better this time, better than before. She gave me her body, her heart, her soul and she gave me her tears.

"No," she whimpered.

But it was too late.

A lot of things are said too late.

The clerk gave us a hard look when we left the hotel but he didn't say anything. Maybe he was happy. He could rent the room again for another five bucks.

It didn't take us long to get to the girl's club and we didn't say much on the way.

"Will I see you again?" she asked when we were standing on the front steps.

I had to give it to her straight.

"What's the use?"

"I don't know. I thought—"

"Look, Ruth. I'm not the kind of a guy for you."

"You don't have to feel guilty."

"I don't. It's just the truth."

Her eyes lingered on my face.

"Why don't you let me judge that?"

I felt uncomfortable.

"Because I'm a sharpie and you don't want anything to do with a guy who's out after a quick buck."

Those eyes of hers were half closed.

"You had plenty to do with me in that hotel."

"I'm not proud of it."

"Aren't you? You didn't refuse."

"I couldn't. I have the urge of the male and you're a female."

"As simple as that?"

"Name me something else."

A couple of girls went up the steps laughing, both of them happy, and I wondered if she was. I had been careless with her—why does a man do such a thing?—and she was in this all by herself.

"We can't stand here," she said.

"No."

She moved up a step and stopped.

"You know where I am now. There's no excuse for not seeing me,"

"Not one."

"Will you?"

"I don't know."

She ran up the steps crying and the door slammed shut behind her. A girl coming out smiled at me and shook her head.

"Mad?" the girl asked.

"Disappointed."

I rode back to the loop on the I. C. and while I was sitting there watching the back porches of the slums rip past the window I couldn't keep my mind free of thoughts. Probably I was part bum and part sharpie but I had a little of the good in me, too. Ruth had tried to find the good side of me, the guy who might marry a nice little girl and settle down with a family of my own and a job where I punched a clock at eight and five. Seeing the good side of me for a moment upset me. That side of me wasn't strong enough to take over and make the rest of me behave. I didn't want to be reminded that I had more than one side. Life was hard enough without driving yourself nuts by trying to find out what you were like inside. I was a two-for-a-nickel-jerk and I'd always been a jerk and I was not going to get all mixed up inside thinking about houses and little white fences.

I got off the train down in the Loop and walked over to the Congress Hotel. Kitty and I might just as well have the first few days in a first-class joint. Maybe it would make things easier for her.

I paid the man at the desk, bought a fifth of bonded bourbon and went the hell up to my room. I didn't get drunk that night, but I got enough of an edge on to keep from thinking anymore.

I wanted the next day to hurry and come so I could have Kitty again. I was awful lonesome that night.

Chapter 11

That lousy feeling left me the next morning when I met Kitty at Field's. I had stood there at the Randolph Street entrance for half an hour waiting for her, and I had about decided that she had changed her mind when suddenly she walked through the revolving door and smiled at me. She looked good that day, like a shiny new penny that had never left the mint. She was dressed up in a pale blue silk dress and wore white earrings and a string of white shell beads. For a minute she just stood there and looked at me and then she ran to me and threw her arms around my neck and held me like she had found the thing that she had always wanted. We were so much in love that we walked down Michigan Boulevard with our arms still around each other. It even made the people happy who saw us. They would look our way and then smile like they were remembering a time when love had been good to them. Only nobody was ever as in love as Kitty and I were that day. There could have been another Chicago fire and an earthquake thrown in on top of that and it wouldn't have pulled us away from each other's arms.

When we got to my room at the Congress Hotel she could hardly wait. The first thing she did after I closed the door was to come to me, her arms around my neck, her hips pushed up against me, moving her hips back and forth, back and forth.

"This is wonderful!" she breathed.

"More than that."

"Love me?"

"Hmmmm."

"You don't kiss like you do."

"How about this one?"

I kissed her, my lips screaming their need for her, and I drove her head back. I held her head with one hand and really slammed one into her, bruising her lips until she started to sob.

"Convinced?"

"I'd be out of my mind if I wasn't."

I wondered how she had gotten away from home, what she had told or written her husband but I didn't ask her. We were together and anything other than that was of no consequence.

"Do it again," she said.

I did it again. We were away from the door now, almost in the middle of the room, and I brought one hand around to the front of her dress. She twisted in my arms as my hand found her, caressing her with a fury that was close to being blind panic. My hand went down inside of her dress, fighting with the bra, wanting to touch her naked flesh.

"You're a little anxious yourself," she said.

"Plenty."

"How many girls have you had up to this room while you've been waiting for me?"

"You're the first."

"Honest?"

"Honest."

"I wouldn't like it but I couldn't blame you if the opposite was true. They say sex is more important to a man than it is to a woman."

"What about yourself?"

She laughed and kissed me.

"They didn't ask me when they wrote that stuff," she said. "If a girl wants a man the way I want you sex is mighty important."

"What would the world do without it?"

"The world would dry up and become nothing. It would be a hollow drum where people just sat around waiting to die."

I had her near the bed.

"I can think of a better way to die," I said.

I ripped something in front with my fingers and then my hand was all over her, lifting, shoving in. We sank to the bed, our mouths fast together.

"I love you," she cried. "You great big animal I love you."

"And I love you."

"We'll make it this way for always."

"You bet we will."

I groaned as her experienced hands did what I wanted them to do. The room seemed to close in on me and the day became endless. My lips crushed against her mouth, forcing it open.

"Don't make me wait, Mike."

"Sometimes the waiting is the best part."

"Don't kid me. You know it isn't."

I intended to make her wait, to make her plead, but there are some things which are beyond the endurance of man. This was one of them.

I couldn't wait.

I had to have her then.

And I did.

Later, when I woke up, I felt the best I'd ever felt. It was like I had taken a bath in a fresh mountain stream. I had everything. I was the richest man in the world. I was the youngest, the strongest, the purest. If I could keep Kitty with me all my life that was all I cared about. The rest of the guys could have their listings in Who's Who and their million bucks as long as I had Kitty. I didn't want to ever look at another woman or take another drink. I didn't need it. I was complete.

That was the way things went all week.

"If we don't start looking for a hash house pretty soon there won't be any money left," I said one night when we came in from blowing forty bucks at the Club Carnival.

"We can use the money I have in the bank."

"How much is that?"

"I don't know."

"How much would you guess?"

"Darling, I don't know much about things like money. I never think about it."

"Like hell you don't."

"All right then I do, but let's not talk about it now."

At breakfast the next morning I bought a paper and settled down to look for a place to buy. Honeymoons were O. K., but a guy couldn't stay on one forever. It was like eating chocolate sundaes three times a day.

"There's a restaurant for sale over on Wilson Avenue."

She didn't say anything. I looked up at her. She was toying with her grapefruit and had a far-away look in her eyes.

"Did you hear me?"

"What was that?"

"I said there's a restaurant for sale over on Wilson Avenue."

"So?"

"Well aren't you interested at all?"

"What do you want me to do, turn handsprings?"

"No, but I expect you to take a little interest."

"All right."

"This place on Wilson can be bought for a grand."

"It sounds like what we want."

"Would you mind being that close to Memorial Hospital?"

"Why not?"

"I thought you might feel funny slinging hash for your old pals."

"They eat at the hospital, but where do you get this slinging hash business? You think I'm going to be a waitress?"

"You are until we can afford to hire one."

She didn't say anything, but I could tell hash slinging wasn't what she expected at the end of the rainbow. Here she'd married a guy worth a million bucks and now she was down to slinging hash to live with the man she loved. Not many dames love a guy enough to give up a million.

"All right, let's get started," she said and got up to dress.

Before we went to the place that was for sale we stopped by the bank to see how much she had in her savings account. It came to $34.05 and the man said she wouldn't be able to get it without her pass book. A hell of a fine note that was. Here I'd been spending my reward money like water with the idea that she had a few hundred tucked away. I checked my wallet and found we had a little over seven hundred left. But that was all right. Nobody ever expected to sell a place for what they asked.

We caught a Ravenswood bus on Michigan Boulevard and got off at the end of the line. This hash joint I had read about was across the street from the Marshall Field Clinic. It was a good neighborhood, but this particular hash joint wasn't much. There was a big sign outside that advertised Coca Cola and in small letters underneath it said: Joe Papanicholo's. Down on the glass by the door there was another sign that said: Ladies Invited. So you know the kind of joint it was.

The place was closed but by the time the door was loose from my knocking, a dumpy little Greek woman with white hair came out from back of the partition in the rear and asked us what we wanted.

"I see in the paper this place is up for sale."

"That's right," she said in a foreign accent and was suddenly all smiles like a sharpie that's found a sucker. "Come right on in."

You should have seen the inside. There was dust all over everything. Nothing had been touched for about a hundred years.

"Looks a little deserted," I said. Kitty looked around like the place made her sick inside.

"My husband he's been sick," the old woman said. "It's a little dirty but everything's she is in fine shape underneath."

"Yeah, I'll bet it is."

"You want to talk to Joe? That's my husband."

Kitty and I followed the white-haired woman to the back where she opened a door and motioned for us to go on in.

A skinny old man lay propped up in a tiny bed with sheets so dirty that they looked like last year's snow. He couldn't move the left side of his body and when he spoke, he drooled out of the corner of his mouth. The woman introduced us but she did all the talking.

"You see you folks can live back here and save money that way. We throw the furniture in the bargain. Eh, Joe?"

"Thatsa right," he said and smiled at us out of the good side of his face.

"You get everything you need for thousand dollar," the wife continued. "Soundsa good, no?"

"We'll think it over," I said. "We have a couple of other places to look at before we make up our minds."

Kitty still had a sour look on her face when we left the joint and took a Damen Avenue bus down to the Polish district around Halsted and Division to look at another place. She didn't say anything about the restaurant and when I asked her what was wrong she wouldn't answer me. Some women are that way. They're all smiles and laughs when it comes to pretty clothes and a night club, but when they see life like it is, they want to close their pretty little eyes and think about something nicer.

The place we looked at on Halsted Street was in about the same class as the one on Wilson, only the neighborhood wasn't nearly as good. But what kind of fixtures could I expect for seven hundred C's? But I didn't plan to spend the rest of my lousy life in one of those fire traps. I just wanted something to get started with. I'd work up from those dumps to the big time.

When we ate lunch and went back to the hotel I tried to explain to Kitty that a guy couldn't start at the top unless he was born with a bankroll. She didn't say anything.

"Well, say something."

She just stayed clammed up.

"God-damn it, if you're going in this with me I want to know what you think about it."

She still wouldn't say anything. I went over to where she was sitting by the window and shook her hard. It didn't do any good. She started crying and I felt like hell.

"Honey, I want you to be happy. Please tell me what you think about the places. Do you want to take one of them or keep on looking?"

"Mike, I can't do it," she sobbed.

"What do you mean?"

"I can't live in one of those filthy holes and wait on tables and cook."

"We can clean up either one of the places. You know, put up some bright red curtains and things and really make them look nice."

She really started crying when I said that.

"What's the matter, honey?"

She went over to the dresser and got a handkerchief from her pocketbook. After she wiped her eyes I asked her again what the trouble was.

"It's just that you're such a nice guy, Mike."

"Nice guy, hell. I'm just another jerk, but it happens that I love you."

"Mike, I can't do it."

"O. K., we'll look for another place."

"I mean I can't live in any kind of place we can buy for the amount of money we have."

"Let's look again tomorrow before you make up your mind."

"I couldn't stand it even if we saw a place that was twice as good as the ones we found today."

I reached in my pocket for a butt, thumped it on the back of my hand and lighted it. I took a long drag. I guess I was stalling for time, because I didn't want to hear the part that I knew was coming next.

"You mean we're all washed up?" I asked.

"Mike, I don't ever want to leave you."

"O. K., tell me your plan."

"Let's go back home. You take the job as body guard and we'll keep on seeing each other."

"We tried that once, and it didn't work."

"But this time it will work. I love you too much to ever live without you again."

"It won't be so easy to go back this time."

"Why?"

"Didn't you tell David that you were running away?"

"No. I told him I was going to see my mother in St. Louis."

"So you never planned to really run away with me after all."

"I wanted to give us a few days to look for a place. I knew that things might not turn out and I didn't want to tell David till I was sure."

I didn't like that. It was one thing for her to leave David and run away with me, but it was something else to be dishonest about it. I may be a jerk and a cheat, but at least I don't try to fool myself about it. I didn't like the way she was dishonest with herself and David, but I didn't say anything about it. Looking back to that day we were talking in our room at the Congress, I now know that it was the first time I had ever seen her dishonest. I should have known enough to pull out and leave her right then.

I did think of calling it quits, of telling her to make up her mind about what she wanted and take the consequences. But she was so damn beautiful and young and innocent that I knew she must be pure and lovely inside. I thought that she was just a poor kid caught in a cross fire that she couldn't handle.

"What if you can't stand living with both of us?"

"I'll be able to handle it this time."

"What if you can't? Suppose you have to decide between me and David?"

"Don't you know the answer?"

"I thought I did."

"I'll take you every time. And just think what we'll have someday. David is a sick man with his diabetes and he can't live very much longer. When he dies we'll be richer than you ever dreamed of. We'll have ten or maybe fifteen million dollars. Just imagine it! Ten million dollars at the very least. Think how we'll be able to live then—Monte Carlo, Paris, Rome, Switzerland. Oh God, Mike can you blame me for wanting to wait for that?"

"I guess not, kid."

But I knew something would go wrong. You just don't get ten million bucks that easy.

Chapter 12

That night we didn't make love. Somehow it just wasn't the same. The next morning Kitty went back to her place on Sheridan Road. I bummed around town for a couple of days and then went back to David and told him I had had enough vacation and was ready to go to work as his body guard. That put me in a different class from a chauffeur, because I would have to be seen in public with him and he wanted me to look like a companion, instead of a body guard.

The first thing he did was to send me to see a gunsmith who had a shop over on West Van Buren. This guy had some of the loveliest heaters I ever set eyes on. I looked them all over, the

Colts, the Smith and Wessons, all of them. When I picked up a blue forty-five revolver I knew I had the right one.

"That's enough to hunt elephants with," the little grey-haired man said when I told him I liked the forty-five. "Why if you just hit a man in the little finger with a bullet from that gun it would be enough to knock him down."

I gripped the gun and aimed it. The balance was perfect.

"Got used to this kind when I was in the army."

"You ever shoot anybody with one of them?"

"Yeah, I killed a German in the Hertgan Forest with a gun like this. I got cut off from my unit one day and walked into a platoon of Krauts. While I was trying to get away from them and find my outfit I lost my carbine, but I still had a forty-five like this in my belt. I ran up a gully and when I came to the end of it there was this damn Kraut standing right in front of me. We saw each other at about the same time. I pulled my forty-five out and almost shot him in two."

I held the gun up and pulled the trigger like I was shooting the guy again. The hammer fell with a loud click.

"I hate to think what a gun like that could do to a man's stomach," the little guy said.

"O.K. if I take this one?"

"Mr. Grey's secretary said to give you anything you wanted."

"Good. I'll take the forty-five."

"You'll need a case. Shoulder or belt?"

"I got used to a belt holder. Any here for me to look at?"

I showed him the gun license David had given me and left the shop with the gun on my side. It was so big you could see it bulge the hell out underneath my coat.

My next stop was at a tailor's joint on the third floor of a building down on State Street.

This tailor was a queer if I ever saw one. He was about thirty-five, tall and skinny with long fingers and hair that would have made Tarzan proud to own. He had to get on his knees to measure my waist, and every time his head came near the forty-five I had belted on my waist he would wrinkle up his nose and pull away a little like he was scared. That gun made me feel like a big son of a bitch.

After leaving there I loaded the gun. I walked a little straighter than usual. There wasn't anything in the world I was afraid of. I wished Danny would sick some more of his goons on me. I had a license to carry a gun and they didn't. Even the law was on my side.

Things changed after I got my new standing. Karl was nicer to me. But I didn't see much of Kitty. That is I didn't see much of her for the first few days.

Then one night about one o'clock the telephone in my room over the garage rang. I pulled myself up and sat on the side of the bed a minute to wake up. I shook my head and staggered over to where the phone sat ringing its head off.

"Yeah?"

"Mike come over right away," Kitty's voice said.

"What's the matter?" Suddenly I was wide awake.

"Just come over right away," she said and banged the receiver down so hard it nearly blew out my ear drum.

I threw on some clothes, ran down the steps three at a time and raced over the lawn to the back door.

Karl was standing there to let me in. He was tall and haughty. He wore a maroon dressing gown and did not seem the least bit upset.

"What's going on?" I asked him.

He looked at me and a thin smile crossed his dark face.

"Mr. Grey is about to die."

"Christ," I said and pushed past him into the house.

I found Kitty walking back and forth in David's room. He lay on his back on the bed. His mouth was open. He was breathing fast and his skin had a lead color to it.

"Is he unconscious?" I asked and ran over to the bed to feel his pulse like feeling his pulse would tell me what to do for him.

"Yes."

"What happened?"

"He's in a diabetic coma."

"Did you call the doctor?"

"Yes. He said to take him to the hospital right away."

"Tell Karl to come up and help me. He's too fat for me to carry downstairs alone."

Kitty just kept walking back and forth like she didn't know where she was. I went out into the hall and shouted down for Karl to come help me.

"I'll be there as soon as I put my shirt on," he called back.

"Well hurry the hell up."

In a couple of minutes he came upstairs. I took David's chest and Karl carried his legs. We managed to get him downstairs, but it wasn't easy because he was so fat and limp. We shoved him in the back seat of the car. I drove. We went down Sheridan Road like a hurricane. When we got to Foster I just held the horn down and kept my foot on the gas.

It wasn't till we got him in the emergency room at the hospital that I laughed at myself and wondered why I was in such a hurry to save his life. I guess it's just a reflex to help people. But my life would have been a lot simpler if he had died then.

We put David on a stretcher and the orderly rolled him upstairs. Kitty and Karl and I sat around the room while Dr. Saunders examined the patient and ordered some lab work.

They kept giving him more insulin and intravenous fluids. By four o'clock he was conscious again. His skin was no longer grey and the breathing was normal, but his face had an ungodly puffiness about it that made you feel like he was a man come back to earth from the next world.

"The doctor says he's going to be all right," Kitty said after talking with Dr. Saunders out in the hall.

"Should I stay here to watch him?"

"Nobody's going to bother him here in the hospital."

Karl kept looking at us like he was storing up every move we made so he could tell it to David later.

"He pays me to watch him."

"Don't worry," she said.

"Do you want me to drive you home?"

"I'm worn out. Let's go. We won't be able to do any more for him now."

Kitty and Karl sat in the back seat of the Caddy while I drove. I didn't mind chauffeuring for Kitty, but it graveled me to have Karl sit back there chatting with Kitty like he owned the string of hotels. It reminded me of the time David was in Hot Springs when I walked in the living room and found Karl sitting in the big chair smoking a cigar. If David ever did die and I married Kitty, I would sure kick Karl to kingdom come.

Kitty and I were real strict around Karl. When I drove up to the mansion, I got out and opened the door. As Karl stepped out he smiled and I was sure he liked it. He and Kitty went in the house. I put the car away and went up to my room over the garage.

I poured a drink, took off my tie and sat there on the bed for a long time thinking of what would have happened to me if David had died. I would have waited for a few months and then married Kitty. I tried to picture ten million bucks. I took a buck out of my wallet and measured it and then multiplied it by ten million and then figured out how many times they would go around the earth if they were put end to end. Ten million bucks is a lot of green stuff. I remembered my old lady when I was a kid. Saturday night was her big night in the tavern. If she didn't make it that night, she didn't make it all week. I remembered when she would count up the dough. If it came to thirty-five, she broke even. If she hit fifty, it was big stuff. But if it was twenty-five, it meant that we ate beans and potatoes all week. Yes, ten million bucks was a lot of money.

I lit a cigarette and looked out over the lake towards the east where a thin grey line was starting the day. There was a soft off-shore breeze and you could hear the birds waking up. I heard a noise behind me and jerked around.

Kitty was standing there in the door. After closing it, she leaned against the door and took a long drag off of the cigarette she held.

"Expecting a cold spell?" I asked.

"You mean the coat I'm wearing?"

"Yes."

She opened it. The coat and the high-heeled shoes were all she was wearing. She was a real blonde all right.

When I got up from the bed and went over to her, she pulled the coat together again and folded her arms.

"I need a drink, Mike."

"You're sure you want to D. F.?"

"Yes. Don't kiss me yet," she said and pulled away from me. She sat down cross-legged on the bed while I threw a couple of drinks together.

We drank about half of it and all the time she kept looking at me in a funny way.

"Mike, how much do you love me?" she asked after a while.

"Don't you know?"

"Tell me."

"I love you with everything there is and you know it. I'd cut it off up to here for you."

"Would you love me no matter what I have done?"

"I love you, period. No ifs, ands or buts about it."

"Would you do anything I asked?"

"Why the hose treatment? You know I love you."

She took another cigarette and lighted it off of the butt of the one she was smoking. Then she sipped the whiskey.

"Mike, I tried to kill David," she said and took a long drag off the cigarette. She squinted her eyes a little and watched me close as she let the blue smoke come lazily out of her mouth.

The words hit me like a ten ton truck. Suddenly when the word KILL is spoken every damn thing is changed. I could feel it change in me. I could feel an icicle start at the base of my brain and work its way down my spinal column and then separate and go down each of my legs.

I didn't say anything. I got up and began walking back and forth like I was trying to get away from the whirling pool inside me. I wanted to open the door and go outside in the cool morning air and then wash all the blackness out of my mind by taking a dip in the lake. Somehow I had felt all along that we would end up by killing David, but now that the time had come to put it into words, I wanted to leave.

I forced myself to sit down on the bed beside Kitty.

"Do you want to hear about it?" she asked.

No, I didn't want to hear about it. I wanted to dump her and leave and then I asked myself what kind of a yellow-hearted jerk I was. This wasn't me turning yellow. I was supposed to be tough. I could take it and I could dish it out. It was like pulling myself down by the collar and telling myself to sit still and listen.

"Yeah, I want to hear about it," I said in a hoarse voice. I lighted a cigarette and looked away from her as she talked.

"I diluted his insulin. I poured three fourths of it out and then filled the bottle up with water."

"So he wasn't getting near enough of the stuff?"

"That's right. In two days he went into a coma. It would have worked. He would have been dead by morning if Karl hadn't discovered him."

"Does Karl suspect anything?"

"No."

"You're certain?"

"How could he?"

"I don't know. I was just checking."

"It's the smoothest plan in the world to kill a diabetic."

"I guess so."

She must have seen the dead look on my face. I still couldn't look at her. After a minute she reached over and turned my face around to her.

"Do you still love me," she asked.

"Sure."

"Sure, but what?" she asked.

"Well, what the hell! I'm new at this killing game. You can't expect me to act like you just told me you had a cup of Lipton's tea after supper."

"But you do still love me?"

"Yes."

"I was doing it for us. If he had died we could have been married and we would have been rich. Not wealthy. Rich."

I kept pulling on the fag and didn't answer her.

"Mike, I tried to make a go of it without killing him. It just wouldn't work out for us as long as he was alive. You know I did it for us."

"Yeah, I know." I wished to hell I had stayed in L. A. and hooked in with the syndicate like a bright boy. With those boys you get professional killers to do your dirty work. I knew what was coming next.

"Mike, he was sick. He won't live much longer anyway. Killing him wouldn't be cruel like it would be to kill a well man."

"What's next?" I asked.

"Mike, you've got to kill him."

Like I said before, I knew what she was going to say next, but still the words hit me like hail stones.

As I poured another drink I had to concentrate hard to keep my hand from shaking. I downed half a glass of the hot stuff.

"Fix me one too," she said.

I mixed two more. I handed her one drink and walked up and down the floor drinking mine.

"Mike, you need guts to get anywhere in this world. It's not easy. If you can't take what you want, you won't have anything." She paused for a minute. "Remember that first day I met you?"

"Yeah." I remembered it. It was about a thousand years ago.

"That very first day I knew you were a man with guts."

"I am. I'll do it," I said. Christ, what else could I say? I was already in it up to here. I was so crazy in love with Kitty that I would do anything. I was so much in love that I would kill a man to take away his wife. It was the world's oldest solution to the world's oldest problem.

"I knew you were man enough to do it. A woman really knows a man loves her when he'll kill for her."

"It isn't just that. It's something that's bigger than I am."

"Tell me."

My hands were shaking and my throat was tight.

"I don't want to talk about it," I said.

She seemed to understand.

"All right, Mike. Come over here and sit down beside me."

She had that same mean look on her face that she had had the first afternoon I had met her. At that time I had thought she was mean. Later I had thought she was just a lonesome kid. Now I knew she was a little bit of both.

When I walked over to the bed I had that same feeling of wanting to hit her that I had had that first afternoon. It was a funny feeling, a strange mixture of hate and love.

We had a couple of drinks and we didn't talk much. We hadn't had anything to eat in a hell of a long time and the drinks boiled through my blood. I had the urge to hit her, to smash her, to drive some sense into her head. I would kill for her—yes, I would do that—but it wasn't necessary. There were other ways and money wasn't everything. Money was only ninety-nine percent of everything.

Suddenly I couldn't stand it any longer. I lifted my head from her lap and got to my feet. I kneeled on the bed and looked down at her for a long time and then I struck her on the side of the face with my open hand. She let out a little scream, tried to cover herself, and I hit her again.

"You bitch," I said.

"Mike!"

"You bitch!" I shouted. "You're a bitch but, God help me, I love you."

"Then love me."

I stopped hitting her and, crying, I fell down beside her, reaching for her, needing her so bad that it hurt.

"Forgive me," I said.

She crept close to me, sobbing deep down inside.

"You're forgiven," she said. "Just love me."

I tasted the blood on her lips and my hands explored her body.

"I'll be better to you than before," I promised.

I was.

Five times better.

Chapter 13

Kitty and I planned to kill David. I knew that it still wasn't too late for me to pull up stakes and haul out of there, but I didn't do it. I wanted Kitty and I wanted ten million bucks. Strange as it sounds, though, I wanted something else more. I wanted to prove to myself that I was man enough to want something and get it.

David looked like hell when he came home from the hospital. He still had the same pudgy face, but it wasn't rosy any longer. It was pale and white and his hair was completely grey like the thin grey hair of an old man. His leg was worse. He walked with a cane and limped more than he had before. Sometimes I felt like Kitty was right when she said we were doing him a favor to kill him. He was like a poor sick dog that should be put away.

Thursday was the new chauffeur's day off. When he was away I drove David. One Thursday afternoon I was taking an after-dinner snooze in my room when the phone rang.

"The chief wants you to drive him to the Loop," Karl said.

"O.K., I'll be there in a minute."

"Make it snappy," Karl said so he would get in the last word.

I backed the Caddy out of the garage and parked it in the drive beside the house while I went up to the door to help David down to the car. By the time I got him out on the porch, Kitty had come out to help me. You should have seen the way she looked when she had on her town clothes. She was wearing a green linen dress and had on a red straw hat as big as an umbrella and she looked as fresh and virginal as a Christmas morning. She took one of his arms and we helped the old man down the stairs. She sort of glanced at me while he was stepping into the car. I wondered what she had planned. I had the method for killing him all worked out in my own mind, but I wanted to see if she had a better plan.

"David, I want Mike to drive me over to Teller's," she said when we stopped in front of the hotel where David's office was located.

"Hadn't I better stick with Mr. Grey?" I said to make it sound O.K.

"Surely I'll be safe in my own office," he said, and laughed with a pained expression on his face like it hurt him to laugh.

"Anything you say, sir."

"You drive Mrs. Grey wherever she wants to go. I'll be all right."

The doorman opened the car door.

"Do you want me to help you inside?"

"Paul will be enough. You two act like I've got one foot in the grave," he said and laughed again as the doorman took his arm.

The David Grey Hotel was located on the Gold Coast not far from the St. Clair. After David got out of the car I drove on down the block towards the lake and then turned north on the Outer Drive.

"You really want to go to Teller's?"

"Let's go someplace where we can talk."

"We can park near the beach on North Avenue."

"That's all right with me."

The rain was coming down in a fine drizzle. The wind was from the northeast and was dashing high waves against the breakwater along the Outer Drive. We were the only ones in sight when I drew up in the parking lot at the North Avenue Beach.

I turned around to look at her.

"What's your plan?" I asked.

"Come on back here with me."

"It would be a pleasure."

I opened the door and crawled in back with her. She looked up at me like she wanted it right there, but we didn't have time. We had to talk and talk it fast.

"O.K., let's stick to business," I said.

"What do you have in mind?"

"I thought we should plan it so the police would think he was killed by the syndicate. It's a good set up for that. He kicked them out of one of his hotels because they were found running a bookie service in one of the suites. After that he hired me as a body guard because he was afraid of them."

"Sounds like a good idea," she said.

"To make it look like a syndicate killing I'd have to shoot him down on the street someplace."

"How could you do that if you were supposed to be his body guard?"

"Easy. I could stop the car in front of a drug store and go in for some cigarettes. I could say that he was knocked off while I was in the store."

"They would check on that. The man who sold you the cigarettes would say he didn't hear the blast while you were in the store."

"That's right. I hadn't thought of an angle like that."

"You could pretend to find something wrong with the car and get out to check on it."

"That's an idea," I said. The whole thing was beginning to take shape now that I was talking about it. I pulled out a pack of butts, gave one to Kitty, and we both leaned back in the seat trying to think the thing through.

"I'd have to use a shot gun. What would I do with it after the killing?"

"You might strap it under the car."

"Too risky. They might search the car."

"I could give it to you. That would be the best plan. You park across the street from where I stop. After I shoot him. I'll give you the gun and you can drive away. It would look better for someone to see a get-away car leaving."

"Would it be safe?"

"Sure. You'd have a good head start on anybody that would follow. Besides who would follow a get-away car other than the police?"

"That's right. We could kill him near the house so I could drive straight home and put the car in the garage."

"This is beginning to sound good."

And it did sound good. The kind of murders that were done on the street with a shot gun blast were hardly ever solved. No clues would be left. Even the cops wouldn't expect to get an arrest. There would be the usual rounding up of hoods for questioning. The papers would play it up for a few days and gradually the whole thing would blow over.

We talked on for a few minutes about our plans. It was taking shape now and I knew I would be able to do it. I felt like we were talking about a movie or something that didn't really have anything to do with me. Pretty soon I looked at my watch and said that it was time for us to go back to pick up David.

Just as I finished kissing Kitty I looked up and saw a cop walking our way. We looked decent, but our faces were still excited enough to give us away.

I rolled down the window.

"What's going on in there?" the angular faced cop asked, looking down at me.

I wanted to blow his head off. What right did he have to go around poking his head in places that were none of his business? He knew damn well what had been going on and now he wanted to come over to enjoy the scene. I guess he got his pleasure out of keeping other people from having any.

I wanted to kill him so bad I couldn't even talk.

"Why nothing, officer," Kitty said and smiled up at him.

"You married to this man?" The cop pointed to me with his night stick.

"Certainly."

"Then why don't you take him home if you want to kiss him?"

"I'm just very sentimental about this spot. You see, we used to come here while we were courting."

"Let's see your driver's license," he said to me.

I showed it to him.

"Chauffeur, eh?"

"That's right."

"This your car?"

"It's the bosses car."

He stood around for five minutes annoying us like that, waiting for Kitty to beg him.

"I really ought to run you two in. There's something funny going on here."

"Please, officer," she said and looked up at him with her blue eyes, "we weren't doing anything. Be a good sport and forget about it."

He thought for a minute and looked Kitty up and down like he was trying to make up his mind about something.

"What's going on, Mac?" the other cop said, strolling up to the window.

"Nothing. It's O.K.," the first cop said.

"You two move on and don't let me catch you down here again," the cop said to us.

"Thank you officer," Kitty said.

They walked back to the Ford patrol car as I climbed out and got in the front seat.

"The damn bastards," I said.

"It's all right," Kitty said and looked back to see if they had gone.

I drove fast going back to the hotel and then I gradually got over my anger and forgot about the incident until later.

That night in my room I thought about our plan a lot. I couldn't see any loop holes. I'd blow his head off some rainy afternoon and that would be the end of the whole thing. Kitty and I would wait a reasonable time before we got married. Then we would take a trip to Europe or somewhere so we could forget about David and everything that was his. Kitty and I would have a good life together. There wouldn't be any more loneliness for me. I would have her in bed every night We would make love and then go to sleep there in each other's arms. Now at last my life was beginning to get some place.

And David—well, he was so sick we would be doing him a favor to put him out of his misery.

I opened a new bottle of cheap bar whiskey and as I sat down by the window to drink the highball I thought about the kind of bourbon I would be drinking the rest of my life. Everything was going to be different. Yes, every damn thing was going to change.

I thought about the gun I would use to kill David. It would have to be a shot gun because that was what the syndicate always used. And besides, it was very efficient. I'd have to buy one and that wouldn't be a very good idea because I planned to kill him right away. I thought of going down on the south side and getting one at a sporting goods shop, but then I changed my mind. I would have to go someplace where the Chicago papers weren't read. My picture might possibly get in the paper some way. The news hounds always played up a juicy killing for all it was worth. They might show a picture of the man who was with him at the time of the killing and I wouldn't want some guy to see me in the paper and then call the police station and tell them that he had sold me a gun the week before the killing. That just wouldn't look good.

Then I got another idea. If I used somebody else's gun nobody would know anything about it.

The next day I got David to call a friend of his on the park commission. He saw to it that I got a membership in the skeet club that overlooks the lake from the Outer Drive. I went a couple of times and shot a few targets. It was good to get a gun in my hands again. After ten minutes I had the swing of the thing and was able to hit target five out of six tries.

The instructor loaned me a Remington repeater that seemed to fit my hands. After practicing with it for two afternoons I was ready for something that walked.

Wednesday night I cleaned the gun, loaded it with five, twelve gauge shells, put the safety catch on and stashed the gun away in the trunk of the Caddy.

The next day was Thursday. The chauffeur would be off and it would be up to me to drive David down to the Loop and back. It would be his last trip.

That night I finished half a bottle of rot gut so I could sleep.

Chapter 14

Kitty and I had it all planned out. When I drove him back from the office I would tell him I wanted to stop on the way home for a package of cigarettes. That would give me an excuse to go over to Broadway instead of on out Sheridan Road like we usually traveled. I would stop for the cigarettes and then cut down Catalpa, a side street that leads to Sheridan Road. I was to say something was wrong with the motor and stop the car on Catalpa. Kitty was to be parked across the street. I would take the gun out of the trunk, shoot David and give her the gun. She was to go up Kenmore in her car, cut over to Sheridan at the next block and then go the three blocks to home where she would put the car in the garage and leave the gun off in my room.

It was a perfect plan because it was the way the professionals did it.

It was a beautiful day for murder. The sky turned a Mediterranean blue and the air was cleaned by a breeze that was fresh from a three-hundred mile sweep across the lake. It was such a nice day that David decided to sit out on the back lawn that overlooked the lake rather than go down to the Loop.

At ten o'clock I went out to the back yard to find out if he was going to sit there all day.

"How is the skeet shooting?" he asked me when he looked up and saw me.

"Fine, sir."

"Great sport skeet shooting. I used to do a bit of it myself."

"Would you like to go down to the club with me for a try at it sometime?"

"Too old for that sort of thing any longer. Shooting's for you young bucks."

He took a cigarette from the jacket he was wearing. I lighted it for him.

"Did I ever tell you about my safari?"

"I don't believe you did, sir."

"Spent six weeks in Africa one time. Beautiful place, Africa. Wonderful shooting in those days. The best part was shooting a rhinoceros. Let the fellow charge right at me. Makes you feel you're being charged by a freight train. Shot him down in his tracks with a .505 caliber rifle. Ever shoot a .505?"

"No, sir. I never have."

"The kick almost knocks you down."

"I'll bet it does."

He went on to tell me about all the gazelles and antelopes that he shot. While he was telling me about the lion he got, Karl brought a pot of coffee and a cup out.

"Have some coffee, Mike?" he asked me when he had pulled his chair up to the table that sat there on the lawn.

"Thank you, sir. That would be swell."

Karl gave me one of his blackest looks. Without saying anything he went back in the house and returned with a cup for me.

"Thanks, Karl," I said.

"Maybe you would like some cream and sugar," David said. "Of course the doctor won't let me have anything but saccharine."

"I could use some cream and sugar," I said. "I'll go in and get it."

"Nothing of the sort. Karl will bring you some. Won't you Karl?"

"Yes, sir," he said and turned stiffly to go back to the house.

I didn't enjoy the coffee very much. It seemed a shame that I was going to have to kill David instead of Karl.

We talked on about shooting while we finished the coffee.

"Plan to go down to the Loop today?" I asked after lighting a cigarette.

"Almost too pretty to spend any time in the office today."

"That's right. Beautiful day."

I got away from him as soon as I could. If we couldn't get him down town we would have to wait until the next Thursday to kill him. I couldn't stand the suspense that long.

I found Kitty upstairs in her studio where she was painting china dolls.

"You shouldn't come up here," she said.

"David's not going downtown today."

"Then we'll just have to wait until next week."

"If we're going to do it, we've got to do it today."

"Getting yellow?"

"Hell no. I just want to finish with it."

"If we have to wait, we just have to wait."

"Can you get out of the house for a few minutes?"

"I guess so."

"Go to the drug store and call the house. Tell whoever answers that you are calling from the office and that you need Mr. Grey to sign some papers. That way he'll have to go downtown."

"They'll recognize my voice."

"Put a pack of gum in your mouth. That will disguise your voice."

She thought for a minute.

"At the inquest someone might mention that he got a phony call."

"So what? The police will think it's somebody from the syndicate."

"All right. I'll leave in a few minutes."

I went back to my room and started walking the floor like a caged lion. I smoked about a hundred fags and finally broke down and took a drink. While I was screwing the top back on I looked out the window and saw Karl come up to David and say something. David then braced himself against his walking stick and pulled his fat body up out of the chair and started walking slowly towards the house.

I smoked another cigarette and took another swig before my phone rang.

"Yes?"

"Mr. Grey would like to go downtown," Karl's voice said.

"O. K." I was about to hang up. "By the way, Karl, I enjoyed the coffee."

"I'll get you," he said in a muffled voice and hung up.

Like hell he would get me. He didn't know that I would be the boss in a couple more hours.

As I drove David downtown he was in a very good humor. He joked with me and asked me questions.

"You never say anything about your girl," he said as we turned right on Foster to go onto the Outer Drive. "You do have a girl?"

"Yes, sir."

"Tell me about her. Are you going to get married one of these days?"

"I'm thinking about it," I said. I didn't say that I was planning to marry his wife in a couple of months.

"What's she like?"

"Blonde, blue eyes, cute."

"Sounds attractive. Sometimes I wish I were a young man again."

"You must not be too old if you married a girl Mrs. Grey's age."

"Just memories, that's all I have anymore."

He lighted a cigar and then leaned back in the seat again with a sigh.

"This is just between you and me," he said.

"Yes, sir."

"If a man can't have a few secrets with his body guard, I don't know who he can have secrets with."

"That's right."

"Kitty was quite a girl when I first married her. She's meant a lot to me as time has gone by. Of course she doesn't mean the same to me now that she once did."

"I don't understand you."

"Well, you know, I'm getting old." He paused for a minute. "Sometimes I think it wasn't fair for me to get her tied down with an old man like me."

"She seems happy most of the time."

"I guess so. But she's just a child. It doesn't take much to make her happy."

No, it didn't take much—only a man my age and ten million bucks!

"Sometimes I feel as though I do not understand her very well," he continued. "There's such a difference in our ages."

He went on talking about her like I was one of his buddies. I guess the poor guy got lonesome sometimes and needed to talk.

"There are some funny things about Kitty, too."

"What do you mean, sir?"

"Did you ever notice the diamond she wears?"

"Yes, sir. It's about the biggest one I ever saw."

"She won't wear it to the hospital."

I thought back to the time she had come to see me in the hospital. She had not worn the ring then and I remembered that she had taken it off and put it in her pocketbook the time we took David to the hospital when he was in a coma.

"I guess she doesn't want to show it off in front of the nurses she went to school with. Might make them think she married you for your money."

"That's not the reason. I didn't give it to her."

"Oh?"

"No, she had that before we were married. I've never been able to find out where she got it. Her parents certainly couldn't have given it to her."

He didn't talk anymore.

There was a lot I didn't know about Kitty, too. I decided to ask her about the ring the next time I saw her.

I let him out at the hotel entrance and then got back in the car to wait for him. I turned the radio on and lighted a cigarette. I got to going over the whole plan, how I would go by the store on Broadway for some cigarettes, then pretend the car was out of order when I got on Catalpa. I would go back to the trunk, take out the shot gun, shoot David and give the gun to Kitty. It was a very simple and fool-proof plan. While I sat there smoking my cigarette I got to thinking about the gun in the trunk. I wasn't certain that I had loaded it. I tried to think back about my actions the night before, but I couldn't remember.

It would sure be one fine note if I pointed the gun at him and got only a dull click when I pulled the trigger.

After awhile I couldn't stand it any longer. I got out of the car and went around to the back. I looked up and down the street. There was no one walking in my direction so I opened the trunk and checked the gun. It was loaded all right. I had the safety on. I would have to remember to take it off safety before I pointed it at him. I closed the trunk. My hands were trembling and when I pulled the key out of the lock, it slipped out of my fingers and fell through a manhole opening.

I said a string of four letter words.

"What's the matter," the doorman asked. He had just come back to his place in front of the hotel entrance.

"I dropped my damned keys down the manhole."

We both got down on our knees and tried to see the keys.

"What's the matter?" David said as he came out and saw us down there on our knees.

"I dropped the keys."

"Then I'll call a taxi and go on home while you look for them." I could tell he was in a bad humor. I guess he thought somebody was pulling a practical joke on him with the phony call to the office. I'll bet he thought it was somebody in his own house, too.

"I'll have them in just a minute, sir," I said. I stood up and helped him in the car.

"Be quick about it," he said.

By that time a crowd was gathered around the manhole. Oh, Christ, I thought.

I hooked a couple of fingers down through the top and heaved the cover away. The key had a chain and goodluck piece attached to it that had caught on one of the wires that ran through the manhole. I lay down on the street, leaned down into the hole and got the key.

The policeman was telling the crowd to shove off. I pulled the top back in place, brushed some of the dirt off my clothes and got back in the car.

David was still mad.

"I thought you were supposed to be my body guard," he said as I put the key in the ignition and started the motor.

"I'm sorry, sir."

"Leave me sitting out there with a crowd like that gathered around."

I told him I was sorry again.

The whole thing had made me nervous. I was tied up enough before, but after that it was all the worse.

As I drove on up Michigan Avenue to the Outer Drive my nerves quieted down a little and I got the strange feeling that it was not me in the car. I was just a character in a movie who was going to shoot a guy. It didn't seem real.

I kept going over the plan in my mind. It had to be perfect. My life depended on it being perfect.

At last we got to the Foster Avenue cutoff. I kept on west on Foster instead of turning right into Sheridan Road.

"Where are you going?" David asked. He was still mad about being called downtown and then having to wait for me to find the keys.

"I need some cigarettes."

"You can get them later. Take me home first."

"Mrs. Grey asked me to get some for her, too."

"Well, get them later."

"I'm sorry, sir, but it's too late for me to turn."

"Damn it, what's up?" It was the first time I had ever heard him swear.

"Nothing, sir."

"Then take me home."

I didn't answer him. He knew something was screwy. He just sort of sensed it, I guess. Now I had to kill him because he would be suspicious if he lived and I wouldn't get another chance.

Like I said, I didn't pay any attention to him when he told me to take him straight home.

I turned right on Broadway and double-parked in front of a cigar store a couple of blocks up the street. I took the keys with me to make sure he wouldn't drive away. I felt so funny inside that I can hardly remember even going into the store.

He was so mad he was red in the face when I got back in the car.

"Mike, you're fired," he said when we drove away. That was all he said.

And I thought it was the last thing he would say. It was sort of funny, him firing me. He didn't know that he was going to be dead in three more minutes and that I was going to marry his wife and share his ten million pieces of green stuff.

I watched close. When we got to Catalpa I turned east. I pushed the accelerator pedal down hard a couple of times so it seemed like there was something the matter with the engine. We crossed Kenmore and I saw Kitty parked across the street ready to take the gun and get away. I stopped the car.

"Something's wrong with the motor," I said and pulled the car up to double park. "I'll have a look under the hood."

He didn't say anything.

I opened the car trunk. As I reached for the gun I could feel my head getting bigger and smaller like somebody was blowing up balloons inside my skull and then letting the air out and blowing them up again.

"What's the matter?" a deep voice said to me from a car that had just eased up beside the caddy.

It felt like I jumped five inches in the air. I looked up and saw a police car with two policemen. I let go the gun and got the wrench that was on the floor.

"Something's wrong with the engine," I said and could feel the trembling come out in my voice.

"Need any help?"

"No thanks."

I watched them drive on down the street towards Sheridan Road. Then I lifted the hood and poked around inside for a couple of minutes like I was fixing something.

I closed the hood and looked around. Kitty was still parked across the street. I wondered if David had spotted her yet. He was sitting up very stiff and looking straight ahead. There were no people on the street to see me. Now was the time to get the gun and blow David's head off. He wouldn't be mad much longer.

I opened the trunk again, put down the wrench and decided to have another look around just to be sure no one was watching.

I saw a jeep turn out of the Shell Oil Station on the corner and head our way. The cops had told somebody there that we needed help.

I closed the trunk.

"What's the matter?" the guy in the jeep asked when he got to us.

"I got it fixed."

"Go on and try it," he said.

I started the engine and drove off. David wouldn't get killed on that trip, and it was going to be hard to get him in a spot like that again.

Chapter 15

By the time I got to my room I damn near had the shakes. I had been able to control myself and feel impersonal about it all up until then. But I was all keyed up for the kill and when it didn't come off things sort of piled up inside of me.

I threw myself down on the bed and gasped for air like I had run back from the Loop. There didn't seem to be enough air in the whole world. At last I covered my face with my arms and tried to feel dead again and fall asleep. But I was too restless to stay that way. I went to the bathroom and then walked back and forth beside the bed, striking my head with my closed fist like I could jar something out of my brain that was bothering me. It took three tries at striking a match before I got one to light a cigarette. There was only a couple of fingers of rot gut left in my fifth bottle. I finished that off, but it wasn't enough to even dent the edge of my feelings.

One thing I knew. I didn't want anything more to do with the job. Kitty could take her sex and go someplace else and she could take the ten million too. It wasn't worth going through what I felt. No dame or nothing was worth that.

I tried to think of some way to see Kitty, but things just wouldn't work right inside my head. I couldn't plan what to do next. I thought of throwing my stuff together and pulling out, but I couldn't even plan things enough to do that. One thing I did know! I had to have a drink pretty quick or I would go out of my mind.

I put on my coat and stumbled down the steps and on out the drive to Sheridan Road. Somehow I got across the street in spite of all the traffic and then I walked on down towards Foster without even knowing where I was going. When I got to a grog shop on the corner of Sheridan and Foster I went in and bought a couple of pints of rot gut, shoved one in each of my coat pockets and walked down to the lake. I sat down on the rocky break water and opened the first bottle. I don't remember drinking it, but I remember I felt better by the time I heaved the empty bottle overboard. Before opening the second bottle I got up from the break water and pulled my dead body under a heavy green bush that grew about ten feet from the edge of the water. I took a couple of drinks from the second bottle and went to sleep.

After going to sleep under the bush down by the lake I stayed there a couple of hours. When I woke up it was dark and I could see the running lights on the yachts out on the lake.

I took another drink and got up. My clothes were all wrinkled and I had dirt in my hair and smeared over my face. At first I couldn't remember what had happened to me and then it all began to come back.

As I walked back towards Foster Avenue, I tried to think ahead and decide what I was going to do then. I had come back to Chicago to get in something good so I could finally make a few bucks and quit throwing away my life, but now I was right back where I had started. Maybe I'd always be a jerk who would always slide back to where I started. Some guys are like that. Nothing ever turns out right.

I was lonesome till I remembered Ruth and wondered what she was doing. She was the only good thing that had ever come into my life. Just being around her made me feel clean inside. Suddenly I wanted to put my head in her arms and tell her all about everything. Somehow I was sure she would understand.

I dragged myself in the drug store on the corner of Foster and Sheridan and gave Ruth a buzz. The house mother said she was not in, but that she expected her back by ten o'clock.

"Do you know where I can reach her?"

"I'm sorry, but I can't give you that information. May I give her a message for you when she comes in?"

"Thanks but I'll call back," I said and told her goodbye.

I looked at my watch. It was almost nine o'clock. What was I going to do the rest of the night?

I walked down Sheridan a couple of blocks to a hotel where I went to the men's room and cleaned up.

Then I got to thinking about Danny and his strip joint. Sure Danny had sent a couple of apes around to beat me up, but I didn't blame him. After all I had run off with one of his women and I had a beating coming for that. Besides Danny was probably drank anyway when he told the boys to pay me a social call. The beating was my own fault. After all Danny was the only friend I had in Chicago outside of Ruth and I couldn't find her. Danny would be opening up his joint just about then and I decided to go by and chew the rag with him for a few minutes before calling Ruth again.

It was hot downtown. When I walked up the subway steps to Grand Avenue the hot damp air oozed up around me like fog. By the time I reached Clark Street I was sweating so hard I had to take off my coat.

Danny's strip joint hadn't changed any. I sat down at the long horse shoe shaped bar and ordered a brew. It was early and the place was only half filled with degenerates. A girl up on the stage was starting her number, but neither she nor the band had their hearts in it.

"If you knew Susie
Like I know Susie . . ."

She was singing only she twisted the words around and made a dirty song out of it.

The beer was nice and cold. It was the only good thing I had hit all day. I ordered another one and asked the bar hop if Danny was in. He said he was out back so I took the bottle and walked back to the office.

Danny was sitting there at his desk playing solitaire. He had his coat off so you could see his beer belly hanging out in front of him like a cow catcher. He had a cigar in the corner of his mouth.

"If it's not Sir Galahad," he said, looking up at me.

"That's right." I pulled up a chair and sat down.

"Didn't think I'd see you again."

"I guess I had it coming to me."

"Yeah, you sure did."

"Ruth's sister still around?"

"She left a couple of weeks ago. Full time hustler now." He relighted his cigar, threw the match on the floor and looked at me. "How are you and Ruth getting along?"

"Haven't seen much of her."

"Very noble."

"Maybe. You're going to leave her alone?"

"Yeah, I figure we came out about even on that deal," Danny said.

He went on laying down the cards on top of others.

"Still working for that guy up on Sheridan?"

"That's right."

"He must have a pile of dough. We ought to figure some way to get a little of it."

"I got fired today."

"Same old Mike."

"What do you mean?"

"Everything you touch turns to dirt. Why don't you put a bullet through your head and call it quits? Some guys like you are always going around from one thing to the next. Nothing ever turns out right for them. Jerks. Here you are thirty years old. Got no car, got no house, got no business, got no money. I'll bet you haven't even got a woman."

That made me burn inside. I'd been saying the same things to myself and it made me mad enough when I said it, but it made me a hundred times madder when he said it. The hell of it was that everything he said was true. I sure took the wrong turn every time I came to a fork in the road.

"Still want to go straight like you said when you came back from L. A.?" he asked.

"I want to make some money. You're right. I haven't got a lousy thing. Have you got a place for me somewhere in your setup?"

"Does it have to be strictly on the up and up?" He pushed his chair back from the table a little and looked at me over the end of the cigar butt that stuck in his mouth.

"No, it doesn't have to be strictly legitimate."

"So you've changed?"

"That's right. I've changed. I can't go on like this the rest of my life. I want something just like other guys."

He leaned back and laughed.

"Sorry, Mike, I got nothing for you in my setup."

"What do you mean?"

"Just what I said."

"Still sore about the dame I stole from you?" I asked.

"Now that don't mean nothing to me. I got over that."

"Then what's the matter?"

"I already told you. You're a jerk and I don't want no jerks in business with me."

I downed the bottle of beer I held in my hand and got up.

"See you around, Mike," he said as I was leaving.

"Yeah," I said and went back through the strip joint where the babes were sweating it out.

I hit the bar next door and got a couple of drinks. Then I sort of worked my way north on Clark Street. I was too restless to stay long at any one place so I'd breeze in a joint, have a couple and work my way on up the street.

I kept trying to forget about myself, and then when I couldn't forget about the kind of person I was I tried to figure myself out, to put my finger on the reason for everything always going wrong for me.

I couldn't figure that out so I just kept hitting the joints. I wasn't feeling much pain by the time I got to North Avenue.

For a while I just stood there on the corner, half blind to the cars that swished past me.

"Jerk," I said to myself after a while and got in a taxi to go home.

I said the same word over and over to myself when I got to my place and looked at myself in the mirror. I took another drink, lit a fag and sat down on the edge of my bed with my elbows on my knees. I had been there, long enough to pull the fag down about an inch when the door opened and Kitty came in. She had on a nightgown and slippers. Her blonde hair was falling down over her face and she looked upset. She brushed the hair out of her face and ran over to where I lay on the bed. I could feel her tremble as she put her arms around me and held me close to her.

"What's the matter, kid?" I asked her.

"Just hold me close to you, Mike."

I held her there for a minute or two and then looked at her face. She was crying and biting her lower lip. It was no act.

"What happened?"

"David."

"What did he do?"

"The same thing he always does."

"What?"

"He hurt me. I didn't tell you before but he likes to hurt me."

"The dirty bastard."

"Mike, you've got to kill him."

I knew I would kill him. I'd show Danny and everybody else that I could start one thing and follow it through to the end. When I got David's money I would buy up Danny's place and kick him out. I'd show all the sons of bitches that I wasn't a jelly fish after all. No. I was Mike Callahan, a guy who had what it took.

"Where is he now?" I asked Kitty.

"Upstairs in his room."

"Is anybody around?"

"No." She was looking up at me with her big blue eyes like I was God.

"Do you think we can get away with it if I kill him now?"

"We could say someone from the syndicate sneaked in the house and shot him."

"Yeah, we could," I said. I was too drunk and crazy and mad to see the holes in it. I didn't care about a master plan any longer. I didn't care about anything except killing David and showing everybody what kind of guts I had. So they called me a jerk. I'd show all of them.

"Let's go," I said. I checked my heater and took off the safety catch.

We walked quietly up the big front stairs and Kitty showed me which room he was in.

I found him asleep on his side of the big double bed. He was snoring and his open mouth looked little surrounded by his fat face. His grey hair was all messed up but there was a little clearing where the pink skin showed through right in front of his ear.

I pulled the gun out and held it close. He must have heard me moving about because right then he opened his eyes and looked at me.

I pulled the trigger. The forty-five blew half his brains out and made a bloody mess against the drapes on the other side of the room. The power of the forty-five was so terrific that it spun him around and shoved the top half of his body off the bed. I saw his arms and legs twitch a couple of times and then he was still.

"Let me have the gun," Kitty said. Without wondering why she wanted it, I handed it over.

Karl, dressed in a maroon smoking jacket, stepped from the closet.

"Mike, you're a very good shot," he said.

Chapter 16

Suddenly I was very sober.

"Give me the gun," I said to Kitty.

"Stay where you are," she said and pointed the gun at me.

"What's going on here?" I asked.

"Don't you get the picture?" Karl said. He lighted a cigarette and began pacing back and forth in front of me.

"I smell a dirty frame."

"Do you now?" He turned to Kitty. "Bright boy, isn't he?"

"Very bright, but it's too late. Mike, we're going to turn you in for murdering David."

"You can't get away with it."

"Oh, yes I can. It was your gun. Both Karl and I saw you kill him. You had the motive because he fired you today."

Lights were flashing through my brain so fast I couldn't think. I knew that there was some way out. There was always a way out of everything if you could just figure it right. I tried to make the lights in my brain go away so I could start thinking again.

"You mean you're in love with Karl?" I asked, stalling for time.

"That's right. I've always been fond of, shall we say, mature men."

"Old men. Karl, she'll do the same thing to you some day. Don't you see the pattern?"

"Let me worry about that," he said. He didn't seem to be worried about anything. He had Kitty and he had the ten million green backs that went with her.

Kitty kept the gun leveled at me while Karl walked over to the phone that sat on the night table by the bed.

"Wait a minute," I said. I tried to think. Now there were no more lights flashing through my brain. In place of them I had pictures, crazy pictures of old men and young girls and guns and red blood. Pictures were better than lights. They were nearer to thinking.

"Well?" he said.

"Put the phone down. I have something to say that will interest you." Oh, Christ, let me think of something, I thought.

"All right, tell me what you have on your mind," he said, lifting the phone off the hook.

"He's just bluffing. Go ahead and call the police," Kitty said. She still stood there dressed in the nightgown with her legs spread apart and pointing the gun at me.

Karl began dialing the number. I started to walk over to him. I knew there was something I must tell him, but I couldn't remember what it was.

"Hold it," I said.

"Hello, I'd like . . ." he said.

"It's about Kitty," I said.

He asked the desk sergeant to hold the line a minute.

"Make it quick," he said.

"Ask Kitty where she got her diamond ring," I said. I still don't know where the words came from, but suddenly I knew they were the right words to say.

"David gave it to me," she said.

"That's a lie. Ask her why she won't ever wear it when she goes to the hospital," I said.

Karl told the desk sergeant that he would call back later and hung up.

"If you turn me in I'll tell them that you were an accomplice," I said to Kitty. "I'll tell them to investigate about the ring, too. How would you like that?"

Karl stood looking at Kitty like he expected her to explain it all.

"We'll have to kill him," she said.

"Maybe that would be best," Karl said. I began edging over toward Kitty so I could make a dive for the gun.

"Go in the other room," she said. Karl turned stiffly and went out through the door.

For a second her eyes followed him. I dived for the gun. An explosion blinded me and almost blew out my ear drums, but I had my hands on the gun. When it went off the second time it was pointed straight up at the ceiling and the flash blinded both of us. I wrenched the gun from her hand and staggered over to the door. My eyes were burning and I could hardly see the outline of the room.

Karl was standing in the hall.

"If you try to pin this on me, I'll kill both of you," I said. I went over to the staircase and began feeling my way downstairs. By the time I reached the street the sight in my right eye was coming back.

I put the gun in my pocket and ran across Sheridan Road like a scared animal. I ran over to Kenmore and turned south. By the time I reached Foster I had come to my senses enough to remember that a running man was more suspicious than one who was walking. My legs ached like a sore tooth but I still wanted to run so bad that it was all I could do to force myself to walk. As I crossed Sheridan again and made my way toward the lake I began to wake up more. My left shoulder had taken the first shot. It would not move and I could feel the blood running down my arm and soaking in the coat sleeve. My face was on fire from the powder burn caused by the second shot.

Finally I made the lake where I heaved the gun as far out over the water as I could. Then I crawled under the bush where I had passed out earlier that day.

It wasn't the coziest night I ever spent. While stopping the blood with a handkerchief stuffed in the torn flesh of my shoulder, the sirens started screaming down the Outer Drive. I wondered what Kitty was telling them. It was my bet that she would try to shove it off on the syndicate boys. At least that was what she would do if she was smart.

By the time things had quieted down some and I was beginning to relax a little, it started to rain. At first the fine mist didn't get to me, but after about half an hour went by the leaves were soaked and dripping on me. I huddled myself together the best I could, but by morning I was cold and wet and hungry. I knew what the word outcast meant. I didn't belong to anyone and I had no place to go. On top of that something from down inside me said: "You killed a man," every few minutes and it would send a sick feeling over me. For all I knew every cop in town was looking for me. I could see why guys would give themselves up just so they could be in a warm jail or be around people to talk with. It was the worst hell I had ever known, even worse than the cold clear nights I had spent in the Sahara Desert during my army days when I knew I was going up front to be shot at the next morning.

I didn't have a mirror or a tooth brush or soap or anything. By morning my mouth felt like fuzzy worms had been crawling in it all night. When it got light I took off my clothes and jumped in the cold lake water to wash the black powder marks off my face. My left eye was swollen shut and my arm was pounding like it was full of a million little devils driving stakes in the bone.

I had to get a place to stay. I couldn't go on sleeping under bushes and not eating. It was a chance I just had to take.

I sat down at the counter of a crummy cafe over on Broadway at about seven-thirty. The Tribune ran headlines about the murder of David Grey. It told about him kicking the wire service system out of his hotel and how he had been so frightened of the syndicate that he had hired a bodyguard. The police suspected the syndicate was mixed up with the killing and they were busy rounding up several men who were known hoodlums. On the back page there were pictures of the house, of Kitty and Karl. There was also a sketch of the room where the body had been found. After looking at all that I couldn't eat any breakfast. Instead I went to a tavern on the corner and downed a couple of quick ones that I chased with beer.

I got on the El that was crowded with office workers and rode down to the Near North Side because I was sure they would be looking for suspicious characters up north where David had been bumped off.

I wanted a cheap hotel room, but decided that was too public. I hit a string of crummy wooden boarding houses over on Hubbard Street not far from Dearborn. The first place I tried wasn't so hot. The man sitting back against the door in a wooden chair looked at me like he wanted to know what had happened. I turned and left without saying anything. There was another lousy joint in the next block that I decided to give a tumble. It was better. The fat sloppy woman who collected my rent money was so batty she wouldn't even be able to read the papers.

I laughed to myself when I saw the room. It was even worse than the flea trap I was living in up on Kenmore when I first met Kitty. Yeah, I'd come a long way. I fell over the iron bed and it sounded like a mortar shell landing in a mess of barbed wire.

I lay still for a long time looking up at the streaked ceiling, hoping that the pain in my shoulder would make me pass out for a few hours. After about an hour I got to the half awake—half asleep stage and suddenly there was the scream of a siren outside on the street. I jumped to my feet and ran to the window. It was a cop alight, but he was just stopping a car for speeding.

When you've killed somebody a siren makes you go weak all over and want to throw up. Your ticker starts in like a riveting machine and you live for a while in hell.

This time I couldn't get back to sleep. I kept turning from side to side looking for a comfortable spot, but there weren't any. Then I got to thinking about all the things that could happen to a wound like mine. I wondered if the bullet was still in my arm and if I'd get lead poisoning from it like the joke said. Then I wondered about tetanus and gangrene. That day I saw myself in some awful pictures, but the worst ones were about my eye. My left eye was swollen tight shut so I couldn't even see light. I wondered if I would lose it and if the other one would gradually dim out on me like it did sometimes in the stories I'd heard. I could see myself sitting on the corner of State and Randolph. My left arm would be gone and I would be blind as I held out a dirty hat full of pencils for people to buy.

No, you can't go to sleep when your skull's full of things like that. Finally I drove those thoughts away, but the one that took their place were even worse. I saw David again as he looked at me before I blew his brains out. I saw Kitty and Karl having a drink together and laughing at me.

"Christ, leave me alone," I said out loud and got up from the bed.

As I walked the floor my stomach was gurgling from hunger, but still the very thought of food nauseated me. I couldn't go on like that much longer. I had to have a drink.

I didn't meet anybody on the street outside and the grog shop on the corner was deserted. For once I'd been lucky.

When I got back to my room I was trembling and out of breath from climbing the two flights of stairs to my room. Yes, I would get a nice drunk on if I finished that fifth bottle in my weakened condition. But I didn't care about how drunk I got. I just wanted to get away from the pain and the pictures. I didn't give a damn if I never woke up.

I ripped off the plastic seal around the neck of the bottle and sat down on the edge of the bed as I unscrewed the top and put the smooth glass top against my mouth.

Yes, that was what I needed. I lay back down on the bed and put the open bottle there on the floor beside me so I could reach it for another long drink. I kept that up till I passed out.

Chapter 17

While I slept a word kept coming back to me. That word was Ruth. It ran around inside my head like the ball on a roulette wheel. And the word had a feeling that went with it. It felt warm and soft and secure. It wasn't a feeling like being in love. Maybe it was more like the feeling a little kid has for its mother. It was the only thing that could make me feel good right then.

When I woke up it was dark and I lay there on the bed for a few minutes letting the word run around some more because it felt good. I put my arm under the pillow on the bed and hugged it to me as I said the one word: "Ruth."

I thought of her with her soft auburn hair and quick soft smile. I wondered what would have happened to me if I had married her and settled down to punching a timeclock some place. If I had done that, I would have turned out to be just another jerk lost in the millions of jerks who punch timeclocks twice a day. But I would have had something real. Now I was a very special person set apart from the common run of men. I was famous. I was a murderer.

I went to the half-dark bathroom at the end of the hall and threw some cold water over my face. I just felt half human when I went back to the grog shop on the corner to give Ruth a ring.

"I can't hear you," she said when I started speaking.

"It's Mike."

"Oh, hello, Mike."

"Ruth, will you do me a favor?"

"Just name it."

"Will you come down to my place? I want to talk to you."

"Is it important that I come tonight?"

"Yes."

"Then give me the address."

I told her the address on Hubbard Street slow so she could write it down.

"Aren't you still working on Sheridan Road?"

"No. Haven't you read the papers?"

"No."

"There's been some trouble. Don't tell anybody that you're coming to meet me."

"Whatever you say," she said in a puzzled voice.

"And Ruth."

"Yes."

"Pick up an evening paper and some sandwiches for me on your way."

We told each other goodbye. Just talking to her made me feel better.

Back at the house I went to sleep and then later jumped up ready to fight when I heard a noise at my door. It was Ruth dressed in a candy striped dress that should have made her look like the kid I had first met. But she had filled out and you could tell she was getting to be more of a woman every day.

I dragged back to the bed and sagged down on it.

"Oh, hell," I said. That wasn't what I wanted to say at all, but that was all that would come out. I put my head up against her and cried like a baby.

I tried to stop. I bit my lip and clenched my fists but it wasn't any use. I shook all over and the tears came out like they had been dammed up there inside me all my life. I must have cried ten minutes like that.

"Do you want to tell me about it?" she asked.

I managed to stop crying enough to talk.

"I got framed. I told you about Kitty, the girl who was married to my boss."

"Yes."

"I fell in love with her and she framed me."

"What happened?"

"She talked me into killing her husband and after it was all over I found that she and the valet were using me to get the old man out of the way. It was so simple and stupid. How a guy that's been around as much as I have could fall for a trick like that, I'll never know. You'd think I'd get some sense in my head, but instead I get dumber every day."

"I always want to be the big shot. I came back from L. A. dead broke and made up my mind to get somewhere. I saw a chance at ten million dollars and I jumped for it. I've always been such a washout at everything. It was almost like I wanted to prove to myself that I could start something and finish it even if it was murder. You don't know what it feels like to be such a failure."

"Mike, you weren't a failure."

"I never made any money."

"Most people never do make any money, but that doesn't mean they're failures. They just go along paying the rent and doing the best they can. They aren't failures. They're the heroes."

"I got all mixed up somewhere along the line."

I opened up the paper she held in her hand and read where the cops were looking for an ex-bodyguard named Mike Callahan for questioning. There was still no mention of my name in connection with the killing. The police were holding several suspects for a lie detector test.

"What are you going to do now?" she asked.

"I don't know. I'm so weak that I can't even think straight."

"Did you eat anything today?"

"No."

"Would you like me to go out and get you some soup?" She looked over at the sandwiches she had brought. "You should have something hot. The sandwiches will keep till tomorrow."

"I'm hungry but I'm not sure I can keep anything down."

"Will you try?"

"Sure," I said. She lighted a cigarette for me and then went out to shop. It was good to see Ruth again. She took over like a mother robin with a nest full of young ones and it was good to have somebody around that cared, somebody that I was sure cared.

The soup tasted good and I was able to keep it down. She brought back a package of medical supplies and started to work on my arm about an hour after I had eaten. It was the first good look I had had at the bullet hole. The flesh at the tip of the shoulder was torn away so that the ragged edges of the muscles was all that was left. She poured some hot stuff over it and then bandaged it. Just smelling the disinfectant and seeing the white bandages made it feel better. She put some ointment over my eye.

"Can you go to sleep now?" she asked when I gave a sigh and lay down on the bed.

"I think so."

"Do you want me to stay with you?"

"Won't they kick you out of the girl's club if you stay out all night?"

"Yes."

"And you don't care?"

"Yes, I care, but I care more about you."

"Ruth, why was I such a fool?"

She didn't say anything. She just looked at me with her big eyes and I knew all the more that I had been such a fool. I had loved Ruth all the time. I must have loved her. She was the only person in the world I ever went out on the limb to help. But I had been such a fool. I had thrown everything away when I could have had Ruth and a nice little home someplace.

"Darling," I said, "Give me your hand."

She stretched out her long moist hand and I took it in mine.

"Ruth."

"Yes."

"I love you," I said and squeezed her hand.

"And I love you too."

"When did you start loving me?" I asked.

"That first night when we left the apartment and sat over by the lake to watch the sun come up. I felt so little and helpless, but I had you beside me. I knew you would help me. I trusted you. I could just feel the goodness inside you."

"The only time in the world I ever had any goodness was when I was with you. You always brought out what little goodness I had."

"You're full of goodness," she said like she really believed it. It was nice to have someone like Ruth believe I was an all right guy. "When did you fall in love with me?"

"I guess it was that first night."

"What about Kitty?"

"It wasn't love with Kitty. It was something else. It was almost like we hated each other and rubbed our bodies together to discharge the hate. It was physical excitement but it wasn't love."

"Did you ever sleep with her?"

"I won't lie to you. I slept with her."

"How did you meet?"

"I was working for a driving school and she came there for lesson. Now that I look back I see how easy she was, that she had been looking for somebody like me all along." I lit another cigarette but it didn't taste good. "I was too blind to see it, too anxious to get my hands on a lot of money." I stubbed out the cigarette. "I had to talk to somebody and that's why I called you. But talking won't help. I killed a man and I'm going to have to pay for it."

She was silent for a long time and I knew she was crying.

"It could have been fine for us," she said after a while.

"Yes."

"We could have gotten an apartment and both of us could have worked."

A pain shot through my shoulder.

"I said I was blind, didn't I?"

"I should have made you love me more, Mike. Then this thing wouldn't have happened."

"It isn't your fault."

"Maybe it isn't but I feel guilty."

"I'm the one who's guilty."

"Of killing a man, yes."

"You must hate me for that."

Her eyes were soft.

"You don't hate somebody you love, Mike. You may feel sorry for what they do or for what they are but you don't hate them. Love lasts beyond anything else that a person can feel."

She was good, the best, and I had traded all of it for a handful of nothing. She was sweet, the way the morning air from the lake was sweet, and when the chips were down she was right there to pick them up.

I had another drink and wished that I could get drunk and stay drunk for the rest of my life. I was sure she didn't approve but I knew she must realize what was going on inside of me. I was thirty years old and if I lived to be thirty-one I would be lucky. Danny had been right. I was a jerk. I had killed for a woman and money and I had lost both. Well, that wasn't right. I hadn't lost them. They hadn't ever belonged to me. The only one who belonged to me was Ruth and I had betrayed her.

"You don't have to stay the night," I said. "You've done enough already."

She walked over to the window and lowered the shade. Slowly she turned and faced me.

"I want to stay the night," she said simply. "I want you to make love to me. It may be the last time," she added, her voice low. "We both know where this is going to end and we can't stop it. The only thing we have is tonight and a few short hours together. If I never do anything in my life again I want to make the most of them."

"I'm a killer," I said.

She shook her head. "To the rest of the world you'll be a killer but to me you are my lover. Why would I desert you now? The time for love is when somebody needs you."

I had another drink and put the bottle aside. I remembered my life as a kid, growing up, and I tried to put my finger on when I had gone wrong. I didn't know. It had been gradual, something which I hadn't been aware of. In school I had wanted a bike and I had stolen one, painting it that same night in the cellar so that it couldn't be recognized. Perhaps it had started then, my brain fired by a desire to have all of the things that were not mine.

"My sister isn't at the club any longer," Ruth said.

"I know."

"There was an opening in our department at the store and I thought I might talk her into taking it. I stopped at the club and saw that man Danny and he told me, without skipping any words, about what she was doing. It's—disgusting."

"A lot of girls go that way."

"But what do they get out of it?"

"They try for the same thing I tried for—money. A few make it for a short time but they grow old fast and afterward they turn to posing for sex pictures or wind up in the slums, selling their bodies for the price of a drink."

"I wish I could help her."

"You can't help her any more than you can help me. She'll lead her own life and nothing you'd be able to say would change her."

"I suppose not."

Ruth left the light on and got out of her dress. She was wearing one of those bras without shoulder straps and she had on a pair of pale blue panties. I looked at her and the pain in my shoulder didn't seem to be as great.

"This may be the last time you'll see me this way," she said.

"Don't say that."

"You have to face it, Mike. This can't go on forever."

The ache wasn't in my shoulder now; it was in my guts. No, it couldn't go on. I would die for killing the old guy and Kitty and her lover would be free. Maybe it wasn't right but that's the way it was. In a sense, except that I had pulled the trigger on the gun, she was as guilty as I was but I'd never be able to prove it. I was alone in this and I was in it up to my neck. No, not my neck. Over the top of my head.

"You're beautiful," I said to her, trying to shove my problems aside.

"Am I?"

She was. Even with the hurt in her eyes, a hurt I had put there, she was beautiful. She reminded me of some of the pictures you see in the men's magazines, pictures of girls you would like to own for a short time. The only difference was that she was there in the room with me and she belonged to me as much as my wounded shoulder.

"Lovely may be the word for it," I said. "I don't know. There's nothing harder in the world to describe than a girl's figure."

"Did that Kitty have a nice one?"

"She was all right."

"As good as mine?"

"Why make yourself miserable?"

"I just want to know."

"No," I said, "I don't think so."

She reached behind her to find the snap on the bra.

"That's good," she said. "I want you to be pleased."

The bra came away from her and I saw the wild red tips of her breasts jutting forward, tips I knew that would get hard when I touched them.

"You must think I'm a hussy," she said.

"No, I don't."

"I'll never do this with another man. Never."

"You can't tell."

Her hands went down to the elastic band on her panties.

"No, I won't, Mike. If you die a little bit of me will die with you." She pushed downward and all of her was there for me to see. "There's only one thing that could prevent it."

"A man?"

"Don't say that. Don't ever say that to me, Mike."

"Well, I didn't know."

She would have made a stripper all right. She was one of the few girls I had known who looked as well with her clothes off as she did with them on. Some people say there isn't anything more glorious than the naked female form, but with most girls I don't go along with that. Generally you think they're firm but after they get off the trimmings they turn out to be sagging and flabby. This, however, wasn't true of Ruth. She was everything she looked to be and then some. She reminded me of a girl I had once seen in a carnival girlie show. She had been young, hardly more than seventeen, and she had been the extra half a buck they had charged for the second show. She had gone down to her skin and she had come along the edge of the platform so that the men could touch her. I had touched her and she had told me that for twenty dollars I could have anything I wanted. When the carnival had closed that night I had met her in back of the tent, paid her the twenty, and she had taken me to her trailer. She had had an exciting body, almost as good as Ruth's, but she had faked the rest of it. I had left there disgusted.

"I want your child," Ruth was saying. She said it as though she had a challenge for the whole word. "It's the only thing that can keep me sane, Mike, the only thing that I'll ever be able to cling to."

"Are you crazy?"

"Far from it." She walked over to the light switch and the movements of her body dripped sex. "Maybe I am that way already. I hope so. At first I was scared, the way any girl would be scared, but then I knew that it was the one thing that I wanted. It's even more important now. I'm going to lose you, Mike—lose you forever—and I want something of you to remember."

I reached for the bottle again. This thing was beyond me.

"You'd ruin your life," I said, taking a drink.

"No, I wouldn't. It would be the start of my life. I would be good to the child, working for it, and I would do all the things that a mother and a father are supposed to do—together."

"What would you tell the kid when it grows up?"

"The truth."

"I see."

"The truth is bigger than any of us, Mike. If you don't have the truth you don't have anything."

"Not much."

She stood there, poised, and I wanted her so badly that I couldn't see straight. But this other—well, I didn't know. You bring a boy or a girl into the world and you have to give them something to live for. What could I give? The record of a killer, a fool? I didn't have anything else and no child would want that. I had so little to give that a kid wouldn't be able to find it if it lived to be a hundred.

"Lights out," she said and flipped the switch.

I was waiting for her when she came to bed. I kissed her and I knew that she was crying. I was crying myself. I was crying for all of the good things that she was and for all of the bad things that I had been.

"You don't know how much I love you," she whispered, kissing me on the face, my neck and around my ears. "You'll never know because there isn't time to find out."

My shoulder bothered me but there wasn't anything wrong with my hand. I started at her throat, moving down, touching her where I knew she liked to be touched. She responded to my touch, whimpering, her whole body belonging to me.

"Please, Mike! Do what I want you to do."

I didn't.

I couldn't.

I was pretty low but not that low. She had her life ahead of her and most of mine was behind me. You don't try to start a family with those odds.

I don't think she knew the difference.

Chapter 18

Ruth spent the night with me. It was a night like I had never known before. The next morning I felt like I'd been touched by an angel.

But the shoulder was bad. Now it was swollen so that I could feel every one of my heart beats pound against it.

"Do you still love me?" Ruth asked. It's funny how women all think you won't love them anymore if you sleep with them.

"More than ever. What about you?"

"I worship you like you were a God."

"Forget it. I'm not."

"You were very tender and sweet."

I laughed. Who would ever think about me being tender and sweet? Danny would really get a buzz out of it if he could hear her say that about me.

"I'm just another jerk and you're crazy to be in love with me."

"I know I'm crazy."

"But you still love me?"

"Yes."

"Then it must be love."

I moved over to kiss her and she saw my face twist with the pain I felt from the shoulder.

"Is it your shoulder?"

"Yes, it hurts worse this morning."

She got out of bed and took the bandage off. I didn't have to look at it to know that it was bad. I could smell it. She put her hand against my forehead and said that I had a fever.

"You've got to see a doctor."

"Fat chance. No doctor would take care of a bullet wound like that without reporting it. Just pour some more of that red stuff on and bandage it."

She looked at it closer.

"Darling, that won't help. The infection's way deep inside. Nothing I put on the outside will help that."

"Maybe you could get some penicillin from the druggist. Ask him how much to give and everything."

"He won't let me have it without a prescription."

"Tell him your grandmother's sick and you can't get a doctor to come to the house."

"I'll try," she said and slipped her dress over her head to go to the bathroom down the hall. She brought me a glass of water and a wet towel to wash with. After that she finished dressing and went out to the drug store.

I got out of bed and went over to the dresser where I kept the whiskey. Yeah, I was sweet and tender as hell, I thought as I turned the bottle up and drank about three inches. Yeah, I was sweet all right.

The druggist wouldn't let her have any penicillin. He told her to have the doctor telephone him.

"Here's the morning paper," she said and put it down on the bed beside me. She looked tired.

GREY'S BODYGUARD SOUGHT IN KILLING the big black headlines said. Now I was famous at last.

My hands shook so I had to put the paper flat on the bed to read it. I almost wish I hadn't read it. There it was, the whole story. Under repeated questioning Kitty had broken down and told everything. Only it was a little mixed up. She told them that she was just a sweet girl who had been taken in by a sharpie by the name of Mike Callahan. She denied any part in the murder. I was just a monster who had sneaked up to the room, shot her husband and run away.

Well, there would be a lot more to add to that story before long. If I got on the spot I would set the cops on her tail but good.

"Mike, what are you going to do?" Ruth asked after I had finished the paper.

"I don't know. I'm so damn sick and weak I can't even think straight. What do you want me to do?"

"That's up to you," she said.

"Would you go with me if I made a run for it?"

"Yes."

"Mike, I do love you. But I love you too much to see you lie there and get blood poisoning."

I had to have some treatment for my shoulder and I had to have it soon. Danny would know all about the kind of doctors who would fix me up without asking any questions. I didn't want him to find out I was with Ruth, but there didn't seem to be any other way.

"You'd better call Danny and tell him I need a doctor," I said.

While Ruth was out making the call I began to get the shakes. Every muscle in my body began quivering like I was standing naked on a windy street corner with the temperature twenty below. I tried to light a fag, but my hand shook so the match waved out before I could take a draw. I gave up on the smoking and threw my twisted body across the bed to wait for Ruth. I guess I must have gone to sleep or something because when she came back it took me a couple of minutes to recognize her and remember what was going on with us.

"Danny said he would call somebody," Ruth said.

"He'd do what?"

"He'll get a doctor for you."

"Yeah, I remember now. Did he recognize your voice?"

"Yes," she said and looked away from me like she didn't want to talk about it any more.

"What did he say to you?"

"Nothing."

I could tell by the look on her face that she didn't want to talk about it, but I wanted to know what he had said so I could guess how he would treat her the next time they met.

"Out with it. What did he say."

"He said that he had something for me."

"The dirty rotten dog. Don't get near him unless I'm with you."

But a lot of good I would be in a fight right then.

Ruth wet a towel with some cold water and began wiping my feverish face after the chilling stopped. I wished that the whole world would go away and leave us alone together like we were then. If I ever got out of the mess I was in, things would certainly be different with me. It made me sick to think how different things would be right then if I had dropped Kitty and gone off with Ruth that first night I met her. She brought out all the good in me and Kitty brought out all the bad.

"It's a damned shame," I said, half delirious with fever.

"What is?"

"That I didn't fall in love with you sooner."

"It's still not too late," she said and I hoped she was right. "You should have known better than to get mixed up with someone like Mrs. Grey, but now that part is all over and things will be better."

She said it like I had only been a bad boy and gotten in a fight at school. But how could she stand me? Didn't she realize I had killed a man?

Suddenly the sound of sirens came up from the street below. Ruth rushed to the window.

"They're just giving it to some jerk for speeding," I said.

"Mike, there're two police cars stopping out in front of the building."

My friend Danny must have turned me in. Maybe there was a two cent reward out for me and Danny wouldn't miss a chance to make two cents. I knew that something had to be done. I made myself sit up on the edge of the bed, but that was as far ahead as I could think. My mind was too burned up from the fever to go on from there. And then I felt Ruth's hands pulling me to my feet and quickly helping me through the door that led into the hall. I followed her to the bathroom at the end of the hall and we were half way out the bathroom window and on the roof of the next building before I fully realized what was going on. She helped me across the roof to the next building where we went down the fire escape to the street below.

"You can make it," Ruth kept saying to me as we walked. "You can make it."

"Make it to where? I might just as well throw in the towel, Ruth. It's not good. I can't make it."

As I was saying those words I found myself stumbling down the steps leading to a subway station. Didn't she know that I wasn't worth this kind of trouble? She put me in the corner of the car and squeezed up tight against me to keep me from falling out of the seat into the aisle when the car started. I don't know how long we rode like that but it seemed forever.

"Christ, it's not worth it," I said at last.

"We get off at the next stop," she said.

"Where are we going?"

"I'm going by the girls' club to borrow some money first, and then we're going to Billings Hospital to get your shoulder taken care of."

"They'll turn me in to the cops when they hear it's a bullet wound."

"We won't tell them it was done by a bullet. The shoulder is swollen so much and so infected now that they won't be able to tell that it was caused by a bullet."

Maybe she was right, I thought, but I was too sick and tired to care what happened to me any longer. Finally I got up and let her shove me off of the El train on to the Platform. She pushed me into a taxi downstairs and told him to go to the girl's club. I folded up in the back seat while she was inside trying to raise some dough. The driver must have wondered what was going on between us. I must have passed out or something because the next thing I remembered I was sitting up in the cab seat and Ruth was slapping my face.

"We're at the hospital," she kept saying.

"Alright, so we're at the hospital. Let me alone. I just want to die."

She and the driver helped me up to the door and Ruth held me there alone as she paid the cabbie and then rang the bell to call the nurse on emergency duty.

"Now remember not to say anything. I'll do all the talking. Do you hear me?"

"Yes," I said. Ruth was surprisingly adult and commanding about this whole thing. Maybe she was getting over this little girl stuff now that she had been in the city alone for awhile.

"Don't say a word."

"O. K., but don't keep telling me everything twice. I'm not a kid."

"I love you, Mike."

"You're nuts."

The door in front of me gave way so that Ruth had to catch me to keep me from falling on the floor.

I was so sick then that I hardly remembered what went on. I remember that they got a sleepy looking intern who acted bored as hell as he filled out the accident report.

"How did you say it happened?" he asked Ruth and then ran a hand through his thick hair as though he were trying to hold his head up. The uniform he wore was still white but you could tell from the wrinkles that it had been slept in.

"We were hanging curtains last night when my husband slipped. The rod stuck in his shoulder."

The intern mumbled something.

"What did you say?" Ruth asked.

"Nasty way to get hurt."

The nurse helped me over to the table and took off my shirt while the intern finished filling out the report. It hurt like hell when he put a drain down in the tissue to keep the pus from backing up. After that he bandaged it up and told me to come back the next day.

"Should I give him a tetanus shot?" the nurse asked the intern.

"Never heard of anybody getting tetanus from a curtain rod," he said and yawned. "Just give him three hundred thousand units of penicillin and let him go home to bed."

"All right," the nurse said and suppressed a smile like there was some kind of joke between them about his bed.

After the nurse stuck me in the butt with the penicillin, Ruth told them that we were on our way to her home in Iowa and wouldn't be able to come back for more penicillin and a fresh dressing the next day.

The intern was putting some papers away and didn't answer.

"What should these folks do, Dr. Farrer?" the nurse asked and then had to tell him that we wouldn't be able to get in the next day.

"Then give them some sulfa tablets."

The last thing I remember it was night time again and I was on another train propped in the corner where I wouldn't fall off the seat. My shoulder was full of atom-hot fire and felt like it would explode any second.

Chapter 19

All night I was awake enough to know that I was traveling; I felt Ruth pushing me about, making me walk or sit or climb stairs; but I was too sick to know just what was happening to me. Certainly I was too sick to care.

When I woke up it was like I had suddenly died and landed in another world. There were smooth clean sheets beneath me and the clean, bright sun was streaming in through an open window. Now the pain in my shoulder was gone.

"Ready for some more pills?" a voice asked me when I tried to sit up. It was a soft sweet voice and I knew that it was friendly towards me but I couldn't place it. When I tried to make my mind go back over what had happened to me, it cut off like an electric motor that wouldn't work. Maybe I felt too good right then to remember any of the bad part that had gone before.

"Here you go, two more pills and a glass of water."

"Ruth?"

"Who else would it be?"

"Yes, it's you, isn't it, Ruth? Thanks."

"For what?"

"Thanks for bringing me here and taking care of me."

"I'll bet you don't even know where we are. We've been here three days and this is the first time you've shown any interest."

"I might not know where it is, but I like it. Am I in the hospital?"

"Goodness no, that was ages ago when we were at the hospital."

"Well, I might not know where it is, but it's the nicest place I ever spent a night," I said, laying back down on the pillow and passed out again.

I dreamed all kinds of evil things. There were sinister men chasing after me. One of the men who was fat and who had small slanting eyes was luring me to a cave that I knew would be full of unspeakable lewdness. I refused to go with him and then he had a beautiful blonde dancing girl come out to the mouth of the cave and dance for me, shedding her veils one by one and beckoning to me with her finger. As I touched her she turned into a haggard witch and the fat man laughed. He grabbed out for me like he was going to carry me down in the cave and then I struck him. We wrestled there at the mouth of the cave and at last I threw him to the ground and ran a sword through his chest.

"Mike, wake up," Ruth's voice was saying to me and she was slapping me on the face.

The other time when I woke up the room and I had been full of goodness and cleanness and it had seemed that there was nothing but goodness inside me, but this time when I woke up it was night time in the room as well as inside me. I suddenly remembered all that had gone before. Kitty and David and the way I had killed him. Now I was filled with vileness.

"Are you awake?" Ruth asked and stopped slapping me.

"Yes."

"What was the matter?"

"I was dreaming about hell and then I woke up and remembered everything that happened. I killed a man."

"That's all in the past."

"Is it?"

"Yes, you did many things in the past, but now that's all gone and we're going to find a new life together. We're going to have each other forever and that will make things inside you."

"You should have turned me over to the cops or let me die on the streets."

"I love you, Mike."

"Why?"

"Maybe part of it is because you helped me one time when I needed you. The other part I can't explain."

"It's no good, Ruth. You'll ruin your life for nothing. If you'd stayed at work and left me alone, you might have had a chance, but this way you're getting the booby prize. I never should have called you, but I didn't know what to do. Now that I'm better why don't you leave me and try to forget you ever met me?"

Then she sat down by the bed and began talking. She told me how much she loved me and said that we would work things out. The shooting of David had taken place because Kitty talked me into it. I had gotten mixed up with the wrong woman and that was what had really happened to me. It wasn't my fault, she said. All that was in the past. We were going somewhere downstate in Indiana and get a job on a farm where I wouldn't be around people like those I had known in Chicago. Maybe someday we would own our own place.

It was all a crazy dream, but I liked it. Ruth was so sold on the whole idea that she got me to believing it just might be possible.

The rest of the week I stayed there in the neat little room that was the tourist cabin she had rented near the Indiana Dunes. My strength came back fast and every day when she dressed the shoulder it looked better. Now I could use the arm without any pain at all. I finished taking the sulfa pills and then the fever didn't come back again so I knew I must be just about well. We'd been there six days when Ruth bought a Chicago Tribune back with her when she brought home the groceries. The story of David's death had dwindled to one column on page three. There was a summary of what had gone before. They were still looking for the chauffeur, and there was a pretty good description of me, but without a picture it wouldn't get them very far. I learned that Kitty and Karl were both free as the air without a trace of suspicion around them. That burned me up to think that Kitty had been in love with Karl all the time, and had just used me to get rid of her husband. Here the two that had really done the killing were scot free to go about their life while I had to keep away from the open and might have to spend all my life hiding. That time she had cut down on David's insulin had only been a fake to make me think she had tried to kill him.

I had gotten a pretty lousy deal and I was going to do something about it.

The next day I got an idea. There had always been something screwy about Kitty and that big damn diamond that she wore. David had said that he didn't give it to her and that he was certain that her family could never have bought it. There must be something big in her past life that accounted for that stone. If I could get the cops to snooping around trying to pick up a lead on that it might take the heat off me and give Kitty and Karl a little of the kind of reward they had coming.

"Ruth, how far are we from Chicago?"

"About sixty miles."

"Will you do me a favor?" I asked.

"What do you think?"

"I want you to take a trip into Chicago and telephone the police station. Ask to speak to Homicide and tell them to investigate the big diamond ring that Kitty Grey wears. Tell them it might have something to do with the time she was in nurse's training at Memorial Hospital."

Ruth said she would give them my message but she couldn't see what sense it made. I wasn't sure myself that it made sense but it seemed to be a strike in the right direction. It might do something to drive a wedge between Karl and Kitty. Any favors I could do for those characters would be strictly what they had coming to them. They expected to walk away from murder with clean hands and let me take the rap for everything. I had a jail record from the time I was in stir out on the coast, and the jury would never take my word for anything. I could shout to the rafters that Karl and Kitty were accessories and nobody would ever believe me.

The day Ruth went to Chicago I began to get restless. I was ready to move on now that my strength was returning. During the week or so that I had been out of circulation I had sprouted quite a respectable beard. I decided to keep the mustache. I gave myself a very short crew hair cut and by the time I got through my old lady herself wouldn't have recognize me.

"Mike! what have you done to yourself?" Ruth said when she got back.

"I thought a little plastic job would be a good idea since I'm about ready to push on. This is too near the city to suit me. What do you say we head downstate tomorrow and start looking for a job?"

"All right."

"How did it go in the city?"

"The police tried to make me keep talking so they could trace the call I was making, but I hung up after I gave them the information about Mrs. Grey's diamond ring."

"Good kid."

It would be interesting to see what the newspapers had to say in the morning.

Chapter 20

If Ruth's call to the police station had any effect on the case it wasn't mentioned in the Tribune the next morning. Now there was only a tiny paragraph on the fifth page.

But still I was a wanted man and every flat foot in a dozen states would be on the outlook for me. I felt restless staying so close to Chicago and wanted to move on downstate in Indiana where we could find a job on a farm that was away from things like cops.

That morning Ruth paid the rest of our bill there at the tourist court and we hopped the next bus south. With my cropped hair and mustache I hoped nobody would recognize me. Just to make things even more certain I bought a big straw beach hat at a novelty shop in front of the tourist court and after we got on the bus I pulled the hat over my face and lay back in the seat like I was sleeping. It wasn't a perfect way to make a run for it, but it was good enough because we got all the way to Plainsville, Indiana, without any trouble. We planned to buy a local paper the next morning and look for a job on one of the farms not too far from the little town where we got a room at a very second class hotel.

When Ruth came in with the paper on the next morning it wasn't the want-ads of the local sheet that took our attention.

BUTLER KILLED DAVID GREY the headlines of the *Chicago Tribune* read. That was a real switch. My hands shook as I read down the column. The cops started tracking down the diamond ring that Kitty wore and she got frightened. They discovered that Kitty had been dismissed from Memorial Hospital when she was a student nurse because a patient had died under mysterious circumstances. Also the patient had owned a large diamond ring that had never been located after her death. That would certainly explain how Kitty got the ring and why she would never wear it around the hospital. She must have been pretty nervous about her own life when the police were able to connect her with a possible murder in her past life. Now there was another dead person connected with her. Yes, she must have been nervous as hell. The newspaper went on to say that Mrs. David Grey confessed that she was in love with Karl, the butler, and that he killed her husband so he could have her and the fortune that went with her.

"What do you make out of that?" Ruth asked from behind my back where she was reading over my shoulder.

"Don't you see what happened?"

"Not at all."

"They were going to accuse Kitty of murdering her husband, but she pulled a fast one and said that Karl did the killing."

"But why Karl? Why didn't she stick to her story about you doing it?"

"Because they weren't able to find me and Kitty knew the cops would come nearer leaving her alone if they had the murderer in their hands. She knew the cops would keep poking around looking for evidence as long as they didn't have the murderer."

It was hard to believe that I was now free to go out in the world again and walk the streets without worrying. I didn't feel too bad about Karl taking the rap for me. After all he had been in on the deal from the first and it may have been Karl who suggested the whole plan to Kitty. Certainly Karl had the most to gain by David's death.

I didn't like to look at myself as the guy who had committed the perfect murder. I didn't like to think of myself as a murderer and after a few days I had myself believing that it wasn't really me who did the killing. I had only been the instrument that the real murderer used.

The next day there was more news in the paper:

BLONDE WIFE HELD AS ACCESSORY
TO MURDER

I read on down the page and learned that the police had dug up some more facts about Kitty. They found out that she had been working for Danny as a stripper before she went into nurses' training. In a signed statement Danny said that she had always had a predilection for older men. Kitty hadn't been a very nice girl. The coppers had put two and two together and decided she was in on the deal to kill her husband. Any fool could see that it figured. She was a girl born to be bad and she was full of rottenness all the way through to the core.

The next column in the paper said that Danny's place had been closed down because it was contributing to the delinquency of minors by recruiting girls under eighteen as strippers.

All my friends were getting paid off with the kind of reward they deserved.

"Ruth, I'm the luckiest man alive," I said. "Now I've learned my lesson damned well and from now on it's the straight and narrow for me. A guy couldn't be that lucky twice and I'm not going to tempt fate again."

"And do you love me?"

"You're the most wonderful girl in the world and I don't want to ever be more than two feet away from you."

"Then come over here and give me a kiss."

I kissed her, but right.

"What do you say we head for the justice of the peace to have a little marriage ceremony performed?"

"I say yes, Mike." She looked like the happiest girl in Indiana.

That night was the first time I noticed any stiffness in my jaw. We had eaten a steak for dinner so I didn't think any more about it at the time.

Chapter 21

"We've got a beautiful day to look for a job," Ruth said the next morning when she came back with the newspaper.

"I don't feel so well. Maybe I'm catching a cold," I said and worked my jaw back and forth to ease the aching I felt there. It was a funny way for a cold to start.

She sat down by the table across the room from where I lay in bed and began going, through the want ad section. Every few minutes she would come over to me and point her finger at an ad, but I couldn't take much interest in the whole thing. By ten o'clock the pain in my jaw was something terrible. I began telling myself that it was a cold and an inflamed tooth together that was making me feel so bad.

"Maybe a couple of shots of whiskey will make it go away," I said at last.

"I think we'd better have a doctor in to see you."

"Doctor, hell. It's only a sore tooth," I said and turned the bottle up to take a couple of long swigs.

"I never heard of a tooth that gave you pain in both jaws at one time," Ruth said.

Of course she was right, but I figured it would all go away in a few minutes if we gave it some time. I took a couple of more shots of whiskey and threw myself back down on the bed to try for a few minutes, sleep. I was still trying to fall off to sleep when Ruth told me it was time for dinner.

"I went out for some nice soup while you were resting," she said.

The word soup was enough to turn my stomach, but she was trying so hard to make me feel better that I didn't have the heart to tell her I wasn't hungry. As I sat up for her to prop the pillows behind my back, I could feel a deep throbbing in my head. I wanted to pull my eyeballs out to make the pain go away.

"Can't you eat some of it? Perhaps you'd feel better if you got some nourishment," she said when I held the soup spoon in front of my lips and just looked at it. I wasn't able to open my mouth. Suddenly I was scared. Then when I tried to talk I wasn't able to do anything except mumble.

"I don't care what you say, I'm going out for a doctor," Ruth said.

This time I didn't argue with her.

I took another drink of the whiskey, letting the hot liquid run between my clenched teeth. It felt good and I did it again. An hour seemed to go by between then and the time Ruth came back with a rummy looking old country doctor who was dressed in a wrinkled black suit that looked like something the local undertaking parlor had thrown away.

He took my temperature by putting the thermometer under my arm.

He felt my clenched jaws.

That was all he needed to make a diagnosis.

"Has he had any kind of injury during the past two weeks?" the doctor asked Ruth.

"He was cut by a curtain rod," she said.

"I never heard of anybody getting tetanus from a curtain rod," he said.

It hit me like a ten-ton truck. The original infection in the gun wound had healed, but now I was getting lock jaw.

"Tetanus usually takes from ten days to two weeks in developing," the doctor said, and I saw him eyeing the bottle that was sitting next to the bed like he was more interested in that than in his patient.

"Will he be alright?" Ruth asked. I could see the color in her face. She didn't know whether or not to tell him the truth about the kind of injury I had gotten.

"Don't know how things will turn out," the doctor said. "We'd better see about getting him to the hospital."

"How long will that take?"

"Hour, maybe two. The nearest hospital is in LaFayette."

"Couldn't you give him something in the meantime?" Ruth asked.

"I don't carry that kind of stuff around with me. I'd get some and bring it back only that would take an hour or so and you might just as well take him in to the hospital."

That was when I had my first convulsion. I could feel it coming on like a giant ocean wave that was breaking over top of me. Light things like sun rays sparkled in the water and then the great green thing came tumbling down on top of me. The last thing I remembered was throwing my head back and making a horrible sound through my clenched teeth as I tried to scream.

After that I was in the ambulance. I woke up and saw Ruth sitting there beside me holding my hand.

"That's alright. Everything will be alright," she was saying and patted my shoulder. The sun showed through her auburn hair and her face looked like the gentle painting of a madonna. I thought: she could have saved me if I'd known her sooner. I wished I was going to have a lifetime to spend with her gentle arms about me.

"How did it start, son," a voice said. I turned my head and saw a priest sitting there beside me. I wanted to tell him that I was about to die, but maybe he knew it and had already given me the last rites of the church.

"How did it start, son?" he asked again.

I looked up at Ruth but I couldn't see her very clearly.

"Tell him," I managed to say. "The truth."

I guess she knew it was about my last request and she started to talk right away. What she was saying would take Karl and Kitty out of jail and give them their freedom. It was only fair, only sense. They had been wrong but I had killed David. I had pulled the trigger on the gun.

"Is that all?"

"That's all." Ruth's voice was far away and unreal. "Isn't it enough?"

I looked for her again but this time I couldn't see her. Night was closing in rapidly, a night that was black and filled with peace.

I closed my eyes and waited for the thing that had to happen.

THE END

SUMMER HOTEL
by Orrie Hitt

Part One

1

I didn't have my hand caught in the cash register, not when Hughie walked into the diner, but he figured it had been there earlier, and that's all the excuse he needed to fire me.

"You know how it is, Mac," he explained, after he'd told me I was finished and I could get the hell out. "Things have been slow enough without somebody getting into the business on the side."

I know where the five bucks had gone, and why it had gone, but there was no point to arguing with him about it. Hughie wouldn't believe me, even if I went out into the middle of Route 29 and stood in front of a truck and took the pledge. Hughie was that kind; he bought what he saw and what he felt and nothing else.

I took off my apron, found five bucks in my wallet and threw it on the counter.

"There's your dough," I told him. "Now you can retire."

It was around ten at night and there was nobody else in the diner. The trucks from the coal mines wouldn't start booming through until around twelve, some of them stopping and some of them going on into town, and it was still too early to catch the teenagers from the late show.

"I could have you arrested," Hughie said, looking at the five. "I could cause you trouble, Mac."

"Go ahead. It won't be the first time."

Hughie wasn't a young man and he wasn't old, either. Put twenty years on my own age, twenty-five, and you'd come within a year or so of his birthday. Take a foot from my own height, six-two, and that's how high he stood. But after that you couldn't add or subtract anything from the way I looked and come up with a close resemblance of Hughie Rowlands. He was overly fat, kitchen white, and he was so greedy for a buck that he'd hang his own mother if the price was right.

"Paying it back doesn't square things," Hughie said, but he picked up the five and rang it up on the register. "One right doesn't make a wrong proper."

"You'll be short another five now," I pointed out. "Don't expect me to make that up, too."

"Well, hell," he said. "What do you know?"

I didn't have many things lying around the diner, just some cigarettes, a jacket that was hardly warm enough and an envelope with some references in it. I could forget about the references; they wouldn't get me a job in a potato field.

"I know I just finished wasting six months," I said. "That's what I know."

"It was a job, Mac."

He was right, of course. Sixty a week is better than nothing. And now I had nothing. Just like before.

"You owe me a week's pay," I reminded him. "Let's have it."

"I'll send it to you."

"You will like hell. Not the way you sent it to Bill Forbes."

"Who's Bill Forbes?"

As though he didn't know.

"The guy I replaced."

"Oh, him."

"Yes, him." I watched Hughie as he shrugged out of his coat and rolled up the sleeves of his shirt over his fat arms. "It took him a month of crawling in here on his belly before you paid off. You try anything like that with me, Hughie, and you'll wind up with your jaw spattered all over the wall."

He retreated to the alleyway that led into the kitchen and hung up his coat.

"You threatening me, Mac?"

"I'm telling you."

"You've got a bad temper, Mac. I've seen you use it around Laura."

Laura was the waitress who worked from noon until eight, half on my shift and half on Al Gordon's shift. She was a blonde tip chaser who had a sick mother and who drank more than she should. You could have the counter full and she'd be at the telephone, out near the washrooms, calling her old lady or a doctor or somebody else, and she'd act like you were asking her the price of it if you told her to hump it up and get on the move.

"You're not paying me for my temper," I told Hughie. "You're paying me for work. Let's have it. Fast."

But he had to complain before he would even consider parting with the money. He had to complain and he had to bitch. It wasn't anything new. He cried like a sick baby every time he parted with more than a dime. You'd think he was being asked to pay for his own funeral.

"You're no short order cook," he said. "You never was."

"Did I ever say so?"

I could fix a hamburger, sure, or some other kind of sandwich, even dish up a dinner that was on the steam table, but I was no cook. My job had been running hotels and resorts, not getting curvature of the spine bending over a soup pot. That is, it had been my job until Miriam. After Miriam I'd been willing to take what I could get. Like running errands in back of the counter in Rowland's Diner.

"My dough," I said. "Count it out. Sixty bucks." Hughie picked up the apron I had taken off, turned it over to the clean side, and wrapped it around his belly. "Now, Mac, you know I don't keep that kind of money in the register."

"No. In your pocket. Let's go."

"I said I'd send it to you, didn't I? I got your address in town. You know I like to pay by check."

Maybe I shouldn't have done it but I was sick of him. He tried to get away from me but I've got long arms and I move fast for a hundred and ninety pounds. I caught him by the front of the shirt and jerked him toward me, lifting him just about up off the floor as I did so.

"My money," I said, shaking him. "Now. No check. Cash. And now."

He paid me, his hands trembling as he counted out the bills.

"Don't use me for a reference," he said. "I won't give you none."

I shoved him away from me. "My life is ruined."

I pocketed the money, got my coat and found my cigarettes under the counter. When I was ready to go he asked me if I cared for a cup of coffee. I don't know if he was going to give it to me or charge me for it but I told him what he could do with his coffee, the diner and anything else that he found lying around loose.

"You won't get another job like this," he said as I jerked the door open.

"If I do," I replied, "I'll drown myself in happiness."

Outside, the warm night held the promise of an early spring. The sky was dark, speckled with a few stars, but it was light enough to see the thumb-like buds of new leaves on the trees.

I walked across the clay-dirt parking area, reached the highway and swung right, moving over onto the other side of the asphalt so that I could walk on the left, facing traffic. That's one thing you learn when you live in the Catskills—you walk on the left. You don't do that, or keep to the ditch, and you have a good chance of some crazy slob decorating his front bumper with your remains.

A car came along a few minutes later but it didn't stop. I didn't expect it to stop. Few people will pick up a stranger at night. If it's a guy driving he's not apt to feel sorry for some other guy who's lifting them up and putting them down. And if it's a girl she's afraid you'll force her off onto the next wood road.

Up ahead, about a mile away, I could see the faint reflection of the lights of the town of Duncan lifting up into the night. But I wasn't paying much attention to the lights or the trees or the road or anything. I was too busy staring at the dark shape of the gas station along the left side of the road.

The little gooseneck lamp on the roll-top desk in the tiny front office was on. I grinned. Her old man was out with the dog chasing foxes again and she was back there in the bedroom waiting for me to come in and give her what her husband didn't have any more.

I continued walking on toward town.

Any other night I would have gone inside—she always left the side door unlocked—turned, cut the light and struck off for the bedroom like the number one man in a hundred yard dash. But this night I was headed for something else—a dame in town. A dame who had been into Hughie's cash register and who had cost me my job.

But I kept on thinking about Julia Edwards, sitting there, waiting for me.

You could say it's funny how you meet a dame like her, but it isn't funny at all; it is, if you aren't a prude, the most natural thing in the world.

Julia had come up from the city the summer before to work for Hughie in the diner. That is, she had come up to work in one of the hotels but the deal had fallen through and she'd gone to work at the diner instead. The first time Elbert Edwards had seen her he'd fallen for Julia like the bottom going out of the stock market.

Elbert was in his fifties, though he didn't look that old, and he was pretty well off financially. I don't know what it was he waved in front of her to make her marry him but I guess it must have been his money. As it turned out, he didn't have anything else to wave.

I met Julia the second night I was with Hughie. She'd come up to the diner to kill some time while her husband was out chasing his fox hound over half of Sullivan County. She'd been pleased to find somebody young around for a change—she was twenty-two—and we'd got to talking. I don't remember what we talked about but what I said must have pleased her because she laughed a lot. The next night she'd returned to the diner and we'd talked some more. The third night she came later, just before twelve. After I knocked off work, walked her home and she let me go inside. Hell, why not be honest about it? She let me do more than that. She was hungry for a man, the way a man gets hungry for a woman sometimes, and those dirty books she read while her husband was out ramming through the hills didn't take the place of the real thing.

I wouldn't say that Julia was pretty but I wouldn't say she was ugly. She was sort of in between, like two cans of different colored paint you throw together and, even though you use it, you aren't really sold on the result. Her face was a little too fat and a little too tired beneath carefully curled brown hair, but her body was all right. Oh, she was slightly heavy if you put her next to a showgirl, but when you're getting it for nothing, and no obligation, you don't notice a thing like that. Besides, she really went for her sex and what she lacked in looks she made up for with ability. Outside of Miriam I'd never met a woman who could ask for the same thing so many times.

But, like I say, this night I kept on moving toward town. She'd have to catch herself a good dream and be happy with that. But more likely, she'd have to look around and find some other guy to tend the fire for her. A thing like that a guy can find almost anywhere.

I got in town around eleven. I didn't have a watch but I knew it was eleven, or slightly after, because the movies were just letting out. Some kids in a rod came down the street, backing off sharply as they reached the corner, and I supposed they were on their way to the diner. Or to one of the dark parking places on the road that curled over the mountain to Groton. Sometimes they went to the diner first and sometimes they went up on the mountain first. It all depended upon who couldn't wait for what.

I followed the main street, all five blocks of it, and turned left on Elm. Like a lot of Catskill towns there wasn't much to Duncan, except in the summer when the vacationists make it look like Times Square on New Year's. At this season, however, it was dead, so dopey that you wouldn't have given it four chances out of five of ever coming back to life again.

A short distance down the street I went into the Crystal Bar. A couple of guys in hunting boots and Woolrich caps were standing at the bar, drinking. I didn't have to look very hard to find Laura. She was sitting in the rear booth, alone, and she smiled when she saw me.

"Beer," I told the bartender.

I carried the drink back to the booth and sat down opposite the blonde. She had her coat off and the two things underneath her white sweater reminded me of a pair of headlights on a Mack truck.

"Hello, Mac," she said.

I drank half of the beer and lit a cigarette.

"You jazzed me up good," I said. "With Hughie. He checked the register, found it short five bucks and threw me out on my pratt."

"You think I took it?"

"I know you took it. When I was arguing with that guy about the stew. When you rang up for that western."

For a second she looked scared. "Did you tell him?"

I drank the rest of the beer. "Why should I tell him? He wouldn't have believed me, anyway. Besides, I was getting tired of his crap."

"What will you do now, Mac?"

"I've got plans."

"What're they?"

"Nothing. But I've got them."

Actually, I'd had the idea for four or five days, but you know how it is when you're working—you get a lead, or think you've got one, and for one reason or another, you just don't follow it up. But I did have the idea, and knew pretty well what I was going to do. The memory of that redhead made my thinking a little easier, too.

She had come into the diner a few nights earlier, and I'd spotted her as soon as she opened the door. Tall, beautiful, long-legged, redheaded—the kind of girl that gives the gloss on the covers of men's magazines. At first, I thought she was alone but before I got her coffee poured an old guy came in and sat down alongside her. Both of them wore plain gold rings on their left hands and they fought like married people fight. It was hard to hear everything they said but by the time they left I knew that they owned Parsons Ranch, that they had been in New York looking for a manager, that they hadn't found one, and that the girl wasn't going to carry the load on her back for another season. I'd meant to call them the next day, or take a cab out there, but I hadn't done anything about it. Now, however, I was out of a job and I intended to do something about their problem the first thing in the morning. Or my own problem. It didn't matter which.

"I didn't mean any harm by borrowing that five," Laura said. "Honest, I didn't." I saw that she was dry and I waved at the bartender for another round of drinks.

"Forget it," I said.

Three drinks later she started to cry. Her old lady had needed some medicine and her tips had been bad that day and she'd just borrowed the five. She'd tried to call Hughie about it but he hadn't answered his phone.

"I was going to tell him tomorrow," she said.

"Don't bother."

"But if you try to get another job and they find out why he let you go, nobody'll hire you."

"I said, don't bother."

I'd asked around about the Parsons Ranch from some cab drivers, and, as far as I could tell, my references were just about perfect for a job out there. They dealt in the same thing that I had been arrested for the previous summer. Flesh.

We had two more drinks and then she said she had to go.

"Mother gets her medicine at one-thirty."

I walked her over to the drab-looking house on Charles Street. There was a glider on the porch, left out from the summer before, and she asked me if I wanted to sit down for a minute.

I sat down.

There was no protest when I kissed her, no preliminaries to what happened afterward.

She got her medicine before the old lady got hers that night.

2

The next morning it was raining and I had to hang around the bus station almost an hour before I could get a cab.

"Parsons Ranch?" the driver repeated as I got in beside him. "That'll cost you ten bucks."

"One way or two ways?"

"It don't matter none. I gotta come back anyway."

"White of you."

We rode out of town and took the county road that led down through the valley to French Creek. The ranch, I understood, was along the creek, a little closer to Midville than it was to Duncan.

"You a guest out there, mister?"

"No."

"I didn't think so. They don't open up for three, maybe four weeks yet." He let out a groan as we hit a chug hole and the rear axle walloped the frame. "Looking for work?"

"Yep."

"Great place to work, I hear. One guy, they say, came out of there last year so skinny you could see right through him."

"A lot of places don't feed their help very good," I said, innocently.

"Food?" He laughed and scratched his head. "What's that got to do with it? Hell, I cart a lot of girls out there during the summer and you should hear how they talk, mister. They've got filthy mouths, that's what they've got. And the fellows! Oh, well—hell, one is as bad as the other. They just come up to the ranch for one thing and that's what they get."

"Well, at least they're not disappointed."

"You wouldn't think so if you could hear them when they're leaving. Of course, sometimes I get a load of fellows and sometimes I get a load of girls. You expect dirty talk from the guys, but the girls charge you. You should hear 'em. They compare the men, how they do it, how often they do it and which man is best. I've heard a lot of things in my time but honest, they embarrass even me. They don't seem to care who's driving the cab. Why, I had one group last summer that was really out of this world. Four girls, sometimes five. They used to sing that old song, 'There's a Chapel in the Moonlight,' and when they got to the part about the organ in the moonlight you should've heard them. I tell you, mister, those people who come out there are really something."

The road leading down to French Creek was typical of many Sullivan County roads: dirt, scraped once a year, and narrow as a snake in spots. In many respects, it was hardly different from the roads in the county where I had been born and raised, Delaware County, a little further upstate.

My folks still lived up there, on the farm, hauling the milk to the creamery and going to bed at nine-thirty or ten every night. They had a good farm, a big one, but I'd never been much interested. I'd helped out with the cows some when I was a kid, but later on during high school I'd summered out in Sullivan County, bussing dishes, horsing around with the waitresses and things like that. I guess neither my father nor mother approved but they hadn't stood in my way when I'd gone to the Cornell hotel school, not to the Aggie school like they wanted. Anyhow, they'd paid my way.

We came down off the mountain, gravel rattling underneath the fenders, made a sharp right turn and continued along French Creek.

"Looking for a job, huh?" the driver mused. "What doing?"

"Anything."

"That ought to be easy. They do anything out here."

The road curved away from the creek and we passed a huge rye field on our left. The rye was short but green and four or five deer were giving it a try on the South end. About a quarter of a mile further on, when we were in the woods again, the driver slowed and dropped the Plymouth into second.

"Rough road," he explained, turning left. "They never fix it."

The road was plenty rough. There were big rocks sticking up in the center and a couple of times he got far over to one side so he wouldn't smash the oil pan.

"They leave it this way," he said. "Keeps curious people out."

We bumped along, and finally he shifted down into low. There was no doubt about it—you had to be Christ-awful curious or have a deposit laid out to want to drive that lane.

Pretty soon, though, the going got better and he changed back into high. We slipped through an oak and pine woods and now there were fields on either side. Up front, along the creek, the trees were big and far apart and I could see a dozen or so buildings scattered around in a horseshoe effect. Some of the buildings were fairly large, one-story, rambling affairs, and some were quite small; all were white and trimmed with green.

"That's it," the driver said.

The ranch looked desolate, deserted.

"Like the end of the world," I said.

"Maybe it is."

The driver parked the cab in front of a small building marked "Office." Leaves covered the foot-high porch, a screen in one of the windows was busted and the door was closed.

"Maybe there's nobody here," I said.

"Must be or that car wouldn't be around."

A green Ford station wagon stood about a hundred feet away, under a low shed. I nodded and got out of the cab.

"You wait here," I said.

"How do I know you're coming back?"

I gave him a five. "How do I know you'll wait? You get the rest on the way in to town."

I walked around some of the buildings, looking things over and, of course, looking for the guy or the girl. I could have shouted or had the cab driver bend his elbow on the horn, but in the spring, when you're looking for the owner of a seasonal resort, you don't do either one. If they made money the year before they get offended if you act so impatient, and if they didn't make any money they think you're a bill collector and they can hide out better than a squirrel in a tree.

The buildings weren't new but they weren't in bad shape, either. Most of them were about ten or twelve inches from the ground, up on cement blocks, and those that were used for sleeping were typical of the bunk houses you see on television or in the movies. There were upper bunks, lower bunks and there weren't any partitions to interfere. They could pack a lot of guests into even the smallest building, and rake in ten times the amount of money that could be earned from the same space in a hotel. Of course, at this time of the year there weren't any mattresses on the bunks, just the springs, and the curtains, if there ever were any, had been removed from the windows. None of the bunk houses held any furniture, not even tables or chairs, but that wasn't unusual; most resorts pull everything they have into one heated central building during the winter so they can paint and make needed repairs.

The mess hall must have been built by somebody who'd been in the army; there were long, bare tables with benches on either side and the whole thing looked about as attractive as a pile of lumber in a dump.

I went from building to building, moving through the rain, and peeked in through the windows. Everything looked out of business; there didn't seem to be anybody around.

When I got half-way along the horseshoe, at the point nearest the creek, I smelled smoke, wood smoke. A few seconds later I saw the smoke coming out of a fireplace chimney at the rear of a building not far from where I had seen the station wagon parked.

This time I didn't look in through one of the windows; I just pushed the door open and walked inside.

There were a lot of things in there—tables, chairs, new tar barrels to be used under a float—but there was only one thing that I really saw.

The girl.

She was at the other end of the open room, not far from the fireplace, slapping some red paint on a battered chair that rested on top of a table.

I started to sweat.

She wore tight green slacks that couldn't have been hiked up another inch on her legs without busting the seams and above the slacks was a green, short-sleeved, low-necked blouse that was just as tight. No wonder she had the chair up on the table; she couldn't have bent over to pick up a hundred dollar bill.

She hadn't heard me come in and for a couple of seconds I just stood there watching her. The reflection of the fire behind her caught at her red hair, making it appear as though she were washed in flame all the way down to her shoulders. Her head turned a little, following the somewhat clumsy strokes of the brush in her right hand, and her hair tumbled forward, almost covering her face. She shook her head, brushing at her hair with her left hand, and it was then that she saw me.

"Oh, hello," she said.

I remembered her voice from that night in the diner but then it had been a trifle high, edged with anger. Now it was soft, as smooth as her hair, and it filled the room with more warmth than you could ever get out of that fireplace.

"Hi," I said.

"Can I help you?"

She turned, facing me, and I could see how her belly sucked in, until it was almost nothing at all, and the way her thighs and hips swelled out against the slacks.

"Maybe," I said, going forward slowly. "I heard you were looking for a manager."

She placed the brush across the top of the paint can and reached for a rag that smelled of turpentine. "Where did you hear that?"

"In town."

"From the employment agency?"

"No." Since she didn't seem to remember me from the diner there was no point of mentioning it. "Just around. I thought it was worth coming out here to see about."

She threw the rag down on top of the table and waved her hands back and forth, drying them. Even when her face registered mild disgust at the strong odor of the turpentine she was pretty. She had blue eyes, very blue, and her lips were like red crayon marks on a pink-white wall. Her face reminded me of some of the faces I'd seen in the cosmetic ads of a woman's magazine—sulky, inviting, ripe. But it wasn't just her face that I noticed. The pink-white skin continued all the way down to where the dark, deep cleavage between her breasts showed over the top of her blouse.

I could tell something else. She was sweating a little under the clinging, green material.

"My husband isn't here," she said. "He drove in to Midville."

"That's too bad."

"But I could talk with you, if you wish."

"All right."

I told her about college, of graduating and some of the jobs I held. She smoked and watched me while I talked. I had the feeling that she wasn't listening to me, not until I mentioned the Hotel Gordon.

"You were there last summer?"

"That's right."

She smiled but her eyes didn't change their expression. "So far, you haven't told me your name, but I think I know what it is."

"If you read the papers, you do."

"It's MacKenzie Osmund."

"Yes."

"And you were arrested."

"No, I wasn't arrested. I mean, they held me for a few days but they didn't prove anything. It cost me my job, though. But that was the reason for the mess, to get me out."

Her smile was amused and this time what she felt inside was in her eyes, too.

"Do you expect me to believe that? As I recall, you had some secretaries out at the hotel—only they weren't secretaries."

"I didn't have them. I knew they were there, of course, but I thought they were legitimate."

Her smile mocked me. "If you didn't bring them there, then who did?"

"My assistant, a fellow by the name of Gromley. Sid Gromley. He hauled them up from New York."

"By himself?"

"No. There was a girl. Miriam. Miriam Samuels."

"What did she do at the hotel?"

"I thought she was going to be my wife."

"Go on."

I hesitated. What was the use? She wouldn't believe me. Nobody would. The cops hadn't, either, but they'd let me go because they couldn't prove anything.

I had met Miriam in New York and I had fallen in love with her the way you fall in love with a girl who is pretty and sweet and who you think loves you. I'd brought her up to the mountains with me the previous spring, paying for her room at the hotel as though she were any other guest, and, when she had suggested Sid as my assistant—an old neighborhood friend, she'd said—I'd gone along with her on it. I guess they had liked the hotel, a year-around place, and wanted to make it their home, because Sid had reported me to the police, saying that I had this string of girls, and I'd been picked up. The girls had gotten away before the raid but one of the guests who had lost a hundred bucks to a "secretary"—I'd often thought he'd been clipped by Miriam or Sid—had put up a big yell with the cops. They'd held me for a couple of days, investigated the charges, and then released me. I'd been fired, of course, and Sid had been moved up into the top slot. I hadn't seen either one of them since that time and I hoped I never would. I've got a hot temper and I couldn't be sure myself what I might do if I did.

"I've got a good record otherwise," I told her. "I never had any trouble like that before."

"Where are you working now?"

"I'm not."

"Haven't you done anything to speak of since last fall?"

I thought of Hughie but I had to skip that one. If there's anything a resort owner doesn't want worse than a bad season it's a dishonest manager.

"Not much to speak of."

"These other places you've worked," she said, "are a lot different than what we have here. This is a peculiar type of operation."

I'd expected something of that sort. "Food costs are the same. The guests are the same. The help is the same. It's just the environment that's different."

She nodded and for a second I thought she was going to show some interest in me. Then, abruptly, she stopped smiling, picked up the paint brush and stuck it down into the can.

"I don't know what we're going to do about a manager," she said, slopping the paint on a rung of the chair. "We haven't made up our minds yet. You might, if you want, leave your address and phone number."

Usually, leaving your name and phone number with a resort owner is about as hopeless as trying to climb a greased pole backwards. Yet I'd had the feeling—I couldn't say just when or why—that I'd almost gotten through to her. Maybe it had been the lift of her eyes, a slight movement of her lips, or—perhaps I had imagined this—her quickened breathing. Whatever it was it had been there and then it had passed. It was obvious, though, that spending more time with her just then could be no more profitable than putting two bucks down on a three-legged horse.

"Sure," I said.

I wrote my name, address and phone number down on a slip of paper and laid it on the table.

"You can call me," I said.

"Are you there all the time?"

"Just about."

"Perhaps we will, then."

I told her so long, that it was nice having met her, and made my way to the door. I hung there for a few moments, unnecessarily fooling with an open pack of cigarettes, and looked back at her. She had some shape, that much was for sure. A shape that a guy would never forget.

"So long," I said again.

She dipped her head in the direction of the scrap of paper I'd left on top of the table.

"Thanks for coming, Mr. Osmund. You may be hearing from us."

"Fine."

"I'll talk it over with my husband."

"Well, I'd appreciate it if you would."

"And Mr. Osmund?"

"Yes?"

There it was again, that smile or something else that I didn't understand.

"Don't get in any more trouble."

I grinned at her. "I won't," I said.

I stepped outside to the porch, closing the door after me. It was raining harder now, coming down in big drops; there was an east wind behind it. I lingered on the porch, feeling the dampness of the storm, and wished I'd brought an umbrella along. Just then a man rounded the corner of the building and came stamping up on the porch. I recognized him as the same man who'd been in the diner with her that night.

We said hello and he griped some about the weather. It was a perfectly natural thing to do.

"My name is Osmund," I said. "Mac Osmund. I was just talking to your wife about applying for the manager's job."

"Oh."

I told him pretty much what I had told her but he didn't recognize my name and I didn't have to go into the bit about the Hotel Gordon. He listened politely. A couple of times when the rain came down very hard, drumming on the roof overhead, I got the impression, from the way he asked me to repeat what I'd said, that he was a little hard of hearing. But he wasn't as old as I'd first imagined. Probably in his early forties which put him about twenty years in front of the girl. And that was quite a distance to be in front of a classy babe like the one inside. A hell of a long way.

"I couldn't say yes or no right now," he informed me. "Diana claims we need somebody but I'm not so sure. We did all right last year, our second season, and I don't know why we couldn't do the same again."

"I suppose you could."

"This isn't like a hotel, Mr.—"

"Call me Mac."

"Well, Mac, it isn't at all like a hotel. The people who come here aren't looking for anything fancy. You don't have to run your legs off up to your knees for them."

"I see."

"It's mostly keeping the books, making charges or ordering the food that bothers us most."

"I've done those things, too."

"I'm sure you have. All right—where could we get in touch with you? We'll let you know."

"I left all that with the lady."

He nodded his head and brushed the rain out of his hair.

"Then there isn't anything more for us to talk about."

"No, I guess not."

I shook hands with him and started down off the porch.

"Don't count on it, though, Mac. If something else turns up, grab it. As I said, it's my wife—"

"I'll take the first thing that comes along," I lied. "You can make book on that."

I hurried through the pouring rain toward the waiting cab. Outside I was getting wet but inside I was hotter than a piece of raw meat in the sun. I could still see how she looked in those green slacks and green blouse, neither of which had concealed very much at all. And I wasn't taking any other job, not for a while. I had a few bucks in the bank, a little in my pocket, and I'd sit it out and wait. The next time, I felt, she would come to me.

That is, she'd come to me—if I had what she wanted.

3

I phoned home and asked the old man for a loan of five hundred dollars and the next day it arrived by Special Delivery. This wasn't the first time I'd borrowed from him. I'd done it before, several times, and I'd always paid him back. That's more than I can say for that loan outfit in Syracuse, the one that charges twelve bucks interest every month on a six hundred dollar note. For all I know, and for all I give a damn, they're still scratching their backsides for the hundred bucks outstanding. They can charge it off to experience; I got plenty of that with them.

The car I bought wasn't a very good one but the tires were new and the motor didn't knock. It was a fifty Ford two-door and the guy who sold it to me said it should take me to California and back. The price was two ninety-five which, I suppose, wasn't too bad.

That's one thing you need in the Catskills, a car. Without a car you might just as well be locked up in the county jail. Oh, there are busses, that's true, but they only run between New York and Monticello, Liberty and the bigger towns. If you live in a place like Duncan you might just as well try to buy a ticket for a ride on a wheelbarrow as catch a bus. And cabs are expensive. The only other way to travel is by your thumb and unless you're a girl with your shorts up to here nobody's going to see you until you've gotten to wherever it is you're going. Girls in the mountains get rides, sometimes a little bit of both kinds. But don't feel sorry about it. A lot of girls want both and a lot of them look for one kind more than they do the other. And they get them.

The day after I bought the car I was lying around in my room, reading the want ads, when Mrs. Herbert's loud voice filled the lower hall.

"Mr. Osmund! Somebody to see you!"

Mrs. Herbert had a hair-raising voice and it was getting worse all the time. I don't mean that she shrieked; she didn't. She just sounded like some excited property owner calling out half the fire engines in the county.

"Okay. Who is it?"

"It's a man."

"Then send him up."

In a lot of private homes you can't have visitors in your room, male or female, but Mrs. Herbert wasn't that way. For all Mrs. Herbert cared it could have been a naked woman standing down there in the hall and she'd have sent her up. There were only two things in life that interested Mrs. Herbert—getting her rent on time, and her pregnant, unmarried daughter who just couldn't, for the life of her, remember the name of the summer boarder who was the poppa-to-be.

I threw the paper aside and sat up on the bed, reaching for a cigarette. Just as I lit the match the door opened and Hughie Rowland came in.

"Well, Mac," he said, noting my shorts. "The life of ease, huh?"

"Nothing like it."

"Feel like going back to work?"

I stared at him through the smoke. "You sick, or something?"

"Naw." He looked uncomfortable. "Laura told me what happened. Stupid thing for her to have done and stupid for me to have thought the way I did. But the register had been running short off and on for over a month. A buck here, another there. That's why I came out and checked it."

"Laura?"

He nodded. "Her old lady's been sick and tips stink during the winter. She didn't do it to be mean. I guess she just couldn't help herself none."

"You fire her?"

"Are you kidding? It's bad enough to be short-ordering two shifts, let alone taking care of the counter. Naw, I didn't fire her. I lent her a few bucks until summer and she said she wouldn't do it no more. She's really a good kid."

I wondered what Laura had given him as security for the loan, but I had to ask myself more than once and even then I didn't get an answer. Hughie wasn't the kind to take it out in trade. Maybe, I decided, the stone had a heart after all.

"Yeah, she's a good kid."

Hughie nodded again. "And she likes you. Said she'd rather work with you than me any day. You could come back at sixty, Mac. And a day off. I could give you more later on."

"No. Thanks anyway, but I'm waiting on something big."

He didn't argue with me. He was smart enough to know that a guy didn't go from hotel manager to short order cook and not want to get back up there again.

"I hope it's good, Mac."

"It'll be good," I said, remembering those tight green slacks. "If I get it."

He hung around for a while, bitching about the rain that had just let up that morning, and then he left.

Later that afternoon, after I'd taken a short nap, I shaved and dressed and went downstairs. Mrs. Herbert's daughter, Sandy, was out on the front porch sweeping away the wet leaves.

"Hello, Mr. Osmond."

"Hello, Sandy."

I don't know what it was about her, she was so big in the belly and everything, but there was something sexy about Sandy. Her breasts were getting bigger every day, running a race with her belly, and that might have had something to do with it.

"Not working, Mr. Osmond?"

"Took some time off."

"That's nice. And you got a car. That's nice, too. After a rain it's always nice to ride."

It sounded like an invitation, as though she was lonely and bored, but I hurried down the porch steps and across the wet grass to the driveway. There was as much sense to taking her out for a ride as there was to letting the air out of my rear tires; neither would get me anything at all.

I didn't pay any attention to where I drove that afternoon. I just kept the Ford moving, thinking and not thinking, looking at the empty hotels and the bungalow colonies and the swimming pools without water in them. At this time of the year the whole countryside was as deserted as a church on Saturday but in a few short weeks it would be spilling over with old people and young people, good people and bad people, whores and showgirls, pimps and bookies, salesmen and promoters. In the fall, winter, and early spring you were lucky if you could get the time of the day in the Catskills, but in the summer there wasn't anything that was off-limits or impossible.

A little after seven I stopped at Rowland's Diner and had supper. Hughie was at the grill and he asked me again about coming back to work but I told him the same thing I'd told him before.

It was fairly busy in the diner, more so than usual, and I didn't have much chance to talk to Laura. But I could see her looking at me whenever she got the chance and every time she did she smiled. I had a second cup of coffee, tried to think of her as pretty and gave it up as a bad job. She was just a girl. But frankly, there wasn't anything else I was looking for at the moment. And she was handy.

At eight, when she went off shift, I told her I'd take her to town.

"You got a car, now?"

"A heap."

I didn't ask her if it was all right to drive up to the mountain road before taking her home and she didn't say anything about not wanting to go. We just went.

"I don't do this with everybody," she said when parked.

"You'd better not."

She crept into my arms. "Would you be mad?" She was warm and soft and after she'd unbuttoned her coat her body fit just right. "Would you, Mac?"

She didn't give me any time to answer because she pulled my head down and her lips burned hard up against my mouth. They moved, getting wetter, pressing in, and then they opened up, filling the night with a sudden, torrid fire. I reached for her. It didn't make any difference if she was pretty or not or if she was the biggest slut in the world.

"Make me happy," she whispered.

I did my damndest.

After I dropped Laura off at her home in town I drove back out along Route 29. She had been good and I should have been satisfied but I was like a hound dog on the loose in mating season. A guy gets that way sometimes. Not often, but sometimes. And when he does there's just one thing to do—get it out of his system. All of it.

The gooseneck lamp in the front of the gasoline station was dark and for some reason this made me violently angry. I cursed Julia, calling her a no-good bitch and pounded my hand against the steering wheel. A couple of miles further on, however, past the diner, I felt sorry for the outburst. It wasn't Julia's fault and it wasn't mine. The blame, if there was any, belonged to a redheaded number who looked like a lipstick ad in a magazine.

I stopped at a bar and had several drinks. I had to think this thing out. It was ridiculous to have a woman I hardly knew bothering me so much. But she did. I couldn't forget the look of those green slacks or the green blouse or the husky sound of her voice. And I couldn't forget that there had been something there that I'd missed, a strange, elusive something that just hadn't quite jelled. She was a whole lot like some of those dolls you see on television—warm and desirable and yet so very, very far away. How do you explain it? One second she's there for you to watch, to think about, and the next instant she's gone.

I had another drink and tried to think about something else. Money. That's always a good subject. You can find more angles to money than you can find in a broken buzz saw in a sawmill.

I had about three hundred bucks in the bank; not much but enough to get along on for a while. My room rent was seven-fifty a week. Add to that another twenty-five for food and drinks, divide the total into the checking account and you came up with a nest egg. A little one.

"Hello," a girl at the bar said when I looked at her. "Feels like spring out, doesn't it?"

I glanced away from the girl. My pass, if there had been one, was unintentional. She was fairly pretty, alone, and any other time I would have been interested. But not tonight. Tonight I had a furnace fire going for somebody I knew wouldn't be around to help put it out.

"Another drink," I told the bartender.

I'd bought the car for just one reason, so I could go out there to see her if she didn't come into town to see me. It was crazy. What would I do if I did drive out there? She had my phone number, my address, and she knew what I was after. Otherwise I didn't mean any more to her than a bale of last year's hay. As I say, it was crazy.

I finished my drink and the bartender bought one for the girl and for me. It gave him the right to start a conversation and to keep pumping away at it until his well ran dry. He lived five miles up the road on a farm, and he'd done some trapping the winter before. Fur prices had been lousy. Most of his traps had been stolen. He was in a mess.

"You got screwed," I told him.

The girl wasn't offended. She was a college kid, or she had been until they'd kicked her out for low grades. She was going to another college in the fall, and this time she'd buckle down and study.

"I want to be a teacher," she said. "Social studies."

I looked at her and she crossed her legs, taking plenty of time about it. Her legs weren't bad under the nylons, either below or above the knees. Only she rolled her stockings and I never cared much for girls who did that. My glance moved up. Thick hips, a narrow stomach and an upper story with two balconies that hung out in space. Not good, not bad. Average. I grinned. I could see it in her eyes, in her smile. There was one thing she didn't have to take any course in.

I had another drink and left. I wasn't sleepy and it was still too early to go to bed so I just drove. It didn't matter where I went. I made a right turn, a left, and then another right. The lighted houses slid by. The night was black up ahead. I was alone and miserable.

I recognized the golf course first, the sixth hole that was too close to the road. I hadn't intended to drive by the Hotel Gordon or anywhere near it. But there it was, standing up on the knoll, looking huge and black against a background of gray sky. A couple of lights burned in bedroom windows and there were a few on the lower floor, back where the kitchen was located and up front in the office. Perhaps it was the effects of the liquor but a wave of nostalgia hit me. I could have stopped the car right there and heaved.

I slowed as I passed the two stone pillars guarding the wide shaled entrance. And then I saw them.

You might think it was funny for them to be walking along the road at that time of the night but it wasn't funny at all. It was a warm night, if you had a blanket—and Sid was toting a blanket under one arm—and Miriam was the kind who liked a change of atmosphere once in a while. It had been pretty cold up until now and this was probably the first chance they'd had, since the previous summer, to get their fun in the open. Miriam was a fine girl behind walls, fine in a car, but out under the trees she was in her element. She'd told me once that it was more primitive, that she could really let herself go. I didn't believe her when she first suggested it, but later on she'd proven it to me. Under the trees there wasn't a thing that she wouldn't do. Not a thing.

I drove past them, and of course, they didn't recognize me. As far as they were concerned I was just another jerk in a heap of a car that would be lucky to make the next gas station.

A quarter of a mile down the road I stopped the car, slammed it into reverse and backed it into a wood road that led up into the hills and a gravel bank. I knew, from experience, that she liked it up there. There was plenty of moss above the gravel bank, as smooth and thick as a Persian rug, and she could play there without scratching up her back or legs.

I cut the motor, turned out the lights, and sat there thinking. This, I told myself, was crazy. This was something I shouldn't do. But I sat. And I waited for them. When you find yourself down in a hole there's a sucker's way of trying to get out—dig deeper.

I rolled down the window and lit a cigarette. The night air was fresh and clear, but to me it smelled just as though I'd shoved my head into a sewer. And the cigarette, no matter what they claimed in their commercials, couldn't have tasted worse if they'd been made from plank-road tobacco. I cursed. To hell with them. I threw the cigarette away.

Presently I heard the two of them coming along the road. They were laughing, talking in low tones, and the heels of their shoes scuffed against the blacktop. By this time my eyes had become accustomed to the darkness and I could make out the blackberry bushes on the left, hanging out over the wood road, and the highway itself. Beyond this, on the other side of the road, was an open field, and further in the distance, the irregular gray of the skyline.

A couple of minutes later they turned off the highway and entered the wood road. I waited until they were about twenty feet away and then I pulled out the button, giving them the high beams. They stopped, standing very still, and blinked into the glare of the lights.

Miriam looked as if she had been sleeping in her clothes—and had just fallen out of bed. Her disheveled hair tossed in the sultry breeze. Her blouse was open and wrinkled. I could see her black bra and the band of white skin below it. She must have realized how she looked, too, because she turned quickly and began to button herself, up.

"Hey!" Sid shouted. "What's going on?"

His face was very white and he looked silly standing there with the blanket under one arm. I pushed the door open and got out.

"Hello, Sid," I said. "Hi, Miriam."

She gasped and swung to face the lights. She'd gotten most of the buttons fastened but the ones at the top of the blouse, the most important ones, were still undone.

"Mac!" she said.

I laughed and walked toward them. Sid dropped the blanket and backed off a couple of feet.

"Don't look at me like that," I said. "I'm no ghost. What the hell, you people didn't bury me in your slime."

"Mac," Miriam said again.

She was pretty, that much I could say for her. She had dark hair, almost black, a peaches-and-cream complexion, and a shape that she could have hired out as a nude model. But only the outside of her was worth a second glance. Inside she was cold and deliberate, worse than any slut who had the guts to put a price on it.

"You certainly make an attractive-looking couple," I sneered, coming closer. "Maybe I should have waited until you got yourselves up in the woods."

"Now, see here, Mac," Sid began. "I don't think you got—"

"You don't think! Stop me from laughing, will you? You've been thinking plenty. If I know you, you've been thinking about when I might show up and clout you one just for kicks. Well, here I am, sonny boy. Here I am. You don't have to wonder anymore."

I won't deny it. I meant to smack him good. I had all set in my mind just how to do it. I'd lay one hard into his face, and then, while he was up straight, I'd dig one into his belly.

"Mac!"

He started to run but I was a lot quicker. He didn't even get close to the highway. But I couldn't do it the way I wanted. I caught him by one shoulder, spinning him around, and I chopped the side of my hand across his throat. It had an instant effect. He began to gag, fighting for breath, and as he doubled over I gave him a knee in the gut. Crouched and retching, he wheeled and staggered toward the highway. I didn't bother following him. He wasn't worth it.

The girl stood in the same place. Her dark eyes were wide and she was breathing very heavily. I guess she thought she was next.

"You don't have to worry any, baby," I told her. "I don't go around messing up women."

You'd think she'd have been grateful but she wasn't. "Damn you," she said. "Why did you have to do that?"

"You know why. He had it coming."

"But, Mac—"

"Shut up!"

I was up close to her now and I could smell her perfume. I stared at her. She was just as big as ever, just as soft and round.

"You cheap slut," I said, pushing her toward the car. "There's nothing I could do to you that would be enough. Nothing."

"Mac!"

"Shut up!"

She stumbled in the darkness and fell against the side of the car.

"Sid! Sid, don't leave me!"

"Go ahead. Call him. He's probably halfway to the hotel by this time. And he hasn't got the nerve to come back."

"Mac, don't!"

"Don't what?"

"Whatever it is you're going to do!"

She was frightened, the way a lot of people get frightened when the chips are flying all over the place. I couldn't blame her any. I was big and she was small. If you know what I mean.

"There's nothing I'm going to do to you." Even there in the darkness I could see the blacker strip of her bra, the white flesh that was on either side of it. "I just want you to know that it's over, finished at last, that you don't count for a damned thing with me anymore. Not that you care, though. I guess you don't."

"But I do, Mac." She tilted her head and I knew that she was looking up into my eyes. "I do! I found out afterward, but I didn't know where to reach you."

"That's tough."

"It's true. True, Mac. I've been sorry, so sorry that I didn't know what to do. Last summer when you were so busy at the hotel—Mac, I can't explain it. I don't know. Every time I turned around Sid was there. You have to believe me, I didn't know about the girls. Not until afterward. And then it was too late. Sid thought it was cute, funny, and—oh, Mac!"

I knocked her hands aside and then, because I was so boiling inside, I slapped her across the face. But the slap didn't bother her any. She just let out a little sigh and rubbed at the spot where my fingers had laced her cheek.

"I know what you think, Mac. I don't blame you. I thought I was in love with Sid then. But I'm not. I know I'm not."

I had to laugh at her.

"I suppose going up into the woods with Sid is one way of telling him that it isn't love," I said. "You can take off your clothes, romp in the moss and give it to him gently. Who do you think you're fooling?"

"You don't understand, Mac!"

"I understand, baby. I understand that I met you, got the yen, and brought you up here so that I could get it regular. The only trouble was that somebody else—maybe a lot of somebodys—began getting it regular, too. It made you so happy to spend half your time on the flat of your back that you wound up making me the biggest sucker in the Catskills. That's what I understand."

"Mac. Oh, Mac!"

The liquor I'd been drinking made my anger swell and I crowded in against her, forcing her back and bending her over the contour of the fender. I could feel the warmth of her legs against mine and I could see how the bra really filled itself out.

"You bitch," I breathed.

I remembered her kisses, how good they'd been, and I wondered if it could ever be the same again.

"I'm taking what I paid for," I told her.

My mouth found her lips, moved away, and returned to tease her. My left hand slid down and did what any left hand might do. She began to tremble, and her hands sought my hair, mussing it.

"Not here," she murmured.

"Why not?"

"We could go up on the bank."

"You might like that," I said, speaking against her mouth. "In the dark you couldn't tell the difference."

She kissed me. "Oh, yes I could."

And then, right there, I gave her a chance to find out one final time. Maybe she could tell the difference and maybe she couldn't. I know I couldn't. She was just a dame who had cost me twice what she was worth.

4

I wasn't sure if I was half-awake, still dreaming, or if I had dropped dead and was in hell.

I opened my eyes, slowly, felt the pain shoot all the way back to my neck as sight collided with the warm sunlight, and hurriedly closed them again. I groaned. My mouth tasted as though I'd eaten all the fish in Sullivan County and washed the whole assortment down with shaving lotion.

I felt terrible.

But I wasn't dead, though at the moment it seemed like a happy prospect.

I rolled toward the wall and pulled the pillow over my head. Somebody, somewhere, was making a terrible noise—not a steady noise but something that kept coming back all the time. Why, for Christ's sakes, didn't they stop?

My head ached, my belly hurt, and my arms and legs had hardly any feeling at all. I had a hangover, the first in months. And it was a beaut.

I tried to think, but when you're fighting your way out of one of these mistakes you don't really think. You remember a little here, a little there. It all adds up to something but it never makes much sense. A guy could do better if he just kept sober and wrote everything down in invisible ink.

There were, however, some things that I did remember. But the things you remember after a drunk are always the things you want to forget.

I remembered getting in the car with her, driving down the road and buying a bottle. I remembered hating her, trying to drink away that hate, then parking on the mountain road. And, in a hazy recollection of passion and disgust, I remembered the devil trying to collect his due again and again.

After that there was nothing except time and then the car was empty. In fact I wasn't even in the car. I was in a bar, sitting on a stool and hanging to the rail that was sometimes close and sometimes very far away. The only thing that never got very far away was a cute little blonde who pressed her knees into my thigh and helped me spend my money. Thinking about the money made my head pound all the more. When it ran out, as it must have, the blonde drifted away and the bartender started yelling. Most bartenders are okay but this one hadn't been; he wouldn't lend his best friend an empty glass to cry in.

Beyond that there was very little. There was a car on the wrong side of the road—mine or did it belong to somebody else?—and there was a tangle of streets that made as much sense as a Chinese fire drill.

The noise started again and I went deeper into the pillow, cursing whoever or whatever it was.

The steps. Oh, those steps had been murder. Up two feet and down one and you never got anywhere at all. Somebody had helped me. A girl. A fat girl whose big stomach got in the way.

"Mr. Osmund. Mr. Osmund!"

This was better than the noise; it didn't clang around in my head so much. I relaxed my grip on the pillow and struggled to a sitting position. I opened my eyes carefully and they still hurt. I closed them again.

"Who is it?"

"Sandy, Mr. Osmund. Are you all right?"

I got my feet over the side of the bed and onto the floor.

"I don't know," I admitted.

"There's a woman downstairs to see you," she said.

No wonder there had been so much noise; no doubt her old lady had stood down at the bottom of the stairs, bellowing her lungs out.

"What woman?"

"A Mrs. Shipton."

That didn't help, not a bit. I didn't know any Mrs. Shipton. Then, with the feeling of coldness, I remembered the blonde at the bar, the uncertainty of what had happened afterward.

"What does she want?"

"She wants to see you."

Practical, I thought that Sandy is practical. She gives you a straight answer and she might just as well have kept her mouth shut.

I lay down again. "Tell her to come back," I said.

"I did, Mr. Osmund, because I know you don't feel so good this morning. But she says it's important."

I opened my eyes and this time it wasn't so bad. I left them open. My head felt unusually large as I sat up but most of the pain was gone. I looked down at myself and managed a grin. The only thing I had on was a pair of socks.

"Okay," I said. "Tell her I'll be down in a couple of minutes."

The knob turned and the door opened a couple of inches, just enough so that she could talk to me without shouting.

"Mr. Osmund, I hope you're not mad at me."

"For what?"

"Last night. You were—kind of mixed-up."

"Yeah. Thanks."

"Your shorts and shirt are on the foot of the bed and your pants are on the chair, the one by the window. I left your shoes under the bed."

After a couple of false, unsteady starts I got into my clothes and fumbled for the shoes. Bending over was only slightly better than falling out of a second story window. I swore softly and grunted.

"Are you sure you're all right, Mr. Osmund?"

"I'm not sure of anything."

"Do you want an aspirin?"

"Maybe later."

She hesitated. "May I come in?"

"If you want to."

She came in, closing the door behind her. I glanced up from tying my shoes and about all I could see of her was that great big belly. It made me near sick, it was so big. Maybe if she wore a maternity dress I wouldn't have noticed it so much but in just a house dress the hem was hiked up in front and drooped down in back.

"You had a ball of it last night," she said.

I finished tying my shoes, "I guess I did."

"It's a good thing Ma took her sleeping pills last night, Mr. Osmund. She'd have heard you, otherwise. And drinking's one thing Ma don't hold with. She says it makes her afraid of having a fire."

"Well, it won't happen again." I stood up, rocking back on my heels. "So help me God, I take the pledge."

"You wanted to sleep on the porch."

"That would have been a neat stunt."

"I heard you fall. You made an awful lot of noise. Didn't you hurt yourself?"

I shook my head. "A drunk never does."

"I heard you," she said again. "I came down. I had an awful time getting you up the stairs. You could walk but you didn't want to. All you wanted me to do was—go to bed with you."

"I did!"

Her smile was forgiving. "I told you what the doctor said, that I couldn't, and after we got in the room you started to cry. You wanted me to be nice to you, you said."

I felt so ashamed I couldn't look at her.

"I tried to be nice to you," she went on. "But it wasn't any use. You fell asleep."

I didn't know what she meant and I didn't ask her. I just stumbled out into the hall and groped my way down the stairs. There are times when a guy can't stand living with himself.

Mrs. Herbert met me in the lower hall.

"You're harder to wake up than the dead," she told me. "You could have heard me from here to Monticello."

"I'll bet."

She took no offense at the remark. "The lady's in the living room."

"Thanks."

I walked around Mrs. Herbert and through the archway. Two feet inside the room I stopped shorter than a passenger train with a yanked emergency cord. "Hi," I said.

The lips of the redhead seated on the davenport parted and revealed a set of very white teeth.

"Well, Mr. Osmund," she said. "The way that woman was shouting I thought I'd have to wait until Resurrection Day."

She must have been partial to green because this time she had on a green dress. And it was tight. It was tight across her breasts and it was tight around the middle. It was even snug and a little high across her knees. Her legs beneath the stockings looked like brown velvet.

"I don't expect people to come around so early in the morning," I said.

"Morning? It's the middle of the afternoon."

I sighed and reached for the cigarettes which I didn't have. I was getting off to a fine start.

"Cigarette, Mr. Osmund?"

"Thanks."

She opened a pocketbook the size of an overnight bag and located a pack of cigarettes without any trouble at all. I had never seen a green bra before but as I leaned over her to get a light, I got a good look at part of one. Her eyes lifted to mine, knew where I was looking and she didn't seem to mind at all.

"A hotel manager ought to be able to tell the difference between morning and afternoon," she said, obviously amused. "Or daylight from dark."

"That's for true."

"Don't be so nervous. Sit down."

"Yeah."

I sat down on the other end of the davenport, losing the view of her legs but getting another one that was even better. She had a long, tapered thigh and its outline was plainly visible beneath the dress. And on top—well, I'd seen plenty of nice ones before, but none like these.

"I thought your name was Parsons," I said.

"No. It's Shipton. Diana Shipton. My husband is George."

Diana, I knew, comes from the Latin and it meant "goddess." Goddess of what?

"I don't get it," I said. "Why the Parsons?"

"That was the name of the ranch before and, for credit purposes, we didn't change it."

"I see."

"But I doubt if you do. We've only had it two years and we bought it on a shoestring. The Parsons credit was already established and the name didn't mean anything to us. We can get as many guests with one name as with another."

It was an old trick in the resort business. A hotel or a boarding house changed hands but the handle remained the same. A creditor, not aware of this, could get burned but good if the season turned sour.

"The place used to be a horse ranch for under-privileged kids," she said. "Can you imagine that?"

"Hardly."

"Why do you say, 'hardly'?"

I stubbed out the cigarette in an ash tray. "Because I've heard a few things about your operation."

"Do you object?"

"I didn't say that."

Outside the sun was bright and inside the house it was getting warm. My head now throbbed with the persistence of rain dripping from a roof. I felt hungry and I felt sick and I wished I hadn't drunk so much the night before.

"You talked with my husband."

"Yes, for a few minutes."

"But you neglected to tell him about the Hotel Gordon."

"I'd already told you. I thought that was enough." She smiled and her hand followed mine to the ash tray. I noticed that in spite of the manual work she did, she kept her fingernails neatly buffed.

"We'll get along," she announced. "We'll get along fine."

My glance went over her body again. We could get along. There was no doubt about that.

"I guess you made up your mind about a manager," I said.

She frowned. "No, that isn't quite so. Actually, George doesn't want to spend the money for more help but I think I need somebody to give me a hand once in a while. Do I make myself clear?"

She could have my hand or anything else that she wanted. "Yeah," I said.

"I can take care of the reservations but it's ordering the food and keeping the books that's got me stuck. That's where you come in." She turned those big blue eyes on me. "If you're interested."

It was the one time in my life that I wasn't too concerned about the money part of a job. I was close enough to her to smell the woman smell, the way a woman smells when she's all woman, and right then I'd have taken on the chore of washing a stack of dishes a yard wide and a mile high. For nothing. For all I could get on the side.

"I'm interested," I said. And then because it was expected of me, "What does it pay? And when do I start?"

"You know how to paint?"

"A little."

"Good. You could start tomorrow. George hates to paint but I like it and you could help me with the rest of the chairs. With the two of us working we can get things in nice shape before the start of the season."

Things, as far as I could see, were already in nice shape.

"And the pay?"

"Seventy-five a week, plus your room and board, until we get some people. A hundred after that. I'll take care of the desk and you'll watch the back of the house and keep the books."

She continued to talk but none of it sounded very important and I didn't listen to much of what she said. A warning chill crept down my back and settled at the base of my spine. Sixty a week was plenty for that kind of a job in a small resort and here she was offering me much more than that. It didn't make sense, not if her husband didn't want to throw his money around. It didn't make sense at all. It could make sense only one way. Somebody was going to ask me to do something I still didn't know about.

"Mr. Osmund?"

"What?"

"Are you listening to me?"

"Naturally. I start tomorrow. And I get seventy-five a week until—"

"No, not that. What I just said. Don't tell my husband how much you're getting. Show fifty dollars on your pay slip and take the rest out of petty cash."

"Got you." I wished I did have.

"Then it's settled, Mr. Osmund?"

"Call me Mac."

"Mac."

"It's settled."

She stood up and the way that green dress hugged her like a bath of lime juice threw sky rockets against the top of my skull.

"Come out early in the morning," she said. "George is driving to New York and there won't be anybody around to bother us. We ought to get a lot done."

I wet my lips with my tongue. "Plenty," I decided.

After she was gone I sat down on the davenport and I started to sweat. I was a fool to go out there, to have anything to do with her. That girl meant trouble, big trouble. I could feel it. But I couldn't help myself. I'd go there for money or I'd go there for nothing.

I had to have her.

5

It rained the next day and George postponed his New York trip. By noon I began to wish that he'd either gone to New York or that he'd jump into a boat and drift down French Creek out of sight.

There wasn't anything really wrong about George, not the way he treated me or anything like that. But the way he fussed around, going from one thing to another, gave me a great big pain in a sensitive spot that made me want to holler at him.

I'm not the world's best painter, and I'm not the worst, either. We used to have a lot of painting to do around the farm, from fences to silos, and anything my father touched always looked like it had been put on with a broom. I'd done most of the painting around the place and even as a kid I'd been pretty good at it. Consequently, I didn't go for it much when George told me to dip the brush just so, clean it off on the edge of the can—don't let it drip on the outside, Mac—and hold the brush as though I were eating potatoes with a fork. When you're painting, especially chairs, it's better to hold the brush real strong so you can hug the paint in around the rungs and cracks.

"What the hell," I said finally, "you want to do this, maybe?"

He said no, he didn't want to do it, that he hated to paint worse than he hated the rain, so he went over and sat down in one of the chairs that had dried, and watched me.

In between brush strokes I watched George and George watched me. When I looked at George, I could look past him and see his wife. I'll tell you the truth: I wasn't looking at George very much.

This wife of his, this Diana Shipton, was built along the lines of the car of tomorrow—smooth, rounded surfaces with little flat places in between. While I painted, glancing at her every chance I got, I tried to remember where I'd ever seen anybody before who looked like her. I was about ready to give it up and settle for what was in the room with me when I remembered. Abbe Lane. She looked like Abbe Lane, although she didn't have Abbe Lane's face. Rita Hayworth's face and Abbe Lane's body. That was it or, anyway, it's close enough to describe how she hit me. She hit me hard.

And I stayed hit.

We worked most of the morning on the chairs, with George watching me silently, but just before lunch he had me all over the lot like a cow being chased by a pack of dogs.

Get a hammer, he said, and nail down the floor board. It took five minutes to find the hammer and the nails and about two seconds to fix a warped board that wouldn't stay in place even if you glued it down.

"Now get a screwdriver," he said, almost before I had finished with the board. "There's something wrong with that light over in the corner."

That was a short job; the thing was busted, the chain snapped off inside, and he'd have to get a new one when he went to town.

"We need some wood for the fire," he said as I got off the step ladder. "It's in a shed, around to the right of the building. You'd better take my raincoat."

All this time I'd kept my eyes on the girl, as much as the law allows when you're measuring up a guy's wife while he's around. She kept on with her painting but I knew she was listening to everything her husband said. A little smile tugged at her lips and once or twice it nearly matched the warmth of the flames in the fireplace. I got the impression that she was amused at me being booted around this way and that she was wondering, secretly, just how much of it I was going to take and what I was going to do about it when I'd had enough.

I put on George's raincoat and brought in the wood, lugging it in on my shoulders and smelling the stink of the wet bark.

"Throw some on the fire," he said.

I threw some on the fire. One of the sticks was an old piece of chestnut and it started to pop and snap like fireworks at a Mount Carmel celebration. Back on the farm we'd never used any chestnut because of the shooting sparks, but around Duncan I guess they did things differently. You could set fire to a place, using the chestnut sparks to start it, and not even annoy the ulcer in an insurance investigator's belly. But I didn't think this of either George or the girl. They were making money at Parsons Ranch, and anyway, you don't burn a joint down in the spring. You burn her up in the fall, giving you enough time to collect the insurance money and stick up another building for the next season. "What do you think of painting this floor in here?" George asked me.

I took off his raincoat and hung it over the back of a chair. The water ran down from it and a half circle of wet began to spot the bare boards.

"Look," I said to George, "you want me to paint chairs, paint floors, drive nails, rewire the building. Just what the hell do you want me to do?"

I was speaking to George but I was staring at the girl. Her eyes, as they met mine, registered approval. "Well," George said, "I didn't mean no harm, Mac."

"No. I'm just asking you, that's all."

"The floor needs to be done," he insisted. "We've never painted it and with no cellar under the building you've got the dampness to think about."

"Sure. Paint the floor. Do a good job on it, make it nice and then we can do the rest of the chairs and we spot it all up. It's none of my business, but why don't we do first things first?"

He backed away from me again, the way he had before, and sat down. He didn't say anything when I picked up the brush and started on the chairs. In fact, he didn't say anything until it was time to knock off for lunch.

"What about pancakes?" he wanted to know. "All right with you people."

I said they were fine with me and his wife nodded, though I had the feeling that she wasn't thinking of food at the moment.

They lived in what they called the "main house," but it wasn't a main house at all. It was just a cottage at one end of the horseshoe circle of buildings, with a kitchen, living room and, obviously, a bedroom. It was neat, modern enough, and it would have been red meat for any newly married couple. But it wasn't that you expected a resort owner to live in.

"We go to New York or Florida during the winter," Diana said, answering a question I hadn't asked.

"Oh."

I washed up in the bathroom, which was off the kitchen, and then sat at the table, waiting. George fixed the pancakes and his wife set the table while he was mussing around with the pots.

I learned, in those few minutes, a hell of a lot about both of them. First, George didn't use ready-mixed pancake stuff but he made up his own. He used sour milk, eggs, flour and some vanilla. I knew right away that he had once been a cook. And Diana, when she set the table, came in behind me from the left, putting the fork and spoon and knife down just right. She had been a waitress and not long enough ago to get out of the habit.

"Stopped raining," George said, looking outside.

It hadn't, not entirely, but if he thought it had and it would chase him off someplace else, it was all right with me.

The pancakes were only fair and I made up my mind that George hadn't been a very good cook. His wife was more professional. She waited on me like I was a duke who had just been elevated to crown prince.

She sat across from me while we ate and now I didn't have to sneak my looks. She wore the green outfit she'd been wearing the first day I'd come out to the ranch and I decided that she must love green. Even the walls of the kitchen were green. And the china was green. Christ, I hadn't seen so much green since my second year in college, when I'd worked extra in the bank and they'd stuck me on a dollar bill project that had lasted for a week.

"I hope you don't think I'm a pain in the can," George said to me over our coffee. "But I get so I can't sit still and I got a bad habit of not letting other people do it, either."

"That's okay." It wasn't okay but just then I was looking at his wife and that was plenty all right. "We all get jazzed up once in a while."

"It really isn't me," George said. "I'm sick."

"You don't look sick." He didn't. He was fat, his face was red and he looked as healthy as a young calf ready for market "You don't look sick at all."

"Well, he is," his wife said. "He takes insulin."

"What's that?"

"For sugar," George said. "I got a dose of sugar."

I'd heard of guys getting a dose of a lot of other things but this sugar angle was a new one on me. I guess I should have known about it but I'd never been sick, not sick enough to have a doctor, and I'd never read any medical books. My mother, now that's another story. She gets a new medical book every year and when she has a pain she sits down and reads the book until the pain either goes away or gets worse. If the pain gets worse she tells my father that she's dying of some horrible disease and the old man sends for the doctor. Then the doctor tells my mother to take a little baking soda, with plenty of water. The soda and the water make her belch and after a while she feels better. After that she's okay, puts the book away and says you can't believe a damn thing you read any more.

"I think I'll run into Midville," George said, rising. "I ought to pick up a new needle and some more insulin. That old needle of mine's getting pretty dull."

"If you'd do it in the light," his wife said, "you wouldn't have so much trouble. You ought to be used to sticking yourself by this time."

He sounded angry. "But I can't do it in the light!" I didn't know what they were talking about.

We did the dishes and George said he was going into the bedroom to get ready. His wife and I, using the big black umbrella from the porch, returned to the cabin where we'd been painting.

"Don't let my husband upset you," she said.

"I won't."

"He goes from one thing to the other."

"You can say that again."

"But he doesn't mean any harm by it. It's his sickness."

"Is it serious?"

"Not if he takes care of himself."

"But he has to keep taking that stuff?"

"Yes. All the time. I guess he'd die if he didn't."

I stirred up the fire, threw on a couple of logs, and we went back to work. I was at one end of a long table and she was at the other end. I kept turning the chair around while painting it so that I didn't miss anything she did. When she stood up straight it was like watching some show girl in a classy floor show and when she bent over, her blouse dipping open, it was better than burlesque.

"How many chairs have we got?" I wanted to know.

"All those along the wall. I don't know how many. Why don't you count them?"

I did. There were eighty-five. I told her.

"There's another hundred or so in another building," she said. "When we finish these we'll have to move them down here."

"You got a truck?"

"No. You'll have to carry them."

There was one thing about it: they were going to get their money's worth from me, even if they had to drain some of my blood to do it.

About two we stopped for a short break and smoked. She told me then all we had to do. The walls and the floor in this building had to be painted and there were three other buildings, one smaller, that needed the same thing. By the time we got done with this the weather would be good and we'd have to get outside. The tennis courts needed doing over, the lawns had to be raked and rolled, and following this, there was more painting.

"You need a handyman," I told her. "Or a guy who's grown four arms."

She laughed. "You getting discouraged, Mac?"

If I was, just looking at her and the flare of her hips cured me.

"No," I said.

"We do need a handyman, though. But George doesn't want to spend the money."

"He ought to do some of the work himself, then."

She demurred about that. "I don't know," she said. "I guess he doesn't feel so hot most of the time. He tries a little, now and then, but it gets him down."

"He doesn't mind how hard you work."

"No. That's one thing about George. No matter how hard anybody else works it doesn't make him sick at all." My brain had been unconsciously considering a conclusion for some while now and, without forcing the issue, I suddenly knew what it was: I didn't like George Shipton worth a good damn.

"Well," I told her, "if we've got to do so much work, why not do it the easy way? Why strain ourselves when we don't have to?"

"What do you mean?"

"You got a flit gun?"

"A flit gun?"

"Yeah. You spray for bugs with it in the summer. And flies. It's got a tank on the bottom, up front, and the handle goes in and out. You know what I mean?"

She tossed her hair. "Yes, I know what you mean."

There wasn't any flit gun around where we were working so we had to go over to the storeroom in back of the dining room to look for one. At this time of the year the storeroom was so empty, a mouse couldn't have survived unless he'd brought his own lunch. The wide, wooden shelves were bare and so was the floor, except for the racks where they piled potato sacks. There was a thick, musty smell. We looked around, pawing through some boxes of junk, and once our hands touched. Another time, when I jumped up in the air to look at a top shelf, I bumped one of those soft hips when I came down. She didn't say anything about it and she wasn't mad.

"Maybe there's one in the kitchen," she said. "I know I saw some around here last year."

The kitchen wasn't good and it wasn't bad. The stoves were jammed up into one end and I noticed that a couple of the lids were warped. It had been swept out the fall before, but not scrubbed, and the floor and the metal canopy over the stoves needed a hell of a lot of cleaning work.

I found a flit gun lying in back of one of the stoves. "I knew I'd seen one," she said again.

We returned to the paint shop and I cleaned the gun with kerosene. After I'd wiped it out with a rag and tested it, I thinned some of the paint down with turpentine and gave it a whirl. The paint came out in a fine, even spray and it only took me a couple of minutes to do one of the chairs.

"You're quite clever, Mac," she said to me. "I'd never have thought of that."

The way she stood, off to one side and leaning forward, there were a lot of things I could have thought of that she never would.

Getting her started with the gun wasn't the easiest thing in the world. I had to show her half a dozen times how to use it and in the end I had to get behind her, circling her with my arms, to get her to hold it just right.

"You don't have to squeeze me, Mac."

"Well, I do if I'm going to show you how to use the thing."

She smelled good, nice and clean, and her hair was soft under my chin. I tried not to do it but I couldn't help myself. My lips brushed the back of her neck, lingering there for a second. She sort of let out her breath and stood just a little straighter.

"You shouldn't have done that," she said.

"I know."

"George would be pretty angry if he knew."

"But George doesn't know. And he won't know, unless you tell him."

"I won't tell him."

I did the same thing again, longer this time.

"What about now?" I demanded.

She squealed and slid down and out from under my arms.

"I will if you're not a good boy, Mac."

She didn't know how good I could be when I threw myself into it.

I walked back to the kitchen, found another gun for myself and fixed that up.

"You're quite an inventor," she said.

"Yeah."

We went through a mess of those chairs like Grant took Richmond—or was it Crosby? Three or four times I had to stop and fix paint for her but other than that there weren't any interruptions.

"I like working with you," she said at quitting time. "You get things done."

We cleaned up with the turpentine, standing quite close together. I tried to tell myself that I shouldn't keep looking at her so much but it didn't do any good. Hell, there was something I could do a lot better and a lot quicker than painting one of those broken down chairs.

"You don't waste any time yourself," I said.

She surveyed the results of our efforts. "George will be pleased," she said.

George. I had almost forgotten about him. "Yeah."

She had a long fine neck and her skin was sea shell-pink and soft. I could still taste it on my lips. I wondered what she'd do if I tried the same thing again. I decided that my luck had been fairly good for the first day and that I'd better not press it.

"You can stay for supper if you want," she said.

The deal was that I'd live at the ranch, as soon as they got the help's quarters opened up, but that I'd keep my room in town until then.

"I'll take a rain check on it," I said.

Actually, I would have liked to stay, if she'd been going to be alone, but I'd had just about enough of her husband for one eight-hour period.

"Of course," she agreed. "Anytime." Then, "You should be able to move out here the first of next week. There's no heat in the cabin but we've got an electric heater you can use."

"Fine." I knew of something else that I could use better. "When do you bring in the rest of the help?"

"In three or four weeks. The cooks first, of course, and then the waitresses and the other girls. The cooks stay next to the kitchen, in three rooms, but the girls are in the building with you."

"With me?"

Her smiled mocked me. "Do you object?"

"How do I know?" I asked her. "I haven't seen any of them yet."

She got a kick out of that and we both laughed. I remembered what the taxi driver had told me about some guy who'd come out so skinny the summer before that you could see through him. I wondered if he'd had my room. That made me laugh some more. There wasn't a dame made—well, only one—who had a chance of making me lose a pound and she wasn't giving me the chance to prove it. Not yet. But she would. Even if I had to fight every itchy male in Sullivan County for the opportunity. And that's saying a lot. You never saw so many itchy people in all your life. You don't think so and you just take a look at the size of some of the families in those Sullivan County hills. They don't count the kids singly or in pairs. They start out with a half a dozen and go on up. A guy with less than half a dozen is considered sterile.

"We're having steak," she said. "I wish you'd stay."

"Some other time."

She laughed again. "Rain check?"

"Rain check."

It had stopped raining and she walked with me to the car. French Creek was high, its red waters swollen, and I could hear it tumbling and roaring as it cut its way down through the valley. The sun had come out, crawling in between the new leaves on the trees, and this splashed across the creek, turning the water to the color of blood.

"I'll be out in the morning," I said.

She nodded. "Eight-thirty is okay."

"Fine."

"We'll get a lot of the chairs done. Now that it's cleared up, I think George will go into the city tomorrow."

"Hiring help?"

"No. On some other business. The hiring is always left up to me."

"I see."

"Next week I thought you could run down to the city with me and we could look for a cook. I think you've had more experience at that sort of thing than I have."

"Anything you say, Mrs. Shipton."

"I wish you'd call me Diana."

"Okay." I got in the car and slammed the door shut. "First names are always easier."

"We'd have to stay overnight."

Together, I wondered, or in separate rooms?

"You pay my expenses," I said, making it sound business like.

"Why, of course."

I started the car and she waved at me as I started down the lane. I waved back and then damned near fell out of the car as I slammed into a chug hole.

On the way to town I kept thinking about her. And I kept thinking about something else, something that hadn't been there before. Something which, no matter how you looked at it, I had no business thinking.

How long could that husband of hers live without his insulin?

6

The weather cleared, getting warm, almost hot, and we buckled down to some real work. It required only two days to knock off the pile of chairs with the flit gun, including those from the other buildings, and then we went outside to fix the lawn and then the tennis court.

"You ought to do the floor in there," George told me. "And the walls. Why don't you stick to one thing and clean up each job as you go along?"

No matter what he said, or how he said it, it always burned me up.

"We can paint when it rains," I pointed out, shortly. "The thing to do is work outside when it's clear and inside when there's a storm. That way, as my old man says, there's no lost motion."

"Mac's right," Diana informed her husband. "That's the way we should do it."

So we got out the rakes and the water roller, and we started to work. Even George picked up a rake, but he just looked at it and threw the thing down again. Maybe he was so sick he couldn't do anything and maybe he wasn't, but there was one thing wrong with him that no medicine could touch—he was so damned lazy he wouldn't have bothered breathing if it hadn't been a habit he couldn't break.

But the girl was a worker. She could do more in five minutes than George could think about doing in an hour. He was as much help as a busted back, if you know what I mean. He stood around, smoking a cigar, and telling you how to hold the rake, and not to dig up the ground, and push the leaves all the way into the water when you take them down to the creek. I got sick of it. I got so sick of his mouth that I couldn't even look at him.

But I didn't say anything, or hardly anything. Because of the girl.

She was five percent girl and ninety-five percent woman.

She'd dress in shorts and halter when we were outside and it's a wonder I got any work done at all.

Those long white legs of hers flashed in the sun and when she bent down, picking up a stone, the shorts got tight across her backside and that halter sort of loosened up, letting her spill down and almost over the top.

"You just dug up a piece of sod," she told me more than once.

You can't use an iron-toothed rake and watch a dame, without raising hell with a lawn.

The third day she caught me staring at her, the hunger there in my eyes, and she knew what I wanted.

For a second I thought she was going to be mad, or club me with the rake, but all she did was smile. Well, not just smiled. Her lips, which were as red as her hair, parted and she gave me the best look I ever had of a set of white, straight teeth.

"Uh-uh," she said, glancing around to make sure that George was too far away to hear. "Mustn't touch." My temperature shot up five degrees.

But that's all that happened. Nothing else. George was around all the time and even if he hadn't been I guess I'd have been careful. I didn't know how to figure this girl. Out there in the yard she was alive, like a little fire that smoked but that you couldn't get to burn, but inside, when we were having lunch, she was so formal that I felt as though I was some dirt she wanted to sweep up off the floor.

I'd get to thinking about this, how she was, and some nights I'd stop at the Crystal Bar and take on a few. One night I drove out along Route 29, not stopping at the diner, but the office in the gasoline station was dark and I continued on as far as Wheaton. There was a little bar in Wheaton, in a big, tumbled down building they called a hotel, and I had some drinks in there. The bartender, a one-eyed character with a limp, asked me if I might be interested in something he had upstairs and after I saw what he had I was interested. She had brown hair but in the half light of the bedroom I could make believe it was red, like the girl at the ranch, and I gave her hell, the way I would have given that redhead hell. Business was bad at this time of the year, and she told me I could stay all night for twenty bucks. In the morning, when I left, I gave her an extra ten. She was worth it. It had been a long winter for her, too, and she knew that the nights were made for something besides sleep.

That morning, about ten, I got into my first real hassle with George Shipton.

If you know anything about fixing a lawn you know that the time to roll it is just after the ground has been raked. The soil is broken up then, soft, and the roller bites down and hard. You can flatten out most of the mole holes and the skunk diggings and if you've got plenty of weight, which we had, you can work the surface as flat as a table top.

"Better start on the tennis courts," George said.

That's the way he was, going from one thing to another, though he'd tell you, to your face, that you ought to stick to one job until it was finished.

I kept right on with the roller, just like I hadn't heard him at all.

There's something else, too. These clay tennis courts are great, real fast if they're put in proper shape, but you can spend a week on one and hardly see what you've done. You have to bust up the crust, pick out the stones, and rake the thing until you're so sick of it that you don't know what to do. Then you should get some fresh clay, mix it with flat sand, and work this in over the top. To anybody else, to somebody who had some sense, a project like that would have been big stuff. But to George who stood around all the time, picking his nose when nobody was looking, it was just another way of wasting money and time.

"You hear me, Mac?"

"I heard you."

"Well, put that roller away. And bring your rake. You can start on the creek side of the first court."

I put the roller away. I was working on the downgrade, towards the woods, and I gave the roller such a hard shove that it nearly ran over him as it went clattering across the uneven ground and into the brush.

"You trying to make life miserable for me?" I demanded.

"Now, Mac."

"Are you?" I guess I was shouting. "First you've got fifty different ideas about the painting and now you've got a hundred about this work outside. Can't you get off my back?"

"I only thought—"

"You thought! Now, tell you what I think. I think you're a big, fat, lazy slob, that's what I think. Why, hell, your wife does more work in five minutes than you do in all day. All you do is stand around and look like somebody is getting ready to steal the shoes off your feet. What's the matter with you, anyway? Don't you know when somebody is trying to help you?"

We got into it good and hot after that. He called me a no-good bastard and I came right back and said he was big enough for two of them. All the while this was going on the girl said nothing. She just stood perfectly still, leaning on her rake handle, watching us.

"Get yourself another boy," I told him.

"Now, Mac."

"I said, get yourself another boy. Somebody who doesn't think for himself."

He backed away from me. "It was just an idea, Mac. You don't have to blow up."

"You get too many ideas. A million of them."

But the steam had, for some reason, gone out of both of us. The argument which, a few minutes before, had seemed so important was now as foolish as two kids fighting over a girl with two heads. George said he was sorry, that he guessed he wasn't feeling so well, and after a while he got me to feeling sorry, too. But I was looking at the girl when I felt sorry. I was looking at her red shorts and yellow halter and her long legs that were slowly getting tanned from the sun. And her slightly amused smile. You couldn't look at her when she was like that and not feel sorry about some other things. "There must be something that I can do," George said, putting on the big brother act.

I told him there was.

"What?"

"Well, we'll finish up the lawn sometime tomorrow and then we can start in on the tennis courts. We'll need some clay and flat sand. The sand you can get in town but you'll have to hunt around for some clay. I don't think you've got any here."

"No, I don't think so."

"You could hop in the car and drive around and ask some people."

He seemed glad of the prospects of getting away from the ranch.

"I could do that," he agreed.

"Don't get the yellow. Get the red. The yellow is too slippery when it's wet and after it dries out it'll crack all to hell."

"Somebody ought to be able to tell me."

"Sure. Just ask around. And when you find out where it is I'll see a guy in town about renting his truck. It would be cheaper than getting a trucker to haul it for you."

George nodded. "Every dollar saved is that much gravy," he said.

After he had driven off in the station wagon I got the roller from the bushes and resumed my work on the lawn. I finished rolling it just before twelve.

George didn't return for lunch and while we were eating—canned soup, bread and coffee—Diana mentioned the disagreement.

"My husband can be impossible at times," she said.

"Not impossible. Miserable."

"I'm glad you didn't quit."

"Are you?"

She looked awfully pretty across the table from me. It was a toss-up as to whether I should look at her face or her knockers. I looked at both.

"Yes. I think you're good for us, Mac. I think you're the kind of a man we need around here. You seem to know what you're doing and how to get things done."

There was one thing I didn't know how to do.

"You just keep plugging," I said. "That's all."

From where I sat at the kitchen table I could look through into the living room and see the door that led into the bedroom. Just the thought of what it would be like to go in there with her made me sweat. And then I thought of her husband and what they probably did when the lights were out. The sweat turned cold.

We spent the afternoon working on the edges of the lawn, places we hadn't touched before, and by three we were done with that.

"God," Diana said, "but I'm tired."

You couldn't tell by looking at her that she was tired. Her eyes were bright blue, her skin smooth and she was something you wanted to hold in your arms. We were on the bank, near the creek, and she relaxed and smiled. I'd seen her smile before, lots of times, but this smile she gave me was the difference between New York and Miami in the winter. It was all warmth and filled with some secret meaning.

I thought about asking her to go for a swim—the creek was lower now and running clear—but he came in, driving the station wagon, and I had to forget about the idea. That was the worst part of being around here—I'd get to thinking, trying to plan something, and then he'd show up, or say something, and I'd have to put it off. But one thing I did know: one of these days, right or wrong or whether she said no or yes, I was going to find out if she was just half as good as she looked.

"You can make arrangements for the truck," he said, coming toward us. "I found some clay. Nice stuff and easy to get at."

"Where?"

"At the Hotel Gordon. They've got a big field down in back and they sell it. Two-fifty a load. I paid for five loads."

"That ought to be enough."

"You just check in at the office every time you go there. That's all. And they've got a kid over there, hanging around with nothing to do. He said for fifty cents he'd give you a hand at loading."

"Not bad."

"That's what I thought, Mac."

He seemed pleased that he had accomplished something but I could have strangled him right there for having gone to the Hotel Gordon. When I went for the clay I'd have to check in with Sid and I'd look like some laborer hanging around for favors. And then there was Miriam. She'd be there, too, and she'd see me working this way. Don't ask me why it was important, but it was, I didn't want to have anything to do with either one of them again.

There was still some time left so Diana and I carried some of the chairs out of the paint shop and put them in a couple of the buildings.

"You oughtn't to figure on working on the tennis courts," I told her. "That's too hard a job for a girl."

"I won't mind," she said. "I want to get out into the sun."

I let it go at that. I wouldn't mind, either.

At five George came around and he had five tens in his hand. He gave them to me.

"Your week's up," he said.

I gave him credit for one thing: he could keep track of time better than I could. I hadn't realized that I'd put in a full week already.

And, then, we got into it again. All of us.

"You ought to be working for forty," he said. "Until the start of the season. Once we get some guests, money coming in, fifty is okay but it ought to be less until then, Mac. I could get a guy out from town for thirty-five or forty. I know I could. I had one last year, fellow from one of the farms who got held up on his plowing."

I was so mad at the crazy fool I couldn't say a word. I looked around for the girl, but she wasn't anywhere in sight.

"Your wife told me fifty," I said, after a while. "And fifty it is. Besides, I've earned it. Every dime. Sure, you can get a guy for forty but you'll get forty bucks worth of work. It's like buying meat—you pay for a pound and you get a pound. Why else would a guy work?"

"Now, Mac—"

"Oh, go to hell!" I shouted at him.

Suddenly I was sick of the whole thing; sick of being a jerk over a woman who didn't know I existed and sick of working for peanuts. As a manager I was worth a hundred or a hundred and fifty of anybody's money, but as a ground digging merchant I wasn't worth fifty a week.

I left him there, with his mouth hanging open, and walked down to the cottage where they stayed. Diana was in the kitchen, drinking coffee.

"Your husband thinks I'm only worth forty a week," I said.

She smiled. "He's a cheapskate. That's another nice thing about him."

There was something about this dame; when I was near her I melted inside like butter under a hot sun. But I was determined not to let it happen this time. This time I was talking about money.

"Our agreement was seventy-five," I reminded her. "Seventy-five before the season and a hundred after that."

"You didn't tell him?"

"No."

"That's good." She drank her coffee slowly, watching me over the rim of the cup. "He'd have a fit if you had."

"I think he must have had one already."

"Oh, it isn't that bad, Mac."

"It isn't? What about my other twenty-five?"

"That comes out of petty cash."

"Well, where's the petty cash?"

"There isn't any, not right now. And there won't be until we open up. He'll put five hundred in it to start it off."

"So what happens to my seventy-five a week between now and then?"

"Well, you'll have to wait."

She offered me a cup of coffee but I didn't take it. I felt as though she had been using me but I couldn't tell her that, because I didn't know the right words to use. After all, she hadn't done anything, not directly. She was pretty, yes, but that didn't have anything to do with it. I'd kissed her on the neck, yes, but she hadn't asked me to and there hadn't been anything else since. Anything beyond that had only been in my mind. She'd given me no reason to believe that she could be had, or that she wanted me to have her. It had all been in my mind so far, and that was all.

"To hell with it," I said.

She'd been using me, the dirty slut, the same way her husband had been using me. They had no more intention of paying top dollar for good work than they had of drowning themselves in French Creek. I'd thought the job worth at least sixty but now they were getting it for less.

"To hell with it," I said again.

"Mac! Where are you going?"

"I'm getting out of here," I said, jerking the door open. "Fast."

"Mac!"

I kept right on going, not just because of the money but because of something else. I had felt it before, the same as I felt it then, and I still didn't know what it was. It was like knowing a thunder shower was coming up even though the sky was a rich blue. Like throwing the dice and knowing you're going to crap out.

I looked back and she was standing in the doorway, staring after me. She wasn't smiling and her face had a dead gray expression on it.

"Now, Mac—"

"Go to hell," I told George, walking past him. "Get yourself another idiot."

Neither one of them waved as I drove away. And neither did I.

They could drop dead in the same grave and I wouldn't shovel dirt on them.

I drove toward town, thinking about it and not thinking about it. It was like a bad dream, something that hadn't happened. Fifty a week. Who did they think they were kidding?

I lit a cigarette and my hand shook. And who did I think I was kidding?

I wasn't running from fifty bucks a week and I wasn't running from George Shipton. I was running from his wife. As far and as fast as I could.

7

They carried Sandy Herbert off to the hospital in the middle of the night. She'd been having pains all evening, hollering and yelling with them, and when her old lady finally got the doctor the doctor said she was losing the kid.

"Thank the Lord," Mrs. Herbert said.

"But I don't want to lose the baby!" Sandy wailed. "I want my baby!"

Her mother showed about as much sympathy as a funeral director sending a bill to an enemy.

"You wanted to find the father, too," Mrs. Herbert said. "But before you could finish counting how many prospects there were you ran out of fingers."

"Oh, Ma!"

"The kid will be better off dead. And so will you."

"I wouldn't say that," the doctor started. "A thing like this can be a great shock to such a young girl."

"Don't worry about her," Mrs. Herbert said. "She's had plenty of shocks."

The next morning at breakfast Mrs. Herbert told me Sandy's baby had been born dead, at about five o'clock.

"Good thing she's got Blue Cross," she said. "Do you suppose they'll pay for it?"

"I don't know."

"Maybe they don't pay for single girls who get pregnant."

"Maybe not."

"Well, they'd better. I've got no money to throw away."

Usually I had two cups of coffee but this morning I had three.

"You going to work this morning, Mr. Osmund?"

"No."

"Laid off?"

"Quit."

Her thin lips narrowed. "I don't know what's the matter with you men. You get a good job and you don't take care of it."

"Sure. That's right."

"Don't think you can lay around here and not pay your board and room."

To shut her up I got out my wallet and paid her for the week. She stuffed the money down inside her dress, putting the bills in a spot where no man's hands had been for a number of years.

"Mr. Fishers wants somebody down at the hardware store," she told me. "Don't pay big money, thirty-five a week, but it's steady."

I knew Fishers. It would be steady all right. It would be steady six days a week, nine hours a day.

I walked down to the corner, got a paper, and came back to the room to read the classifieds. There were lots of jobs, but that mess the summer before had queered me for most of them.

I threw the paper aside, closed my eyes and smoked. The more I thought about it the more I hated Sid and that witch Miriam. They had fixed me good. I had about as much get up and go to me as a car with both hind wheels jacked up off the ground.

When I finished the cigarette I tried to forget about everything and went to sleep. I awoke to find Mrs. Herbert standing over me.

"You sure you didn't know Sandy last summer, Mr. Osmund?"

That was a hell of a question to wake up to.

"No. I didn't know her. Why?"

"I thought maybe you did and that maybe you was the guy."

That made me sit up. "Say," I wanted to know, "what right have you got to come busting in here like this?"

"You didn't answer me when I knocked."

"Even so." I found a cigarette and lit it. "The money I give you counterfeit or something?"

"You're very funny, Mr. Osmund. You get them off with a straight face just like Bob Hope."

"Or Jack Benny?"

"I don't watch Jack Benny. Him and his violin, he makes me nervous."

"Me too."

"The hospital called, Mr. Osmund. My daughter wants to see you."

"Me?"

"That's what they said."

I tried to figure that and couldn't. I hardly knew the girl. But I didn't have anything to do that afternoon and if she wanted to see me I guessed it was all right.

"What hospital is she in?"

They'd taken her in to Monticello.

"She's on the third floor."

"Okay," I said.

I had lunch in a restaurant in Duncan and then drove on over to Monticello. I got there about two, just as visiting hours were starting.

She looked awfully small and weak in the big hospital bed but when she saw me her face brightened and her eyes took on a shine.

"It was nice of you to come," she said.

I pulled up a chair and sat down.

"Your mother said you wanted to see me."

"It seems silly, now that you're here."

"Why?"

"I don't know. It just does. I was lying here, trying to think of somebody who could help me with something and I thought of you. But you're almost a stranger. I shouldn't ask you for anything."

"What difference does that make?"

"A lot."

I thought she was going to talk about the kid, or start crying, but she didn't. I made up my mind that she had more guts than her old lady would ever have. "What's the trouble?" I asked her.

It was a short and bitter story. She hadn't been working all fall or winter and she hadn't had the money to keep up her hospitalization insurance.

"They wouldn't pay for this, anyway," she said. "The doctor told me they wouldn't."

You couldn't blame them for that. A single girl gets herself knocked up and she's on her own, from scratch to finish.

"Go on."

"I'll owe the doctor some money and the hospital about two hundred dollars. They've been around already asking me about it. Not the doctor. The hospital. They say I have to pay before I can get out."

That was no problem. "They can't keep you here forever," I said.

"No. But they can go to my mother and that would make it worse. I don't know if she's got that much money or not but even if she had it she wouldn't give it to me for this."

"I see."

"There's nobody I can turn to, nobody at all." She turned her head away and this time she was ready to burst out into tears. "I thought of you and—well, it's silly. You wouldn't help me."

Nothing has ever come easy for me and I'm not generally a soft touch. But I felt sorry for this girl. She was all by herself and, as she said, she had nobody. Her mother was less than nobody. She was somebody who should have cared and who didn't.

"What makes you say that?"

"I don't know. It's just—oh, would you?" Her face was lifted to me, filled with hope. "Would you?"

"Two hundred bucks. For the hospital."

"And the doctor."

"The doctor can wait. Doctors don't mind waiting; they're used to it. But a hospital can be rugged."

I tried to remember just how much I had in my bank account and couldn't. My little budget had gone down the drain, what with drinking and chasing a little female flesh here and there. And the fifty bucks, instead of seventy-five, didn't help. It didn't help a bit.

"I'll do what I can," I promised her. "When are you getting out?"

"Day after tomorrow."

"Don't worry. I'll square it with them by then."

"Oh, thank you!"

We talked some more and I guess she told me more about herself than she'd ever told her mother. There hadn't been a lot of guys the summer before, just one. He'd been a college student, playing in an orchestra out where she worked, and she'd fallen in love with him.

"I did wrong," she admitted. "But I'd do the same thing over again. I'm not sorry."

She'd told him about her condition and he'd wanted to marry her but that had meant leaving college and giving up everything he'd worked for. She'd thought too much of him for that.

"I told him I didn't love him," she said, "and I chased him away. I thought I could go through this all by myself. But that was wrong. A girl just can't, not when she's got nothing and nobody."

"I said I'd help you."

She grabbed up one of my hands and pressed it to her lips. The way I had made her feel good was worth two hundred dollars any day.

"I know you did, Mac. You're wonderful. And I'll pay you back. I really will."

"Let's not talk about that now."

"But I will. This summer I'll get a job and I'll work hard. You won't be sorry."

"I'm sure I won't."

She clung to my hand. "You'll never be sorry," she repeated. "I'll do anything I can to make it up to you."

I left the hospital and drove back to Duncan. The bank was closed. When I phoned them some guy said, sure, he'd check my account for me. I felt like ripping the phone out and hitting myself over the head with it when he told me how much there was left. One hundred and six dollars.

"Thanks," I told him. "For nothing."

In the summer you can send a carrier pigeon out of Sullivan County faster than you can make a long distance phone call, but during the off season you don't have any trouble at all. Less than five minutes later I was talking to the old man up in Delaware County.

"I'm glad you called," he said. "Your mother is poorly again."

"What is it this time?"

"Same thing. A bellyache and that book she's always reading."

"You ought to take it away from her."

"I did once. But she sent away for another one."

We talked some more, about the weather and things like that, and then I told him I was driving up for overnight. It had been several months since I'd been home and he said he was glad I was breaking down at last. Of course, he didn't know I was going to ask him for another touch. But that would come later.

I didn't get up to the farm until around eight that night. My father, smelling of pipe tobacco, came out to meet me and my mother stood on the porch, waiting. I kissed both of them. In a way, it was good to be home.

They had held up on supper and we sat around eating fried chicken and talking. My father said I could do better on the farm than I could running a hotel. I told him I couldn't and we let it go at that. Both of them knew about my trouble the summer before but neither one of them mentioned it. I guess they were ashamed or they were trying to help me forget. I don't know.

My mother looked pretty good, older and grayer than when I had last seen her, but keeping her age fairly well. She ate heartily, as she always did following one of those gas attacks, and I wondered if she'd get through the night without having another one.

While we were doing the dishes I put the hammer on the old man for another five hundred. I don't think he exactly approved but he got his checkbook and came across with the dough right away.

"I was saving that for new siding on the house," he said.

I folded the check. "You'll have it back before the end of the summer. Every dime."

"You take your time about it," my mother said. "We don't need the siding until next year."

They were good, honest, hard-working people. At nine-thirty they went to bed.

By ten o'clock I was reading my mother's medical book.

It was crazy, I told myself. I didn't care anything about insulin, or sugar, or George Shipton. But I read it all, every bit of it. And I read more. I read about needles and their use. One paragraph I read four or five times. It gave me the creeps. The poor slob could kill himself and not even know it. Nobody else would know the reason, either.

I read the paragraph again. Then I put the book aside.

What business was it of mine?

8

On the way back to Duncan the next morning I drove around by Monticello and paid Sandy's hospital bill. It was a hundred eighty-seven dollars and fifty cents. The woman at the desk gave me a receipt and coughed once or twice.

"Would you like to see Miss Duncan?"

She made sure to put a lot of emphasis on the Miss. The girl was single, she'd gotten herself into a jam and the old hag was having a ball of it.

"That's one thing you'll never have to worry about," I told her, getting sore. "Nobody in his right mind is ever going to waste his strength to get you that way."

"Young man," she said, sternly, "if you think for one minute you can talk to me like that, why—"

"I'll talk to you any way I want," I said, leaning over the counter. "Who the hell are you, a saint or something to throw a slur at a nice kid?"

"Nice kid! Indeed!"

"Button your mouth," I said, turning away.

After I left the desk and started up the stairs I regretted having squabbled with the woman. It was just one of those unimportant things you get involved in, because of somebody's stupidity, and it gets you all worked up. Hell, I told myself, what's this young chicken to you? And I answered it right away. Nothing. Not a thing. But that didn't mean I had to listen to somebody slam it into her when she wasn't around to defend herself.

I guess I've always been like that, getting all steamed up in a matter of seconds. Sometimes it concerns me and sometimes, like then, it doesn't. But that doesn't prevent me from getting mad. I hate people who've got so much of other people's business to take care of that they haven't got time for their own.

She was asleep, her soft brown hair lying deep and thick on the white pillow, and I didn't awaken her. I thought she had more color in her face, almost flushed. I hoped she didn't have a fever. All she had to do was get sick and conk off and I'd be out nearly two hundred bucks quicker than if I'd flushed it down a john.

Outside, I hung around Monticello for a while, visited the state employment agency, which knew nothing from nothing, and had a few beers in a couple of gin mills.

I drove along the road toward Duncan.

My biggest problem at the moment was getting a job. I couldn't hit the old man up for any more loot—a grand is plenty, even for a prosperous Delaware County farmer—and, besides, what I had already borrowed would be enough to pay back. If the girl got a break undoubtedly she would come through with her share but if she didn't, and she might not, I could kiss that loan goodbye. Or I could take it out in trade. But one way or another, she was good for it.

The road was fairly good, the Ford ran as well as could be expected, and I rolled right along. On both sides of the road spring had come to the woods. The leaves on the trees were all out, a couple of dogwood blossoms had made an early start and overhead the sky was like a blue bowl turned upside down over the world.

Yes, I had to get a job. There was no question about that.

There are a lot of things you can get to do in the mountains for the spring and summer. You can work for the county, pimp for a broad or, if you're really down on your luck, work in a place like Hughie Rowland's diner. I didn't want to go back to Hughie's, or any sixty buck a week job, but it didn't seem like I had much choice about it. There was no use fooling myself; I had to look at my situation logically. That farce at the Hotel Gordon had done me in as a hotel manager in the sticks. The association knew about it, the cops knew about it and, even worse, if I filed an application with anybody, I knew about it. It showed on my face, the way I talked, affecting my self-confidence, and when you're dealing with a resort owner you don't want to be hiding anything. The only person in this world smarter than a resort owner is a Philadelphia lawyer with a client who's got a minister for an alibi.

It was around five when I reached Mrs. Herbert's, parked the car, went into the house and started up the stairs. Two steps up and I stopped as though I'd been shot. Mrs. Herbert was screaming at me like a bear with its left hind foot caught in a trap.

"Damn you!" she screamed. "Damn you, Mr. Osmund, but you're the man!"

I didn't know what she was talking about. I wasn't her man and I never would be, not if I aged twenty years and she became ten years younger.

"You'll blow a blood vessel," I told her.

Mrs. Herbert's red face looked up at me from down below.

"Damn you," she said again, but with somewhat less hate. "I knew there was some reason you moved in on me. I knew there was some reason why you stayed here. Damn you, damn you, you're the man who went and done it."

"Did what?"

"Made Sandy pregnant."

"Oh, for Christ's sake!"

"Don't you lie to me, Mr. Osmund. You didn't pay no hospital bill for her out of the goodness of your heart. I know your kind. You wouldn't have paid it unless you had to."

She was smarter than I had thought. "How do you know I paid it?"

"I went over there, you damn fool. I was there just after you left and the woman at the desk told me that the bill had been paid. She described you perfectly and then she showed me the check. There it was, your name right on it."

See what I mean? You do one thing, for one particular reason, and some nosey bitch thinks it's because of something else. How do you win?

"I did it because I wanted to," I said.

"That's a likely story!" she sneered.

"Well, you can believe it or not," I said, starting up the stairs again. "But that's the way it is."

"Oh, it is, is it?"

"Yeah."

"Don't you give me that 'yeah' stuff," she hollered. "Don't you give me that. I don't like it. You hear that, Mr. Osmund? I don't like it!"

I stopped at the top of the stairs, turned and faced her. I wasn't shaking outside but I was shaking inside. Like I say, you do something one way, for one reason, and it comes out entirely different.

"Look," I argued, "I didn't have anything to do with your daughter. I never saw her until I came here. Believe me, that's the truth."

"Then why would she send for you when her own mother was here in the house?"

"I don't know."

"Because you were responsible, that's why!"

"No."

"You lie, Mr. Osmund. You lie. I say you lie!"

What was the use?

"Go ahead and say it if it makes you feel any better. It won't do you any good."

In disgust, I swung around and started for my room.

"You get out of here!" she shouted. "You get your things together and get out. I won't have the likes of you in my house, I won't. I've heard plenty of things about you, Mr. Osmund, I have. And now this. My God, how do you think I feel, my daughter lying there in the hospital and you here in this house, under my own roof, acting for all the world as though nothing had happened?"

I slammed the bedroom door and shut her off. I could still hear her making some noise down there but I couldn't tell what she was doing. I didn't want to hear. She was just as wrong as a drunken cop directing traffic on a one way street.

It didn't take me very long to pack and get out of there. She wasn't anywhere in sight when I carried my bags down and I didn't look for her. I just toted the stuff out to the car, threw the bags in back and drove out of there.

My hassle with her hadn't destroyed my appetite so I rode out Route 26 to Hughie's diner. Laura was working behind the counter and the place was empty.

"Hughie around?" I asked her.

She said no, Hughie hadn't been feeling well and that he'd gone home early. He wouldn't be back until morning.

"You want something?" she asked me.

I looked her over. She wasn't a shade near being like the redhead but then I didn't have a claim on the redhead and, as far as I knew, Laura was available. But I didn't know if I wanted anything that way or not.

"Couple of burgers," I said.

She fixed the burgers and leaned her elbows on the counter while I ate and drank coffee. The nylon uniform dipped down a little but I couldn't see anything. I felt more cheated than if I'd gone to a Marilyn Monroe movie and not seen her walk from the rear.

"Hughie told me to stay open until twelve and then close up," she said. "But how would he know if I closed before then? You think he would?"

It was an invitation. We could turn off the steam table, slam the door, jump in the car and ride up to the mountain road.

"He might," I said.

At first, I couldn't figure out just why I'd put her off. She had everything a guy could use or want and it was there for the taking. But I knew, without analyzing myself, what was wrong. Every time I looked at a dame I saw that redhead. She was burning inside me like a loaf of bread in an untended Dutch oven.

I threw a buck on the counter and walked to the door.

"You coming back at twelve, Mac?"

"Maybe."

She looked hurt. "I'll have to call a cab if you don't."

"Maybe," I said again.

I nosed the Ford toward town and spun her into high when I broke fifty. I gave the car hell going past the gas station but that didn't stop me from looking. The little goose neck lamp was turned on in the front office.

I grinned, and kept on going. Julia must have it bad for me the way I had it for the redhead. I supposed I was missing a good bet by not stopping. She could be hot when she was starved and I'd kept her on a hunger strike for more than a week. I grinned again. It was a safe guess that she had read those dirty books at least a dozen times and looked at all the dirty pictures she could get her hands on. I wondered, vaguely, what either did for her. Did they charge her batteries up or run them down?

I kept on driving.

Some night I'd go back there.

Some night when I was really hard up.

Back in town I thought of looking for a room but quickly gave up the idea. I could always get a room. The town's only hotel was open all night and I could check in any time I felt like it. What I needed was a drink. No, not one drink. A lot of them. Enough to make me forget, at least for a little while, the part of my own private world which had died.

I turned right and parked in front of the Crystal Bar. There were two guys sitting at the bar and talking about trout fishing. One said the state was stocking all the streams and the other said the state wasn't. It was a stupid conversation.

Trout fishing, of course, is big business in Sullivan County. It's spring business more than it is summer business but it's pretty big. In the spring you get a different type of vacationist slogging through the hills. They wear hip boots and crazy hats and they carry nets that make them look a little like butterfly chasers. They drink in the hotels and they get their butts wet in the streams and they buy all kinds of hand-tied flies that are guaranteed to excite any fish within fifty miles. The people who make the most dough out of this wild-eyed exodus from the city are the people who tie the flies, and every hick has a sure-fire fly, the best in the county. But the city sucker learns soon that the fish don't hear the publicity. Worms, of course, are the best bait but the sport frowns on worms and his friends frown on worms. He only uses a worm when nobody is looking. He makes a catch, sneaks the fish into his creel, and proudly announces to the world that he made the haul on a dipsy-doodle fly, his own secret weapon. The rush is on then for dipsy-doodles. Everybody buys one, nobody catches anything, and everybody goes back to the city sore as a boil.

That's trout fishing in Sullivan County.

And you can have it.

I moved down the bar, away from the two guys, and kept the bartender jumping around with a bottle of rye.

"You new around here?" he wanted to know.

"Born and raised in the county."

That's one thing you learn about Sullivan County: don't ever be an immigrant, be a native. If they know you're from Delaware County they treat you as though you were born in the dark ages, and if they know you're from Orange County, or any other place, they wet their sucker knives for you. No, in Sullivan County, be a native.

"You want another, mister?"

"Sure."

"It'd be cheaper for you to buy a bottle."

"I guess it would."

"And you're from around here?"

"Born and raised in the county."

"Have one on me."

See what I mean? You become a brother right away. Even bartenders open up their hearts.

I don't know how many I had but it must have been a lot. I was trying to think and not to think, and I was all mixed-up inside.

I arrived at one conclusion, though. Maybe my folks were right. Maybe I'd be better off if I went back to the farm. But I couldn't remember the cows without remembering that I didn't like them, and that ruined everything. No, I had to stick it out in this hotel business. It was my life. I got a kick out of seeing people come and go, listening to their problems—the cream turned, or the room was noisy, or a dame had lifted somebody's wallet—and helping them when I could. It was in my blood, like a disease—like sugar was in George Shipton's blood—and I couldn't drain it off just by feeling sorry for myself.

"Another, mister?"

"Another."

"Jesus, you've got a tank."

"I must have."

The fishermen were gone and it was quiet in the bar. On the way out they had left the door open and the spring night air crept inside. It felt good, with a hint of warmth, and it pushed the beer smell back into one dark corner.

I didn't hear her come in and I didn't see her. She was there beside me, on the stool, before I knew of it. "Hello, Mac," she said.

I glanced into the mirror first. All I could see was that red hair and a soft, smiling face. It was enough. The liquor turned over inside of my stomach and I began to sweat worse than a bull on his way to the herd.

"Hi," I said.

"I saw your car out front. I thought I'd find you in here."

"Oh?"

"I stopped by your place but the lady said you didn't live there anymore. She sounded upset."

"She was."

"What about? Didn't you pay your rent?"

I gave it to her head-on. "She thinks I played with her daughter and made her that way."

There was no surprise in the blue eyes. "And did you?"

"No."

"Was she pretty?"

"A little."

"Maybe you were just unlucky, that's all."

"Maybe."

I swung around on the stool and faced her. My foot bumped against something and I looked down. The liquor rolled some more. She had her legs crossed, her right one over her left, and I could see all the way from above her knee to her toes. Her leg had the shape of a piece of polished driftwood, all curves and bumps. I had all I could do to keep my hands on the bar. I wanted to put them down there, feel the leg and go up higher to see where the nylon ended.

"You've got no right here," I said.

"Why not? I've got as much right as you."

"This is a dump."

"Well, we don't have to stay here."

I thought about that. This wasn't any accident. She was after something. I waved to the bartender. "What'll you have?" I asked her.

"Scotch."

I should have known.

The bartender fixed us up and then went down to the far end of the bar and began work on a crossword puzzle. He knew when he wasn't wanted.

"You owe me twenty-five bucks," I said, thinking it sounded cute.

"You're not worried about the money, Mac."

"Who says I'm not?"

"I do."

She was right, of course. The money had about as much significance to me as a hole in somebody else's sock. She was right there, close to me and smelling nice, and nothing else seemed to be worth thinking about.

"You must like green," I said.

"Yes." It wasn't the same green dress as she had worn before but it fit just as tight and, if anything, it hugged her pointed breasts more snugly. I was pretty damn sure that she didn't have anything on underneath except her skin.

"Here's your twenty-five bucks," she said, opening her pocketbook. "If it makes you feel any better."

I took the money. "Thanks."

"Only don't tell George."

"I won't be seeing George."

"You will if you come back to work."

"Who said I was coming back to work?"

Those blue eyes cut a hole right through my skull into my brain.

"I did, Mac."

"Yeah?"

"That's why I came looking for you."

"What about your husband?"

"He's sorry he argued with you. We talked about it and he says he knows it wasn't right and that he won't do it again. He wasn't feeling well."

"He don't have to take his sickness out on me."

She was silent for a moment. "You're not the only one," she said. "I get mine too."

I wondered what she meant.

We had a couple of more drinks and we didn't say very much. We just sat there drinking and smoking and every chance I got I looked down at that leg. You can have all of your Hollywood actresses and your Copa cuties. This girl had a pair of pins to knock you as flat as water on a dry board. Slim ankles, good calves just the right size, and a smooth round knee with the hint of a dimple in the center. Above that, from what I could see, she was even better. Long, trim thighs filling out near the top and flowing up into a pair of hips that did things to you even when they sat still.

And her belly—well, there was hardly any belly at all. It was rounded below the navel, flattening out as it swept up to her luscious womanhood.

"Nuts to it," I said.

I wasn't thinking about the job just then but about the impressions that had raced through my mind before. Somehow, she didn't seem to fit with this guy George, she didn't fit at all. Nothing seemed to fit. She could have had her pick of any man, with or without dough, and she had selected this slob. It didn't make sense. She didn't love him. And when a dame is married to a guy she doesn't love it can mean only one thing: trouble. You can get into the trouble or you can stay away from it but if you jump in with both feet you have to be prepared to ride downhill for a long trip. A married woman can do that to you. She gets ideas about her husband that drag her down and she takes you right along with her.

"You don't mean that," she said, patiently, fingering her drink.

"But I do."

"No you don't, Mac. You're sore right now and I don't blame you for being sore, but you don't mean it. You have to work somewhere and both of us know that you won't be able to get a hotel to manage until this thing about you has died down. What are you going to do? Work for fifty or sixty dollars a week when you can make seventy-five and a hundred? Isn't that silly?"

I didn't have any answer for that. It was.

"Forget whatever you think of me or George," she continued. "Think of yourself."

That was a neat trick, forgetting about her.

"Yeah," I said.

"You won't have the expense of a room. We've got the place fixed up out there for you, and you'll have good food. You won't have to spend a dime. Everything you make will be yours. Isn't that better than—"

She went on and on, through two more drinks. She said the same thing over two or three times and it began to register. It was a better job than I could get any place else. And, I said to myself, I could look at her and not get all jammed up. I didn't have to fool around with her. All I had to do was do my work, collect my pay and find a dame to take her place in the sheets. It was that simple.

"And there'll be something else for you," she said.

"What?"

"That's for you to find out."

"You serious?"

"I'm serious."

I thought about it again. I thought about it a lot. I thought about it so much that my head started to ache. There were two answers. I was a sucker if I didn't do it. And I was a sucker if I did.

"I'll be out in the morning," I said, finally.

"Oh, Mac!"

We had another drink together and then she left. I didn't watch her go. I couldn't stand the physical pressure of seeing her body sway back and forth. I might not be able to work off the steam. There was a good chance that the goose neck lamp was turned off by this time.

"Closing up," the bartender said. "You've had enough." I agreed with him and staggered outside. I got into the Ford and headed back toward the gas station. The light was still on.

I went inside, using the side door, and flipped off the lamp as I passed through the office.

"That you?" Julia called from the darkness of the bedroom.

I told her it was me.

"Mac! Where have you been?"

"Around."

I entered the bedroom. I didn't need a light. She moved on the bed and the springs made a funny noise.

Even in the dark I couldn't miss.

"Your old man running foxes?" I inquired.

"Him and his damned dogs!"

"Bless the dogs," I said and got down on the bed beside her.

She was silent, waiting for me, and her lips under my mouth were hot and wet. She moved her lips in tiny circles, forcing my mouth open, driving her tongue inside.

"Oh, Mac!"

My hands slid down over her body. She began to tremble as I fondled her, caressed her. My lips followed my hands and she lifted herself to me.

"Mac, Mac, Mac!"

My hands kept moving and my lips returned to her mouth.

"Love me good," she whispered.

"You been waiting for me, baby?"

"Have I!"

I kissed her in between the words. "You going to be good to me?"

"Am I! Ummmm!"

And she was.

She was warm and definitely wonderful and more eager than a couple of dozen women should have been. My back hurt and my legs hurt and my arms were nearly numb. But she left me as cold as a snow storm in the dead of winter.

"Mac?"

I paused in the doorway. "Yeah?"

"Next time remember."

"Remember what?"

"My name isn't Diana."

I stumbled through the office and kicked the side door open. I no longer felt cold. I felt hot, covered with prickly heat.

It was then that I should have run. But I didn't.
I didn't have the sense.
Or the guts.

Part Two

9

I got a truck in Duncan at a pretty low figure. The guy wanted fifteen bucks a day for it, but he was laid up with a bad foot and after I showed him he wasn't making anything with it standing in his driveway he gave it to me for eight. George thought that was a buy, a real steal, and that's about the only time I ever saw him pleased.

"You've got the hang of it," he said. "Save a buck here and another buck there."

That was okay with me as long as he didn't try it on yours truly again.

The surfaces of the courts were hard like rock, but I told him we ought to haul in the clay first, put it in little piles and let it dry out while we were busting up the crust.

"You're thinking," he said, complimenting me for the second time in almost as many minutes.

I was thinking of myself. The clay, no matter how good it was, would have to be sifted through a wire screen and if you've ever sifted wet clay through a wire screen you know it can make a pretzel out of even a strong man's back. I didn't mind working, and I was willing to do my share, but I wanted to do it as easily as I could and not poke a rib through my side.

Diana said she would start working on the courts, roughing them up with the back of a rake, but I told her it was too much work for a girl.

"You could paint some of the floors," I said. "Or the walls. You get one of those roller things and you can do the walls slick as a cat."

George stayed out of our discussion. I guess he didn't care what his wife did as long as she worked. "I'd rather be out in the sun," she said.

"Well, suit yourself."

"We can both paint inside when it rains."

"Yeah."

Of course, this is what I was trying to get away from, both of us working close together. If I could keep her inside, out of sight, I wouldn't think about her so much. But she was the boss, or one of the bosses, and I could argue just so much with her.

"I'll work on the courts," she said.

"And maybe I'll help," George said.

I knew he wouldn't.

The truck was old, and it rattled like crazy but it had a dump body and that's what we needed. Of course, the clay had to be shoveled onto it, which was a tough job, but it could be dumped off and that would save a lot of effort.

I hated to go out there to the Hotel Gordon the first time but I forced myself to do it. I left the truck parked in the driveway, right smack in front of the entrance, and I went in to pay for the load.

Sid was behind the desk.

"Hello, Mac," he said.

I told him what I wanted and gave him the dough. "You look like a working man," he said.

I guess I did, dressed in sun tans and a T-shirt.

"There's supposed to be some kid around here who wants to make half a buck helping out. Where is he?"

But Sid said the kid was busy washing windows. I had an idea he wouldn't have told me where to find any help if the kid had been hiding under the desk.

The clay was at the end of a field, way down past the hotel near a little stream of water. It was easy enough loading on the slope, shoveling downhill, but when I started to pull out of there the old truck bellowed like the engine ahead of a long freight. I finally got out, though, back onto solid ground, and after that the going was fairly good.

It was about six miles between the Hotel Gordon and Parsons Ranch and I made two trips that morning. Each time I arrived at the tennis court it seemed as though the redhead had less and less on. When I'd left she'd been wearing a half-skirt over the shorts and a little jacket affair over her shoulders. The end of the first trip found the jacket off and when I pulled in with the second load I saw that she had the skirt off. She was wearing pink shorts and a pink halter and from a distance she looked naked.

I dumped the second load and tore back up the road.

When I arrived at the ranch after the third trip she came over to the truck and stood there while I dumped the clay.

"Aren't you going to eat lunch, Mac?"

"I'm not hungry."

"You can have a steak if you want. He's not here. He went into town for some more medicine."

We were all alone. My head thumped.

"No," I said. "I'll keep on rolling."

I had to keep rolling. Christ, what was the matter with me, anyway? I was getting so I didn't know up from down or right from left. She was in my blood, as dangerous as the sugar in her husband's blood, and I couldn't get her out of it. She filled me with need and desire and fear, all at the same time. It was worse than having an arm splintered. An arm you could get fixed.

"There's nobody else here," she said softly as I got into the cab.

I gave the truck hell going back to the Hotel Gordon. I didn't try to miss any of the chug holes and I bounced around like change in a tin cup. The owner of the truck had been right; he ought to get fifteen bucks a day. At eight he was being taken.

I loaded the body up, all the way to the top, and then heaped on some more. Every time I added another shovelful I could hear the springs creak.

But I fooled myself. Fifty feet up the incline and the truck buried itself up to the hubs in back.

I had to unload the whole thing.

I cursed and sweated and cursed some more. By the time I got the clay off and the wheels jacked up out of the holes I was so mad that I could have wrapped the shovel handle around the front of the truck.

I didn't load the truck again.

I drove back to the ranch.

I was done, finished with both of them. This time when I quit I'd stay quit. Maybe I couldn't get seventy-five a week any place else, but that wasn't the important thing. I had to get out of there while I still had part of my sanity and all of my hide.

I parked the truck alongside the tennis courts and got out. I looked around for her but I didn't see her. At first, I thought she'd changed her mind about the sun and gone inside of one of the buildings.

And then I saw her.

She was lying on one of the piles of clay, all spread out, and I could tell from the position of her halter that it was untied and that she'd had it off so that she could get tanned up there, too.

"Hello," she said.

I walked toward her. My knees were weak.

"Hello, Mac," she said.

I wet my lips. My mouth was so dry I could have swallowed slop and it would have felt good. My brain kept telling me to quit but I couldn't answer I was going to quit. The hell with my brain. Body was boss now.

She lifted her arms, placing them beneath her head, and the movement caused the halter to move down just a little.

"Mac, what's the matter with you? You're so white."

"Sweet Jesus," I said, thickly.

I've never been able to figure out if she wanted me then and there or not but there is one thing I do know: she couldn't have stopped me if she'd had a shotgun and a knife and she'd used both of them.

"Mac!"

I was down there beside her, my knees buried in the soft, cool clay, and my mouth was coming down over her lips.

Those blue eyes of hers were wide open, staring straight up into my face.

I kissed her. Her lips had looked soft but never so soft as they felt. They were as smooth as wet satin, alive with fire, and when they moved they forced my mouth open so wide I thought my jaw would crack.

"Sweet Jesus," I said again.

She laughed and twisted her head aside.

I tried to kiss her again but she wouldn't let me.

"I'm married," she said.

"To a guy with sugar in his blood."

"What's that got to do with it?"

"I don't know. You tell me."

She shrugged and when I glanced down I saw that the halter wasn't there anymore. Just Diana Shipton.

Just Diana Shipton, as bare as you please.

"Mac," she sighed. "Mac, oh, Mac!"

There was no doubt about it now. I was going to have her.

"Mac! Oh, Mac!"

"Baby," I told her, "you've driven me nuts. I look at you and I see the sun and the sky and everything good. No fooling. I look at you and the whole world stands right on end."

"Yes." Her lips came against my mouth, greedily. "Oh, yes! Yes, Mac!"

"You, too?"

"Me, too."

"Since when?"

"Since that first day."

"Me, too."

"George mustn't know," she whispered.

"Well, I won't tell him."

"No. But there are other ways."

"How?"

"One in particular."

"Tell me."

"George is sterile."

"And I'm not. Is that it?"

She laughed and clung to me, rocking back and forth.

"That's what I like about you. You don't have to be drawn a picture."

"You're a picture, baby."

"Am I?"

"You know you are."

She argued a little about staying out there in the sun, where everybody could see us, but there wasn't anybody around.

She clung to me like I was a log and she was caught in a great big whirlpool that threatened to destroy her.

The sun became a bright, red fire, and then big and dark and wonderful.

It was good. Oh, God, was it good!

Later, we got out the rakes and started working on the tennis courts as though nothing had happened.

But something had.

Plenty.

10

It's great the amount of work two people can do, just a man and a woman working together.

We used up a week leveling the tennis courts and then we moved back inside to finish off the floors and the walls in some of the buildings. Diana got to be nearly a professional with the roller and while she did the walls I slapped paint on the floors. It took us about a day for each setup, except when we got to the smaller ones, and before we were aware of it we were done.

"Now to put up the cots, and get some mattresses on the bunks," George said.

George was no help at all. He stood around with one finger in his nose and watched us work. When he got tired of doing that he thought up some excuse and rode into town. I liked it when he went into town. We kept up our work but we kept up something else, too. By the end of the second week I'd had her in every building on the grounds, including the bedroom in the cottage.

"He'd kill us if he ever found us in here," she said. "He'd kill, us, anyway."

Now that I was living out at the ranch, hanging around in the evening, I had learned quite a bit about George Shipton. He was in love with his wife, just as crazy as one man can get over a woman, and he trusted her. You violate a combination like that and it's like holding a stick of dynamite with a short fuse.

Nights were bad. Nights I couldn't get near her. I could lie on my bed in the help's quarters and look over there across the horseshoe and see them in the kitchen. He had a habit of sneaking up behind her when she was doing the dishes, putting his fat arms around her and kissing her on the neck or maybe it was the lobe of her ear. When I saw him do that I'd get tight inside and I'd feel as empty as a smashed barrel of rain water.

On Wednesday, at breakfast, he announced he was driving down to Newburgh, in Orange County, for the day. He'd had a letter from the cook who'd been with them the summer before and he wanted to see the guy about coming back to work for the summer.

"He wants a hundred and a quarter this time," George said to his wife.

"He got a hundred last year."

"Yeah. But this time he'll bring his own rassler with him. Of course, I know how that goes, too. A cook comes on with his own rassler, keeps him a week, fires the guy and then you have to pay for one anyway. That's one thing I want to get squared up with Sam; I don't want him to think he's coming in here and cracking the nut at a hundred a quarter."

If you know anything about hotels you know that some chefs prefer to bring their own pot and pan man along, some fellow who's familiar with how they work, rather than depend upon a drunk or a ridge runner you pick up in the hills. But George was right about the gimmick. A lot of chefs used it and got away with it.

"I never liked that Sam," Diana said. "You know that, George. I haven't got any use for him."

George filled his big mouth with one entire egg. "I don't know why not, hon."

"He's dirty around the food."

"No dirtier than any of the others."

They argued some about Sam, Diana sticking to her guns about not liking the man, but it was obvious that George was going to have his way.

"You can hire all the rest of the help," George told her. "But the cook is my baby. The cook can make us or break us. You know that. You get a saving cook like Sam and he'll avoid a lot of waste. The profits in a place like this are made between the kitchen and the garbage can."

George was no fool; he was right again.

"Such as pulling corn out of the garbage can, washing it off and throwing it back on the table?" Diana wanted to know.

George looked perturbed. "You still harping about that little thing?"

"I saw him do it."

"I don't care if you did." George finished his coffee and stood up. "I'm taking Sam on if I can get him. If I can't, I've gotta shag my butt around and make some connections. Like I say, the rest of the help is up to you. But the cook is mine. I don't care if he feeds them swill as long as they don't die of poison and they pay their bills."

"You wouldn't."

George looked at me. "That right, Mac?"

"I guess so," I said, and earned a frown from Diana. Then I added, "But it doesn't cost anything to be clean."

"You trying to tell me my business, too?"

Brother, he was temperamental.

"No," I said. "Not at all, George. I can always eat eggs. There's not much you can do to mess up an egg."

He nodded. "That's the idea. What the hell do we care?"

He went in to dress and I helped Diana with the dishes. I was tempted to slide my arms around her, the way her husband did, but thought better of it. I settled for a great big fat kiss on the back of her neck.

"Don't do that," she whispered, drawing away.

"Why not?"

"Not with him here."

"To hell with him."

"You don't mean that, Mac."

"No."

When he came out he looked as though he was on his way to a funeral. He had on a black suit, black tie and he was wearing a black homburg.

"What's the program today?" he asked me.

"Putting the mattresses on the bunks," I replied. Then I brought up a subject I had mentioned the night before at supper. "Too bad we still don't have that truck," I said. "It would save a lot of time carting them. Or you can drive my car and we'll use the station wagon."

"We've got a wheelbarrow," he said. "Take that."

See what I mean? He was a human hog with two legs. He wouldn't have cared if I'd had to move one of the buildings on my back.

"Sure," I agreed. There was no sense of chewing with him about it. "Or maybe I can bounce them from place to place," I said, looking right at his wife.

"What's that, Mac?"

"Oh, never mind."

He kissed Diana goodbye but I didn't watch him while he did it. It made me sick enough to hear him slobbering over her.

"The dirty bastard," I said, after he was gone.

She listened for the sound of his car starting and she laughed.

"You hate him worse every day, don't you, Mac?"

"I hate his guts."

"Why?"

"You know why. You work like a hired hand and he treats you like dirt."

She drifted across the kitchen and crept into my arms. Her shoulders, above the tiny halter, were bare. "Is that the only reason, Mac?"

I listened to the sounds of the departing car. "I hate the bastard," I said.

"Because I belong to him?"

"Because he's got no right to you. Any guy who thinks the way George does hasn't got the right to any woman."

"But you do?" She was teasing me.

"I love you." It just slipped out.

"I like that," she said and kissed me on the mouth. "You never told me that before."

I kissed her back. "Don't tell me you didn't know it."

She was in a playful mood and she jerked free of my arms. She turned, racing into the bedroom, and I followed her.

"Tell me again," she said, throwing herself down on the bed.

I told her in the only way that she could completely understand and appreciate.

We didn't leave the cottage until after ten.

The rest of the day we moved mattresses, trying out some of them for bounce and size.

"We'll break them in," she said.

"They're probably already broken in."

"You can say that again, Mac. We had nine pregnancies that I know about last year."

"Help or guests?"

"Half and half."

I decided the cab driver had been right; this place was sex from the word go.

Shortly after five, when we went in to make supper, the phone rang. It was George. The man Sam had been out of town that day, wouldn't get home until late that night and George was staying over. "I'll see you tomorrow, honey," she said, winking at me. "Drive carefully."

I could have puked.

"The bastard," she said, after she'd put the phone down. She came into my arms. "He thinks I miss him."

It was my turn to tease. "And you don't?"

She nibbled on my ear. "After supper I'll show you how much I miss him."

"Show me now."

Her little hands strained against my chest. "No. Later." She tossed her hair back away from her ears. "I never saw a guy like you, Mac."

"I never had a girl like you before, either."

"Have you had many girls?"

"Enough."

"Were any of them like me?"

"Not even all put together."

"You're kidding me."

"No, I'm not. I mean it."

"You're sweet." Her face hardened and she laid her hand against my chest. "He's a slob. Oh, God, he's a slob. Mac, you'll get a kick out of this. The last few times when he's tried, he hasn't been able to."

George was right; he was a sick man. A guy got that far gone, with something like this in his arms, and he was the next thing to being dead.

"I'm glad," I said, huskily.

"I thought you would be. That's why I told you."

"That makes you mine."

"Gee, but you're possessive tonight."

"Well, aren't you?"

She kissed me her answer. "I want to be yours," she said. "If I didn't you'd never have gotten this far."

"I know that."

She cuddled in close. "Just remember it, Mac. I'm yours as long as you want me."

Supper was the best that night. We had steak, French fries, broccoli, and strawberry shortcake. I helped with the dishes, playing around with her some while I dried, and once she put a soapy hand to my mouth.

"You're cute," I said.

"You're not so bad yourself."

After the dishes had been put away we went into the living room and watched television for a while. I fixed a couple of drinks, rye, and we curled up on the davenport together. I don't know what show was on and it didn't matter. She was there with me and for a little bit it was a whole lot more than just a cheap love affair.

I tried to think of us as married, that this was our home and that we had a couple of kids sleeping in that bedroom, but I didn't have much luck at it. I guess the fact that she was married to George prevented the vision from coming out good and clear. Once, a long time ago, there had been another girl I'd been able to think of in that way. We'd been kids, just out of high school, and she'd been as pretty and as saucy as they come. It hadn't lasted, of course, because we had been too young and the summer had been too short, but since then, usually when I was drinking, the memory of that summer came back. The memory was good and there was a clean feeling to it but there was something lonely about it, too. It wasn't the kind of loneliness that makes you sick or ugly, but like a little hollow inside that never seems to fill up regardless of anything that happened.

Maybe it was crazy but that's how I wanted it to be for Diana and me. If things didn't last, if something happened and killed it for us, I wanted the memory of her to be just as good as the one I had of that other girl. I wanted the warmth to come through me when I thought of her, I wanted to see the kids that weren't there, to feel the touch of her hands, the softness of her body, the luxury of her kisses.

"You're so quiet, Mac. What are you thinking about?"

"Us."

"Is that all?"

"Isn't that enough?"

"Hmmmm."

And then I was kissing her again, forgetting about the television, and George, and forgetting about everything. "You excite me, too."

"You do things to me, too."

"We're burning out George's picture tube for nothing."

"Yeah."

"George wouldn't like that."

"Damn George."

"You hate George, don't you?"

"I hate the bastard."

"He's my husband."

Cold sweat was on my forehead, under my arms, across my belly.

"That's why I hate him. Not only that, but he's a hog. You know what my father used to say? He used to say from a pig you get a grunt. That's George. From a pig you get a grunt. How else do you figure it? No wonder the damned bastard has so little to say."

"You shouldn't swear so much, Mac."

"I can't help it. He's a bastard. I call him a bastard because he is a bastard. What else do you want me to call him?"

"He's a bastard," she said, pulling my head down.

"Now you're saying it."

"I've got a right to say it. He lives with me. And I hate him."

I had to know. "Enough to divorce him?"

She bent down and kissed me furiously on the mouth, "Let's not talk about that right now."

"But I want to know."

"Why?"

It was a hell of a question.

"Because I want to marry you," I said.

She put her arms around me and held me tight.

"I wanted you to say that, Mac. I honestly did."

"Well?"

"I don't know." Her voice was huskier than usual. "I don't know. There's more than what you see here, more than what you realize."

"Go on."

"You don't know how I met George. You don't know how we got into this thing together. You don't know anything about it."

"No."

"You'd hate me if you did."

I kissed her, trying to make her feel the way I felt. "No, I wouldn't," I said.

"You'll have to know someday," she decided, weakening.

"Yes."

And so she told me.

She had been born outside Scranton, Pennsylvania, in the guts of the coal fields. She had been an only child. Her parents had wanted more children but her mother had had such a bad time at Diana's birth the doctor had advised against it.

"She died when I was seventeen. But not because of that. Something else. I don't know what. I came home from school one day and my father came home from work and we found her there in the kitchen, dead."

After that she'd continued with her schooling, kept house for her father and studied every night.

"I didn't go out with the boys much," she said. "When you live in the coal fields there's only one thing a boy wants from a girl. You can't blame the boys too much. Most of the girls do it. But I didn't. I minded my own business and kept what I had to myself."

"Somebody got cheated."

"Don't be nasty."

"I'm only saying."

After graduating from high school she hung around the house for a few days, making up her mind about what she could do. A girlfriend of hers, a year older, had been working at some of the resorts down in Pike County and it was through this girl that Diana got her first job.

"I was scared to death waiting on tables," she confided. "I didn't know which side of the plate the silver went on. But they were nice to me and they showed me. By the end of the summer I was doing fine and I was making more tips than anybody."

That winter she went to Florida and this established a pattern which she followed for the next three years.

Florida in the winter and the Pennsylvania resorts during the summer. She bought new clothes, a second hand car, and she fought off the wolves.

"It's the only trouble being a waitress," she said. "Every man who sits down at a table has read that there are more waitresses doing it than girls in any other line of work. It isn't so and I don't know who started it but it sure makes the job interesting."

Two years before her father had been killed in a mine accident, leaving her ten thousand dollars insurance. "That's when I met George."

George had been a friend of her father, a man her father trusted, and at his death George had offered to help the girl in any way he could.

"I didn't know what it was all about," she said. "There were insurance papers and forms and a dozen and one other things. He helped me with everything and I thought he was a nice guy."

At the time George had been drinking quite a bit, working as a chef in one of the hotels and playing the horses on the side. He'd just made a big killing on a couple of lucky races.

"He didn't know about having sugar then," she said. "He found out about that when we took our blood tests before our marriage."

George's conquest of a girl much younger than himself had been both direct and sudden. Four nights after the funeral of her father, George had taken her to dinner, encouraged her to drink, and then, while she was under the influence of the liquor, assaulted her.

"The morning when I woke up and found him in bed with me I thought I'd die," she said, quietly. "I hadn't gotten over my father's death and here this man had done this to me. It was the first time it ever happened." Her laugh was bitter. "And with him. God, I was sick!"

"The bastard!"

"Yes. The bastard."

"But you didn't have to marry him just because of that."

"He told me I might be pregnant. I was scared."

"But you said he's sterile."

"How was I to know that?"

The question didn't need an answer. It wasn't hard to imagine how she had felt.

"I married him a week later," she said. "And when I didn't show up pregnant I was furious at myself. I could have killed him when I found out that it was impossible. But then it was too late. We were married and we were into this thing."

The rest of the story was obvious. Diana had wanted to run a nice place but her husband always overruled her. Anybody who could wave a dollar bill in front of his face was a top-ranking guest. Advertising was hardly necessary. Once the wild crowd found out about the ranch they had more business than they could handle.

"I hate it," Diana said. "Why, we have one cottage which George calls the mating lodge where the girls and boys sleep together. And they don't even know each other. They come up, get off the bus or the train, and go to bed with the first one they find. It's terrible."

"The cops will knock you off one of these days," I said. "They raised the roof at the Hotel Gordon. The cops won't put up with that kind of stuff."

"But there was a complaint up there."

"Yes."

"Here there's no danger of that. None of the guests do anything they don't want to do. The girls aren't professionals. They come up here looking for fun and they get it. If they turn up pregnant they don't yell. Most of the time they've had so many men they wouldn't be able to prove anything anyway. And they take the risk. For every one who gets pregnant there are fifteen or twenty who don't. The law of averages is pretty good."

"Well, it's a lousy business."

"I agree. But what can I do?"

"Nothing. Not with George in the saddle."

"He doesn't care about anything except money, Mac."

"So it would seem."

"He even sells those rubbers to the guests."

"Thoughtful of him."

"One night he sold over three hundred."

"This is a hot place."

"You'll find out this summer." Her lips lingered against my mouth. "But I just want you to look. I don't want you finding out for yourself. You're handsome, you know, and it wouldn't be hard for you to find out."

"I won't," I said, kissing her back.

"I ought to be all you can handle."

"Hell, yes."

We laughed and kissed and lay there together on the davenport. The television might just as well have been turned the other way. Who cared?

"I can see now why you can't just walk out on him," I said seriously. "You've got a bundle tied up in here and you could lose every dime."

"No, I wouldn't lose it, but I'd still be in business with him. I'd hate that."

"So would I."

"This isn't just a marriage thing, Mac. He had legal papers drawn up and all. He owns half and I own half. Getting a divorce from him wouldn't change that."

"No, I guess not."

"And there's an insurance policy."

I nodded. "You have to be protected against fire."

"No. I mean life insurance. We've got one policy for twenty-five thousand, but it insures both of us. They call it a joint life, or something like that."

"How could he get insurance if he's sick?"

"He lied to them. He didn't tell the doctor and the doctor didn't give us much of an exam."

"Then it isn't any good," I said. "I read once that if you lied to an insurance company, they don't have to pay off."

"Not after two years," she cut in. "After two years they can't fight the claim."

"So if you die he gets twenty-five thousand?"

"Yes."

"And if he dies you get it?"

"That's right."

"Well."

We had some more to drink, tried to watch the television, and finally gave up on the whole thing.

"I love you," I said as I carried her into the darkened bedroom.

"I love you, too, Mac."

I turned on the bed lamp and she let me undress her. I had never undressed her before, not this way, and I took my time about it, torturing both of us.

"You've got the most beautiful body I've ever seen," I said.

"Now you're kidding me."

"No, I'm not. How big are you around the hips?"

"Thirty-six."

"They're child-bearing hips."

"Are they?"

I crushed her to me. "I could give you a kid."

"Don't do it."

I laughed, feeling wonderful, and stood back, looking at her.

"How big are you around the belly?"

"Twenty-two."

"Small."

"You'd better not make it any bigger."

I started to push her down onto the bed but she stood firm and her lips sought out my mouth.

"Now it's my turn," she said.

She damned near drove me crazy.

"We don't have to worry about him tonight," she said as she got down there with me.

We left the light on for a while but after I turned it off we both agreed that it was better in the dark. "Give me love," she begged.

I did.

I don't remember too much after that except pretty soon the gray of the new dawn crept in through the windows and we hadn't slept at all.

Later, when I held her in my arms and we finally did try to go to sleep, I wasn't thinking much about her at all. I was thinking of a guy and twenty-five thousand dollars and a mail order house medical book. A fat guy, a fatter twenty-five grand and a medical book.

It didn't, just then, make sense.

11

If I hadn't gotten drunk it wouldn't have happened and if they hadn't done what they did I wouldn't have gotten drunk.

George returned from Newburgh all fired up with you-know-what and vinegar. He had gotten Sam for a hundred a week across the season and he, George, would supply the pot rassler.

"I even got him to let me hold back two weeks on his pay," George bragged. "That'll tie him down until after Labor Day."

"It was an old trick still used by many of the hotels. They hold back two weeks' pay on the help and then keep that hanging over their heads if they ever decided to quit."

"I still think we would have done better with somebody else," Diana said. "You don't see much of the kitchen, George, but I do and he's filthy."

George hit the ceiling. "My God Almighty," he yelled, "What are you, a sanitary engineer, for Christ's sake?"

"It doesn't cost anything to be clean," she insisted.

"Forget it," George said. "He's hired."

They argued some more about Sam and then she hit on a point I hadn't considered.

"You've got to make my life tough, haven't you?" she threw in his face. "That means I'll have to do all the ordering."

"Why?"

"Because he's the hardest cook this side of hell to order for. A new man like Mac wouldn't be able to keep up with him."

I could see her point. She had plenty to do and she didn't want any more. I couldn't blame her for that. Do one job at a resort and do it well and you're lucky.

"Forget it," George said again. "He's hired."

"That doesn't make it any easier to order for him. He can be awful when he wants to be."

"Forget it. Mac's experienced."

"Not with Sam."

They went at it again, knocking my name around like I was a baseball. She said I wouldn't be able to order for Sam and George said I would. Finally, George threw up his hands and walked away.

"To hell with it," he said. "You do what you want." He went storming into the cottage.

"You know how some cooks are," Diana said.

"Yeah."

I did. Ordering stock that's bound to go up on the stock market is easier than ordering for some cooks. You can work up an ulcer over one short season with some of those characters.

"It might be better if you did the registrations and I did the ordering," Diana said.

"Anything is okay with me. I just don't want you knocking your brains out."

Her eyes turned toward the cottage.

"The bastard," she said.

I nodded.

But I still couldn't understand what all the rumpus over the cook had been about. One way or the other I had to work; what difference did it make what I did?

By the next day George had calmed down and even helped us with some of the mattresses. He couldn't understand why we hadn't gotten them all out and he bitched to me about that.

"Your wife isn't any horse," I told him, "and neither am I."

"Who said you were, Mac?"

"You just did. There's a lot of mattresses."

"And there was a lot of time, too."

I could have spit in his face, or laughed in it, or slugged him right there. He wouldn't be so smart if he knew what his wife and I had been doing while he was away.

We used the station wagon and that made the moving lot easier and faster.

"I'd like to have a dollar for every time the mattresses catch it this summer," he said.

"You'll get more than that," I reminded him.

Just before supper I changed into swim trunks and went down to French Creek. I'd been doing this almost for a week now and while the girl had wanted to go in with me George had objected, saying that the water was too cold. It was cold, far out, but along the shore it wasn't too bad.

I dove in, downstream from a pile of stones, and hit the water clean, going fast, churning it with my feet. The water was good, about the temperature of the air, and I swam to the opposite shore, about a hundred and fifty feet distant. I turned around, submerging, and swam half the way back under water.

Diana was waiting for me on the bank.

"Mac."

"What?"

"Come here."

I swam in to shore, stood up, and walked to her. "He cut his throat?" I wanted to know.

She made a face. "We'll never be that lucky. He uses an electric shaver."

"Maybe he'll get electrocuted, then."

The bank was high enough so that he couldn't see us from the cottage. She tipped her head back, waiting, and I planted a long kiss on her mouth.

"He wants to go away for the weekend," she said.

"What!"

"He wants to leave tomorrow, Friday. He says we won't have a chance once the season starts." She laughed, shortly. "Know why? The bastard says I've been working so hard that I need a couple of days rest. Isn't that a hot one?"

"The bastard wouldn't give his mother a rest," I said.

That wasn't swearing to us. As far as we were concerned his name was "the bastard." I guess it seemed like a more fitting name than the one his family had given him. George Shipton. But "the bastard" was better. It fully described him for just what he was.

"I'll miss you," I said.

"I'll miss you, too."

I hadn't been able to have her since he'd returned from Newburgh, and it was driving me wild.

I stood, facing the bank, watching the rim of it, and put my arms around her.

"I ought to give you a going away present," I said. "Something you can take with you."

"Mac, not here!"

"Why not here?"

"You'll get me all wet."

I sealed her mouth for a second.

"You'll dry."

"Mac . . ."

I pulled her to me and let my hands go down to the small of her back, lifting her and pressing her to me.

It was so good to hold her in my arms again.

"He'll see us, Mac."

"I can watch for him."

"How do you mean, Mac?"

I showed her.

The next morning, shortly before ten, they left. It made me sick, watching them load the car with their bags, and her all dressed up ready to go off with him. Even when George came over to talk to me before they drove away, I couldn't look at him without wanting to drag him down to French Creek and shove his head under the water.

"There's a lawn mower in the shed," he said. "Cut the grass."

"Okay."

"There's some weeds coming up in the tennis courts. Dig them out!"

"Sure."

"And I got two gallons of outside green for the corral fence. Give it a lick and a promise."

You'd think they were going to be gone for a week instead of a couple of days.

"Anything else?"

"Don't be sarcastic."

"I only asked."

He stared at me. "No," he said, turning away, "I don't think there's anything else." A couple of feet off he stopped and spoke over his shoulder. "We'll leave the cottage unlocked so you can get your meals."

"Thanks."

Waving at me, they drove away.

The lawn mower was a mess. I had to take the thing apart, oil it and sharpen the blades. Even then it didn't cut worth a damn. I did half the lawn in the middle of the horseshoe and it looked like a French barber had been at it with a sickle and a rake. At four I pushed the lawn mower into the shed and went down to the cottage.

I wasn't hungry.

But Christ, I was thirsty.

I found a bottle of rye and drank some of that. At first, I used some water in a glass with the rye, but after that I drank right from the bottle.

I sat down at the kitchen table and thought. My thoughts weren't good but I couldn't control them. I thought about the girl, sure, but I also thought about something else. The more I drank the clearer it became.

I saw the guy and the needle and I saw twenty-five grand. My hands were shaking so hard I could hardly hold the bottle. It was terrible.

I finished the bottle, which had only been half full, and wandered around the cottage. I went first into the living room but there was nothing of interest in there. Then I entered the bedroom.

The bed was rumpled, just the way they had left it. I closed my eyes, trying to shut it out, but I couldn't. I could see them there in that bed, the two of them, and I remembered her telling me about how he had tried and how he couldn't. It was almost obscene, thinking about a man that way. A man was supposed to be virile, ready to take care of a woman, to please her and make her happy. Not that I objected. I didn't. I didn't want him to dirty her body with his own.

I swung away from the bed and looked at the rest of the room. There were two dressers in there, one which belonged to Diana and the other which was used by George. Scattered around on the top of hers were perfume bottles, lipsticks, some face powder, a few bobby pins, a half empty pack of cigarettes and a couple of safety pins. There was nothing on top of George's dresser.

You could say I didn't have any right looking into the drawers of either dresser, but I did. I looked into hers first. I saw some slips and bras and panties, and my head hit the ceiling. I closed my eyes, touching the soft material and trying to think of her as being somewhere inside. But it wasn't any good.

There wasn't much in George's dresser, except some shirts, ties, shorts and things like that.

And a hypodermic needle.

I stared at the needle, fascinated.

Then I slammed the drawer shut.

I was thinking of the medical book and what it had said and I knew that I mustn't. Christ, I told myself, I must never let myself think that way again.

An air bubble, it had said. You had to be careful with these needles. An air bubble that got into the blood stream could kill you quicker than poison. The air bubble hit your heart and you died.

I jerked the drawer open and looked at the needle again.

Then I slammed it shut.

Jesus, sweet Jesus, I had to quit thinking this way. I got out of the cottage in a hurry.

Driving in toward town I felt better. I had the windows down, both front and back, and the air was clear and fresh.

I stopped at the Crystal Bar and had a few drinks. The bartender asked me again if I was from around those parts and

I said, yes, born and raised in the county. He set up one on the house.

"Soon'll be summer," he said.

"Won't be long."

"Everybody and his brother will be coming up from the city."

"Yeah."

"That's what I hate about this place. They run over you like cattle from the Fourth until Labor Day."

"True. Very true."

"You working around here, fellow?"

"Out at Parsons Ranch."

"Some place in the summer."

"So I heard."

"They got women out there just hollering to get taken care of."

"That a fact?"

"You'll find out."

When it got to be seven I drank up and got out of the Crystal Bar. The bartender was still talking about the ranch, and how you could get your ashes hauled for nothing, and I was getting fed up with it. Anyway, I was hungry and I had to put something in my stomach to keep the liquor company.

I drove out to the diner and found Laura and Hughie behind the counter. As usual at this time of the night, there wasn't any business.

"Meatloaf," I told Hughie.

I'll say one thing for Hughie, he made good meatloaf. He didn't load it up with a lot of sage, trying to kill the taste of some old meat. He used the best quality pork, veal and beef and he used just enough seasoning to bring out the flavor.

"You working?" he inquired.

"Like a dog."

"The offer's still good here, Mac."

"Thanks, but no."

He shrugged and went back to the kitchen. Laura moved down the counter and sat beside me.

"Long time no see, Mac."

"Been busy." The meatloaf was fine.

"Hughie misses you, Mac."

"I miss him. I think we'll go steady."

"Always kidding."

"A little." I reached down and pinched her on the knee. "Except about one thing. About that I never can settle down and take it seriously."

"Oh, you!"

"Oh, me!"

Laura was no good, not the way you measure goodness and badness in a girl, but we understood each other.

You might say I shouldn't have been interested in her, not that way and not after all I'd been through out at the ranch, but the fact is that I don't discourage easily. That's one thing in life that I believe in: giving all I've got. And, if I do say so myself, I've got a lot to give.

"I get off at eight."

"That's good."

I hung around drinking coffee and talking to Hughie until she went off shift, and then we walked outside. "Spring is in the air," she said.

She was right, it was. The late evening shadows were warm and soft and the air was thick with the scent of new life in the woods.

She didn't ask me where we were going and I didn't have to tell her. I buzzed down the highway, turned left and hit the mountain road.

"I knew it," she said, laughing and creeping in closer to me.

It wasn't easy to find a parking place. Spring was in the air, there was no doubt about that. Every fifty or a hundred feet a car was pulled off to the side of the road and some couple was having the usual fun. One could look right into the car of a couple—it was on a downhill slope—and see what they were doing. I slowed the car and grinned.

I found a place alongside a little creek and the water hadn't stopped bubbling in the radiator before it was all over. I was shocked. With Diana this sort of a thing could go on for hours. But then, with Diana, everything was better.

I drove down to the village and parked in front of Laura's house. I waited for her to get out but she seemed to hesitate.

"Mac," she asked, not looking at me, "do you have five dollars?"

"Why, sure."

She stared straight ahead. "Tips have been terrible lately and this medicine for my mother costs like the devil."

I pressed a five into her hand. "I understand," I said.

And I did.

She had just sold herself.

I rode back to the Crystal Bar and started drinking.

By the time I left, bumping into the door on my way out, I had narrowed my thoughts down to just four things.

The girl.
The needle.
The book.
And the dough.
It was hell.

12

I've said that it wouldn't have happened if I hadn't gotten drunk, but I think I should change that. It wouldn't have happened if I hadn't stayed that way. Or maybe it would have. I don't know. Sometimes there are things that go on that you can't be sure about.

When I woke up Saturday morning I was sort of half and half, a little bit in the loop yet, but part of me had both feet on the ground. I tried to keep them there. I tried like fury.

It was hot outside, the sun blazing down, and I stripped to the waist. I pushed that beat up lawn mower like a maniac escaping over the hills and by noon I had been over the lawn once. It looked pretty bad, ragged and uneven, but what did George want me to do about it? Chew the grass down with my teeth?

I sat down in some shade and thought about a lot of things. It was confusing. I was remembering that medical book and a lot of other things and I tried to forget about them, too. The only thing I didn't want to forget about was the girl. I never wanted to forget about her.

I didn't stop for lunch but went up and yanked the weeds out of the tennis courts. That's the worst thing about clay; you always get weeds. When I finished I stood back and looked at the courts. They were nice and flat and they had plenty of life. But he still hadn't gotten the sand for me. Well, I thought, to hell with him. If he was too cheap to buy it I was too lazy to put it on.

I had all good intentions of painting the corral fence that afternoon but, somehow, I never got down there . . . I got as far as the cottage and then I ran out of gas. Like a dog without his sputnik.

After ten minutes in the cottage I made up my mind that there wasn't a jug hidden anywhere.

I had to go to town.

Up in the help's quarters I shaved in cold water, showered in cold water and dressed in a hurry.

Let me tell you about the help's quarters. It was quite a set up and it had all the prospects of being mighty interesting come summer.

There were two bedrooms at the south end of the building, past the two johns, but the rest of thing was wide open, barracks-style. There were eighteen cots in the big room, all waiting for nice little waitresses to come prancing up from the city or wherever it was the came from. There wasn't any door between the johns and room section and the barracks section, just wide, empty space that you could look through without straining an eyeball.

"We're pretty crowded up here in the summer," Diana had told me, "and those are the only two extra rooms we've got. The other one is used by the head waitress, so she can have a place to keep her papers and keep track of the girls."

"But there ought to be a door or something in there?"

"Why?"

"I don't know. Hell, it just seems so open, that's all. You'd think the girls would bitch about it."

"Are you worried about the girls?"

"Not particularly. It's just an observation. I can see myself going blind in there during the summer."

"You hadn't better."

"I was only kidding. You're enough for me, baby."

"I hope so."

"But a guy can always have the yen."

"Oh, shut up!"

Yes, it looked interesting for the summer, to say the least. What if I was in love with her? It wouldn't cut much ice if something hot came along. After all, hell, I'm a male and I can resist just so much. And I've got a low resistance in that department. I might as well admit it.

I drove into town but I didn't go to the Crystal Bar. It was costing me too much, drinking that way and there was always some character hanging around wanting a free one. I settled on three bottles, two for myself and the other to replace the one I'd taken from the cottage. I noticed that I had ten bucks left in my wallet. That reminded me that I hadn't been paid for the past week and that I hadn't received the extra twenty-five since the first time. But I wasn't worried about it. George was good for the money and his wife was good for something that was a lot better than money.

I started drinking on the way back to the ranch. I had the bottle propped on the seat beside me, open, and every quarter of a mile, maybe less, I put one away.

Generally, although you may not believe this, I'm not a heavy drinker. Oh, I'll tie one on and get sick and not know what the hell it's all about the next day but it isn't a habit with me. At least, not a habit that I couldn't break if I had one good reason for doing so. Or it hadn't been a habit until that moment. Maybe, just then, it was the most important thing in the world, being able to drink and hoping to forget.

To forget George.

The needle.

The book.

And the money.

They all seemed associated with an unyielding tie, and I couldn't quite understand it. I had his wife, or as much of her as I could get under the circumstances. In some way, she could work things out and we could eventually marry. It wasn't as though it was the end of the world or anything like that. There was always tomorrow. And tomorrow would be better.

I had another drink.

I cursed.

The drinks hadn't helped.

Nothing helped.

My whole body felt like a mess of silage being pulled into a huge grinder. I needed her so badly, I wanted her so much, and there was this guy George standing in my way. Or was he? Who was George, anyhow? He was nothing but a big fat slob with sugar in his blood. She didn't love him. She had never loved him. He had forced her into the marriage, probably for the ten grand she'd inherited from her father, and nothing built that way ever lasted.

I slowed the car and had another drink.

What the hell.

I tried to think about the way you could get a divorce in New York State but I wasn't clear on a lot of things. Adultery, I knew that much. You could get a divorce if one or the other went to bed with somebody else. But that was no good. That was a laugh. She had gone to bed with me but George couldn't do anything even if he did go to bed with somebody else. Was that adultery, when a guy tried and couldn't? I laughed and lifted the bottle. That was a technical point. Oh, Jesus, that was a good one.

If you drink a lot, the way I was doing, you reach one plateau, just before you go from sense to nonsense, when everything is clear. They say liquor dulls you, twists the meaning of things, but there is always that one fine point, that brief instant, when everything is so sharply in focus that you wonder why it's never been that way before.

That instant hit me, lingering a little bit, as I drove up to the ranch.

She didn't have to get a divorce in New York State. She could get one in Reno, or Mexico, or someplace like that. All right, so a trip cost money, hanging around cost money, but I wasn't any cripple. I could go with her. I could get a job, both of us could work for a while, and somehow we'd manage. You can always manage to do those things that you want to do. Nobody can stop you. If you love somebody and you want each other, there isn't anything a third party can do to prevent it. So it would take time and it would mean work but what doesn't take time and what doesn't mean work? In this life you get out of it what you put into it. You stick a nickel in the slot and you get five pennies back. Nobody bugs you. You get what you buy.

See what I mean?

It was clean, simple, direct. There were no complications. She had only to tell him that she was done, finished, and then the two of us could blow out of there. Maybe she'd be giving up her interest in the ranch, but she was parting with something that would bring her trouble someday, anyway. The cops wouldn't let a thing like this go on. They'd crack down hard, some night, and then the whole bubble would burst. As one of the owners she could be sent to jail. But if she was away from there, she could disclaim any knowledge of what her husband had been doing, there wasn't anything they could do about it.

Yes, for that instant it was as plain to see as the hand at the end of my arm, the hand that reached for the bottle.

And then it got all fouled up again. The liquor really twisted itself around my brain.

I parked the car in front of the cottage and stumbled outside. I had a bottle in both hands and when I fell down I was lucky that one of them didn't break.

Somehow I got the door of the cottage open and walked inside. I put the bottles on the kitchen table and sat down. A glass got in my way and I just pushed it off of the table and on the floor. It broke and the sound of it smashing made me jump.

I don't know what stopped me. I wanted to crush the kitchen table, and the chairs, and the pots and pans, and I wanted to go into that bedroom and rip that bed apart. I wanted to destroy something here that I couldn't see, a strange something that I could feel, and I wanted to destroy it before it destroyed me. I didn't know what it was—oh, Christ, I didn't know what it was—but it laughed back at me from the walls and the ceiling and the floor.

I had to drink. There was nothing else I could do. I upset one of the bottles but it didn't break and I laughed at it. I remember opening both bottles, setting them side by side, and taking turns drinking from each. I remember the shadows of the evening filling the room, then the darkness, and falling off the chair. I remember falling off the chair because it was funny how it happened. I sat there, lying over the table like a sick man hanging on the railing of a ship, and the chair just skidded out from in under me. I must have landed with my hand in the broken glass because pretty soon I could smell the blood and when I ran my fingers across my mouth I could taste it.

I didn't turn on the light; I didn't want to see the mess or the kitchen or anything. It was dark, good and dark, and I wanted the world to stay that way. I could find the bottles all right, but after a while it didn't do me any good even when I did. They were empty.

I had a hell of a time getting out to the car. I went on my hands and knees, knowing that if I stood up I'd only go down again.

It took me a while to get the door of the car open and as soon as I stuck my head inside I knew that I had gone to all this trouble for nothing. It smelled like a gin mill inside, a gin mill with its doors and windows closed for a week.

"You dirty bastard!" I shouted into the night. "You dirty, dirty bastard!"

The bottle had upset and drained itself off into the upholstery on the seat.

Back on my hands and knees again, back toward the cottage. I cursed bitterly, angrily. I couldn't drive into town for more liquor. I knew that. If I could get the car started I'd only make like a squirrel going up a tree and half kill myself. Or somebody else. Thinking of somebody else did something to me that nothing else had done. I started to cry. I didn't want to kill somebody else. If it was the last thing I could ever do, I wouldn't do it. I hadn't been brought up that way. That made me cry some more, thinking of my mother and father. What would they say if I killed somebody? That was easy; they'd say the same thing that everybody else would say.

"You murderer you," they'd say. "You stinking murderer! And all for a woman. You must be crazy." Crazy?

I cried some more.

Was I?

That was the worst part. I didn't know.

I could taste the tears and smell the blood on my hand as I crawled across the doorsill into the kitchen.

I tried to find the chair but it was a far away and it seemed stupid to go through the motions.

I lay down on the floor, still crying.

After a while I went to sleep.

There are one of two ways that you can wake up the next morning or, as in this case, the next day. If you've done a little bowling, had two or three drinks with the boys, you can get up with a head as big as a kid's balloon at a fireman's parade. Or you can put a gallon away and get up with your head fairly clear. I'm no doctor and no doctor has ever told me this but I think it has a lot to do with the reason for drinking in the first place. If it's a little fun you want you get up feeling like a bum, and if you're trying to drown something you wake up feeling so good you've got every right to be disgusted with yourself all over again.

I woke up sort of between these two. My head hurt, my right hand hurt, but I could see everything quite clearly.

And I wasn't alone.

"What the hell are you doing here?" I wanted to know.

Sandy Herbert was not at all offended by the way I spoke. She stood over me, smiling down, and the smile went all the way up into her dark eyes. I was, of course, sitting on the floor, looking up at her, and feeling like the biggest jerk in Sullivan County. Maybe I was.

"Two pitchers of water," she said, "and you never moved. But the third one really shook you."

I realized then that I was as wet as a muskrat on his way upstream in French Creek.

"Hell," I said.

"Can you get up?"

"I guess."

"Be careful of that glass and don't get into it again. You must have cut your hand in it last night."

"Yeah."

I didn't move right away. I just sat there looking up at her. Now that she had lost the kid she was as trim as a race horse in spring. The red skirt flowed around her thighs and hips, molding them, and the white, sleeveless sweater was just about as full as you could want it. Staring up at her they looked like the headlights on a bus coming out of nowhere.

"You didn't have to drown me," I said.

"Well, you wouldn't move, otherwise."

"What are you doing here?"

"I came out to see you. I thought you wouldn't be working on Sunday and I didn't want to bother you when you were busy."

"Your mother know about this?"

"No. She thinks I'm out looking for work."

"On Sunday?"

"You know my mother. She doesn't care what day it is just so long as I look."

I started to get up but it wasn't as easy as I thought. My whole body ached. I must have slept on the floor for the night. I finally made it into the chair.

"You drive out here?"

"No, I took a cab."

"It'll cost you money if he waits for you."

"I let him go," she said. "I came in here and found you on the floor, out cold, and I didn't know what to do. I tried to wake you, just by talking, but it didn't do any good. So I told the driver to go on without me."

"You shouldn't have done that," I said.

"Why not? You were nice to me and I hated to see you here like this." She smiled again. "You must have had a real time for yourself."

"I guess I did, but you couldn't prove it by me."

She looked around. "This place is a mess."

It was.

"I'll clean it up, Mac. You just sit still and get hold of yourself."

She got a broom, a mop and a dust cloth and it didn't take her very long. I felt like helping her but that's as far as it went; I didn't do anything about it.

"There," she said when she was finished. "That's better."

After she put the broom, the mop and the cloth away she made a pot of coffee. There wasn't any cream, but the coffee was better for me black, anyway. By the time I'd had two cups of it, I began to get the idea that I might live.

"Don't you want one?" I asked her.

"No. I had my breakfast. You know Ma. She had me up at seven-thirty."

"What time is it now?" The clock in the kitchen had stopped.

"It must be about three."

"Jeeze!"

I lit a cigarette; it tasted worse than a piece of string soaked in gasoline.

"Your mother and I had a set-to."

Sandy looked away, ashamed. "I know. She told me. That's one of the things I wanted to see you about. I didn't want you to think that I—"

"I didn't."

"I know you didn't, because you're much too fine man for that."

"Thanks."

"I mean it, Mac."

"Sure."

She pulled out a chair and sat down on the opposite side of the table. Her eyes were wet and her lower lip trembled just a little. I noticed for the first time what a nice mouth she had; it was soft and oval and the lips were darkly full.

"No one has ever been so good to me as you, Mac. Not even my own mother. I feel as though I can tell you things I never told anybody else, that you understand."

"I can try."

"This boy who caused me all the trouble—it really wasn't all his fault. He wanted to be careful. But I didn't want him to. I knew that he was going away after the summer was over, that I could never really have him, and I wanted to keep a little bit of him for me."

I didn't say anything. She'd done more than keep just a small part of the guy. She'd kept a lot of him.

"I know now that it was wrong, because now that it's over and the baby is—dead—and I can see how wrong it was. It wouldn't have been fair to my mother, or to the baby, or me, or anybody. But at the time—Mac, you don't know how scared I've been!"

"I can imagine."

"And when I lay there in that hospital, people looking at me as though I was an animal or something, I wanted to die."

"Nobody wants to die, not really."

She frowned prettily. "No, I guess that's right. I guess you get afraid and weak and it seems like the best way, only it isn't."

"Something like that."

"You don't mind me talking to you this way, Mac?"

"No."

It was funny, but I didn't. It made me feel bigger to have her tell me these things, to depend upon me that much. How do you explain it? You lose yourself, get mixed-up, you don't know a square from a circle and then somebody comes along, telling you their own troubles, and you get a lift.

"I thought you might help me get a job, Mac."

"Me?"

"Yes. Out here. They'll be putting some waitresses on in a week or so."

I shook my head. "This is no place for you, Sandy. It's going to be rugged."

"I know. I've heard. But that doesn't matter. Honestly, it doesn't, Mac. I won't do the same thing again. I won't ever let another man, not unless I want him to."

I should have seen it then, but I didn't. I should have seen it in the way she smiled, the way she looked at me, soft and dreamy like, but I was too stupid to spot the signs.

After she cleaned up the dishes, because there was nothing else to do, I said I'd show her around the place.

Once out in the air and the hot sun I began to feel better.

We looked in most of the buildings and I showed her the tennis courts and made a joke out of my lawn cutting job. She was more interested, however, in the interior arrangements of the buildings.

"They all sleep in one big room?"

"That's right."

"Boys and girls?"

"That's what I've heard."

"Well!"

She wasn't shocked but there was no reason why she should be. Sandy was no juvenile. She knew the rumors about the birds and the bees pretty well, believe me.

"Where do you stay, Mac?"

Again, I should have seen it, but once again, I didn't.

"It's classic," I said, steering her to the right. "Wait until you see it."

"Oh, would you?"

"Why, sure."

She was quite amused at my room being at the end of the building which would be occupied by a flock of waitresses.

"You'll have a party," she said.

"I don't think so."

"You sound serious, Mac."

"I guess I am."

All the while I'd been talking to her, all the while I'd been awake, I'd been thinking about it. Diana could get her divorce and we would make out somehow. And I'd been thinking about something else, too; she was all the woman I'd ever want.

How wrong can you be?

"Where's your room?"

"In here."

It wasn't much of a room but I did keep it neat and clean and that was something. I'd scrubbed the bare boards on the floor with Clorox and they'd come out white and clean. Although I'd intended to put a coat of paint on the plasterboard walls and ceiling I hadn't gotten around to that. The bed was unmade, as though somebody had just gotten out of it. Or was getting ready to crawl into it.

"Nothing fancy," I said, needlessly.

"No, but it isn't bad."

She walked to the window and stood looking out. From the window you could see French Creek, one corner of the corral fence and the woods beyond. It was a nice view, typical of Sullivan County, and it rolled off into the nothingness of the world beyond.

"Mac?" She didn't turn as she spoke. "Mac?"

"Yes?"

"Do you—like me?"

It was the question of a little girl, a question that a child might put to you. And yet, it wasn't a little girl or a child speaking. I felt it right away. It was a woman and she asked it from somewhere deep inside.

"Why, yes, I like you," I said.

"A little? Or a lot?"

Now that was a pointed inquiry. If I told her I liked her a little she would be hurt and mad and if I told her I liked her a lot—well, people have got no business asking things that leave you little or no choice.

"I like you," I said.

"But you didn't answer me."

"No, I suppose I didn't"

She continued to look out of the window. "I'm twenty-two, Mac. I know my own mind. I know what I want."

"Most of us do."

"No, not all of us. Few of us. You have to feel something very terribly to know what you want."

It was then that it came drifting over me like a fog rolling up from the belly of the swamp. It was in the room, all around us, and it sort of took my breath away.

True, I had been good to her but not good to her for the reason which she so obviously thought.

"Look," I began, "I—"

"No, Mac. No. Don't say it. Let me say it."

Sweat tumbled out onto my forehead.

"I don't want you to say it."

"But I have to."

"No!"

"Mac." She turned to me and her face was pale. "Mac, I think a lot of you, an awful lot of you. It wasn't easy for me to come out here, not with what I had in mind, not with what I had to tell you."

"Please!"

"Mac, you have to listen. I can't stop now."

You try to shut up a girl and you've got your hands full. You might just as well ride out the storm and the lightning flash.

"Go ahead."

She took a deep breath.

"I told you about the boy last summer."

"Yes."

"I didn't love him. I thought I did but I didn't. He was the first. Maybe that was it. They say you never forget the first."

She was right. You never forget the first. You always remember, even if you're a male. There's never anything quite like it again, the world opening up and falling in on you.

"I've been through hell, Mac. Hell! You can't know what it was like, getting big, having my mother holler at me, having everybody in Duncan calling me a whore. And I'm not, Mac. I'm not!"

"Of course you're not."

"I wouldn't have cared if I'd loved him. I'm sure of that. If I had loved him it would have been beautiful and wonderful, anyway. How do you explain it? Getting pregnant is the finest thing that a girl can feel. She feels whole for the first time, complete, but without love you have a dirty feeling, too."

I was sweating all over, under my arms, across my back, and there was a ridge of cold sweat on my belly, just above the belt line.

"You don't have to tell me this, Sandy."

"No. And I won't bother you with it more. I just wanted you to know how it was, the way it was. As I got bigger I hated the baby and myself. I hated my mother. I hated everybody. I wanted it to die. I prayed for it to die. I did a terrible thing. I got down on my knees at night and prayed for God to take it from me."

"God wouldn't do that," I said. "God doesn't kill. You had no right to pray that way."

Her eyes searched my face. "It sounds funny for you to say such a thing."

"Does it?"

"Yes. You're big and strong and to look at you you'd never think that you knew what fear was. But you do, Mac. I can tell. You're just as afraid as I am, but you're afraid of something else. You drink because you're afraid, because you're trying to hide from something."

"Are you trying to figure me out?"

"No. I know you, Mac. I know you better than you think. I learned a lot about you that day when you came to the hospital. No matter what you think, you're not afraid of anything."

Now it was her turn to be wrong.

"You'd better be getting back to town," I said, but I didn't move.

"No, Mac, I don't want to go. Not yet."

"But—"

"Mac, please." She came toward me across the room, moving slowly, her whole body alive and fluid with motion. "Mac, I love you. Please don't chase me away."

"For Christ's sake!"

"I do, Mac. I do!"

Yes, I should have seen it before, but I hadn't. It had been there all along, staring me in the face, and I hadn't paid any attention. She was just a kid and she was on fire and it was all my fault.

"You don't know what you're saying."

"I do. I've thought it all out, Mac. I'm no fool. I don't believe you feel that way about me, or that you can, but that doesn't matter. I want you, Mac."

All right, I should have run or I should have up-ended her and walloped her little fanny good and hard. I was in love with Diana, I owed her some respect for that love, but I couldn't pull my eyes away from that girl there in the room with me. She smelled of woman, she looked like a woman, and she was a woman.

She turned away from me and walked over to the bed. Her little hands gripped the bottom of the sweater tightly.

"You're not afraid of me, are you, Mac?"

As if I'd say I was. "No," I said, "I'm not afraid of you."

"Do you think I'm pretty?"

"Yes, you're pretty."

"Promiscuous?" Her voice nearly faltered.

"I wouldn't say that."

She wheeled and faced me and her eyes were bright.

"Remember that night at the house? The night you asked me?" Her lips curved in a smile. "I would have that night, Mac, if I could. Even then I was beginning to feel this way about you."

I should have considered myself lucky; I had two dames in love with me and they both wanted to give me what a man needs. But I didn't. The one I wanted forever, not just for now and this one, Sandy, I wasn't sure whether or not I wanted at all.

"I don't remember," I said. "I was drunk."

"I—I tried to help you, but—"

"You ought to go," I said, interrupting her.

"No, Mac."

She knew what she wanted and how she was going to get it. Slowly, ever so slowly, she pulled the sweater up over her head and tossed it onto a chair back. She was as bare as a seal's skin underneath. I wet my lips and stared at her.

My God!

"You're not pretty," I said between clenched teeth. "You're beautiful!"

This pleased her. She reached for the zipper on the skirt.

"Do you want to undress me, Mac?"

Fire filled my eyes. "No. You do it."

And then she was out of the skirt. My head thumped and the ache of it echoed in my legs. She was just so beautiful.

"Mac! Oh, Mac, am I beautiful?"

The words were thick in my mouth, sticking as though they had been jammed down into a pot of glue. I attempted to say something, anything, and I couldn't. She smiled at and lay down on the rumpled bed. "I'm waiting," she said. "I'm waiting for you, Mac." She didn't have to wait long.

It wasn't the same as it had been with the redhead. Maybe it's because she had asked me for it. I don't know. Or maybe it was because I was a little scared of her. It could have been that, too.

But it didn't take long for all hell to break loose. She became wild and passionate and a bundle of unrestrained fury. She bit me with her teeth and dug with her fingernails, raking my back, left long scratches.

She surprised me. She really did.

We were lying there on the bed, totally and completely exhausted, when somebody stepped into the doorway and stopped short.

It was George Shipton.

"Well, hell," he said, not knowing whether to stand still or jump outside. "Well, hell."

I tried to cover us with a sheet but it was too late. And I couldn't be mad at him. I should have closed the door.

"Damnit," I said, "what are you doing here?"

He looked at me, at the girl who cowered beside me, and then backed out of sight.

"I wanted to tell you that we were back," he said. "And that supper will be ready in an hour."

"Thanks," I said, drily. "You could have yelled."

"I did. But you didn't answer. I thought you were asleep."

His voice faded away as I slammed the door in his face.

"Crummy bastard," I said.

"It's all right," Sandy told me. "Nobody means to do a thing like that."

"He would."

"Is he your boss?"

"Yes."

"I'm sorry. I hope you won't get in any trouble over it."

Trouble? That was a laugh. After he told Diana about it there would be plenty of trouble.

"No," I said. "Don't worry about it." Then, "I'm sorry, too. For you."

She began putting on her clothes.

"Don't be. I'm not ashamed."

"Aren't you sorry it happened?"

"With us? No. Never."

I drove her back to town and we didn't talk a great deal on the way in. She asked me to see what I could do for her about getting a job and I said I would, though I wasn't sure just then what I would be able to do about it, if anything. I could just picture Diana hiring a girl I had just shacked up with. Sure.

"About this afternoon," she said when I let her out at the corner near the house. "I'm glad it happened."

"So am I." Why lie about it? Those moments with her hadn't been wasted; some of them had been a lot of fun.

"And you'll see about the job?"

"Yes. I'll try."

She got out and blew a kiss toward me.

"'Bye, Mac."

"So long."

I returned to the ranch and parked the car near the cottage. I didn't want to go into the cottage and face Diana, but there was no sense putting it off. It wouldn't be any better or worse one time than it would be another.

"There's the old stud now," George said when I entered. He winked at his wife. "What do you think of a guy who gets his in the afternoon?"

You crazy bastard, you, I thought, you wouldn't be able to do it morning, noon, night or in hell. "Let's eat," Diana said stiffly.

We ate. George kidded me some about the girl and I dug down into a shell of silence. Once or twice the redhead looked at me and I saw that her eyes were filled with anger.

"Somebody drank up the whiskey," she said once.

"To hell with the whiskey," George retorted. "Mac did a lot of work while we were away. Maybe he needed it." George laughed. "Maybe he needed it the way he needed the other thing."

"George!"

"Knock it off," I told George, getting sore. "So you peeked in my room and you got yourself a thrill. Knock it off."

"You don't have to get mad, Mac."

"Well, I am."

I didn't look at the girl again and I didn't hang around to help with the dishes after we'd finished eating. I just took off.

I didn't know what to think or what to do. I'd made a mess of things.

How big a mess I couldn't even realize at the time.

13

I thought the trip into New York would be murder but it wasn't. Even before we got to the highway, with me driving the station wagon, I learned a couple of things about Diana Shipton. She could forgive and she could forget.

"Mac," she said, "I don't blame you. We aren't married and I don't have a claim to you. But it came to me so suddenly last night, about the girl, that I was mad."

"You had a right to be. I was a damned fool."

"We're all damned fools at times."

"Yes. But there was no excuse for this. I knew better and I didn't stop it."

"George got quite a kick out of finding you that way."

"He's a bastard."

"A dirty bastard."

"To hell with the slob," I said, feeling the hot morning air around me, feeling good. "We've got today, tonight and tomorrow."

She slid across the seat toward me. "And we've got a lot to do," she said.

I deliberately misinterpreted her.

"You can say that again," I told her, laughing. "We've got plenty to do."

We rolled through Duncan, picked up the county road and rolled on in the direction of Monticello. At Monticello I took Route 42, and from there to New Jersey 23.

We arrived in New York early in the afternoon, and drove downtown to an employment agency in the fruit and vegetable section, not far from the Chambers Street ferry, or where the Erie used to have a ferry. There were a lot of people hanging around in the waiting room, looking for jobs.

"I called them this morning, before we left," Diana said. "They're expecting us."

A dame with a pair of thick glasses and a limp put us in a little empty room and sent in some characters for interviews. I'll say one thing for the agency, the applicants had been carefully screened.

We picked up a baker, for rolls and bread, who had a good employment record. He said he wanted to go to the mountains, because there was a girl in Liberty whom he liked. His explanation was reasonable, his qualifications good and there was no reason why we shouldn't hire him. We did.

As for a desk clerk, we went through five or six guys before we found one who seemed to fill the bill. He was young, in his early twenties, and good looking. Not only that, but he had worked the summer circuit before and he indicated, from the way he talked, that you got more screwballs than sensible people and that you had to treat them as though they were in their right minds. "I wouldn't take a check from my own mother," he said, firmly.

That clinched it. We hired him.

It was after four before we got down to where there was nobody left. The woman with the glasses seemed pleased that we had put some money in her till—she'd get a percentage of the employee's wages for the first month—and she walked with us to the door, promising us anything short of an atomic expert if we should require additional help.

On the way uptown I spoke to Diana about something that had been bothering me.

"What about waitresses?" I wanted to know. "Aren't you looking for them, too?"

"We've already got the waitresses."

"You work fast. You work so fast that I didn't even see you do it."

She laughed. "You'll meet Ester tonight. And then you won't wonder anymore."

We checked in at an uptown hotel, taking a big room with a double bed, and then had dinner in the dining room. After we had eaten Diana made a phone call from the lobby and we went into the bar to wait.

Three drinks later this Ester appeared, smelling of perfume, her high heels clicking.

"Well, honey," she said to Diana. "How good to see you!"

It didn't take me long to find out that everybody was "honey." She had a faint southern accent that went very well with her bleached blonde hair and her light gray eyes. With some words, when she was talking, you'd think she was pouting her mouth formed such a great big oval. I made up my mind that the farthest south she had ever been had been the Battery, or possibly Atlantic City, and let it go at that.

She didn't stay very long but it didn't require much time for her to say what she had to say. She had eighteen girls lined up, all hot numbers, and they were just raring to get up into the mountains.

"Same arrangement as last summer?" she wanted to know.

"Same arrangement," Diana replied. "The girls get forty percent and the house gets forty percent."

"And I get twenty?"

"You get twenty."

Neither one of them had drawn me a picture about what they were discussing but I knew. The girls sold it when they got a chance and everybody picked up an odd buck.

"Mac will be sleeping across the hall from you," Diana said.

This Ester looked at me and smiled. I didn't like her smile. Her teeth were too white, as though they were capped or something.

"He's a handsome thing," she purred. "He doesn't have to sleep across any old hall."

Diana laughed but it was the sort of laugh that told me I'd better keep plenty of space between my sheets and this dame. She didn't have to bother telling me. A real natural blonde is a pleasure to behold, but these phony ones are as bad as finding a chocolate drop in a package of marshmallows.

This Ester didn't hang around long. She had one drink, something I didn't know the name of, and then excused herself.

"She the madam?" I asked Diana after the woman was gone.

"Don't be crude."

"Me? Who's being crude? Look, Diana, if the cops—"

"I know. I hate it, too. It isn't my idea. I don't think there's anything worse than a girl selling her body for a fee. It's George. Don't forget, darling, George is my partner as well as my husband."

"Please, you don't have to remind me."

She smiled and lifted her glass. "The bastard," she said.

"The bastard," I agreed and drank.

We had two more, until we began to feel the edge and I began playing with her legs under the table, before we took the elevator up to the tenth floor.

"You're sweet," I murmured, kissing her on the neck as she began to undress. "And forgiving. I thought you'd be sore at me about that kid."

She fell back into my arms, sighing. She took my hands and placed them against her lovely body.

"Don't do it again, Mac."

"I won't."

"Promise?"

"Promise!"

Clumsily, I fumbled.

"Baby," I said, "please!"

We made long love, wonderful love, not caring about what we did and not being afraid.

It was sweet.

Just two people in love.

14

Two days before the Fourth the ranch started jumping like a Mexican jumping bean stranded in the middle of Arizona.

Ten horses arrived by truck. They were big, powerful, sleek animals out of the west, but gentle, and there wasn't one of them that wasn't better looking than the owner. He was a short, grubby little man who slept in the stables, smelled like an uncombed horse and spit tobacco juice in two directions at once.

The waitresses came by bus and train and a couple of them managed to make it in private cars. The help's quarters bulged at the seams and every time I went to shave some dame had the door locked while she changed her underwear.

If I worried about the absence of a door the girls didn't. They pulled off dresses, unsnapped bras and jumped in and out of panties whenever they felt like it. I began to think I was in a burlesque house where everybody ran around naked.

All of the girls were hotter than a high bid at an auction and some of them went into town to take on the local yokels for practice before any of the guests arrived. One, a fiery little brunette, caught Sam while he was unpacking and caused his first meal at the ranch to burn up like a stick of wood caught in a bonfire.

"Jesus," Sam exclaimed later, "they're a pack of vultures."

Sam was a good cook, a non-drinker, and he tended to his pots and pans. He had worked on ships, in a score of different hotels, and he said he liked to be busy.

"We'll be packed for the Fourth," I told him. "To the rafters and past."

"Good."

It kept me on the move, answering the phone for reservations, assigning bunks, and getting a set of books worked up. I didn't see much of George but there were a couple of things about him that I did know. He was chasing every girl on the place, trying to do with one what he couldn't successfully do with the other. To top it off, he was hitting the bottle.

"He hadn't ought to drink," Diana said. "It's bad for his sugar."

"Maybe the bastard will drop dead."

"Yes, maybe the bastard will."

I met Diana every chance I got, along the bank of French Creek, in one of the empty buildings, and even a couple of times out in my car.

I stayed close to the ranch, not going into town and not drinking at all. I had plenty to do and since things were rolling along so well I didn't have the urge to do either one.

We started to fill up the day before the Fourth. Some of the girls wanted to be alone but some of them wanted to be in a bunkhouse with the fellows. No matter what they desired we could accommodate them. The girls who wanted to keep it reasonable were put in Cherry House and the girls who were out for a ball with any guy who could get up his share of the fun were put in the Cow Yard. The Bull Pen was for guys who liked to play the field, getting a little from the female guests and a little from the waitresses. The Third Section was for the girls who played only with girls and the Twilight Corral was for the boys who didn't know what girls were for.

It was an assortment, I tell you. We have everything at Parsons Ranch. Guys held hands with guys and girls held hands with girls—or something else. I don't know. I didn't watch them.

"If the legion of something-or-other ever gets wind of this," I told Diana, "we'll be doing time from here to the grave."

"Not you. Me and George."

"To hell with George. I don't care about him. It's you I'm worried about."

We got more people on the Fourth and we got stuck for rooms. I found Diana in the kitchen.

"What do we do now?" I inquired. "Set up tents or rent the lawn out by the square foot?"

She laughed. "No. We can get four in the cottage, two in the bed and two on the davenport. I'll sleep up with Ester tonight and you can put up a cot and George can stay in with you."

I didn't like the idea of sharing my room with George but there wasn't much I could do about it. I went ahead, and did the best I could with the guests—in the end I had to turn five away—and that afternoon when I saw George I told him about the arrangements. He was about as drunk as a prince at a coronation and I wasn't sure he understood me.

"Got you," he mumbled, staggering off toward the tennis court. "Like a glove on my hand, old buddy."

Things went along all right until supper but then, just as I was eating, all hell broke loose.

There were a half a dozen girls at the table, the second cook, the clerk and Sam was lounging in the doorway, rubbing his hands on his apron. Diana squeezed past Sam and stood there, just inside the room, looking at me.

"Mac?"

"Yes."

"Mac, what's got into you?"

The dullness of her eyes and the stern lines of her lips made the meat in my mouth turn into sand.

"Me?"

"Yes, you!"

"I don't know what you're talking about."

She crossed her arms over her breasts. "You rented out our cottage to four guests."

"Well, sure. You said for me to do it."

"And put my husband up there with you in your room?"

"Why, sure."

Everybody at the table sat very still, very quiet, looking at Diana.

"I don't know what the hell's the matter with you, Mac," she said. "I never told you any such thing."

"Well, now, Jesus—"

"Don't swear, Mac."

I sat there numb, unable to speak.

"I don't like to bawl anybody else out in front of other people," she went on, "but this is just one time I couldn't help it, Mac. If you think for one minute that doing anything to my husband will change things between us—Mac, he knows about how you've been acting. He does. And he doesn't like it. After all, I am his wife."

She hadn't said so in so many words, but there was no mistaking the impression she conveyed. I'd been chasing her and she didn't like it. Her husband didn't like it. I was being told to keep my nose fastened to my own face.

"Sure," I said, not knowing what else to say.

After she had gone some of the girls started kidding me and I told them all to go to hell. I got up from the table and wandered out into the kitchen.

"Don't let it get you down," Sam said. "You ain't the first guy who's made a play for her and you won't be the last one, either."

"Shut up!"

"Don't boil at me, Mac."

"I said to shut up!"

I went outside, into the sun. It didn't feel any better out there. I was hot and I was cold and I was everything all at once.

I looked all over the ranch for Diana but I couldn't find her. There was something wrong here, terribly wrong, and I didn't know what it was.

I returned to the office and hung around until almost nine o'clock. Then I looked for her again, but I still couldn't find her. Nobody had seen her and everybody laughed when I asked.

Cursing, I walked up to my room.

There was a waitress coming out of the johns, not a stitch on her body, but I didn't pay any attention to her. I charged inside of my bedroom, still swearing, and damned near fell over George who lay on a cot right in front of the door.

He was drunk and he was snoring like a hog after a full meal.

I changed clothes, dressing fast, and put on a new pair of shoes. As I leaned over to tie the shoes I noticed a piece of paper lying on the floor alongside George's cot. There was something on the paper.

I started to sweat.

It was the needle.

The sweat came out of me in a profusion of huge drops.

I thought of the book, the needle, the twenty-five grand and that big fat slob lying there on the cot. But something was missing, something that made me sweat all the more. The girl was missing.

I walked down to where the car was parked, angled around a number of other cars and drove out the lane to the road. The lane was still rough, even worse now from all the recent traffic, and at one place the oil pan hit bottom. I guess the lane was the only thing around the ranch that George didn't want fixed. Well, when he got around to wanting that he could fix it himself. To hell with him, to hell with the girl and to hell with the whole bunch of them.

I tried to think of what she had done logically but there was no logic to it. She'd just sailed into the help's dining room and given me hell for no reason at all. And had lied like an escaping husband caught with his pants down.

It was impossible for me to get through Duncan without stopping in at the Crystal Bar. Except for the bartender the only one in the place was Laura. She was sitting at her favorite booth in the rear. I stopped at the bar, got a bottle of beer and a glass and walked back to her.

"Hi, baby," I said.

She jumped, startled, and then smiled when she saw who it was.

"Hi," she said.

I sat down and poured the beer. I wished I'd ordered something else, something stronger. I sure needed it just then.

"You expecting somebody else?" I wanted to know.

She nodded. "A boy."

"Well, hell, you switching from girls?"

"That wasn't nice, Mac."

"No, I guess it wasn't. Sorry."

"You're in a foul mood. I can tell."

"How?"

"There's a little nerve along the right side of your face that twitches. It's twitching now. It used to do that out at the diner when you got mad at Hughie. Or mad at me."

"Yeah?"

"See? You're in a foul mood, Mac. I don't like when you're that way."

I polished off the beer and stood up.

"That's tough," I said.

"Mac?"

"What?"

"Something's wrong. You can tell me."

"Skip it."

I walked over to the bar and ordered rye, double, and some soda. I sat down on a stool and watched a fresh-faced kid come in and go back to the table with Laura. A few minutes later they left. She said good night, I said good night and as far as I was concerned it was the end of a beautiful friendship.

"Another," I told the bartender. "And keep the glass filled. You've got nothing else to do."

Laura, I decided, was quite a little philosopher. Something was wrong, dead wrong. Or maybe it wasn't. Maybe Diana had pulled that stunt because somebody was getting wise to us and she'd only hoped to head them off. It was a warm, pleasant thought while it lasted but it slipped away as quickly as it had come. I was reaching for the stars when I thought that. There was another reason, much bigger. I wished I knew what it was.

"You said you were from around here, didn't you, mister?"

"Born and raised in the county."

"Have one on me."

"Would a man in his right mind say no?"

"You're getting loaded."

"A little. Give me a bottle."

"What?"

"I want to buy a bottle."

"We can't sell bottles at a bar. Not in New York State. It's against the law."

"Maybe ten bucks changes the law, huh?"

"Ten bucks changes a lot of things."

I left the bar and drove out to Hughie's diner. I didn't open the bottle but left it on the seat beside me. A couple of times I got over onto the wrong side of the road and I damned near got killed in one spot. I was trying to drive and look to see if the light was on in the gas station, all at the same time. The light wasn't on. Hughie was glad to see me even if I was drunk. He looked tired, working two shifts, and before I even sat down he offered me seventy a week to come back to work.

"That's what I wanted to see you about," I said. "I think I might."

"Honest?"

"Yeah."

"Jeeze, that's good."

I tried to get interested in the coffee but the liquor was out there in the car, waiting for me, and I couldn't. I stayed only a few minutes.

"I'll let you know in a couple of days," I said.

He nodded. "Your apron's still here. Hey Mac, take it easy on the bottle, will you?"

"Sure."

I drove down the road a short distance and parked on the side. Then I went to work on the bottle. I hadn't eaten much supper, my stomach was empty, and on top of what I'd had at the Crystal Bar the contents of the bottle hit me hard.

I remember throwing the empty bottle out into the bushes but beyond that everything else is hazy. I remember driving, stopping, and then driving some more. I remember crawling up a pair of steps, or knocking on a door, and I remember some old woman hollering at me. The woman had a hell of a loud voice, filling the night, and even through the fog of the booze it shook me. But something else shook me even more. There was a younger woman, a girl, and she was crying. I don't know what she was crying about—who knows why a woman cries?—but she was going at it pretty good.

Whoever it was, I got the hell out of there.

I don't remember driving back to the ranch, either, or parking the car, or anything. That is, I don't remember anything much until I walked into that room and saw him lying there.

I was too drunk to think of taking his pulse, and maybe I couldn't have located his arm if I had thought about it, but there was one thing that even I knew. George Shipton would never bother anybody again. He was dead.

15

Nothing much happened for the next couple of days. I mean, nothing much that concerned me directly. And then it hit.

George's death was accepted by the guests as being just one of those things. They continued to drink, jump beds like members of a flea circus, and eat the way city people eat when they're in the country and get a good dose of that mountain air.

Sam felt pretty bad about George but he said that George had been drinking too much, anyway, and that it wasn't unexpected.

"You've got sugar in your blood and you've got to leave the booze alone," he said.

The whole operation of the ranch during that time fell squarely on my shoulders. Nobody else wanted to assume the responsibility and Diana was running around, into town and back, dressed in black, and tears clinging to her eyes. I spoke to her once and then only casually and she said for me to carry on as best I could. I told her I would. I guess I felt sorry for her, and maybe even forgave her for how she had treated me.

The day after the Fourth, I was sitting in the little office in back of the registration desk, fooling around with the payroll book, when a guy in a blue sport shirt came in and introduced himself.

"I'm Saunders," he said. "From Midland Grocers." I nodded. I knew that Midland Grocers supplied the ranch with groceries and I had seen the young fellow in the sport shirt out near the kitchen a couple of times. I had never talked to him, though, since Diana had done all the ordering, but, as I say, I knew who he was. "You'd better see the chef," I told him.

"I already saw the chef. And he said to see you."

"Well."

I don't know just why I did but in that moment I put six and six together and came up with a dozen, just the way I should. I'd heard Diana ordering from this guy, overheard some of the conversation with Sam, and it had struck me then that Sam wasn't a difficult chef to order for at all. Now, his sending the salesman out to see me meant just this one thing: Sam didn't know how to order. A lot of chefs don't, which isn't anything against them. They know how to cook, to get the food on the tables, but when it comes to figuring the amount of stuff they need they're up against a brick wall.

"Well," I said again.

Any other time it wouldn't have been important; sending the salesman out to me was the most logical thing for most chefs to do. But Diana had said Sam was tough to work with. Something, somewhere, just didn't fit.

"Sorry to bother you on Saturday," the salesman said, apparently annoyed by my silence. "Tuesday is my regular day but with the long weekend the boss thought you might need something."

"Okay," I said. "We'll make it short and sweet."

Out in the kitchen I checked Sam's menus against the supplies in the storeroom and the refrigerator and gave the salesman an order. When we had finished I walked with the salesman to the back door and stood looking out into the hot sun.

"I'll add on the usual ten percent," the salesman said.

"What?"

"You know, the kick-back." He laughed. "For the lady. Pin money, she calls it."

The reason why Diana hadn't wanted me to do the ordering hit me right square in the belly. She'd been pulling down on her husband on the side.

"I doubt if it's necessary anymore," I said. "He's dead."

"Yeah. I hadn't thought about that."

I thought of mentioning the incident to Sam, decided against it, and chalked the entire thing up as something that wasn't any of my business. Actually, I couldn't blame her for having done such a thing. George had been plenty tight and possibly it had been her only way of getting hold of some dough.

That afternoon the state cops hit us like honey bees at a swarming party. They were all over the place, talking to everybody. Or almost everybody. They didn't talk to me. Not until after dinner, when it was time to close the office.

I can tell you I wasn't happy about what they had to say.

They arrested me for the murder of George Shipton.

"You almost got away with it," the sergeant told me. "But not quite."

My guts hurt worse than if somebody had stomped on them. I didn't know what to do, what to say. I wanted to run but that was the silliest thing I'd ever thought of. I wouldn't have gotten five feet without getting shot up for a crime I hadn't committed.

"No," I said. "I didn't do it."

"All murderers say that."

I told them again and again that I hadn't done it, that he'd been dead when I entered the bedroom, but nobody seemed to believe me or pay any attention. When I saw it was useless I gave up.

"What do you want me to do?" I said.

"Come with us. And tell the truth."

I went with the sergeant in a car with two other troopers, but all the way into town I didn't say a word. Now that the initial shock had passed I was no longer frightened. I hadn't killed George. Nobody had killed George. He'd been drinking when he shouldn't have been drinking and he'd just dropped down dead. This thing was a crazy, mixed-up affair. It would soon be straightened out. I didn't have anything to worry about.

Like hell I didn't.

They had me good.

And they had me all the way.

Shortly after we arrived at the police station the sergeant gave it to me right between the eyes.

"Here's what we've got, fellow," the sergeant said. "Enough to send you to the chair."

"Tell me." At that point I couldn't believe it, couldn't understand.

"Don't be so cocky."

"I'm not."

"Sure, you are. But you won't be. MacKenzie, you'll be ready for the chair when I'm finished with you."

"Go on."

"You were having an affair with this Shipton's wife, weren't you?"

"I won't deny it."

"A one-sided affair, wasn't it? You were after her but she chased you off."

"No. It was both of us."

"Can you prove that?"

I thought about it. Who had seen us together, who had known? The only public place I'd ever gone with her had been that hotel in New York, but the Mr. and Mrs. registration at the desk wouldn't prove anything. I'd been in the hotel business long enough to know that. The Mrs. with me could have been any woman.

"That's the way it was," I said lamely.

"She says different."

"What!" I came up out of that chair as though it had suddenly been electrified.

"Sit down!"

"But I don't get it."

"You'll get it, fellow. She says you were bothering her all this spring, that her husband was sore about it. She says she even jumped on you the other night in front of a lot of other people. We've talked to these other people, and they say the same thing. She came into the help's dining room and read you off, didn't she?"

There's no use saying I'd started to sweat; my pores were working in double time.

"Go on," I said, wanting to know it all now, wanting to get down to the last bit of it.

"You arranged for her husband to sleep in your room."

"That was her idea."

"She says it wasn't. She says she got after you about it because she was afraid of what you might do to him. She thought coming right out into the open with it would make you change your mind. But it didn't. You got yourself loaded and you killed him."

I laughed. "He wasn't killed," I said. "He just died."

"Everybody dies, killed or not."

I didn't say anything. The sergeant moved around the narrow office. His belt made a loud creaking sound when he breathed.

"He was murdered," the sergeant said. "By you. Oh, it was a clever job and it would have worked except that you made one mistake. You shot the bubble of air into his right arm and not his left. He always took his insulin shots in his left arm because he was right handed. It was the only mistake you made. If it hadn't been for the bruise and the hole in the right arm the doctor might not have suspected anything."

I tried to act dumb. "How do you kill a guy that way?" I wanted to know.

The sergeant glared at me. "I don't have to tell you, MacKenzie. You almost qualified as an expert. But I will. I'll tell you. We've done a lot of checking on you and you'd be surprised about what we know. We even went so far as to talk to your father and mother. They're nice people, fellow, real nice. They don't deserve you. We found out something when we talked to them. You were up there to see them just a little while ago, to borrow some money. Your father has been worried about you ever since that time. He said when you didn't come to bed right away he said he came to the top of the stairs and looked down to see if you'd maybe fallen asleep. But you weren't asleep. You were reading a medical book—a medical book that tells you all about people who have sugar and the dangers of air getting into the blood stream. Of course, he didn't know at the time why you were reading it. He thought you might be sick. That's why he went back to bed and didn't say anything to you."

I guess this is when I felt it, the way they were building this up and tying me down.

"That's no proof," I said.

"It can help establish premeditation."

"Go on," I said thickly, "what else have you got?"

The sergeant smiled for the first time. "Turnabout's fair play," he said. "Supposing you tell me a few things? Where were you the night Shipton got killed?"

"I got drunk."

"I'm listening."

"In town. At the Crystal Bar. Then I drove out to Rowland's Diner."

"And—after that?"

I shook my head. "I don't know. I had a bottle. I remember drinking all of it. Then I went somewhere, I don't know where. There was a woman hollering, it seems like, and a girl crying. I don't know. I've tried to think about it since then, but I haven't been able to. There was just all this noise."

"And then you came back to the ranch?"

"I guess so."

"And killed Shipton?"

"No!"

He didn't appear unhappy that I denied it. I guess he didn't expect me to break down and tell the world that I had killed the guy.

"We can check your story," he said. "In fairness to you, we'll do that."

I waited while he made a few phone calls but when he had completed them I was just as bad off as before. Or worse.

The doctor had placed the time of Shipton's death as around eleven thirty. I'd left the diner, the last place I'd been seen, before ten. The sergeant didn't have to explain to me that this was no alibi at all.

"You got in trouble at the Hotel Gordon last year," he said. "That little piece of business won't help you any in this jam you're now in."

"I suppose not."

They threw me in a cell and kept me locked up over the weekend. Sunday was as long as all of the yesterdays put together and all of the tomorrows laid end to end. Nobody, except the guy who brought my food, came to see me.

The weekly newspaper came out on Monday morning and the jailer brought me a copy so I could read it. I rated a lot of space on the front page but there was one other item that was of interest to me. Miriam Samuels and Sid Gromley had been married in a big ceremony at the Hotel Gordon over the Fourth. Maybe I was in a tough spot but I counted my blessings. Sid might have married her but he wouldn't be able to keep her. No one man would.

Shortly before noon the sergeant came around and let me out of the cell.

"You're free," he said.

I couldn't move. "Tell me that again!"

"You're free. By the Grace of God and the love of a beautiful girl."

"I don't get it."

"You will when you see her. And, MacKenzie, don't drink so much next time that you can't remember where you've been. It confuses things."

I didn't know what he was talking about and I still couldn't move.

"Come on. You want to stay in there the rest of your life?"

For the first time in hours I laughed.

"I should say not!"

And I walked out of that cell, feeling good.

We'll never get rich managing the Channing Hotel but the owners are nice, elderly, and we have a cottage on the grounds where we can live by ourselves in privacy. It's in Sullivan County, the best county in the world, and from our bedroom window you can see for miles and miles on a clear day.

You've probably read about Diana Shipton and that she's doing a life sentence for the murder of her husband. No doubt you have also read that the thing that broke her was the fact there wasn't any insurance. George had let the policy lapse the winter before, without her knowledge, and although he had picked it up again it made the thing contestable once more, which relieved the company of the responsibility of paying the claim since George wasn't an insurable risk.

We talk about it sometimes, how she tried to frame me for his death, but there isn't any bitterness in us about it. She was a crazy fool and she did what she thought she had to do.

"It's a good thing you came knocking on our door that night," Sandy often reminds me. "And it's a good thing mother got mad and shouted at you. I wouldn't have awakened and you wouldn't have had an alibi if I hadn't."

As soon as she had read about my arrest in the paper both Sandy and her mother had come forward, proving that I was still at the Herbert's house almost until one o'clock, long after George was killed.

"Yeah," I tell her, "I was lucky."

But, mostly, we don't talk about the past. We talk about today and tomorrow and the tomorrow that will come. She's a good wife, planning ahead, keeping to the budget and, believe it or not, keeping me in line.

This doesn't mean, however, that we've forgotten about the mistakes both of us have made. We haven't, and they will always be there. The main thing is to be sure they don't happen again. It's wonderful being together, working together, making certain that every tomorrow will be better.

THE END

ORRIE HITT BIBLIOGRAPHY

(all paperbacks unless noted)

I'll Call Every Monday (Red Lantern HC, 1953; Avon, 1954)

Love in the Arctic (Red Lantern HC, 1953)

Leased w/Jack Woodford (Signature HC, 1954; 1958 revised by Hitt & retitled Trapped as by Orrie Hitt)

Cabin Fever (Uni-Book, 1954; Beacon, 1959, as Tawny; Softcover Library UK, 1974, as Lovers at Night)

She Got What She Wanted (Beacon, 1954)

Shabby Street (Beacon, 1954)

Teaser (Woodford HC, 1956; Beacon, 1957; Lancer, 1963)

Unfaithful Wives (Beacon, 1956)

The Sucker (Beacon, 1957)

Nudist Camp (Beacon, 1957)

Pushover (Beacon, 1957)

The Promoter (Beacon, 1957)

Ladies' Man (Beacon, 1957), as Summer of Sin (Beacon 1961)

Dolls and Dues (Beacon, 1957)

Trailer Tramp (Beacon, 1957)

Devil in the Flesh (Valentine HC, 1957; Kozy, 1960, as Sins of Flesh)

Ellie's Shack (Beacon, 1958)

Suburban Wife (Beacon, 1958)

Summer Hotel (Beacon, 1958)

Wild Oats (Beacon, 1958)

Affairs of a Beauty Queen (Beacon, 1958)

Call South 3300: Ask for Molly! (Beacon, 1958)

Burlesque Girl (Beacon, 1958)

Girl's Dormitory (Beacon, 1958)

Woman Hunt (Beacon, 1958)

Hot Cargo (Beacon, 1958)

The Cheat (Beacon, 1958)

Rotten to the Core (Beacon, 1958)

Love Princess (Saber, 1958)

Hotel Women (Vantage HC, 1958)

Hotel Confidential (Vantage HC, 1958)

Sheba (Beacon, 1959)

The Widow (Beacon, 1959)

Add Flesh to the Fire (Beacon, 1959)

Private Club (Beacon, 1959)

Carnival Girl (Beacon, 1959)

The Peeper (Beacon, 1959; Softcover Library UK, 1973, as Twisted Passion)

Too Hot to Handle (Beacon, 1959)

Sin Doll (Beacon, 1959; Softcover Library UK, 1973, as The Excesses of Cherry)

Ex-Virgin (Beacon, 1959; UK Softcover Library, 1969, as Made for Man)

Suburban Sin (Beacon, 1959)

Pleasure Ground (Bedside, 1959; Kozy, 1961)

Affair With Lucy (Midwood, 1959; Midwood, 1961, as Married Mistress)

Girl of the Streets (Midwood, 1959)

Summer Romance (Midwood, 1959)

As Bad as They Come (Midwood, 1959; Midwood, 1962, as Mail Order Sex)

Hotel Woman (Valentine HC, 1959; Kozy, 1960, as Hotel Hostess)

Wayward Girl (Beacon, 1960)

The Torrid Teens (Beacon, 1960)

From Door to Door (Beacon, 1960)

Motel Girls (Beacon, 1960)

Tell Them Anything (Beacon, 1960)

Call Me Bad (Beacon, 1960; Softcover Library, 1970)

Untamed Lust (Beacon, 1960)
Never Cheat Alone (Beacon, 1960)
The Lady is a Lush (Beacon, 1960)
Sexurbia County (Beacon, 1960)
Tramp Wife (Chariot, 1960)
Hotel Girl (Chariot, 1960)
Lonely Flesh (Chariot, 1960; reprinted 1963 as Lola)
Suburban Interlude (Kozy, 1960)
The Cheaters (Midwood, 1960)
A Doctor and His Mistress (Midwood, 1960)
Two of a Kind (Midwood, 1960)
I Prowl by Night (Beacon, 1961)
Dirt Farm (Beacon, 1961; Softcover Library UK, 1968, as The Hired Man)
Four Women (Beacon, 1961)
The Love Season (Beacon, 1961)
Frigid Wife (Beacon, 1961)
Virgins No More (Beacon, 1961)
Party Doll (Chariot, 1961)
Strange Longing (Chariot, 1961; reprinted as Female Doctor, 1963)
Man's Nurse (Chariot, 1961)
Hot Blood (Chariot, 1961)
Diploma Dolls (Kozy, 1961)
Dark Passions (Kozy, 1961)
Twisted Lovers (Kozy, 1961)
Suburban Trap (Kozy, 1961)
Carnival Honey (Kozy, 1961)
Wild Lovers (Kozy, 1961)
Easy Women! (Novel, 1961; reprinted 1963 as Inflamed Dames, 1964 as Love Seekers, 1965 as Jenkins' Lovers)
Shocking Mistress! (Novel, 1961)
Peeping Tom (Wisdom House, 1961)
Love Thief (Beacon, 1962)
Dial "M" for Man (Beacon, 1962)
Torrid Cheat (Chariot, 1962)
Twin Beds (Chariot, 1962)
Naked Model (Chariot, 1962)
Libby Sin (Chariot, 1962)
Passion Street (Chariot, 1962)
Bad Wife (Chariot, 1962)
Passion Hostess (Chariot, 1962)
Bold Affair (Kozy, 1962)
Campus Tramp (Kozy, 1962)
The Naked Flesh (Kozy, 1962)
Violent Sinners (Kozy, 1962)
Love Slave (Kozy, 1962)
Frustrated Females! (Novel, 1962; reprinted 1963 as I Need a Man!)
Warped Woman (Novel, 1962; reprinted 1963 as Taboo Thrills, 1964 as Wilma's Wants)
Abnormal Norma (Novel, 1962)
Bed Crazy (Novel, 1962; reprinted 1964 as Perverted Doctors)
Man-Hungry Female (Novel, 1962; reprinted 1964 as More! More! More!)
Carnival Sin/Playpet (Vest-Pocket, 1962)
Torrid Wench (Kozy, 1963)
Strip Alley (Kozy, 1963)
Nude Doll (Kozy, 1963)
Loose Women (Lancer Domino, 1963)
An American Sodom (Novel, 1963)
Male Lover (Gaslight, 1964)
Passion Pool (Lancer Domino, 1964)
The Color of Lust (Lancer Domino, 1964)
The Passion Hunters (Lancer Domino, 1964; Domino, 1966 as This Wild Desire)
Lust Prowl (Lancer Domino, 1964)
The Love Seekers (Novel, 1964)
The Tavern (Softcover Library, 1966)
Woman's Ward (Softcover Library, 1966)
While the City Sins (Ember Library, 1967)

The Sex Pros (Beacon, 1968;
   Softcover Library UK as
   Cindy)
Panda Bear Passion (P.E.C.,
   1968)
Nude Model (MacFadden, 1970)

As by Kay Addams
Queer Patterns (Beacon, 1959)
Warped Desire (Beacon, 1960;
   Softcover Library UK as
   Night of Desire, 1975)
Lucy (Beacon, 1960; Softcover
   Library UK as Beautiful
   Tramp, 1972)
Three Strange Women (Beacon,
   1960)
The Strangest Sin (Beacon, 1961)
The Autobiography of Kay
   Addams (Novel, 1962; aka The
   Secret Perversions of Kay
   Addams, possible reprint as
   My Lesbian Loves, Novel,
   1964)
My Secret Perversions (Novel,
   1962; reprinted as Hidden
   Hungers)
My Wild Nights With Nine
   Nudists! (Novel, 1963;
   reprinted as Nocturnal
   Nudists)
My Two Strangest Lovers (Novel,
   1963; reprinted 1964 as
   Beyond Love)
Cherry (Novel, 1963)

As by Joe Black (as told to Hitt)
Unnatural Urge (Midwood, 1962)

As by Roger Normandie (co-
   authored with Joe Weiss)
Run for Cover (Key HC, 1957; as
   Race With Lust, Kozy, 1959)
Web of Evil (Key HC, 1957)
The Lion's Den (Key HC, 1957; as
   Tormented Passions, Kozy,
   1959)

As by Charles Verne (co-authored
   with Joe Weiss)
Mr. Hot Rod (Key HC, 1957)
The Wheel of Passion (Key HC,
   1957)

As by Fred Martin
Hired Lover (Midwood, 1959)

As by Nicky Weaver
Love, Blood and Tears (Kozy,
   1963)
Love or Kill Them All (Kozy,
   1963)

Short Stories
Nothing in My Way (Smashing
   Detective Stories, July 1955)